THE CALL OF THE
MAN-EATER

Kenneth Anderson (1910-1974) was a hunter, nature enthusiast and chronicler of wildlife. His hunting expeditions involved several close encounters with man-eating tigers, rogue elephants, leopards and other wild animals. He wrote about eight books and sixty short stories which recount many of his real-life adventures and hunting exploits in the jungles of South India. In 2000, his collected works, *The Kenneth Anderson Omnibus*, were published in two volumes.

He spent most of his life in Bangalore, where he was employed with an aeronautics company. Anderson's invaluable contribution to shikar literature in India continues to inspire scores of wildlife lovers.

Visit www.facebook.com/groups/kennethanderson to know more about the author.

KENNETH ANDERSON
THE CALL OF THE MAN-EATER

Published by
Rupa Publications India Pvt. Ltd 1976
161-B/4, Gulmohar House,
Yusuf Sarai Community Centre,
New Delhi 110049

Sales centres:
Bengaluru Chennai
Hyderabad Kolkata Mumbai

Copyright © Literary Estate of Kenneth Anderson

The views and opinions expressed in this book are the author's own and
the facts are as reported by him/her which have been verified to the extent
possible, and the publishers are not in any way liable for the same.

All rights reserved.
No part of this publication may be reproduced, transmitted,
or stored in a retrieval system, in any form or by any means, electronic,
mechanical, photocopying, recording or otherwise, without the prior
permission of the publisher.

ISBN: 978-81-716-7469-5

Eleventh impression 2025

15 14 13 12 11

The moral right of the author has been asserted.

This edition is for sale in the Indian subcontinent only.

Typeset in Classical Garamond by Mindways Design, New Delhi

Printed in India

This book is sold subject to the condition that it shall not, by way
of trade or otherwise, be lent, resold, hired out, or otherwise circulated,
without the publisher's prior consent, in any form of binding or cover other
than that in which it is published.

Contents

Introduction	*vii*
The Call of the Man-Eater	1
The Evil One of Umbalmeru	46
A Night by the Camp Fire	100
The Black Rogue of the Moyar Valley	143
Jungle Days and Nights	170
The Creatures of the Jungle	205
The Sulekunta Panther	261
From Mauler to Man-Eater	286

Introduction

IN THIS NEW BOOK OF ADVENTURE STORIES I HAVE STRIVEN TO DO something more than provide an account of the pursuit of some of the larger wild animals of the beautiful land in which I live. I have endeavoured to recapture and portray to the reader's mind not only the events as they happened but also the background in which they took place.

The chapter entitled 'A Night by the Camp Fire' is a description of what has occurred many times when I have spent such a night in the forest, and I have tried to take the reader with me on such an excursion, and to introduce him to the sights, sounds and incidents that are likely to be experienced. In two later chapters I have let myself go, so to speak, in thinking aloud about the many wonderful days and nights in which strange or amusing incidents, and even some foolish ones too, have taken place. These memories are very precious indeed to me, and I trust I shall never live to outgrow or forget them. If in recording these musings of mine I have been able to bring to the reader even a fraction of the pleasure I have derived from recounting them, I will be more than satisfied.

INTRODUCTION

I have also related some of the habits of a few of the lesser-known creatures of this wonderful land, and of some of the better-known creatures too, in order to bring them to the reader more intimately—my humble friends of the jungle in whose company I am very happy and contented.

A big movement has just started in India, although unfortunately very late, to instil into the public mind a love of the wild creatures around them, priceless living gems in the diadem of India that have all but vanished for ever. Many places that once teemed with game and resounded to their joyful and melodious voices are now realms of silence. Before this unique heritage becomes altogether a thing of the past, it is the duty of the government, and more particularly of every Indian, to put an end to the wanton slaughter that still goes on, night after night and every day of the year. For the sportsman of the future, I would strongly advocate the camera instead of the rifle and gun. It can give you every bit as much fun—clean fun, unstained by the smell of blood, the sight of death, and the pricking conscience of regret.

So I invite you on a wonderful journey to places that may be new to you and are vastly beautiful to behold—the jungle that throbs with life, although hidden from your view. At night you can feel it around you, just outside the range of your flickering camp fire, where the wall of blackness begins and stretches far into the moonlit forest aisles and glades, or into the deep shadows of the jungle on a moonless night, where, to quote Lawrence Hope:

> There was no sound; he gave no cry,
> The careless stars looked on serene.
> The jungle's sudden tragedy
> Remained unheard, unknown, unseen.

INTRODUCTION

The soughing of the night wind through the boughs of the lofty trees, the quiver of a million leaves that whisper like a distant ocean; the flash and flicker of fireflies that dart among the branches; the blackness all around, and the deeper blackness that moves stealthily within it unseen; and the weird, unearthly cry of the distant jackal pack: 'Ooooo-ooh! Ooh-where? Ooh-where? Where? Where?' And the answer of the leader, punctuated by the chorus of vixens: 'Yes, Here! Hee-re! Hee-ee-yah! Yah! Yah! Yah!' Then at last that awesome but thrilling call that sweeps across the hills and echoes through the mist-laden valleys: 'A-oongh! O-o-n-oon! Augh-ha! Ugh! Ugh! U-u-u-gh!' The call of the man-eater!

So put your man-made cares aside and visit these wondrous regions with me, where the jungle presides and the laws of nature hold sway. In the words of still another poet, let the wild places speak to you in the silence of your heart and mind:

> So ye learn within my arbours
> Where the sleeping wild things lie,
> A reverence for nature
> Which the city's streets deny,
> Ye learn the real value
> Of the man made from the loam;
> And ye kneel and thank your Maker
> As ye wend your footsteps home.

W.J.K.S.

One

The Call of the Man-Eater

IT WAS JUST AFTER MIDNIGHT, AND THE DARKNESS OUTSIDE WAS intense. I lay comfortably stretched in the long armchair on the verandah of the forest bungalow at Joldahl, with both feet upon its wooden rests, smoking my pipe and listening to the sound that is music to the ears of every jungle lover in India and a challenge to every *shikari* and hunter.

It moaned across the forest range; and then, as the creature padded its silent way through the jungle, clearly to my ears came the softer sigh of contentment in the knowledge that it was the supreme lord of all it surveyed. 'Ugh! Ugh! Ughaugh!'

In my imagination I could picture the caller. In that intense darkness its tawny coat, with the bold black stripes and the white spots behind the ears and at the base of its throat and belly, would hold no colour to an observer were he able to see them. Indeed, it would be unrecognizable as a tiger at all. The watcher would only see, if he could see at all, a black shadow, blacker if possible than the surrounding jungle.

If the watcher happened to be a man, unaided by a torch or moonlight, he would see nothing, for human sight is not made to see more blackness where the blackness is already complete. He would know, however, and unmistakably, that a tiger was near. The roars that seemed to make the very jungle tremble would tell him; and the watcher would tremble himself. If he was a trained and experienced hunter with exceptionally acute hearing, he might catch the faint rustle of grass, or the sound of a leaf brushing against some heavy body as it passed. He would not hear the crackle of a twig, because the tiger would not be so careless as to step on such a thing, for he is himself a hunter, and hunters do not betray their presence nor make mistakes.

Should the observer be seated on a low branch of a tree and the tiger pass directly beneath, and should he have a really keen sense of smell, he might possibly wonder at the sudden, very strong 'greenish' odour that might be carried briefly to his nostrils. Then, if he is a religious man, he might be wise to raise a hurried prayer and hold his breath, and not move a muscle nor flicker an eyelid. For although a tiger has practically no sense of smell, he has abnormally acute hearing and marvellous sight, to catch the minutest of movements in his vicinity. Should he hear or see the watcher at that instant, the watcher might watch no more.

For the tiger to whose roars I was listening was no ordinary tiger. He was a man-eater!

You may well ask what was the use of all this stealth, this wonderful hearing and sight, this uncanny sixth sense that all tigers possess, when the stupid brute was advertising his presence by moaning and sighing and roaring? Which is a fair question, and one which is difficult for me to answer

THE CALL OF THE MAN-EATER

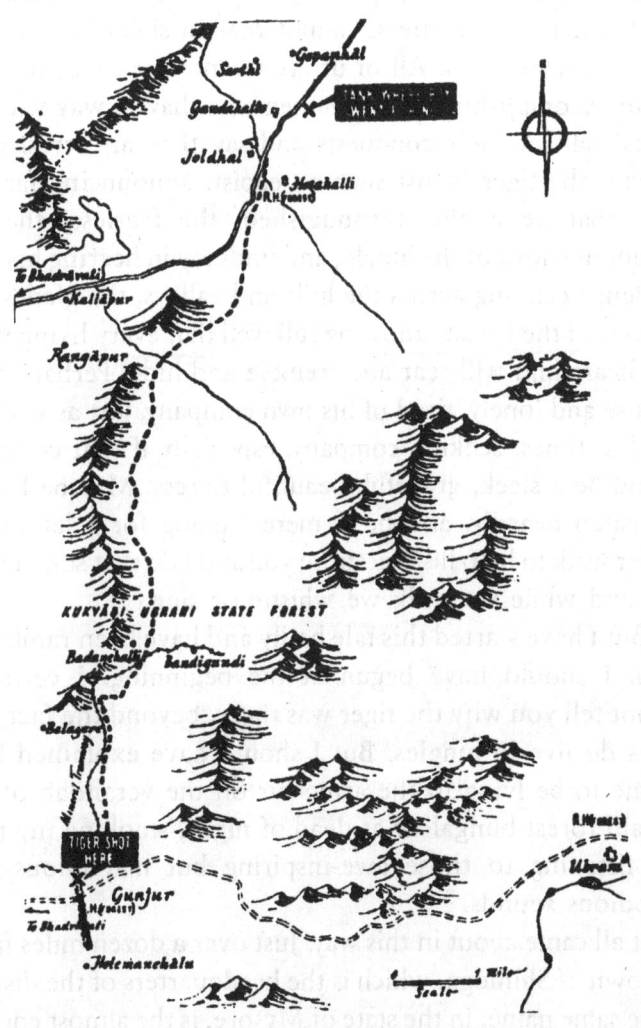

convincingly, not being a tiger myself. I can only make a suggestion. Most strong people, well developed muscularly, good boxers or wrestlers, cannot remain silent and modest about their prowess. All of us are tempted at times to boast of our accomplishments. Even men who 'have a way with the ladies' talk of their conquests and say they are irresistible. Perhaps the tiger is just such an egoist, announcing far and wide that he is the unvanquished, the fearless, the all-conquering lord of the jungle, and finds joy in hearing his own challenge echoing across the hills and valleys, the glades and thickets of the forest, knowing full well that every living thing that hears him will fear and tremble and hide. Perhaps he is morose and lonely, tired of his own company, just as you and I feel at times, seeking company, especially if that company should be a sleek, graceful, beautiful tigress. May be he has just eaten heartily, and he is merely going for a late after-dinner walk to help his digestion; you and I do that sometimes, too, and while we walk we whistle or sing.

But I have started this tale badly and have been rambling, when I should have begun at the beginning. I certainly cannot tell you why the tiger was there, beyond the fact that tigers do live in jungles. But I should have explained how I came to be lying in the armchair on the verandah of the Joldahl forest bungalow at dead of night, smoking my pipe and listening to those awe-inspiring but marvellous and melodious sounds.

It all came about in this way. Just over a dozen miles from the town of Shimoga, which is the headquarters of the district of the same name, in the state of Mysore, is the almost equally large town of Bhadravati, which has become an industrial centre of considerable importance, boasting a large iron and steel foundry. The iron ore, mined at a place named Kemangondi, some miles away on the Baba Budan mountain range, is conveyed downhill by a succession of cable-buckets to the works at Bhadravati. Fuel is provided by charcoal from wood constantly felled in the extensive surrounding forests. The glow from the blast furnaces of Bhadravati is visible for many miles reddening the horizon and reflecting against the clouds in the sky.

Joldahl is about fifteen miles from Bhadravati, on a road that leads more or less eastwards to Chitaldroug. It is completely surrounded by dense jungle and boasts a delightful Forest department bungalow. About ten miles southwest of Joldahl, and also in dense forest, is another forest bungalow, slightly less picturesque. This is situated at a place called Gunjur.

I had often camped at Gunjur in the old days. It is a pretty spot. But the only word to describe the road that leads directly to Gunjur is 'vile'. It branches off to the east from the main road from Bangalore to Tarikere and Bhadravati, about five miles before reaching Bhadravati. From that point it is no longer a road but a cart-track, and a very bad cart-track at that. I have negotiated it in my Model T Ford in early years, and in my Studebaker since then. In all its twenty miles my sympathies and unstinted praise have gone to Henry Ford and the Studebaker brothers. My nerves were at breaking point all the time, yet I never broke a spring or an axle on any of the trips I made there.

At the Gunjur bungalow there lived a very hard-working and obliging caretaker who did all he could on every occasion to make my stay comfortable. This caretaker had a lovely little daughter. She was about twelve years old when I first met her, and she was very interested in watching the cars and in scanning my firearms at a respectful distance. Also, like her father she was very helpful. She would fill her waterpot at a spring nearly a furlong away and carry the load to pour into the old zinc tub in the bathroom of the bungalow, for my use.

This child grew up into a lovely girl of about seventeen years. Her father had, customarily and painstakingly, made all the arrangements for her to marry a respectable villager at Joldahl, and the marriage was soon to take place.

One day she took her waterpot to the spring to fill it for the use of her father and herself. They lived in the humble outhouse (known as a 'godown'), sandwiched between the kitchen and the garage at the rear of the forest bungalow. But she never returned. For, as she stooped to dip the pot in the spring, the man-eater got her.

He carried her away, screaming, into the jungle that grows to the edge of the spring. Her father heard her. He had no gun. Grabbing a woodchopper as his only weapon, he gave chase, running as fast as he could, till he actually overtook the tiger.

He shouted at it in Kanarese—his native tongue: 'Let go my child, you brute. I will slay you for this.'

The tiger heard and turned. He saw the man running behind. The cowardly streak that is latent in the heart of every man-eater filled him with fear. But the feebly struggling victim in his mouth offered too tempting a meal to be so easily relinquished. So the tiger increased his pace and bounded away into the jungle, while the poor girl's cries grew fainter and feebler and soon died away. I was later told by the bereaved man that he never found his daughter's remains.

There is no road connecting Gunjur and Joldahl, only a winding footpath that creeps down densely forested valleys and across hills for about ten miles. Joldahl itself, as I have said, is fifteen miles from Bhadravati, on the road to Chitaldroog, and roughly northeast of Gunjur. That road at least is quite a good one.

THE CALL OF THE MAN-EATER

I am told that it was about two months later that a little Muslim boy went fishing in the small lake that lies about six furlongs from the cluster of huts that form Joldahl hamlet. He must have had quite a bit of luck, for a dozen fish, including murral, cat-fish and small carp, were found afterwards in the basket he had brought, together with the two rods he was using.

Fishing in India, by the way, is not done with reels, or by using bait such as 'spoons' and 'fly'. The rod is a thin length of bamboo; the reel a length of string; the float a quill, made from the wing-feathers of a peafowl, horned-owl or hawk; and the bait is an earthworm dug up in the ditch by the wayside.

Perhaps the luck he had met with had caused the boy to dally further into the evening than he would have done had he caught fewer fish. He stayed till it was getting dark. But dusk is the time when tigers come out. And the man-eater was no exception.

The boy never returned home. Eight o'clock came and it was time for food. His father and eldest brother, who knew he had gone to the tank to fish, took lanterns and sticks and went to fetch him. Probably they intended to beat him with the sticks. They found the two rods and the basket of fish. But not the little boy. Instead, the light from their flickering lamps revealed the pug-marks of a large tiger in the ooze. The tiger had come out of the jungle, had slipped in the mud, and had gone back to the jungle. But not alone. The tiger had taken the boy with him.

On the grass was something that looked black and shiny. When they stooped and touched the shiny blackness and looked at their fingers, they found them red. It was blood. Father and son ran back to the village.

Then there was a third killing, but nobody worried about it. A madman had turned up at Joldahl; no one knew who

THE CALL OF THE MAN-EATER

he was or whence he came, and being quite mad he could not tell them. In India, lunatics are treated with a certain toleration. Little boys and girls may sometimes tease them. The elders check the children and give the madman a handful of food. Beyond that they take little notice of him.

So the madman ate such food as was given him in charity and slept by the wayside at night, outside the locked doors of the huts. But one morning he was found to be missing; nobody showed any concern. Two days later, a couple of forest guards patrolling the jungle that surrounds the village, saw vultures circling in the sky and swooping to earth. So they thought at once that some animal had been killed, perhaps a deer, and that there might be some flesh left on the carcase — enough to sell, or anyway to eat. They hurried to the place where the vultures were gathered and found there, not the remains of a deer, but the whitening bones of the madman. Only his head, that lay at a little distance and grinned at them as stupidly in death as in life, provided the clue that identified the bones as those of the missing lunatic. Imprinted in the soft sand around the head were the pug-marks of a tiger, a fairly large one.

I had not even heard of these killings till a friend of a friend of mine, who had been motoring from Chitaldroog to Bhadravati, stopped for a couple of days at the Joldahl bungalow to do a little hunting. There he heard about the tiger and its three victims. The bungalow caretaker at Joldahl, being distantly related to his counterpart at Gunjur, had told him that the first victim had been the promising daughter of the man who looked after the Gunjur bungalow. When he returned to Bangalore, the gentleman told a friend of mine all about it. Knowing I am in the habit of following up such information, Joe Thompson, the friend in question, passed the story on.

THE CALL OF THE MAN-EATER

The death of the girl whom I remembered so well prompted me to write a letter to the Forest Range Officer at Joldahl, asking for details and particularly whether the rumour I had heard, that the daughter of the caretaker at Gunjur had been the first victim, was really true. His reply, five days later, confirmed the sad tale.

So I went in the Studebaker direct to Joldahl, where I learnt the story I have just related. That had been forty-eight hours earlier. Since then I had walked to Gunjur by the ten-mile footpath and met my old friend, the caretaker, there. He wept bitterly as he recounted his daughter's tragic end. I promised him that I would try to avenge her and asked him to let me know at Joldahl should he hear or see signs of the tiger within the next week.

He had suggested that I should camp at Gunjur, but I said I preferred Joldahl for two reasons. Firstly, there had been two killings there. Secondly, the Studebaker was available for quick transport and the roads were usable. Then I returned by the same path to Joldahl.

I had been sleeping inside the bungalow that night when I awakened shortly after midnight to hear the tiger calling in the jungle, and I had come out to the armchair on the verandah, to smoke and think and listen to that awesome sound. As I heard it I could not refrain from thinking back a few years to the happy face of the pert little girl who had been so interested in my cars and my guns each time I visited Gunjur; who had fetched water for me of her own accord; who had grown into a handsome lass on the eve of marriage; who had now fallen prey to the magnificent but cruel beast to whose call I was at that very moment listening.

It came again! 'A-oongh! Aungh-ha! O-o-o-n-o-on!'

Involuntarily, I shuddered. The sound faded into the distance, and as far as I could judge the tiger was going towards Gunjur, probably walking along the very footpath that led there. I determined to check this first thing in the morning and fell asleep as I thought about it.

The mosquitoes were active until dawn and prevented my sleep from being particularly sound. But I was up before daylight, and after swallowing some coffee and *chappatties*, waited for the sun to rise a little before setting out to try to pick up the trail of the animal that had been calling the night before. It would not have been safe to have set out earlier with the possibility of the tiger lurking anywhere in the bushes beside the path. The half-light of early dawn can be as deceptive as the evening twilight, whereas I knew that with the rising of the sun the man-eater, in all probability, would retire till evening to some sheltered and remote spot to avoid the heat of the day.

I found what I was seeking a little over a mile from the bungalow. The tiger had walked along a narrow ravine, then leapt on to its bank and had started to follow the very path I was traversing, which led to Gunjur. His fresh saucer-like pugmarks, that had been made a little after midnight, were clearly imprinted in the powdery earth as he walked along the centre of the track. He had been disdainful of any interference, for he had been calling as he had walked, knowing well enough that every living creature would keep out of his way.

There was no conclusive evidence that this tiger was the man-eater; but something about his haughty manner told me that it was so, and I was reasonably certain that I was correct. I decided to follow the pug-marks to discover whether the tiger had indeed gone all the way to Gunjur or had turned back after covering part of the distance.

I found that for two miles or more the beast, whose pugmarks showed that he was a large male, had walked along the centre of the footpath. Then the tracks dipped to the dry bed of a stream, which the tiger then began to follow. As far as I could judge by the position of the sun, which was climbing higher and growing hotter every moment, the stream led roughly southeastwards, so that tiger track were now moving away from both Gunjur and Joldahl. But this was not for long. After about half a mile he had climbed the right-hand bank of the stream and had entered the forest, where I soon lost sight of his tracks on the hard, dry gound.

It occurred to me that he might have doubled back on his trail and had returned through the jungle to rejoin the footpath to Gunjur which he had been following before he had met the stream. With this idea, rather than flounder about in the undergrowth, I retraced my footsteps till I met once again the pathway leading to Gunjur. I began to follow it and was delighted, after I had walked nearly a mile from the stream, to find the tiger's pug-marks again in the sand before me. I had guessed correctly. He had taken a short cut through the forest to resume his former course towards Gunjur.

This action clearly revealed that he had made up his mind to go there, and I knew from my experience that he would not change it unless something extraordinary occurred to make him do so. My surmise proved to be right for, excepting a deviation here and there, the tiger had followed the footpath all the way to Gunjur. Keeping sight of his tracks had prevented me from walking as fast as I might have done, so that it took me four hours to cover those ten miles, and I presented myself to the caretaker of the bungalow just after eleven o'clock.

This man's name, I must tell you, was Ananthaswamy, and I told him how I had heard the tiger calling at Joldahl shortly after midnight and had followed the pug-marks that morning direct to Gunjur. Ananthaswamy told me he had been awake since four in the morning but had heard no sound from the tiger. However, two or three sambar had belled shortly after

4.30 a.m., while the spotted deer had been restless at dawn, sounding their calls of alarm from the base of a small hill to the south of the bungalow. We agreed that the tiger's silence, together with the alarm cries of the two species of deer, showed that he had come to Gunjur on serious business.

Now it is a mistake to think that every man-eating tiger or panther subsists on human flesh alone. Both species, particularly the former, are voracious eaters, and if they should decide to live on human flesh only, two things would happen. In the earlier stages the number of people who would die would be enormous, as on an average a tiger makes a kill at least twice a week. After that, when people had become so cautious as not to afford the tiger the opportunity of killing them, he would eventually starve to death. What really happens is that the man-eater takes a liking to the flavour of human flesh, encouraged all the more by the fact that he soon finds human prey much easier to catch and kill than wild animals. So a stage is reached when he will prefer killing and devouring a man, woman or child to killing domestic cattle or wild animals like deer and wild pig. But when he cannot easily find a human being he has no hesitation in reverting to his natural diet till the next opportunity offers. Added to this is the strange fact that, no matter how many people he may kill and eat, a man-eating tiger and panther remain basically afraid of the human race. This has been proved over and over again when a man—or sometimes a woman—has resisted or attempted to resist and even retaliate. Often enough the fiercest of man-eaters has turned tail and fled. But never at any time does a tiger fear domestic cattle or the wild beasts he preys upon, with the exception of the adult bull bison and the elephant.

So, not having had the luck to catch another human being at Joldahl, the tiger had evidently decided to come to Gunjur,

THE CALL OF THE MAN-EATER

where the low hills and wide grassy valleys are heavily stocked with deer. The chances were that he would stay there for some days, slay and eat a few sambar and spotted deer, and when well-filled would start thinking once more of indulging his newly-acquired taste for human flesh.

Except for the caretaker, who was now living alone, there were no other people at Gunjur, for there was no village. So after the few days were over, the tiger would probably go back to Joldahl, or try his luck around one of the other small villages bordering the main Bhadravati-Chitaldroog road. There was thus every hope that the man-eater would remain in the vicinity of Gunjur for the next two or three days at least. This hope would be strengthened if he succeeded in killing a deer and satisfying his immediate hunger, when he would lie up and feed on the remains during the following forty-eight hours. And there was no reason why he should not succeed, for Gunjur, as I have already said, abounds in deer: sambar, spotted deer, jungle sheep and four-horned antelope.

It is also a favourable place in which to bait for tiger, because the clearing in which the forest bungalow stands, and also the spring not far away, are encircled by small hillocks, which would afford the tiger a grand-stand view of any bait that might be placed conspicuously in the open valley below.

Unfortunately, apart from my rifle, I had brought no kit with me. My torch, my warm dark clothes for sitting up at night, my primus stove and stock of provisions were all at Joldahl bungalow. But that was ten miles away and I had just covered the distance. To go back for these things and then return again with them meant a thirty-mile trip altogether. The prospect was not enticing. Besides, I could not complete the trip before nightfall.

Ananthaswamy offered to lend me his torch, although it was only a two-cell affair. He also offered free board and lodging if I was prepared to share the only food he had—*ragi* balls. *Ragi* balls are prepared from ground *ragi* grain made into a dry porridge and then pressed together with both hands into a ball about the size of a cannon ball. It is very wholesome and sustaining, but quite tasteless.

Having accepted his invitation, there was another and greater snag to be overcome. Ananthaswamy had no animal of any sort to tie up as bait. He did have a dog—a rank, mangy cur. But a dog is useless as bait for tiger. Besides, as a dog lover myself, I refuse to use one as bait under any circumstances.

There was one more question. Was I not being rather over-optimistic? How did I know for certain that the tiger I had followed was the man-eater? He might be just a normal, extremely well-behaved and inoffensive game-killing and cattle-lifting beast. I talked the whole thing over with Ananthaswamy. His dark eyes glistened with pleasure when I accepted his hospitality and said I would stay with him for a couple of days. He said he was sure the quarry was the man-eater because there were no other tigers in the vicinity at that time. As for bait, he said that could easily be solved. He would himself sit or stand in the open as bait while I hid under cover or on a tree-*machan* to shoot the tiger—if possible before it leapt upon him. And in the same breath he said: 'Don't think, *dorai*, that I am doing this for your sake. Don't think I am doing it because I am brave and have no fear—for I am terribly afraid too. But I am doing it—and doing it cheerfully—in an attempt to avenge my little daughter. She was everything to me—all I had in the world after her mother died at childbirth and her elder brother, just a little later, of smallpox. I will gladly sacrifice my life to bring about the death of her cruel slayer.'

His simple and magnificent courage was touching and affected me deeply. But this was no time to indulge in sentiment; nor did I want a brave man's blood on my hands. Remember: the nights were dark and I would be using his two-cell torch. Nor had I brought the clamps with which to fix the torch to the rifle. I would have to hold it in my left hand and try to shine it along the barrel of the rifle while shooting. That would entail delay—at least a couple of seconds in which to get the beam correct. And even one second would be long enough for the tiger to pounce on Ananthaswamy and kill him.

Very emphatically, I answered: 'No.' Then, in order not to hurt his feelings while concealing my real reason, I added: 'I shall need you beside me to shine the torch on the tiger when he comes, while I fire at him.'

Ananthaswamy appeared dissatisfied with the explanation I had given him. He said: '*Dorai* can hold the torch in his own left hand up against the rifle, and still shoot.'

Sensing the beginning of an argument I replied: 'No, absolutely and finally, no!'

After that we sat in silence for some time. We were each thinking deeply. Then an idea occurred to me. The man-eater had carried off this man's daughter at the spring where she had gone for water. Perhaps the tiger would remember the kill he had succeeded in making there. Also he had probably seen the girl, and even Ananthaswamy for that matter, go to the spring for water on several occasions. At least he would associate that spring with the occasional visit of a human being. The spring was just a furlong from the bungalow and in a slight depression clearly visible from the surroundings hills. Yes, indeed; the spring would be the best place at which to prepare the bait. As the nights were dark and I had no torch-clamp, that bait could not be either Ananthaswamy or myself. So the only alternative would be to make a dummy to resemble a man in the act of drawing water from the spring, while I would hide myself as near as possible. Near enough for the dim light from the two-cell torch to be effective.

I detailed my thoughts to Ananthaswamy, who was elated. He said: 'Come, *dorai*; we will go at once to the spring and you can select the place where you will hide and shoot the tiger when he attacks the dummy this very night.'

I looked at him squarely, and he returned my look equally squarely. There was frankness and eagerness in his eyes and not a trace of fear, and I knew that this man would not again take 'no' for an answer.

We rose and walked to the spring. The water trickled out from a crack in a flattish rock that lay on the ground. It flowed down a slight slope to a small pool almost three feet deep and about ten feet across. It was from this pool that both father and daughter had been drawing their water throughout the years during which he had been caretaker of the Gunjur bungalow. The overflow of water spread into the jungle where, being insufficient to form a stream, it was absorbed by the earth. The continuous dampness had caused a growth of lush green grass for about twenty-five yards. Then the jungle began again. Ananthaswamy told me that when he first came to Gunjur the undergrowth grew right up to the pool and had enveloped it. With his daughter's help he had cut this away for about twenty-five yards, so that now only the grass grew there.

The problem that presented itself was: where were we going to hide? The nearest tree in which a *machan* could be built was well over 100 yards away. That distance was much too great to cover with the beam of a torch that held only two cells that were far from fresh. It appeared that the whole plan we had hatched of sitting over the dummy was about to fizzle out, for there just did not seem any place in which we could hide.

THE CALL OF THE MAN-EATER

I asked the caretaker if he had any ideas. He replied very ruefully that he had not. One fact emerged as quite unavoidable. We would have to sit on the ground somewhere and conceal ourselves as best we could. Or we would have to abandon the whole scheme. The nearest sizeable tree was too far from the pool and the feeble light of Ananthaswamy's torch could not possibly cover that distance. I had tested it in the caretaker's godown and could see that its cells were already half-exhausted.

By common consent, we walked across the twenty-five yards or so of grassy ground to where the undergrowth began. Neither of us had spoken a word, but it was as if we both accepted the inevitable. Here was where we would have to sit—if at all—to await the tiger.

The undergrowth was of the usual sort; wait-a-bit thorn bushes, lantana and other jungly shrubs, all matted together in close and dense profusion. The wait-a-bit thorn is unpopular with everyone, both human beings as well as animals, as it offers an impossible barrier when it grows really thickly; while even a solitary tendril, should it come in contact with your clothing will hold you up for quite a while. If it comes in contact with your flesh, you must be prepared to leave some of your skin behind, impaled on the numerous needle-sharp, hook-like thorns.

At one spot, just where the undergrowth commenced, there was just a wait-a-bit thorn bush; quite a large one, in fact. No man without a knife could possibly pass through it. No animal could do so either, for that matter, except an elephant. So at that moment I looked upon the bush with great favour. It seemed to have saved the situation.

'Ananthaswamy,' I asked, 'are the two iron spring-cots still in the bungalow?'

'Yes, *dorai*,' he replied. Then, as the strangeness of the sudden question registered itself in his mind, he added: 'If the master is tired, I will open the door of the bungalow and he can lie down and sleep undisturbed.'

Apparently quite irrelevantly, I continued: 'Is there a third such cot on the premises?'

I could see his eyes widen with surprise, and I almost laughed aloud. His thoughts at that moment were written large upon his frank countenance. What on earth can this man want a third cot for? There are two as it is, and being alone he can only sleep on one of them. He did not answer my question.

I repeated it: 'Is there a third such cot available, Ananthaswamy?'

His eyes opened still wider; but he held himself in check admirably, 'No,' he answered. 'Just the two that have always been here.'

'Come, Ananthaswamy,' I said, turning towards the bungalow. 'Open the door. I want to go inside and look over the furniture.'

Sunstroke, undoubtedly; or some other form of madness. The poor *dorai*! How unfortunate that this should happen at such a critical moment! The caretaker could not disguise his thoughts. This time I did laugh openly.

'Don't be alarmed, Ananthaswamy,' I explained as we retraced our steps to the little lodge. 'I am not going mad. It is in my mind to form a sort of cage for you and me to sit in, right where that wait-a-bit thorn-bush now grows. The two cots turned up on their sides—the longer sides by the way—will form a sort of barrier for us. In between the springs we will weave the wait-a-bit thorn branches and tendrils that you will have to cut. The front will be open, for in that direction we will face the dummy.

'But there is one snag, Ananthaswamy. A mighty big one. We will have to find something, some third article of furniture, to form the third barrier on the third side. For we can only

THE CALL OF THE MAN-EATER

watch in one direction, and not in two, my friend. Don't forget the nights at this time are dark; very, very dark. And your torch is in poor shape.'

It took quite a time for the plan I had outlined to sink into his mind. We were walking while we talked, and when finally he did catch on, he reacted rather unexpectedly. Coming to an abrupt halt, the caretaker bent double, slapped his thighs with the palms of his hands, and laughed and laughed and laughed.

'By Krishna!' he chortled, 'I never heard of such a plan before. We are to make a cage of the two beds and some other furniture and sit inside it to wait for the tiger? And the beds will be covered with the wait-a-bit thorn? *Dorai*, I will tell this plan to my children, and my children's children, after them. I swear it.'

Poor Ananthaswamy. He quite forgot he had no children. The tiger had devoured his only remaining one. Besides, there was little prospect of being able to make good his intentions. For he did not even have a wife!

He opened the door of the bungalow and we went inside. The two iron spring cots were there, one in each of the bedrooms. The other furniture consisted of a large dining table, two smaller tables, two dressing tables (one with a cracked mirror and the other with no mirror at all), one fairly large almirah, the usual armchair common to all bungalows, and about half-a-dozen old, wooden-bottomed chairs. In the bathroom was an ancient zinc tub, a brass wash-basin on an iron stand, and a towel-rack. There were no commodes; for purposes of that sort one had to go outside to a mud-walled latrine, where there was a hole in the ground topped by two flag-stones.

I looked at this array of furniture with sinking feelings. For one thing, the almirah was too massive and the two of us could not carry it for a furlong to the spring. The small tables were too small. So we had to choose between the dining table and the armchair for our third barrier. The dining table was certainly the safer and more sturdy alternative. But the trouble lay in the fact that its flat top, when laid sideways, could not easily be hidden by the thorns or even with leaves. It would prove a very conspicuous object that would not only arouse the suspicions of the tiger, but might frighten if off altogether. But at least the shape of the armchair lent itself to a little disguising.

'We will take the armchair,' I decided, explaining my reason to the caretaker.

I looked at my wristwatch. The time was 12.25. 'If your *ragi* balls are ready, Ananthaswamy, we will eat them. Then we must set to work. We have a terrible lot to do.'

I ate half a *ragi* ball. It was as much as I could manage. Swallowing the tasteless stuff was aided by frequent gulps of water. But Ananthaswamy ate two. Then he put water in a *degchie* and left it over the remains of his fire. This was to make tea when we returned. We would need it then; we certainly would be tired.

Ananthaswamy brought his hatchet and handed me a spare chopper of sorts, rather a blunt one. We traced our steps to the spring and set to work in earnest. First we cut down the wait-a-bit thorn bush, a task that left us bleeding from many scratches and perspiring from our exertions. Then we went about 200 yards away and cut undergrowth of the same nature as that which was growing at the place where we intended to sit up. This consisted of lantana and other bushes, but certainly no more wait-a-bit thorn. We carried—but not dragged—this stuff to where we had cut down the thorn bush. Dragging would leave a trail that might make the tiger suspicious. It was two o'clock by the time we had assembled all the necessary camouflage.

Next we returned to the bungalow, from which we carried the beds one at a time, one of us at either end, to our selected spot. The rear would naturally be the weakest link in our defence. There we laid one of the cots on its longer side, legs facing outwards. The second cot we placed on its side at right-angles to the first, its legs also facing outwards. Then we returned to the bungalow for the armchair, which we took back and laid on its side, again with legs facing outwards, on the third side of our rough cage—the side facing the bungalow. This we did because we knew it was the flimsiest of our three flimsy barricades, while it was least likely that the tiger would approach from the direction of the bungalow itself. The fourth side of our 'square' was of course open. It faced the grassy patch before the pool where we were going to place our dummy.

Now began the painful task of threading the branches and tendrils of the wait-a-bit thorns into the springs of the two cots, and between the legs and through the canework bottom of the armchair. To conceal the outside of the three articles of furniture completely, we added the undergrowth we had cut and brought from two hundred yards away.

It soon became evident that we did not have nearly enough camouflage to do this task effectively. We had to make another half-dozen trips for more, and even then we had barely enough. Anyway, the task was finished by 4 p.m. Looked at from a distance and from various angles, our *zareba* appeared to be more or less the same wait-a-bit thorn bush that had been growing there a few hours ago. But I was not happy about it. It seemed too much like wishful thinking to accept to deceive such a cautious animal as a tiger with such poor and very obvious camouflage.

Our only hope lay in making the dummy so realistic as to attract the tiger's attention and keep him from looking too keenly in our direction. Success I knew would also, to a large extent, depend on the angle from which he approached. If this was from either flank, there might be a chance that he would not notice our place of concealment. If he came directly from the opposite direction, our hide would be plainly in view and the chances would be ninety per cent against us. But he came from behind and discovered us, what then? Well, we would not be long in doubt, anyway. Either he would become afraid and just slink away, or he would attack. The chances were about fifty-fifty.

We had to hurry and make the dummy. It was very late already. Getting back to Ananthaswamy's little room, we ransacked his boxes, his bedding, and everything he had. There was no time, and sufficient material, to make anything like a realistic dummy. His filthy old pillow, black with oil from his hair, formed the torso of the dummy. I punctured this at either side, greatly to his consternation, and stuck a bamboo through the holes; protruding at both sides this bamboo would form the two arms. Another short one at the end of the pillow, into which the rim of a small earthenware cooking-pot was inserted, would be the head. There were no bamboos for the legs, so the dummy would have to appear to be squatting beside the pool; a natural enough position, anyway, for a man to be in when drawing water.

On to the pillow went one of the caretaker's old torn shirts, the bamboo arms protruding through its sleeves. Over that a white coat, to make it conspicuous. Around the earthenware pot, a turban of sorts. That was easy enough, anyhow.

But how on earth were we to keep the dummy sitting up? I looked around desperately. Then an idea struck me and I dived into the bathroom coming back with the wooden cross-member from the towel-rack. A final hole at the bottom of the pillow, which was almost ruined anyway, and the cross-member from the towel-rack was forced through the cotton, past the bamboo that formed the arms, and through the opening at the base of the earthenware head, to reinforce the bamboo that was already there. That made quite a good neck. At least it was strong.

It only remained to plant the other end of the cross-member firmly in the ground. But it was five o'clock already. There was no time for food. Who wanted another dose of *ragi* ball, anyhow? And no time for tea. That was tragedy. In our hurry we forgot about the tea and the water became cold again.

'Bring the hatchet and the other chopper, Ananthaswamy. Put on a warm coat, too. Don't forget the torch. And bring two water-pots to make it appear the dummy is drawing water. Hurry, man, hurry!'

We hastened back to the pool, at the edge of which the caretaker scooped a hole in the ground with the chopper. I stuck the 'backbone' of the dummy into this hole and pressed the earth back firmly once more. We placed the two water-pots on the ground, one on each side. *Mafiz feluce*; lo and behold! The dummy sat beside the pool. Very sincerely we hoped that to the eyes of a hungry man-eater it might appear like a human being squatting there and drawing water. To my eyes it looked only a ludicrous mess. One more look around, to see that everything was in order, then from in front we carefully stepped into our 'stronghold'.

We sat down, the caretaker to my right, while I was next to the armchair. I needed him to my right, as he was to shine the torch when the tiger came. For purposes of aligning the sights of the rifle, the light would be too far away if he had sat on my left, for I fire from the right shoulder.

It was just three minutes short of 5.30 p.m. and I knew we should have been in position at least an hour earlier. We were facing east and the sun had already dipped below the rim of hills behind us. In a few hurried and whispered sentences I gave Ananthaswamy his final instructions.

'On no account should you move your head, arms or legs. If the mosquitoes bite, blow them off. Don't slap at them. If you hear or see anything, nudge me gently with your left knee. On no account should you even whisper. If the tiger comes. I will tell you by prodding you twice. That will be the signal. It will probably growl when it leaps upon the dummy and finds no flesh and blood beneath its talons. Then shine the torch and keep it on the animal, whatever happens thereafter. Remember, you should not waver or let the torch go out. If you do that, we are dead men; because I cannot see in the dark and the tiger can.'

His reply was reassuring, 'Do not fear, *dorai*. I shall not let you down. Certainly not, for Rajamma's sake.'

Rajamma had been his daughter's name. After that we did not speak again.

'Tok-tok-tok-tok.' A green and red woodpecker tapped away with his powerful beak at the bole of a tree in the forest behind us. Then the belligerent little spurfowl began to quarrel in the bushes around. 'Kaaw-wick-a-wack,' said the challenging cockbird, and his challenge was taken up in all directions. 'Kukurruka-wack! Kukurruka-wack!' The quarrelsome little cocks were just spoiling for a fight. Far away a koel, a member of the cuckoo family, issued his plaintive cry, calling for rain, as the jungle-folk say. 'Koel! Koel! Ko-yel! Ko-yel!', he screeched in rising crescendo. His cousin, the brain-fever bird, also of the cuckoo family, decided that the call of the koel was nothing to the crescendo he could raise, if he really tried. And he did, 'Brain-fever! Brain-fever; Brain-fever!' The crescendo was almost hysterical, nerve-wracking, far eclipsing the effort the koel had made. There was silence for a while,

THE CALL OF THE MAN-EATER

and before the brain-fever bird could start again came a fresh and pleasant sound; the clarion call of the silver-hackled junglecock. 'Whee-e-e-ew! Kuck-kaya-kya-kuck'm,' he crowed lustily. That silenced the spurfowl for a second or two. Then they began their wrangling again, while other junglecocks crowed their farewell to the dying day.

Dusk fell rapidly, as it always does in the jungle. At one moment it was daylight. Then the forest before me assumed a hazy, smoky-purplish hue. A few moments later it was growing dark and it was becoming difficult to see.

The final call from the birds of the day came from a peacock roosting on some high tree far away. Mia-a-oo! Mia-a-oo! Aaow! Aaow!' he cried, and his cry was hauntingly sad. As if to assert that the time for the peacock to be active was now over, a bird of the night gave answer while it flitted like a bunch of brown soft feathers into the long grass before me. 'Chuck. Chuck. Chuck. Chuck-o-o-o-o.' My little friends, the nightsjars, were active and on the wing once more. A moment later it was night.

I have often noticed that the final calls of day-birds are answered by the early cries of the birds of the night. Then for a while comes total silence. The day-birds have gone to sleep, while those of the night are undoubtedly too busy feeding, except for the small insect-eating bats that flit swiftly overhead as they utter their sharp squeaks. 'Chee-e-ck. Chee-e-ck.' I was grateful to the little wood-cricket that started chirping almost at my feet: 'Sizz.Sizz. Sizz-z-z!.Sizz-z-z!'

The stars shone brightly now, the evening star being prominent among them. The sky was cloudless and of a gun-metal hue, a perfect setting for the myriad twinkling gems that shone so serenely, the incomparable lamps of heaven. There were other scintillating 'gems too, that moved and flitted in the jungle about us; now here, now there; now gone, but only to reappear. They were the fireflies that hung momentarily in the heavy all-pervading blackness of night, only to be gone the next instant. Then they would momentarily reappear to synchronize their flashes into one sudden, fleeting, instantaneous glare, bright enough to outline the trees far away. Once again they were gone; leaving the darkness behind.

We sat motionless. By and by the mosquitoes came, huming and buzzing around us till the air seemed filled with clouds of them. I could feel the faint but sharp pain as one after the other stung me—my face, my neck, my hands; in fact, wherever they could reach my skin. I blew gently against my own face and tried hard not to move my head or arms. Fortunately my pants, socks and shoes protected my feet. I could hear my companion blowing also, just as I had instructed him.

It was very uncomfortable and trying, to say the least of it. But it was not dangerous. For these were not malaria-carrying mosquitoes. When such an insect stings you, it almost stands on its head with its tail in the air, and you do not feel the pain of the sting. By that very same token, how was I to know how many malarial mosquitoes had already stung me that evening, and how many more would sting me before the night was over?

I glanced at my watch. It was nearly 8.30 p.m. There were many hours yet ahead of us. Ten o'clock came very, disconcertingly quiet—almost peaceful. It was as if there were no other living creatures out there in the darkness. But still we knew that the most dangerous of them all lurked in the darkness, a man-eating tiger which had already accounted for several people. But did the silence mean that he had wandered away elsewhere? Was that the reason why we had heard no alarm calls from the frightened deer? It was a cheerless and depressing thought.

THE CALL OF THE MAN-EATER

As if to dispel such ideas I heard a queer cry. Rather, I should say, a distinctive call, of a kind that I had not heard for quite a while now, and is not always heard in the jungle: 'Ba-oooh-ah! Ba-oooh-ah!'

Unmistakably, it was the cry of the 'lone jackal', the mysterious and unexplainable jackal which the jungle tribes say has entered into partnership with a tiger or panther, guiding the carnivore unerringly to a victim. The jackal's share of the partnership is permission, unmolested and freely, to pick the bones of the kill after the senior partner has eaten his fill.

The jackal was drawing closer with each minute, and rapidly too, for his cry every time was louder and more distinct! 'Ba-ooh-ah! Ba-ooh-ah!'

I thought of the rest of the strange rumour: that no victim could ever escape this terrible and diabolical alliance, once the lone jackal had located him or her and the hunt had begun. I shivered involuntarily, and at that instant felt Ananthaswamy's left knee pressing hard against my right thigh. The knee was trembling very violently.

I stared out into the pitch-darkness, attuning my ears to catch the slightest sound. But I could see or hear nothing beyond that ghastly cry that came nearer and louder with repetition: 'Ba-ooh-ah!'

Had my companion seen or heard something? Or was he trying to tell me about the lone jackal? Undoubtedly, he knew the strange tale himself. Perhaps he was not aware that I also knew it. Maybe he was trying to keep me alert, as I had cautioned him not to speak or even whisper at any cost. I forced my mind to put aside all thought of the rumour—true or false, mere superstition or not. To me, now, just one hard fact remained. A jackal was calling strangely, not at all in his usual manner. It was coming closer each second and would be near us very soon. It was up to me to try to find out if it was alone or was accompanied by another animal — perhaps only a pack of jackals like itself.

Once again, and extremely close this time, came that weird cry: 'Ba-oooh-ah! Ba-oooh-ah!'

Did I imagine a note of malevolent gloating in it? Almost a chuckle of derision? A laugh of triumph? Angrily I checked these absurd thoughts and forced myself to be more alert than ever. After that the weird cry was repeated no more. There was just silence, One could almost feel it. Heavy, oppressive silence, very heavy and very real.

Ananthaswamy was trembling violently. His knee beat a tattoo against my thigh. His whole body, which he had pressed against my right arm and side, shook as if with ague. I could hear him breathing hard; in short, sobbing gasps. I slipped my left arm across my lap, closed my hand over his kneecap softly and firmly, and then patted it reassuringly. I did not want a repitition of my experience many years before at a place called Closepet, just thirty miles from Bangalore. That episode had been rather funny, with little danger attached to it. An experience of the same kind now, but under the present circumstances, would certainly not be funny. On the other hand, it might well be the last experience of this or of any other kind that either the caretaker or myself would ever have.

A certain friend, who incidentally was a lady of some repute, had come to me wanting to shoot a panther. We had motored to Closepet, where we had arranged to tie up a couple of donkeys as bait. Two days later, information was brought that one of them had been killed. We drove to the spot to find the donkey had not been tethered properly, with the result that after killing it the panther had succeeded in dragging the donkey away from the foot of the tree where we had tied it to a place where there were only bushes and no trees. So we were faced with the alternatives of sitting on the ground to await his return or going back to Bangalore without further ado. My acquaintance enthusiastically agreed to sit anywhere I decided.

It was a certificate of high merit that the *Shikari* Thangavelu and his brother, whom we had brought with us, earned that day. For they built such a beautiful hide that the panther, when he turned up, never dreamed we were inside. Nor did we ever dream he was outside—or at least not for quite a while.

That night, too, had been dark and moonless. We could not see each other in that dense but marvellously efficient hide-out. After some time I began to hear a faint sound that came from the other side of the bush and to the left of my friend, who was sitting to the left of me.

Rub-rub-rasp-rasp. Something rather rough gliding over something rather soft. What could it be? A snake? Bush-mice? No; the first would rustle for a prolonged time; the second would cause intermittent, jerky noises as they scampered in the lantana. Could it be termites, eating the fallen leaves and dried wood? No; for they would make a sound like rain-drops pattering against the leaves of trees, diminished a hundred times in volume. Could it be caterpillars or night-beetles feeding? No; for caterpillars, when they eat, make no sound. At least, no sound capable of registering itself on the human ear. Some beetles make a very faint sound, like the clicking of fairy castnets: the mandibles of the beetles clicking together as they sever a leaf, and cause a sharp and brittle sound.

But this was something different. Rasp-rasp. Pause. Rub-rub. Pause again. Silence for some seconds. Then once more. Rasp-rasp-rasp. What the devil could it be?

Suddenly enlightenment came. It was the panther, licking himself with his rough tongue. And he was seated just outside the hide. What was more, he had no idea we were within less than two feet of him.

I remember that I nudged my friend, squeezed her arm, brought my forefinger close to her eyes and pointed towards the apparent source of the noise. Of course, she did not catch on.

Then I had another idea. I dared not whisper, for the panther would have heard me. So, with my left hand I seized one of hers. I unclenched the fingers and turned the palm upwards. All by the sense of feel. I have often wondered what she must have thought had gone wrong with me, what she must have wondered was coming next.

But I did not leave her long in doubt. With my right index finger I started tracing capital letters of the alphabet on the palm of her hand. I traced a P. Then A. Then N, and then T and H.

Then she caught on. And in real earnest. I have never seen a human being spring quite so fast to a standing position from a sitting one. Literally like lightning, she threw herself into the air, tripped over me, and fell head over heels into the bushes at my back, giving me a nasty kick in my face with her boot.

But that was not all that happened. Not by a long chalk. For the panther emulated her feat—and very creditably. Hearing what could only have been Satan himself, or whatever name Satan bears in the language of panthers, spring from the earth beside him, the panther did likewise in sheer alarm. He jumped into the air, somersaulted, and fell on top of the left side of 'wall' of our hide, next to which my companion had been seated a split second before. Realizing he was terrified and might strike out blindly with his claws or even bite, I then gave the grand finale to the entertainment by springing into the air and toppling backwards myself.

THE CALL OF THE MAN-EATER

Well, it had all ended very happily and safely. We sorted ourselves out without getting too close to each other, at least, so far as the panther was concerned, and he was good enough to reciprocate. He simply vanished.

We had a great laugh over it. My friend avowed she would not have missed the incident for anything—not even for a thousand rupees. But—and here was a real question—would it have ended thus if we had been dealing with a man-eating tiger instead of an inoffensive panther?

Coming back to realities and the present, I feared the caretaker's nerves might suddenly snap. He might do anything: jump up, cry out, or even scream. And then it might not be so good—remembering we had the 'unholy partners' to deal with, and not just a very ordinary panther. I knew that Ananthaswamy was a brave man and was certainly not afraid of the tiger. But it was the supernatural part of what was happening that was unnerving him—rather, I should say, what he thought to be supernatural: the diabolical partnership, the inhuman, or rather superhuman intelligence of that uncanny 'lone jackal' in leading the man-eater directly to us. I squeezed his knee harder than ever, then tapped it gently, over and over again, to reassure him, to try to calm him.

After that things began to happen fast. I heard the pitter-patter of quick footfalls on the dried leaves of the undergrowth to my left; that was the least fortified side of our absurd little fort, the armchair side, facing towards the bungalow, from which direction we had not anticipated that anything would approach us.

They were coming towards us, and in the undergrowth; for it was the dried leaves that were making the sound. Had it come from in front or even half-left, we would not have heard it, for there the grass was thick and soft and green, and the earth was damp from the proximity of the pool.

The pattering hesitated, came forward again, and then hesitated; forward it came two or three steps, and then it ceased altogether.

The only animal that could have made the pitter-pattering sound was the jackal—that lone jackal. And he had now halted. Why? Was it because he had become suspicious? Had he located us? Or had he stopped for quite another reason? Was his role of 'guide' and junior member now over? Was it the turn of the senior partner to take over?

We had not heard a sound from the tiger. But I was certain—as certain as I was of my own name—that the tiger was there too. Every instinct in me, every fibre of my being, furiously and insistently telegraphed the message. Beware! Danger! The man-eater is close.

Another and still more disconcerting thought flashed to my brain. Perhaps the junior partner, the cunning one, the lone jackal, had deliberately walked through the leaves to make a noise and distract our attention. Perhaps at that very moment the senior partner, the executioner, who meant business, was creeping soundlessly across the damp earth and the green grass in front, to get near enough for the last fatal charge. Worse still, he was perhaps creeping up behind.

I removed my hand from the caretaker' knee, because my hand was trembling almost as much. I stared out into the darkness before me, eyes burning, ears alert. I could see nothing, hear nothing. The seconds ticked away, perhaps the last seconds I would spend on this earth. Sweat ran down my face, trickled from my cheek on to the stock of the .405 which nestled against my shoulder, its muzzle pointing vainly outwards into the black darkness, seeing nothing. My hands, holding the rifle, were clammy with sweat.

How he got behind us we never knew, but suddenly from that direction burst, with startling suddenness, the weird, diabolical challenge: 'Ba-oooh-ah! Ba-oooh-ah!'

THE CALL OF THE MAN-EATER

And for the first time that evening, the unholy partner answered. We heard the tiger roar as he sprang upon the dummy. In our excitement we had quite forgotten it. We had overlooked the possibility that the jackal—if indeed he had led the tiger to his 'prey'—had led him to the dummy, and not to us. Our ruse had actually worked.

But Ananthaswamy was so frightened that he did not, or perhaps just could not, shine the torch. He appeared to be paralysed as we sat in inky darkness and heard the tiger worrying his 'victim'.

And at that critical moment we heard another sound—but a comforting, reassuring, homely sound, this time. The caretaker's mongrel dog began to bark vigorously. He must have come in search of his master. He had heard the noise made by the jackal, followed by the tiger roaring and tearing at the dummy. But instead of running away as he should have done, he had started barking for all he was worth.

I prodded Ananthaswamy's thigh vigorously with my clenched fist and whispered very faintly: 'Battery *Podu* (shine the torch).'

He shone it, poor fellow. But not at the tiger. He shone it directly in my face. Blinded, I grabbed the torch from him with my left hand and turned it into the darkness before us, where the dummy had been sitting. It reflected the eyes of the tiger and outlined his form very faintly behind. Raising the torch up with my left hand, I tried to hold it against the barrel of my rifle to outline the foresight while still lighting the tiger and his glaring eyes.

But luck was dead against us that night. Once again the tiger showed the man-eater's inherent fear of the man who pursues him. A loud 'Wr-r-oof!' rent the air, and the next second the tiger had gone.

I shone the torch in all directions, hoping to be able to pick up his eyes at some other spot. But he had disappeared.

I shone the torch behind us, hoping to locate that accursed jackal, which most certainly I would have shot had I but seen it. But like his partner he had vanished. Then something small and brown and white ran whimpering towards us. Could it be the lone jackal? At last at our mercy? But it whimpered and barked as it came. It was only Ananthaswamy's little dog.

Fifteen minutes later the three of us got up and started walking back to the bungalow. It was obviously useless to stay any longer. The trick of the dummy had been exposed. Both tiger and jackal now knew that men were there—not unwary men—who would slay them first. So they had decided to decamp.

As we walked back to the bungalow I reversed the conclusion I had made only a few minutes earlier. I had thought that this had been my unlucky night. Now I was sure that it had, indeed, been a very lucky one. For one thing, the so-called cunning partner, the jackal, had not proved so very cunning after all. He had warned us of the tiger's coming. Secondly, when I shone the torch, but was not ready to take the shot, the tiger had accommodatingly decided to run away. Supposing he had attacked us instead? Thirdly, perhaps by his sharp bark the little dog had helped to unnerve the tiger and had made him decide to bolt when he could have sprung upon us very easily.

Yes indeed, it had been a lucky, rather than an unlucky, night! We had both been scared stiff. We had both bungled and therefore lost the tiger. But recriminations are useless anyway. So we went to sleep.

The sun, shining brightly and warmly next morning, helped us to forget our disappointment of the night before. Ananthaswamy was thoroughly ashamed of himself. He assured me, repeatedly, that it was not the man-eater he had been terrified of, but the uncanny evil spirit, the lone jackal, the inexorable brain behind the diabolical partnership. I assured him, in turn, that I had been equally afraid, but of the tiger and not of the evil spirit or lone jackal with the calculating brain. Thus, with the air cleared between us by a mutual confession of cowardice, we started planning afresh.

It was very doubtful if the trick with the dummy could be tried again with any chance of success. The tiger, having discovered that, instead of leaping upon a living man, he had attacked a bundle of old clothes and a water-pot, would not be so foolish as to be taken in a second time within twenty-four hours. So we would have to think—and think really hard—of some fresh line of action.

I studied the pug-marks of the tiger, or such of them as we could find near the edge of the pool. He had leapt upon the dummy and then slipped in the mud as it had crumbled beneath his weight, so that there were just two fairly clear impressions of his forefeet—probably at the spot where he had stood still for a second while I had tried to align the small torch with my left hand along the barrel of my rifle. They appeared to be of the same size as the tracks left by the animal I had followed the previous day along the footpath to Gunjur. On the green grass he left no trail, while the jungle behind was dry and stony, showing no marks at all.

One fact was evident. With or without the aid of the jackal, the tiger had been pretty hungry. He had attacked the dummy straight away, and that had left him more hungry than ever. He would have to eat, and soon. Therefore, either he must have killed some animal during the later hours of the night, or he would do so in the early hours of the night to come. As a rule tigers do not hunt wild game during daylight, and there were no domestic cattle at Gunjur. Alternatively he had already left, or would leave the locality at sunset, because of his fright, and take himself elsewhere.

Together we walked back along the footpath to Joldahl for about a mile. But the tiger had not returned that way. We went back to Gunjur and climbed up a knoll half a mile from the bungalow. From this elevation we carefully scanned the sky and it would betray the presence of a kill, if there had been one. But no vultures were to be seen in any direction.

Midday found us much more disconsolate, and quite unsuccessful; and then we did what seemed a very silly thing. We rigged up the dummy afresh and sat in the same hide. This seemed silly for two reasons. Firstly, it was scarcely likely that the tiger would be taken in by the dummy a second time. But, what was far more important, and what did not occur to us till we had actually taken up our positions, was the fact that, if the tiger did return, he would know where we were because of the episode of the night before.

The spotted deer called shortly after 8 p.m. The jungle at the foot of the knoll we had climbed that morning resounded to their sharp, frightened cries of alarm: 'Aiow! Aiow! Aiow!' A stag started first, and then the others took it up. 'Aiow! Aiow! Aiow!'

Undoubtedly they had seen or smelt the tiger. This caused our morale to rise greatly. At least he was still here and had not gone away. But not a sound did we hear from the tiger himself, or from his partner, the lone jackal.

Ten o'clock came, and once more it seemed the predetermined hour for the curtain to rise on the tiger's activities. From a direction a little to the south of us we heard an agonizing, pitiful scream; a shriek that was but twice repeated, ending on a muffled, sobbing note. An animal had just been done to death; probably a spotted deer or a young sambar. The tiger had succeeded in finding his meal. We made a mental note of the approximate direction from which the sound had come.

THE CALL OF THE MAN-EATER

After that nothing happened for the rest of the night, nor did the spotted deer call again. Ananthaswamy fell asleep after two o'clock, while I could hardly keep my eyes open. But just had to remain awake. For both of us to go to sleep would have been very dangerous indeed.

As soon as it was light enough to see, we left the hide and started walking in the direction of the death-call of the previous night. If we were very lucky we might flush the tiger while still on his kill. But there was only one thing wrong with this plan. We had no idea where the kill really was or where to look for it. We searched till nearly nine o'clock. Then the sun began to get hot, and I was very tired. I had not slept the whole night and had slept only half the night before that. So we went back to the bungalow.

Ananthaswamy started to cook his *ragi* balls, which I had begun to look upon more as cannon balls than anything else. Without waiting for this frightful food, I went to sleep. It was after one o'clock in the afternoon when I awoke to find an unusually large *ragi* ball left thoughtfully beside me on a plate with a bowl of tea that had gone quite cold. Ananthaswamy was curled up asleep in the further corner of the room. Resignedly, I nibbled at the glutinous, tasteless mess. If only it had a little sugar with it, or even salt. I turned to the cold tea and emptied the bowl. At least it had some flavour.

Walking out on the verandah of the bungalow, I looked hopefully towards the south. No vultures circled in the sky. There was not a clue to lead us to the kill of the night before. And that meant that again we could not plan any definite line of action for the coming hours of darkness.

For one fact I was grateful, however. Even if the deer the tiger had killed had been a fairly small one, and he had consumed it all, the chances were that he would linger for another twenty-four hours in the vicinity before hunger again drove him out to seek another kill.

It was too late for me to walk the ten miles back to Joldahl, purchase a live bait, and bring it back to tie up before nightfall. That, I determined, was what I would do the following day. For that night there seemed nothing better to do than sit once again in our old hide near the spring, changing the position of the dummy this time. Meanwhile, as it was not yet two o'clock and the caretaker was still asleep. I decided to spend the next two hours of the afternoon in walking along some of the game-trails that led into the foothills surrounding the little bungalow.

I was sure the tiger had killed the night before, for both Ananthaswamy and I had heard the victim's death-cry. If only I could locate the spot before nightfall and sit up over it, there was reasonable certainty that the tiger would return.

With this idea in mind I once more walked south towards the hillock from which that dying scream had sounded. This time I approached it from another angle, my attention divided between scanning any ground sandy enough to show pug-marks and looking around for vultures or even a crow perched on a tree to indicate the spot where the tiger had hidden the carcass. And all the time I had to watch carefully where I was walking, avoiding passing too close to a thicket or bush that might conceal a tiger lying in wait behind it.

For just as certainly as I was hunting him, the tiger, being a man-eater, would hunt me. It was a game in which neither could afford to make the slightest error, which would mean not only the end of the game but the end of the one that made it. Such caution made my progress very slow. Eventually I reached a sandy *nullah* that wound around the base of the hillock. Here I stopped and turned to my left to follow the *nullah* for a short distance to see if the tiger had crossed it.

After a while I saw pug-marks in the sand, but they certainly had not been made the night before. These were at least a week old; perhaps ten days. Disappointed, I crossed the *nullah* and started climbing the hillock.

The ground became pebbly, covered with the red laterite gravel that abounds on so many of the lesser hills throughout Mysore state. Because of this the vegetation became sparse, the undergrowth giving way to isolated 'vallary' plants, dwarf grass, and lantana mixed with prickly pear growing intermittently. I was glad of it because the tiger could no longer spring a surprise on me in this comparatively open terrain. By the same token, he would not have brought his kill up here, for there was nowhere to hide it. So it was useless for me to continue my search. When I looked at my watch I was surprised to find it was 3.20 p.m. I would have to hurry back, for we should arrange the dummy and be in our hide by five.

The return journey was quicker, for I did not look for pug-marks or vultures although I certainly continued to give a wide berth to large clumps of bushes or grass behind which the tiger might be hiding. It was just after four when I got back to a very anxious Ananthaswamy. Fortunately he had prepared some fresh tea, which I drank gratefully, although I could not respond to his invitation to try another *ragi* ball. We titivated the dummy a little and carried it back to the stream. This time we did not put it at the edge of the pool, but on the grassy patch about twenty yards from our hide. This particular spot had no merit beyond being a few yards closer to our zareba, behind which we settled ourselves shortly after five.

Knowing that, in spite of the hours he had already slept that afternoon, Ananthaswamy would fall asleep again by midnight, I asked him to keep watch till seven, when it would be dark, while I took a short nap to prepare myself for an all-night vigil. Thus it came about that I was deprived on that occasion, of listening to the full-throated notes of the birds of the day gradually fall into diminuendo, giving place to the crescendo of calls of the birds and beasts of the night.

I awoke tardily, with the caretaker shaking my shoulder. Above me, in the clear velvety sky, the stars twinkled serenely. It was inky dark and I knew that Anathaswamy had had compassion on me and let me sleep beyond the time at which I had told him to awaken me. I glanced at my watch. It was 8.12 p.m. Gently, and as soundlessly as possible, I sat up.

And then I heard it. Although far away, the sound carried clearly in the cool night air: 'Ba-oooh-ah! Ba-oooh-ah!'

Involuntarily, instinctively, my hand closed on the stock of my rifle, as the old, frightening thoughts, born of the age-old jungle rumour, once more impinged themselves on my mind. The ghastly partners were on the prowl again. Would that uncanny jackal guide the tiger to us, just as he had done two nights previously?

The answer came, almost like a spoken reply to my unvoiced thoughts: 'A-oongh! O-o-n-ooh! Aungh-ha! Aungh-ha!'

The tiger was roaring, and his voice came from exactly the same direction as had that of the lone jackal, hardly a couple of minutes earlier. The jungle-folk sounded the alarm in every direction. To the north and beyond the bungalow a sambar stag bellowed his deep-throated nasal warning, beginning with a startled 'Ponk!,' then 'Whee-onk! Whee-onk!' Finally he settled down to voicing a steady alarm-call that floated across the hills and far, far away: 'Dhank! Dhank! Dhank!' Far closer to us a muntjac, or barking-deer, uttered the hoarse, almost dog-like bark which has given him his name: 'Kharr! Kharr! Kharr!'

Hearing the calls of fear, a spotted deer hind, hidden in the thickets behind us, screamed her preliminary warning, a grating, sharp, whistling-like sound; 'Phrew! Phrew!' Then the stag, leader of the heard, took it up with a startled 'Aiow! Aiow! Aiow!' Even a peacock, roosting and fast asleep on some distant bough, was disturbed. 'Pe-haun! Pe-haun!', he squawked as he awakened, changing to his usual 'Mia-a-oo! Aaow! Mia-a-oo!'

The whole jungle was alarmed and alert. The frogs in the pool ceased their croaking. Even the crickets in the damp grass stopped chirping. Every living creature, big or small, thinks and knows the same thing: Beware! Tiger! Danger!

But for us there was no fleeing. We were there with a set purpose—to destroy the man-eater. With tensed nerves and muscles we awaited the drama that was to be played out in the next few minutes or hours.

The cries of alarm died away in the distance as the animals that uttered them made for safer regions, as far as possible from the presence of that striped terror which to them, as to every living creature at that moment, spelled violent death. The jungle fell into a silence that was full of menace. I thought about Ananthaswamy's feeble two-cell torch, the light from which had become even weaker after the use we had lately given it. It was the one and only means of showing up the tiger to enable me to take a shot.

Nothing happened. An hour passed, an hour of utter, complete silence. Even the frogs and crickets had not begun their relatively homely noises again. More time passed, and with the lessening of tension I stole a glance at my watch. It was 10.5 p.m. and I was feeling inordinately hungry.

Then the hair at the back of my neck seemed of its own volition to stand on end. Ananthaswamy's cold and clammy hand reached out to catch my arm. He was trembling violently.

Pitter-patter. Pitter-patter. Pitter-patter. The noise came from behind us this time, once again in the undergrowth. The same undergrowth in which we were hiding, protected by our flimsy cage. Some animal was walking swiftly over the carpet of dried leaves that covered the ground. A few twigs snapped as it forced its way through the bushes and shrubs.

What could it be? Certainly not the tiger. The footfalls were too light, too swift. Could it be the lone jackal showing the way once more? Wistfully I longed for the little mongrel that yapped and so, perhaps, saved our lives only forty-eight hours before. Alas, we had made certain he would not again interfere at a critical time by locking him in the caretaker's room.

Then silence fell again. The glow from the stars enabled me to distinguish the dummy faintly, only twenty yards away: a dim, white object, almost invisible to my tired eyes. It was impossible to penetrate the undergrowth behind us from which the pitter-pattering sound had come.

After a while we heard the quick light footsteps scampering to our right, south of where we were sitting. Again silence and then a grey, wraith-like shape seemed to flit across the grass in front of us, and between us and the dummy. It seemed rather small, and it moved in a swift, peculiarly jerky, manner. It came to a stop almost opposite us.

The reflected glow of the stars did not shed enough light to enable me to see clearly what the animal was up to. It seemed suddenly to shrink to half its size, but I realized this was because the creature had turned to face us. What was apparently the head seemed to bob up and down quickly as the eyes strove to pierce the screen of undergrowth that hid us, to determine what manner of creatures we were.

One thing was certain: our position was no longer secret. The animal knew there was something or someone behind the camouflage. This was corroborated by the fact that it took no notice whatever of the dummy. It had turned its back upon the dummy and was staring at us intently.

The next moment I not only heard the cry of the lone jackal but saw the animal raise his head towards the sky to utter it: 'Ba-oooh-ah! Ba-oooh-ah!'

Immediately after, as if galvanized into action, the jackal sped some yards away, where it stopped abruptly, turned around and stared intently in our direction.

So interested had I been in this animal's movements that it was Ananthaswamy's hand, squeezing my arm in a vice-like, painful grip, that made me half-turn my head towards him. And as I did so, my glance took in an apparition that momentarily paralysed me with shock. On the very spot where the jackal had been but a second before was a beast of apparently colossal size. In that unreal light it looked as big as a horse.

I knew that I was gazing at the tiger as he stood before us in the grass, broadside on, looking at us intently, just as the jackal had done a moment earlier.

Twice I nudged Ananthaswamy, hard and quickly. It was the prearranged signal for him to shine his torch on the animal. There was no response. The caretaker could not move. Ruefully I realized that once more he had failed me just when I needed his help. I nudged him again, with the same lack of response. With closed fist I pummelled him. But Ananthaswamy just sat and gaped. I cursed myself for having left my own torch behind. But how could I have foreseen events as they happened?

The tiger spotted my movement. Or he may have heard the infinitesimal sound of my fist on Ananthaswamy's thigh. He growled menacingly and his silhouette grew smaller and seemed to merge with the grass. I knew he had sunk to the ground preparatory to charging upon us. Two or three bounds and he would be on top of us, through the unprotected front of our hide.

The tiger's action and my conclusions were almost simultaneous. Perhaps it all took less than ten seconds.

Grabbing the torch from the caretaker's nerveless fingers, I pressed the button even before I had aligned it against the barrel of my rifle. The beam certainly did not show up my foresight, but did shine directly into the tiger's eyes. Although it was a far from powerful light, the tiger baulked appreciably. Perhaps it associated the light with the surprise it had received two nights earlier, when it had leapt upon the dummy. Whatever caused it to hesitate gave me the split-second I needed to put the bead of the foresight in a direct line between the backsight and the gleaming eyes.

Such a shot is by no means ideal, particularly as I was holding both torch and rifle together with my left hand. If placed too high, the bullet was apt to glance off the receding forehead of the tiger. But there was no time for anything else, and I squeezed the trigger.

The report of the rifle was followed by an ear-splitting roar as the tiger reared on its hind feet, its front paws clawing at its smashed face. Feverishly I worked the under-lever and fired into the exposed white fur of its chest.

It came down to earth after that, floundering around blindly while clods of mud and grass were torn up by the threshing talons as they struck wildly into the ground, and by the gaping jaws as they bit savagely in agony. Roar after roar rent the air, while I fired every bullet the magazine held. Losing count of my shots, I heard the click of the firing-pin against the empty chamber. The tiger was still writhing and squirming, but the roars had given place to a gurgle, the unmistakable death-rattle of an expiring tiger.

'Hold the torch.' I whispered hurriedly, thrusting it into the caretaker's numbed hand, while I feverishly loaded three rounds into the magazine.

THE CALL OF THE MAN-EATER

I could just see the heaving flank of the tiger as it lay on its side in the long grass. The gurgle became irregular. Suddenly it ceased and I knew the tiger was dead. We waited another fifteen minutes, but there was no further movement.

The lone jackal never reappeared. Perhaps he knew by instinct that he had led his partner to his death and was sorry. Maybe he hurried away after that to find another partner, remembering that the association had hitherto brought him easy and big dividends.

We examined the tiger carefully next morning. He was a very old male with worn canines. But apart from that he appeared to have no other defects. What had turned him against the human race? Maybe it was just a whim in the first place. Perhaps he had felt old age creeping up on him and had discovered a convenient way of procuring his food. Possibly it was the jackal that had in the first place tempted him by leading him to easy prey—the caretaker's unfortunate daughter. Who can tell?

Two

The Evil One of Umbalmeru

THE GOLDEN-BROWN OF THE JUNGLE GRASSES, MELLOWED AT FIRST by the rains and then burnt dry by the merciless heat of the midday sun, covers the sides of the sloping hills that appear to have raised themselves haphazardly in this jungly corner of the land. At the base of each hill, narrow, sharp valleys have been formed by the rain-water during centuries of storms that have burst against the steeper heights and then cascaded in turbulent, muddy streams down the jungle-clad slopes to the valleys below, where, joining together, they have eventually formed the northeastern branch of the little Kalyani river.

These small valleys are choked with undergrowth: cane-bamboo, lantana and the clinging vines of the 'killer' creeper, which certainly has earned its name.

Years ago some little bird may have eaten a few of its brown berries and had then rested on a leafy perch. The meat of the berries was soon assimilated, and the little bird

THE EVIL ONE OF UMBALMERU

passed out the undigested seeds. One such seed would have fallen at the foot of the mighty tree where it had rested. Then the rains came and the little seed sprouted and a baby 'killer' was born, no bigger at first than the nail on your little finger.

But the seedling grows apace and puts out its tendrils when a month old, thus revealing itself for the first time as a plant that creeps and supports its weight on other plants and trees. It grows and grows, and by the end of the first year it has perhaps climbed a third of the way up the big tree which has sheltered it. But its stem is still no thicker than your middle finger. Within two years it has reached the top of the tree, whence its tendrils reach out hungrily towards the neighbouring forest giants, all of them, like the host tree, possibly two or three centuries old. And the stem of the creeper is now about the thickness of your wrist.

The years roll by and the creeper has completely covered and enmeshed the old tree that supports it. The stem, which was as thick as your finger and then your wrist, has now become as thick as your thigh, and it continues to grow till it becomes as thick as your body. Its weight is colossal. It has wound even tighter around the trunk and branches of its host, biting through the soft outer bark into the very heart of the wood.

Slowly, inexorably, it strangles its host to death. Years later the rains and storms come again. Perhaps on a night very similar to the one on which the 'killer' was born, the grand old tree that had played host to the innocent-looking killer crashes to earth, devoured by the 'baby' to which it once gave shelter. From amid the fallen debris the tendrils of the 'killer' reach out voraciously towards the stems of neighbouring trees, there to repeat the grim story and to earn its name of 'killer' over and over again.

THE CALL OF THE MAN-EATER

Because of the heavy undergrowth in the narrow valleys, it is impossible for a man, and almost out of the question for an animal of any size to penetrate the leafy tangle. It is the home of rodents and other such tiny creatures, and the many species of snakes that prey upon them. It is always green there, despite the driest summer months and hottest tropical sun. For the weight of the surrounding hills seems to press the moisture out of the very earth itself, to make slushy marshes in the tangled verdure where the crickets chirp all day and there is perpetual twilight. No rays from the sun can penetrate the canopy of greenery. A moment's delay in sprouting and upward thrusting means that the neighbouring bush, vine or shrub has seized the opportunity and the laggard is doomed to an existence of perpetual shade and eventual death from rot and decay.

But above the valleys, on the slopes of the hills, it is different. There the sun beats down mercilessly, and in the summer months the leaves of the trees dry up and fall to the ground to form a rustling carpet upon the earth, till the rains bring decay and turn them into mould to feed the very trees from which they have fallen.

Higher up on the hills it is cooler and rockier: a region of tumbled boulders and lichens and mosses, while orchids hang from boles and branches, and the large blue-black bird, known as the 'whistling schoolboy', thrills the listening ear with his wondrous, rambling, warbling notes, carrying never quite the same melody twice.

It is shortly after midday when my story begins: and the whistling schoolboy, together with most other birds and nearly all the beasts, both large and small, is taking his afternoon siesta under some shady boulder overlooking the crystal-clear icy-cold water that trickles from a crack in the face of a rock at the foot of an overhanging escarpment. Hardly a puff of

THE EVIL ONE OF UMBALMERU

air can be felt, and the twigs on the trees and the barbed stems of the tall grasses are motionless. It is strangely quiet at this noonday hour. Even the crickets are silent, and not a leaf stirs or rustles in the neighbourhood. It is as if all the world had been lulled into a deep torpor.

But there comes a faint sound after a while, audible above the gentle murmuring of the waters of the stream as they glide over the smoothly-worn, moss-green, slippery rocks that form their bed. It is a staccato, intermittent sound. The noise of someone or something digging, and it comes from the farther bank of the brook and about fifty yards away.

A human figure can be seen there, crouched on its haunches and almost hidden from view among the huge leaves of the 'elephant-ear' lily that grows in profusion along the banks of the stream. Only the jerky movements, as the man wields his short crowbar, and the sound of the digging itself, betray his presence; for his jet-black body, naked except for a small strip of dirty *loincloth,* blends perfectly with the dark shadows beneath and around the huge leaves of the lilies.

Old Kothanda Reddy has come a long way from his village—the village of Rangampet—nearly twelve miles distant, to dig up the rare bulbs of the kuloo water-plant, famed as an aphrodisiac of rare and magical power, that grow here and there among the giant lilies. He has to search carefully for the kuloo water-plant, with its three-petalled, shamrock-like leaf, so tiny as to be almost completely hidden from view by its huge bedfellow. And when he finds one he has to dig deep into the mire after levering aside the movable stones in order to reach the slender bulbous white roots of the little plant. These roots, when dried thoroughly and later powdered and mixed with male semen and finally treated with magical incantations on the night of the new moon (called 'Amavasa night'), assume their full potency.

It is said that a pinch of this powder, mixed with the loved one's food, or better still administered in coffee without milk and liberally sweetened with jaggery or brown sugar to hide the slightly acrid taste, would so excite the woman as to cause her to throw all modesty to the winds, and incidentally herself, unreservedly and unashamedly, into the arms of her eager and already-prepared lover. The concoction evidently has some value—or at least a reputation for value—for old Kothanda Reddy had been selling it for some years for one rupee per pinch. He is secretly proud of the number of illegitimate children in the village of Rangampet—living testimonials in his opinion to the efficacy of the kuloo roots.

So Kothanda Reddy bends himself to the task and digs deeply, while the dull and intermittent sound of his crowbar is almost drowned, but not quite, by the gurgling and burbling sounds from the hurrying waters of the rivulet. And being thus engrossed he does not notice the malevolently cruel eyes that glare down upon him from a point immediately above and higher up the bank of the rocky little rill.

The creature that watches him makes not the slightest sound that might betray its presence. No growl of any sort issues from the cavernous chest and throat. Nor do the eyes blink once in their searching and merciless gaze.

The point of the crowbar finally lays bare the tender white roots. Old Kothanda Reddy sets it aside and stoops forward to reach with both hands into the hole he has made to disentangle the roots from the surrounding ooze.

The silent watcher above, who has been observing his every movement, notices the action and knows that the man, with his head bent forward and downward, cannot possibly see it now. A red tongue swiftly licks the lips of the upper jaw. Then the creature crouches lower before committing the first of a series of murders that will give it the name of the 'Evil One' in a score of villages and hamlets that border the three forest ranges known as the Bhakarapet Reserve, the Chamala valley, and the Mamandur High Range forests of the Chittoor district, now belonging to the state of Andhra Pradesh.

A moment later the deed is done. Kothanda Reddy never saw the massive form that hurtled through the air and down upon him, although for a second he did feel its stupendous weight, and the agony from the deep wounds inflicted by its talons as they embedded themselves in his exposed back and sides. But that was only for a moment, because the next instant powerful jaws, armed with massive fangs, crunched through his neck and the back of his skull. So Kothanda Reddy died, and he did not know the moment of his passing to another realm where aphrodisiacs are not in demand and the kuloo roots have no value.

It was quite a long time before the old man was missed at Rangampet. It had been his habit to wander off into the jungle to look for his mysterious roots and herbs, or go on a round of the neighbouring villages to sell his concoctions and magical powders and charms and amulets which had spread his reputation far and wide as a great magician or *mantramkara*, as he was called. And when eventually he was missed his bones were never found to associate his passing with the Evil One. But, weeks later, two wandering forest guards, who had climbed the slopes of the hill and stopped at the little brook for a drink of its icy-cold water, noticed the crowbar and beside it a dirty cloth bag that had been partly devoured by termites which, however, had not eaten the evil-looking and mouldering roots that now spilled out and lay scattered on the moist ground of the streambed. Then they remembered that Kothanda Reddy had been missing for quite a long while, causing some people to say he had left Rangampet suddenly and for good. Now, for the first time, the forest guards knew why he had never returned.

The tragedy had evidently taken place quite a long while before, and there were no traces to indicate the nature or identity of his murderer. The forest guards duly reported their find to the police *chowki* at Rangampet, where a note was made of what they had said.

No very definite or proper record was kept of the activities of the Evil One, at least at the beginning of its career; but reports say that the next event occurred in the following manner.

It was again afternoon and around three o'clock, when a line of seven bullock-carts were returning from the jungle along the rough forest track that led to Rangampet from a well seven miles away in the jungle at a place called Pulibonu. About a quarter-of-a-mile off the roadway, and almost opposite the fourth milestone from the village, is a perennial water hole known as Narasimha Cheruvu. The seven men halted their carts beside the fourth milestone and descended the two furlongs to the water hole, chatting as they went, to wash their faces and hands and legs in the limpid, lukewarm brown water, and then their mouths by the simple process of holding a handful of water to their lips, gargling without swallowing it, and ejecting it into the pool.

Finally, the seven men squatted down beneath a *babul* tree near the water's edge for a brief smoke of *beedies*. The *beedies* finished, they got up and returned to their carts in single file. They reached the carts all right. At least, six of them did—but there was no sign of the seventh man. What could he be about, and where had he got to? His half-dozen companions, with the stoical indifference and patience of the Indian villager, time being of no consequence anyhow, sat down at the roadside to wait for him and smoke some more *beedies*. Idly one of them remarked that Puttoo Reddy, the missing cartman, had been walking last in the file. The speaker had happened to turn around for a moment and had noticed Puttoo Reddy stop to light a *beedi*. He was a very heavy smoker.

Time passed and the missing man did not put in an appearance. It would have been safe to wait for him indefinitely under normal circumstances. But if they now dallied too long it would be dark before they were out of the jungle and among the fields surrounding Rangampet. That did not appeal to them.

They began to call him: 'Puttoo Reddy! Hurry up, man; where the devil are you?'—'Puttoo Reddy!'—'Puttoo Reddy!' Puttoo Reddy did not appear.

Panic seized the six cartmen. It was unthinkable to go back the short distance to the water hole to look for their missing companion. Perhaps some evil spirit had seized him. Maybe a snake had bitten him. Perhaps he had been taken by a tiger. Or a panther. Or a bear. But the majority of them ascribed his disappearance to supernatural agencies.

Within a few moments each of them had scrambled into his bullock-cart and the six pairs of bullocks rattled off with their carts as fast as they could, urged on by constant whipping. Left alone at the fourth milestone was the seventh cart— Puttoo Reddy's, the bulls waiting patiently for their owner. He never came.

During the night it grew cold and the dew was heavy. The two bulls that were still yoked to the cart forgot their owner and remembered their dry, cosy stalls at Rangampet. They travelled through the night and reached the village at about 4 a.m. There could be no tigers about, for they were unmolested.

Nevertheless Puttoo Reddy—just like Kothanda Reddy before him—had apparently vanished into thin air without

THE CALL OF THE MAN-EATER

leaving a trace. When a third man, and then a fourth, disappeared within the next two months, people began to say the Chamala Valley was haunted by an 'Evil One', who left no evidence of his coming or of his going, except that he took a human being with him on each occasion.

The third victim was a petty trader who had been driving a pack of ten or twelve donkeys, laden with gram, from Rangampet to a small hamlet thirteen miles away to the northwest. He had been seen eating his midday meal at the well at Pulibonu, which was just beyond the seventh milestone along this track. In fact, he had requested one of a number of bamboo-cutters who had been camped there to draw some water for him from the well, as he had no rope. The man had obliged and the petty merchant had drunk his fill. Then he had been seen reloading his donkeys and had finally moved off, driving them before him.

The following day some other travellers, coming from the opposite direction, had found the pack of donkeys scattered but browsing contentedly in the vicinity of the tenth milestone. They were still carrying the sacks of gram on their backs. But there was no trace of their owner.

The fourth man to vanish had done so at Pulibonu itself. And by a quirk of fate he was the very bamboo-cutter who had obliged by drawing water from the well for the owner of the donkeys. A party of cutters, engaged on contract to fell bamboos in what is known as a 'coupe' in the vicinity of Pulibonu itself, had been camping there for over a month. Just a few days after he had obliged the vanished merchant, this very bamboo-cutter had assembled with his companions beside the Pulibonu well to eat his midday meal and drink water. Thereafter all of them had returned to their respective tasks. But later in the evening, when the day's work was over, he had not rejoined his companions in the small huts

THE EVIL ONE OF UMBALMERU

they had temporarily built close to the roadside. Nor was he ever seen again.

The other bamboo-cutters had not immediately panicked. In fact, the following morning they set out in a body to look for him. They had come to the place where he had been lopping bamboos. A short distance away they had found his *koitha* or chopping-knife. Close to it was the white cloth of his turban where it had fallen off, still shaped to his head. It looked just as if he had taken off the turban carefully and set it aside on the ground, rather than as if it had fallen off.

Spreading out fanwise, his companions had thoroughly searched the jungle, the ground, even the leaves of the trees and blades of grass for a clue to his mysterious disappearance. If he had been attacked and killed by a wild animal there would surely be some traces, a smear of blood, a pug-mark, or a drag-mark where his body had been hauled through the undergrowth. But there were none of these things.

It looked as if he had just taken off his turban deliberately and neatly, laid it on the ground, and then decided to vanish into thin air. But no one would, or could, do that, and in the absence of any trace of violence, the only other conclusion that could be reached—at least in the minds of the other bamboo-cutters—was that supernatural agencies had once again been at work and had whisked away their companion just like the petty merchant before him, and the cartman before that. Even their reputed village magician, Kothanda Reddy, had been helpless before these evil spirits or spirit— this Evil One—which had now come into their jungles, and had come apparently to stay.

Once panic had seized the inhabitants of Rangampet, it gripped them in real earnest. From alarm it soon turned into terror, and it spread through all the villages. The police were alerted, as were the officials of the Forest department. Even the Collector at Chittoor was informed. But the ancients living in Rangampet wagged their heads sadly, if not amusedly. What could the police and other officials do against the Evil One?

Obviously, the only remedy was to appease the Evil One. And the only method of appeasement was by sacrifice—by blood! The police officials in the vicinity grew apprehensive. When the question of sacrifice in a case such as this arose, it was a moot point whether the frightened villagers would consider the life of an animal, such as a fowl or a goat, which were the creatures generally used for a sacrificial ceremony, of sufficient importance to propitiate this Evil Spirit that now haunted the jungle. They might get the impression that a sacrifice of a higher order was called for. A human sacrifice; perhaps a child. Such things had happened before.

So the police *daffedar* (head constable, who ranked as a sergeant) incharge of the tiny Police *Chowki* at Rangampet warned Krishnappa Reddy—the new village voodoo-man, magician and witch-doctor combined, upon whose shoulders the mantle of old Kothanda Reddy had automatically fallen as he was the only eligible candidate in the vicinity—that they would lock him up and then hang him if any of the village children were found missing.

Faced with this curb to his professional activities, Krishnappa Reddy was not easily upset. Whatever conclusion he reached is not known. It was not long afterwards that Adiraj, the nine-year-old son of a Harijan woman named Adima, who was of the 'scavenger' or 'sweeper' class, was reported by his mother as missing from the town of Chandragiri.

Now Chandragiri is hardly six miles from Rangampet, and is the headquarters of the district. A weekly market-fair, called a *shandy*, is held there every Monday. The people from the surrounding villages are in the habit of attending this weekly shandy to buy such provisions and other odds and ends as are not procurable in their own hamlets. What was more to the point, Krishnappa Reddy had been seen by several people at the *shandy* on a Monday morning. The small boy, Adiraj, had slept the previous Sunday night beside his mother. On Monday morning he had told her he intended to wander off to the *shandy* to see what was to be seen, and he had not been seen by anyone after that.

It was not till Friday that Adima screwed up enough courage to report to the police that her son had been missing since Monday morning. The sub-inspector, hot on the scent, requisitioned a *jutka*—a two-wheeled conveyance drawn by a pony—and ordered the driver to make his pony go at a gallop all the six miles to the hamlet of Rangampet. There he searched Krishnappa Reddy's hut very painstakingly, hoping to find some clue to the missing lad's fate—perhaps a blood-stained cloth or knife, or some part of his anatomy, such as his liver or heart or other organs, as these are known to play an important role in sacrificial rights. But he found nothing.

Very indignant and disappointed at his failure, the annoyed sub-inspector took Krishnappa Reddy back to Chandragiri in handcuffs and kept him there over a week. But nobody had come forward to say they had seen him talking to the missing boy, Adiraj. Worse still, nobody could be found who would at least say he thought he had seen the man and the child together. After all, remember, Krishnappa Reddy was a magician! Suppose he laid a curse upon the man or woman who volunteered such witness, false or true, against him?

So on the ninth morning the sub-inspector released the magician and told him to walk back the six miles to his village, where he was to remain and not leave without the permission of the police. To this Krishnappa Reddy had said enigmatically: 'The fox is cunning; but can he outwit a jackal?'

The sub-inspector pondered over those words for several days. Had he been alluded to as the jackal? Or was he only the fox? Whatever fate befell Adiraj was never known. But if he had, indeed, been used as a secret sacrifice, apparently the Evil One would have no part of him. For within a week the fifth victim disappeared.

This time it was a woman. And she vanished near the turning where the footpath, leading to a *nullah* named Ragimankonar, branches off the road from Rangampet to Pulibonu. This turning is within three miles of the village.

The woman, whose name was Venkatamma, had prepared the midday meal for her husband, who had left earlier in the morning with their cattle to graze them in the jungle where he had grazing rights. She set forth at noon to take the meal to the rendezvous they had agreed upon before he left—the sacred peepul tree that grew on the bank of the Ragimankonar *nullah,* where it dropped some thirty feet into a wide sandy hollow where water only gathered during the rainy season.

The man grew angry, because he was hungry; and his anger increased in direct proportion to his hunger, when his spouse never showed up with the long-overdue midday meal. He decided to beat the lazy wench soundly when she did appear. That would encourage her to be more prompt in future.

But the beating never took place. Venkatamma never came to receive it.

It was a highly indignant and furious grazier who drove the herd home much earlier than usual that afternoon, both to eat a belated lunch and to administer the thrashing his wife would long remember, instead of just a normal beating, which was the usual corrective. Once again he was doomed to disappointment. There was no lunch awaiting him—and no Venkatamma. His little daughter told him that mother had left exactly at noon, carrying the meal in an earthen 'chatty' pot.

Some days later searchers found the *chatty* pot lying broken beside the footpath less than half-a-mile from the peepul tree beneath which the herdsman had been waiting all afternoon. But of Venkatamma there was not a trace.

I came one day with an Indian friend to camp for a week at the Forest Bungalow at Nagapatla, which is built near the outskirts of the jungle one mile from Rangampet, on the track that led to Pulibonu. The manner of my coming and the purpose of my visit on that occasion had certainly been unusual. Although I had brought my rifle and gun as a matter of course, we had not planned a serious hunting trip. My friend, Deva Sundram, was in trouble, and I had brought him to Nagapatla to help him out of it. For, of all things, Deva Sundram had contracted whooping-cough, and by his own admission he was thirty-eight years of age.

I know little of sicknesses and far less of doctoring. But I understand that whooping-cough is a child's complaint and seldom, if ever, affects adults. Nevertheless, Deva Sundram had most certainly contracted it in real earnest from his own little son. All the known remedies had apparently not helped the poor man, nor had they allayed his fits of coughing and wheezing and whooping. I had happened to visit him one evening at his home in Bangalore. He was crouched on a sofa, his eyes popping out of his head, spluttering and making strange noises in his throat. Between spasms he waved me frantically away and stuttered: 'Go away. I have whooping-cough. If you come near me you will catch it. Go away—go away.' His wife anxiously explained that they had tried every remedy on the market and several doctors, but Dev seemed to be getting worse.

Now it so transpired that not so many years previously my own daughter, June, and son, Donald, had contracted whooping cough. I had planned to go to Nagapatla on a hunting trip about that time. My wife, who is a bit of a nurse, had thought that the dry, hot climate of the place would shorten the malady and suggested we take the children along. We did so, and she had been right. Both of them had stopped whooping within forty-eight hours.

I mentioned this to Mrs. Sundram. Dev ceased trying to choke to death long enough to listen. Being a lover of the jungle himself, he had just been able to stutter: 'Capital; let's start today,' when off he went into another paroxysm of whooping. It was rather funny to watch him and I could barely repress a smile. Later, he told me he did not think much of my sense of humour.

However, as a result of all this, we left for Nagapatla the following morning in the T Model Ford I owned in those days. We left Bangalore rather early in order not to expose Dev to the chill of the night air. For the Model T, in spite of all its virtues, is not a fast-moving vehicle, and we would never have reached Nagapatla till late at night, the distance being about 170 miles. By leaving in the morning and chugging along at an average twenty miles an hour, stopping now and then to pour water into the radiator, and for lunch, we got to the bungalow shortly before five in the evening. It was noticeably warm even then, and Dev was delighted that I had suggested coming to this place. In spite of the long and somewhat uncomfortable and bumpy journey on the hard springs of the Model T, he had been coughing less since the time we had reached low country after passing Chittoor.

Eating dinner by lantern-light on the wide verandah of the thatched bungalow, I began to chat to the 'bungalow-keeper', a humble servant of the Forest department and an old friend of mine, and asked him for *jungly khubbar*, the latest news of what had been happening in the jungles surrounding the little bungalow.

THE EVIL ONE OF UMBALMERU

He was absolutely bursting with excitement and in a torrent of speech began to tell of the exploits of the Evil One that had come to the forest during the past few months and had accounted for the disappearance of five people already.

Mixed with what he had picked up in the way of rumours, and his own conjectures, plus the centuries-old background of superstition and the tales of witchcraft he had learned as a child, the old bungalow watcher told us an interesting and romantic tale, filled with fantastic details of how each of the five victims had disappeared.

Dev and I were thrilled; and to make it even more thrilling as we listened, a panther began its sawing call as it walked down to the Kalyani river that skirted the forest less than half a mile from where we were sitting. 'Ah-hah! Ah-hah!' he called, uttering a sound almost exactly like someone sawing wood, only it was far louder and deeper.

By his calls we could follow the movements of the panther in our minds, padding softly from bamboo-clump to *muthee* tree, and from the sheltering bushes through the long grasses to the waving belt of rushes that border the banks of the Kalyani and its softly rippling stream of water, that speeds on its way through the dense, silent and mysterious labyrinths of the darkened forest, with only the stars in a velvety-black sky to cast their reflections upon the restless current.

We tried sleeping inside the bungalow that night, but it was far too hot, with not a breath of air to relieve the stifling atmosphere. Further, the gambolling rats in the grass thatch above our heads squeaked as they chased one another about. Suddenly one of them cried out in fright and then pain. We were both lying awake on the hard-boarded cots that furnished the room. The rat had squealed loudly and pitifully for a few seconds and then stopped. Dev asked me if I could think why it had cried out. To me the answer was only too obvious. It

THE CALL OF THE MAN-EATER

had been bitten, caught, and was now in the process of being swallowed by some snake which had crawled into the thatch for that very purpose.

When I told him this, Dev scrambled out of bed and suggested pulling the cots on to the verandah. I thought that a good idea, too. The verandah was not only cooler, but it had a zinc roof where rats would not gambol all night, and snakes would not pursue them.

We fell asleep after that, and Dev did not disturb me much during the night. His cough was already better.

'Whe-e-e-ew! Kuck-kaya-kaya-khuck'm.' It was the old familiar call of the junglecock that awoke me next morning, just as the false dawn was fading, to give way to a short renewed spell of darkness. Then came the real dawn, spreading over the eastern horizon, to outline the distant jungle-clad hills in all the glories of shell-pink, vermilion, red and indigo blue, blending into peacock green, tinged with yellow, orange and purple. I had watched many dawns and sunsets before, but I have never tired of seeing another as the golden orb of the rising sun dispels the wreaths of mist that rise from the rich damp mould of the forest.

'Cock-a doodle-doo.' The cry came from south of the bungalow, where the hamlet of Rangampet nestled a mile away. The village rooster, hearing the challenge of his jungle cousin, could not resist the impulse to reply, although nearly two miles of cultivated lands divided them. The forest, a mile to the north, awoke to the new life of another day as Deva Sundram shook his sleepy head and raised himself on his elbows to listen.

'Mia-a-oo. Mia-oo,' called a peacock, fresh from roosting on some far distant forest tree. Spotted dear, frightened by something, insistently cried, 'Aiow! Aiow! Aiow!' Perhaps the panther we had heard the night before was returning homewards and had alarmed them.

THE EVIL ONE OF UMBALMERU

I fried some bacon on my primus stove, which we ate with the *chappatties* we had brought from Bangalore, while waiting for the hot water to boil for the special coffee that Dev said he was going to make that morning. And he carried out his promise. It was delicious.

We took a walk into the jungle a little later, going as far as the peepul tree on the bank of Ragimankonar, near which the woman, Venkatamma, had so mysteriously disappeared. I scanned the ground on the outward journey and the sandy bed of the *nullah* at Ragimankonar itself, to see what animals had passed in the night. We picked up the trail of the panther as soon as we came to the bank of the Kalyani River. He had been a large male. A mile further on a female sloth bear had rested under a *jumlum* tree, while her two cubs had frolicked around her. Their tiny childlike footpads were quite distinct on the sand. Isolated sambar, spotted deer and wild-pig tracks showed the other beasts that had been abroad during the hours of darkness.

But I entirely failed to find what I had particularly sought and had hoped to discover: tiger pugs. No tiger had passed that way. Dev and I returned to the bungalow, swallowed more coffee and then walked southwards to Rangampet. We wanted to hear other versions of the strange tale that old Dadoo, the bungalow-keeper, had recounted over our dinner the previous night. Both the *patel* and village *munsiff* made us welcome with more coffee, and the villagers clustered around. The advent of visitors, especially from afar, was always an occasion for a chat.

'The Evil One, *dorailu*?' queried an ancient, bent and tottering and leaning on his staff. 'Aye, he is in the jungle in real earnest, and has taken five people already. But he will never fall to your firearms, sirs, for he will never give you a chance by appearing before you. He is cunning—very, very cunning indeed. Although your bullets would have no effect on him even should he show himself, he will never do that. For you are strangers, foreigners, and different from us. But he will lurk in the jungle, hiding behind a bush or in a hole in the ground, or perhaps he will shrink to the size of a beetle and climb to the top of a lofty tree, where he will watch, watch for one of us; man, woman or child, whoever happens to pass alone. Then in the twinkling of an eye he will change in size and shape. From a tiny beetle he will become a giant ogre. He will seize the unfortunate and eat him up and leave not a trace behind. It will go on like this till we are all taken or leave this accursed forest to him and never enter it again.'

The throng of onlookers nodded their heads in melancholy agreement. Face to face with such deep superstition, we felt very helpless indeed. I tried to appear disdainful and said: 'Nonsense, ancient one; I am surprised that a man of your years and wisdom should talk like a little child. Doubtless it is a tiger or panther that has turned man-eater and is causing all the mischief.'

He smiled superciliously. 'Man-eaters, *dorailu*, I have met before. When I was a youth one attacked me at the foot of the escarpment beyond Umbalmeru. Fortunately I was carrying a wood-cutter's axe at the time and threw it at the brute. By still greater luck the blade struck it full between the eyes. That tiger's liver turned to water that day. It whirled around and fled. So I am here to tell the tale. Ho. Ho. Ho.' He cackled toothlessly at the recollection of the incident.

'But this is entirely different, sir,' he went on. 'Look: you know something about tigers and panthers, and we know you are a hunter who has visited these forests before. Have you ever met a tiger or a panther that leaves no pug-marks; no trail of any kind? Not a drop of blood is to be found where

THE EVIL ONE OF UMBALMERU

any of the five victims were taken. Not even a drag-mark, where he pulls or carries their bodies into the jungle. If there is a tiger in these parts just now, particularly a man-eater, would we not have found his tracks in the forest, or along the dusty footpaths, in the sandy *nullahs*, or the moist earth on the banks of the Kalyani river? Would we not have heard his moaning calls at night while searching for his prey? And the same goes for a panther, too, although there are some harmless ones around. Besides, as you know well enough, *dorailu*, it is not the habit of a panther to drag his victim very far from the place he kills it. For one thing, he has not the strength.

'Finally, man-eaters invariably strike during the hours of darkness or in the evening, when the shades of night are not far off. But in this case every one of the five victims has been taken in broad daylight, and that, too, in the blazing heat of the noon or afternoon, when all carnivora are resting.

'You can't explain that, can you, *dorailu*? But I can; and the explanation is simple and obvious. We are up against the Evil One himself—a spirit that can appear and disappear at will, and can assume any form or shape he wishes, from that of an insect to that of a monster, which he is. Your guns will be useless, sirs. For you are not dealing with any flesh-and-blood tiger or panther. I advise you to go home. Perhaps if you annoy him too much, he may even take one of you; maybe both of you.'

And so saying the ancient again grinned mirthlessly. To signify he had spoken the last word, the old man spat a mouthful of betel-nut and pan-leaf against the foundation of the wall of the *munsiff's* little brick-and-mud villa with unerring aim. There was a chorus of assent and approval from the bystanders. Even the *patel* and the village *munsiff* nodded their heads dolefully.

THE CALL OF THE MAN-EATER

Dev and I made our way back to Nagapatla in silence. The old man's words rang in my ears. What manner of creature was this that left no pug-marks, no blood-trail, no drag-mark of any kind, that operated in complete silence, that murdered at the hottest hour of the day? No man-eaters in my experience had behaved in this manner. Yet I knew there was no such thing as an evil spirit responsible for the attacks. There must be a rational explanation.

The five people had been done to death at irregular intervals. The common factor in each case was that the killing—or disappearance—of every victim had always taken place soon after midday. Secondly, there had been no other human witness to the incident. The disappearance of Kothanda Reddy was largely a matter of conjecture; but certainly the cart-man, the trader, the bamboo-cutter, and the woman carrying food to her husband, had each been alone. In the case of the petty merchant, his donkeys were with him when it had happened. They, of course, could not speak. Significantly, none of them had been attacked, hurt or killed. And apparently they had not even been alarmed unduly when their owner vanished, for they had all been found grazing closely together the next day. If they had received a fright, they would naturally have scattered in every direction. And most certainly the sudden advent of a tiger, or even a panther, would have scared the wits out of any donkey.

We got back to the bungalow where we prepared our frugal lunch. Dev asked me: 'Jock,'—he always calls me 'Jock' for the twenty-eight years I have known him—'what do you think it is?'

'It can't be anything but a tiger or panther, Dev,' I replied, 'although I must admit it is certainly a peculiar and unusual beast. There are no elephants or bison in this particular forest, and the only other animal that might attack without provocation

THE EVIL ONE OF UMBALMERU

would be a sloth bear. And a sloth bear is a stupid, clumsy beast. He would certainly have left some sort of trail. Besides he would not have carried away the bodies of his victims. He would have left them where he had killed them.'

After lunch I said to Dev: 'This mystery intrigues me. I would certainly like to solve it. Tell me, would Leela'—Mrs Deva Sundram—'object to you staying another ten days?'

He was enthusiastic about it. As a matter of fact, since hearing about the Evil One, Dev had completely forgotten his whooping-cough, which had almost subsided anyhow. So each of us wrote to his better half saying we were staying rather longer than originally planned. Although we did not say so, we hoped they would conjecture that Dev's whooping cough attack was the only reason for prolonging our stay.

By three o'clock in the afternoon we were back in the jungle, searching for evidence of a tiger. We found none. We walked up the roadway as far as the fourth milestone and then broke off into the jungle to the east, walking the two furlongs to the water hole known as Narasimha Cheruvu. Even on the muddy edge of the pool we found no tiger pug-marks. A panther had come for water recently and, of course, quite a number of deer of varying sorts.

Instead of returning by the road, we came back along the banks of the Kalyani River. Here we picked up the trail of another panther in several places. He was quite a large beast, and certainly not the animal whose tracks we had found at Narasimha Cheruvu. Perhaps the large panther had been the one that had been calling the previous night.

Of one thing we were now almost certain. No tiger appeared to be in residence at that time in that part of the jungle. But there were definitely two panthers; probably more.

Was one of them a man-eater? If the answer to this question was 'yes', then there was all the more reason that at least in one or more of the five instances of the vanished people, some evidence of the attack should have been found. For a man-eating panther, although a deadly antagonist, lacks the great physical strength of a tiger to carry his human prey away bodily. Occasionally he will begin to eat it on the spot, but generally drags the remains into a thicket to consume them there. In either case there would be ample signs for even almost inexperienced searchers to pick up a trail of some sort.

We were immensely intrigued.

Early next morning we walked the seven miles to Pulibonu and pursued our inquiries at the bamboo-cutters' camp, which was still there. Nobody could suggest a rational explanation, and that some malevolent evil spirit was responsible was the universal belief.

We searched the banks of the Kalyani, the game trails, and the footpaths that bifurcate from Pulibonu. One of these leads in a northwesterly direction, and it was along this track that the petty merchant had parted company with his donkeys. The other footpath branched off towards the northeast, skirted a rocky pool known as Gundalpenta and led to another pool, named Umbalmeru, at the foot of a lofty, frowning escarpment. It was somewhere in this latter region that the first victim, old Kothanda Reddy, the village wizard, had disappeared.

These two pathways, branching off at Pulibonu, form a letter Y with the main track leading from Rangampet to Pulibonu. We had walked along the tail of this letter Y for the seven miles from the village of Rangampet to Pulibonu. From there we followed each of the top branches of the Y for more than a mile. On the section leading to Umbalmeru we came across the first tiger pug-marks. They were some days old, but they confirmed that at least one tiger was in the area. On both the bifurcating sections, as well as along the tail of the Y, we had seen the pugs of panthers, and the imprints of what was undoubtedly an outstandingly large hyaena, but no tiger tracks whatever.

Dev asked me if I thought the hyaena might be responsible for what had occurred, and I very definitely rejected the suggestion. I had met hyaenas many times and in many places, and had found them not only quite harmless towards human beings, but particularly cowardly. They would eat only carrion, such as the kills of tigers and panthers, or animals that had otherwise died. I have heard rumours of them encroaching on village burial-grounds and exhuming corpses, and I had read once or twice in the newspapers that in certain jungles in Madhya Pradesh they were credited with carrying off children from the outskirts of villages. But in all my experience in southern India I had never heard of even a single case of this sort. The hyaenas of the south appear to confine themselves exclusively to a diet of carrion, excreta of any sort from beast or bird, and filth of every description, together with such small animals as rodents, lizards and nesting birds as they were able to surprise and catch. Once or twice they have been reputed to have attacked goats and sheep.

We were dead-beat when we got back to the bungalow at Nagapatla after dark that evening, having walked a distance of over eighteen miles. And we were ravenously hungry, too. Dev and I slept so soundly that night that the sun was shining brightly the next morning when we awoke.

Three days later our friends, the bamboo-cutters, provided the first tangible clue to the identity of the Evil One. They had finished their felling operations in the *coupe* near the well at Pulibonu, and the bamboo-contractor, who employed them, shifted the whole party to the next *coupe* at which he had secured the right to cut. This *coupe* was at the very end of the right-hand branch of the letter Y, after leaving the main path at Pulibonu. It was within half a mile of the rocky pool that bore the name of Umbalmeru, and almost at the base of the lofty escarpment which formed the natural northeastern boundary of the Chamala Valley Reserve Forest, where the Evil One at last revealed his identity.

The whole region abounds in bamboo and the Forest department had apportioned it into blocks or *coupes*. When the stems grow to a certain height and thickness, that particular block or *coupe* is auctioned for cutting, and the contractor who employed the party of bamboo-cutters, as the highest bidder at the auction, had obtained the right to fell and sell the bamboos in that area. Time meant money to him and so he did not delay in shifting his employees to the site where they were to begin felling operations at once.

The very first afternoon, one of the men resting from his task had happened to look up. On top of a shelf of rock, and regarding him malevolently, he saw the head and face of a tiger. He fled.

The bamboo-cutters refused to camp in the forest that night, or any longer for that matter. They told their employer that they would rather walk back all the twelve miles to the safety or Rangampet each evening and return next morning until the *coupe* was cleared.

The contractor was not impressed. He argued that, even walking very fast, it would take them two and a half hours each way. That meant the loss of five working hours every day, which in turn implied that so many less bamboos would be cut daily. The less bamboos, the less money for him, he reminded them. They replied that, if he did not agree, they would quit in a body. Then no more bamboos would be felled and there would be no money for him at all. They stressed that their own lives meant more to them than the bamboos they cut and the money he earned. The contractor tried to compromise by saying he would agree if they consented to a proportionate reduction in the daily wages he was paying them. But the men seemed to him unreasonably determined. They demanded the same scale of wages, threatening again to quit work.

'Ah, yes,' the contractor thought to himself. 'Times are certainly bad. Labour is getting more unreasonable, more troublesome and more difficult to manage all the world over. If I don't give in, these fellows will leave and then there will be nobody to cut bamboos for me. My curses on this beastly tiger. May it die a very painful death, and that soon.'

So he agreed to their demand and that evening at dusk the whole band, including the contractor, came home to Rangampet. On the way they had to pass the gate of the Nagapatla forest lodge where Dev and I were camped. All of them trooped inside and the man who had seen the tiger told us about it. The contractor also poured out his tale of woe. We were elated. The mystery was solved at last. The Evil One was no evil spirit, intangible and unreal, as everyone had thought. It was a flesh-and-blood tiger, as I had more than half-anticipated it would be.

The tiger chose to strike the very next day. The bamboo-cutters had returned in the morning and were working at their allotted tasks. By common consent they gave the spot, where one of them had seen the tiger the previous evening, a wide berth. The *maistry*, or foreman in charge of the coolies, announced the midday hour for them to stop work and gather beneath the grove of tamarind trees for their meal, by a series of long, sharp whistles, which he made with the aid of his tongue and teeth. One hour was allowed for this purpose and the bamboo-cutters made the most of it. After eating their curry and rice, washed down by bowlfuls of muddy water drawn from a passing stream that trickled from the pool at Umbalmeru, they sat and smoked, or chewed betel leaves, or dozed.

THE CALL OF THE MAN-EATER

At the end of the hour the *maistry* gave the signal for them to return to work by a similar series of whistles, and soon the sound of the chop-chopping of bamboos, and the crash of falling stems, echoed from the glen in which they were working.

But the story of the man who had reported seeing the tiger the previous day made them nervous and kept them unusually alert. And to that fact alone did one of their number owe his life that day. For as he chopped he glanced apprehensively around him now and then. Thus he noticed the slight shaking of some fronds of tender bamboo that sprang from the ground at the base of a larger clump, and the glaring, greenish-yellow eyes that gazed at him hungrily from a background of russet brown and black and white.

The man whirled around with raised *koitha* just as the tiger leapt. The movement of its quarry told the feline that it had been discovered and the man was ready to defend himself. It checked its spring in midair by a convulsive twisting of its spinal cord and tail, landing just short of its victim whose sharp-bladed chopper swished harmlessly through the air, missing the animal by a hairsbreadth.

But the tiger had no stomach for this kind of reception. It had hoped to seize its quarry unawares. When it landed on the ground it snarled viciously, crouched for a moment as if about to attack again, and then turned tail and leapt back into the bamboos from which it had come and was immediately lost to sight.

The man raised the alarm by screaming at the top of his voice, '*Aiyo! Aiyo! Pilli! Pilli!*' (Help! Help! Tiger! Tiger!), and then made a run for the sheltering tamarind grove. His fellow workers in all directions, hearing his cries, joined in the general pandemonium and stampeded for the tamarinds. The contractor, who had just fallen asleep there, was rudely

THE EVIL ONE OF UMBALMERU

awakened by the hubbub and the men running headlong through the bamboos till they reached him.

There was no thought of work for the rest of the day. The coolies, this time headed by the contractor himself, put their best feet forward to place as great a distance as possible between themselves and the dreaded feline that lurked in the fastnesses of Umbalmeru.

Dev and I had had an early tea and were near the third milestone on the road to Pulibonu when we met the chattering batch of men making at a jog trot for the safety of the village. They all began to jabber at once and it took at least a minute to sort things out and find the man who had been through such a harrowing experience. He described the tiger as having stood 'that high' on its four feet, indicating his chest as he did so. Truly a brute of mammoth proportions.

It was 3.45 p.m. when all this happened. I told the man to hurry, because he was to come back with Dev and myself and show us the spot where the tiger had appeared. I had a reason for wanting to do this. In plain words, I wanted to verify his story if possible, by seeing the tiger's footprints for myself. You must remember that up to that time we had only heard the most exaggerated tales about this weird beast, without the smallest shred of evidence as to its factual existence. And I know from experience to what lengths exaggeration can go when allowed to run riot in the minds of the simple jungle folk.

The man was aghast. Go back to that fearsome place? Not on your life! To hell with the very idea! He said all this and much more to me in his vernacular, and I really could not blame him for feeling that way about it. But I just had to have verification of his story. So I got tough.

I will not tell you what I said, but in a little while Dev and the bamboo-cutter and myself were walking at our best

THE CALL OF THE MAN-EATER

pace up the road that led to Pulibonu, and from there along the righthand branch of the letter Y to Umbalmeru.

We had nine miles to cover and we did it just before 6.30 p.m. It would soon be dark, but that did not worry us unduly as both Dev and I had brought our electric torches with us in case we might return late from our long walk. Also it would not be particularly cold at night except for Dev, who, as a whooping-cough patient, really should not expose himself to the night air and the dew-fall that went with it. I muttered a word of warning to this effect.

'Whooping-cough!' he exclaimed. 'Who said I have whooping-cough? I did have it, but that was long ago.'

The coolie pointed out the place where he had been cutting bamboos, and the fronds of young bamboo that he had noticed moving and from which the tiger had emerged. We examined the ground around and behind it. In spite of the growing dusk we clearly saw the pug-marks of a tiger. Not a very large one it is true, and whether a male or female I could not distinguish because of the fading light and the wisps of fallen, rotting bamboo leaves on which it had trodden. But they were the footprints of a tiger all right.

From scrutinizing the ground I stood up a happy and satisfied man. The mystery was indeed solved. The Evil One that had puzzled us for so long was nothing supernatural or uncanny. It was just a tiger; but an extraordinarily shy, cunning and elusive tiger at that. Also a coward.

We had no bait; nothing to sit up over. Water was to be found in abundance in all directions. To go back to the bungalow meant walking twelve miles in darkness and exhausting our torch cells. So, why not spend the night in the jungle just for the fun of it? We might hear or see something, or we might hear or see nothing at all. At least it would be fun. Better than spending another night in the rat and snake-infested rest-house at Nagapatla.

I made the suggestion. Dev was enthusiastic. The man we had brought with us was shocked. But there was nothing he could do about it, poor fellow, unless he chose to walk back alone—which he most definitely did not.

The next question was where to sit. The pool at Umbalmeru itself would be as good a place as any. At least I hoped we could find a suitable spot there. The jungle where we were was too dense and the bamboos were too close. With nightfall we would be enveloped.

It was getting decidedly dark by the time we covered the short distance to the pool. There was no time to construct a hide on the ground, much less to build a platform or *machan* of any kind on a tree. But a banyan grew not far away, and it was quite a large old tree.

The banyan is a tree that drops roots from its branches. These in turn reach the ground, penetrate, and in due course form the trunks of other trees. So the banyan grows ever wider, covering more and more ground, and consists of many trunks, the original parent one and any number of others that have taken root subsequently. A beautiful specimen of this tree—the largest of its kind in India—grows in the Botanical Gardens at Calcutta. It covers an enormous area. It is one of the landmarks for which the Gardens there have become famous. A similarly mighty banyan grows about forty-two miles from Bangalore and two miles from a village named Thali. A stone temple originally stood at its base. The pendant roots have entirely covered the stone walls of this temple, although its entrance has been kept clear. At a casual glance the roots appear to have formed a natural cave. Incidentally a black cobra, supposed to be a hundred years old, is reputed to live in a hole at the back of the cave. He is fed with bowls of milk and half a dozen eggs at a time by the Brahmin priest who looks after the temple. The priest told me the tree is 2,000 years old.

But to return to Umbalmeru. A banyan grew not far from the pool. Not nearly such a large and old one, but it had quite a number of root-trunks which had started growing in the ground around the main stem. Two of these grew about four feet apart; in diameter each may have been about eight feet.

We took up our position sitting on the ground between the two root-trunks. I kept my rifle and faced the jungle. Dev sat with his back to me, facing the pool, and on his lap lay my .12 bore shotgun, loaded with a lethal ball in the right barrel and an L.G. cartridge in the left. The bamboo-cutter sat on Dev's right and faced in the same direction. Dev and I each had our own torches, but whereas I had remembered to bring the clamps which held the torch to my rifle, there were no clamps for Dev and the shotgun. So the woodcutter was to hold the torch for Dev and shine it if occasion arose. Except for our two flanks, protected by the root-trunks of the banyan, we were completely exposed and visible.

In front of Dev lay the pool. Unless the tiger came along the nearer bank, he would have to cross the water, which afforded some protection. At least we could hear him. In front of me was the jungle into which I could not see once it had become dark unless I flashed my torch. All three of us would have to rely on our sense of hearing alone. The tiger, if he approached either from the side of the pool or from the jungle I faced, would immediately see us. What happened next was a matter of chance and depended on the tiger's courage. Would he attack three men together or slink away?

Dev was as elated and as excited as a schoolboy at a fair.

In no time it was pitch-dark. My feathered friends, the birds, had gone to roost long before we had taken up our positions. After a while the only audible sound was the faraway hooting of a horned owl. Somewhere high above us, in the fastnesses of the towering escarpment, maybe a mile away, he

THE EVIL ONE OF UMBALMERU

sat complacently regarding the valley that stretched below him. And as he sat he hooted: 'Whooo-oooo! Whooo-oooo!'

Suddenly a bull-frog began to croak in the pool. 'Khor! Khor! Khor! Khor! Khor!' Others joined in, one by one. It became a throbbing pulsating chorus.

'Skitch! Skitch! Skitch! Skitch!' The bamboo-cutter, whose back touched my left arm, started violently. I could imagine him staring hard into the darkness. But it was only a water-frog.

Much smaller than the bull-frog and with long, slender hindlegs, this species of frog sits half-submerged at the edge of pools and lakes. Occasionally one of them will skim across the top of the water, barely touching the surface with violent kicks of its hind legs for some yards, before coming to a halt and floating with its eyes and half its head out of the water. It was this act of skimming or leaping along the water that had made the sound that had caused the coolie to start so violently.

I knew that so long as one such frog skimmed the surface of the water now and then, there was nothing to worry about. But if several of the frogs were to do that together, it would be a very reliable signal that something was coming and had frightened them, causing them to take shelter in the middle of the water.

The Umbalmeru pool itself is not very large. Oval in shape, it is about sixty feet by thirty feet. At the northern and narrower end it is bounded by rock, being a continuation of the terrain that lies at the foot of the escarpment. On the other three sides is jungle. We were sitting on the eastern bank. It was too dark to see now, but before settling down I had looked up and noticed the escarpment looming above us, perhaps to a height of 500 feet.

The bull-frogs croaked noisily beside the water behind me. Otherwise there was silence. Then the horned-owl began his eerie call again: 'Whooo-oooo! Whooo-oooo! Whooo-oooo!'

In the dell below us a plover suddenly started screeching: 'Did-you-do-it! Did-you-do-it! Quick! Quick! Quick! Quick!' Something had alarmed the bird. What could it have been? Almost together, I felt the backs of Deva Sundram and the coolie straighten and tauten behind mine. But I knew there was time yet. Whatever had frightened the plover, if it happened to be coming towards us, would take at least another five minutes, maybe ten, to arrive.

A small animal rustled the leaves in the jungle before me. Perhaps a mongoose, or one of those creatures that are distinctly rare in south Indian jungles—a ratel. The rustling alternated with silence as the small mammal stopped its search for food every now and then and listened for possible enemies. Then it began again to scratch the earth and scrape the leaves.

All at once it stopped and remained quiet. The five minutes were about up. Could it have sensed something approaching? Coinciding with the thought I felt the elbows of both my companions excitedly digging me in the small of my back.

Very slowly I turned my head. At first I could see nothing. And then, forming a silhouette like a shifting black blur against the faint lighter outline that was the surface of the water, something seemed to be moving towards us.

It merged into a black background of shadows cast by the outer fringes of the main banyan tree and was completely lost to sight. But it had been approaching us when this happened. The thought was a most disconcerting one. I felt certain it was the tiger, and to be helpless in the dark while a man-eater came on and attacked us at close quarters would indeed be an ignominious end.

I turned around, balancing on my right knee. Placing the stock of my rifle to my shoulder, I pointed the muzzle in the direction where I judged the killer would be and quickly pressed the button of my torch with my left thumb. The bright beam lit a ghoulish head, from which two bluish-green eyes stared back at me in surprise, fully reflecting the torch-light. But they were cowardly, sly, scheming eyes, albeit a bit foolish in their startled expression. The enormous head, out of all proportion to the sloping body of a large hyaena, looked up at us. I could clearly see the long, upright ears, the dark muzzle and the black patch under its throat, although being head-on to us, most of the grey body, with its straggling black stripes, was hidden.

I kept the torch burning. All three of us remained motionless and silent.

'Grr-rr-rr! Goo-doo! Goo-doo! Goo-doo!' growled the amazed beast, not being able to understand for a moment the origin of the light, nor its association with human agency.

Then perhaps his nose, or maybe just instinct, told him.

'Pfoof! Pfoof!' he snorted, darting to cover with his peculiar undulating gait, caused by his ridiculously short and weak hind legs trying to keep pace with his long and powerful front ones. He ran with an awkwardly loping motion, while the mane of hair along his neck and back stood erect, giving the illusion that he had suddenly grown to twice his size before our very eyes. His grey tail, bristling all over like the rest of him, fanned out behind like a feather-brush.

The hyaena vanished in the undergrowth, but he certainly did not leave the scene. He scampered around us in a wide circle, crackling the thickets as he forced his way through them, while making the most curious and disconcerting medley of sounds imaginable: 'Ha! Ha! Ha! Ha! Ha!' he cackled, 'What-have-we-here? Ha! Ha!'

When he came to the windward side of us and finally got our scent, he was able to realize at last that human beings sat close by. He changed his cries to a series of disdainful remarks: 'Cheey! Shee-ay! Shee-ay!' as he scurried about hoping that we would go away. But we did not go away and he was not happy about it. In fact, he grew displeased. 'Garrar! Garrar!' he growled, then breaking into a gargling-like series of protests, 'Guddar! Guddar! Guddar! Guddar! Guddar!'

In his indignant displeasure at our persistent refusal to budge, he fairly made the jungle ring, scampering around and around and making his ridiculous noises till we were about sick of hearing him. One fact began to stick out a mile. If we did not drive this garrulous visitor away, we might as well pack our traps and walk back to the bungalow to put in a few undisturbed hours of sleep.

'Shoo! Shoo!' I said. 'Shoo! Shoo!' cried Dev. '*Chee! po phissach*! (go devil),' repeated the coolie. But it was all to no effect; for go he certainly would not.

I groped in the earth beside me for a clod, found it and hurled it at the noisy intruder. He made more noise than ever.

'*Goalee utchoodoo thaywoolee maylay*!' advised the bamboo-cutter, which means. 'Shoot the so-and-so!' But he was only a poor hyaena, although he was certainly not minding his own business, and I did not want to do so. The din was shocking.

The hyaena came into view again—a dark shadow against the lighter sheen of the pool of water reflecting the starlight.

Just then the tiger growled on the other side of the water: 'Aa-ooo-om! Aa-ooo-om!'

The effect on the hyaena was instantaneous. He stopped dead in his tracks, as if turned into stone. His long ears were clearly outlined as he turned his head away to look for the dreaded author of that ominous sound. The next instant he was gone!

We heard a scrambling patter for a few seconds as he dashed over the fallen leaves. Then came silence: intense and frightening.

THE EVIL ONE OF UMBALMERU

We knew the tiger had been somewhere in front of us and across the water when he had growled. But was he still there? He might be, but just as likely he might now be behind us or on either side. For tigers do not advertise their movements as the hyaena had done. Or he might have gone away.

The hyaena had warned him and he knew that all was not well. The question was: would he want to investigate? Or would he slink off, just as the hyaena had done? The next few moments would give us the answer, and it was very important to us. So we kept silent and remained watchful.

The minutes dragged by and an hour had passed. Except for the distant chirping of wood-crickets and the closer croaking of the frogs, there was no other sound to be heard. I began to wish the hyaena was back. The noise he had made, although ridiculous, had been something tangible and concrete. But this silence was disconcerting and unnerving! We grew fidgety.

Midnight came and passed, and then it became chill. We heard slight rustlings and faint scampering sounds on the dried leaves and in the undergrowth. Rats perhaps, or other small animals, feeding and quenching their thirst at the water.

A shadow glided overhead. We heard the heavy flapping of wings. Then came silence again.

'Whooo-oooo! Whooo-oooo!' The horned owl was now our companion. No doubt he knew the time when the small creatures would come for water and thus expose themselves for a few seconds. We never knew when he attacked; but we certainly heard the result.

A rabbit (called a 'hare' in India) was the victim. We heard his plaintive scream for mercy as the cruel talons of the owl drove into his tender back, and we heard the faint 'thud, thud', as the powerful beak struck his skull. Then the hare shrieked no more. For he was dead.

The hours dragged by and it grew more chilly. We could not see the sky immediately overhead because of the canopy of branches formed by the banyan; but through the clearing over the water hole, across which the giant owl had lately flapped his way, we caught glimpses of it. There were no clouds, and one or two stars twinkled distantly.

The clear sky assisted the earth in radiating what little heat had remained since the hours of sunlight. Rapidly it became colder and colder. This caused a heavy dew-fall and we could hear the moisture dripping from the leaves of the trees around us, although we were protected by the two trunks of the banyan and its branches above our heads.

The coolie, poor fellow, was the thinnest clad and he began to react to the cold in real earnest. I could feel him shivering against my back and hear the faint chattering of his teeth. The barrel of the rifle in my hands was like ice and the dew ran down it in a little trickle. I pointed the muzzle downwards to keep the moisture from running inside.

To a certain extent the cold discouraged the mosquitoes which had been very active since sunset. Even the faint scratching sounds made by the rats and other small animals subsided. No doubt they were feeling the cold too. The chorus of the bullfrogs died away to a spasmodic individual effort by one or other of their number. It was that hour, early in the morning, when even the denizens of the night appear to rest.

After 3 a.m. the wind began to blow. The warm air in the valley below us, which had cooled by now, had long risen from the ground to be replaced by the cold air from the lofty escarpment to the north and northeast. It soughed and moaned and bent the tops of the lesser trees as it blew into the valley in short violent gusts.

I began to forget about the tiger and felt sleepy. But it was too cold even to doze. The distant crow of a single jungle-

THE EVIL ONE OF UMBALMERU

cock indicated the time as past 4 a.m. Our vigil was drawing to a close and the tiger had not come.

The false dawn came at about five o'clock, with its hopes of an early sunrise. Then, as usual, followed a few minutes of renewed, intensified darkness. The faint outline of the summit of the escarpment to the east showed that the night hours were coming to an end at last. The valley below was still enveloped in darkness as the crags above began to show up in the most delicate hues of pale pink, curiously mixed with a mauve and blue background, before which wisps of mist spiralled upwards from the trees growing on the slopes like the smoke-signals of a band of marauding Red Indians.

'Whoomp! Whoomp! Whoomp!' The rousing cry reverberated across the ragged perpendicular face of the escarpment and boomed with a hollow echo in the wooded valley below. It was the joyous call of the male langur, the large grey monkey with the whiskered black face and abnormally long, curved tail, that lives in the forests of south India, as he awoke to greet the coming day. Soon other langurs joined in and call after call echoed from crag to cliff and then re-echoed across the forested valley to fade away in the distance.

It was quite bright where we were sitting, although the sun had not topped the serrated line of rocks and boulders that marked the summit of the escarpment to the east, when at last we rose to our feet, stamped and stretched and yawned to dispel the effects of a sleepless, uncomfortable night, and began the twelve-mile march to the bungalow at Nagapatla. None of us was in a good mood, nor did we feel like talking.

At the bungalow gates we met some of our friends, the bamboo-cutters, who had come there from the village to await our return. 'What happened?' asked someone. 'Did the tiger come?' queried another. 'Did it attack you?' asked a third.

THE CALL OF THE MAN-EATER

'Damn the tiger,' I replied crossly. Then, relenting, I told our coolie to acquaint his colleagues with the details of all that had happened. They were discussing it loudly as I placed the kettle on the primus stove to make hot water for tea. And they were still discussing it when Dev and I tumbled onto the hard beds and fell asleep at once.

We slept through the afternoon and awoke about 4 p.m. to eat a late lunch, washed down with more tea. Then we put our heads together to think out some way of settling accounts with the tiger.

Marshalling the facts, or rather as many of them as were known to us, we found we were up against an animal that did not follow the normal habits of a man-eater in the least. Firstly, all its human kills had been made in the afternoon, during the heat of the day. Secondly, they were all more or less localized and within a few miles of the Umbalmeru pool and escarpment where he appeared to be living. Ordinarily, man-eaters cover a large area and follow a more or less distinct beat, which sometimes extends for more than a hundred miles. Thirdly, those of his victims whom he took he made away with completely and mysteriously. Not a single body had been recovered. Fourthly, he appeared an abnormally shy animal, with more than the usual degree of cowardice that all man-eaters evince towards the human being who fights back. In this case the bamboo-cutter had frightened it off with his *koitha*, while the hyaena's warnings of the previous night had caused it to slink away when it could easily have attacked us. Fifthly, it did not seem to have the habit of wandering about its jungle domain as tigers usually do. We had not found this animal's tracks along any of the jungle-paths or streambeds which we had searched for that very purpose. Sixthly, we had not received any reports of cattle being killed in the surrounding area.

THE EVIL ONE OF UMBALMERU

We could make nothing of it, so we decided to do the only possible thing—tie up a live bait or two in the vicinity of the Umbalmeru water hole, although we scarcely expected they would be taken.

With this in view we went down to Rangampet village after dinner that night. The villagers co-operated readily, and Dev and I each bought a three-quarters-grown bull for the sum (in those days) of about forty rupees. In English currency this ran to about three pounds apiece! One of them was brown in colour, the other ash-grey. We deliberately avoided animals that were white, or even black, as some tigers shun baits of either colour, but especially white. We wanted to take no chances. Having completed the deal, we led our animals back to the forest lodge and quartered them for the night in the motor-shed, pushing the Model T into the open.

Early the following morning we got busy and with the help of two of the bamboo-cutters led our animals all the way back to Umbalmeru. We tied one under the banyan at the side of the water hole, and the other about two miles away, near the track leading back to Pulibonu. Here also we tied it close to a selected tree. We did this deliberately so that in the event of either animal being killed, a suitable tree would be readily available in which we could sit and await the tiger's return.

All this took us till past midday, so that it was evening by the time we returned to the rest house at Nagapatla.

The following morning we used the Ford to cover the first seven miles of rough track to Pulibonu. The car could go no further for the simple reason that the road ended there. So we visited our baits on foot. They were both alive.

Untying each in turn, we led them to water, and then retied them, leaving both with enough to eat until the next day. There was nothing more we could do after that. Dev said he would like to visit some of the temples at the town of

Tirupati, which was about fifteen miles from the bungalow. So we did that.

Tirupati is a centre of Hindu pilgrimage, devotees coming there in their thousands throughout the year to pay homage to the god Govinda, whose name they keep chanting aloud. All the women who visit these shrines are required to shave their heads entirely as an outward token of having made the pilgrimage. Considering they arrive in hundreds daily, the quantity of hair removed must be colossal.

Just before returning we dropped in at the refreshment room on the railway station for tea. No train being due for some time, the manager was at a loose end for the moment. So he came over to the table where we were sitting and opened a conversation to pass the time. In the usual easygoing manner of India he began asking who we were, where we had come from, why we had come, and numerous other questions.

Dev good-naturedly gave him all the details. The manager, who professed to know a great deal about *shikar*, also agreed that the tiger's general conduct was most unusual and not in keeping with a man-eater's normal behaviour.

Then he said something that made me sit up with a jerk. 'I wonder if it could be the tigress that escaped some months ago from a circus that came to town.'

Now it was my turn to ask the questions, and I fairly rained them on him. What circus? How long ago? At which place had the tigress escaped? Had a report been made? Had she been recaptured?

He answered my questions piecemeal, and from the information he gave we gleaned the following facts. A small travelling circus with a tigress and a few other animals had visited Tirupati and had camped a mile or so outside town. The proprietor of the circus had come to make friends with the manager of the refreshment room at the railway station because they were not teetotallers, and in a district where prohibition prevails people who are not teetotallers find much in common in their search for that of which they both feel in need.

One evening, after a few glasses had been surreptitiously consumed, the proprietor of the circus had loosened up a bit and had confided to the manager of the refreshment room that two nights before the tigress had escaped. The stupid fellow who looked after her had not closed the door of her cage properly. The proprietor had been afraid to inform the police, and as he was a likeable fellow, held in esteem among his own artists and employees, he was confident that they would not divulge the secret. Nobody had. A half-hearted attempt had been made to find the missing tigress, but no one appeared to have seen her. As the jungle lies within a mile of Tirupati, the proprietor naturally concluded that his tigress had found her way back into the forest where she would be able to look after herself. He became reconciled to his loss and the circus moved on.

I asked the manager if he had ever seen this animal before her escape. He replied that he had, as the circus owner had given him a free pass to visit the show as often as he pleased. She was not a very big tigress, but she was full-grown. He added that he thought she was unusually fierce, having often seen her snarling and growling as she ate her usual single meal of beef each day. He also felt she had never been thoroughly broken in, as he never saw her put through the usual acts of circus tigers.

A curious thought entered my mind and I asked him: 'About what time did this tigress receive her daily meal?'

He glanced at me rather in surprise, but answered promptly enough: 'In the afternoon, after the circus-people had finished their own lunch.'

The enigma was solved, and the animal's peculiar habits were no longer a mystery. For I was sure now that the man-eater was the escaped tigress and no other beast.

She maintained her habit of eating at midday. She was terrified of people—unless she could spring upon them unawares and kill them quickly. She could not hunt properly and hence had not developed a specific line of beat like a normal man-eating tiger. Being fundamentally still afraid of people, she made off with her human kills as quickly as she could, leaving no traces behind, in order to devour her victim very far from the scene of the crime. And, still not completely rid of her habits after living so long in a cage, she had found some shelter for herself, probably a cave, and had made it a permanent abode, instead of wandering from one area of forest to another, after the manner of normal tigers, whether man-eaters or not.

The more I thought about it, the more certain I felt that my theory was correct. And her abode was doubtless somewhere in the vicinity of Umbalmeru; probably a cave or rocky hollow of some kind at the base of the escarpment. After all, as the crow flies, the distance from Tirupati to the escarpment near Umbalmeru could not be more than twenty miles, if as much. And that is no great distance for a tiger to cover.

I did not confide my ideas to Dev just then, but kept plying the manager of the refreshment room with more questions. But it was soon evident that he had told us all he knew. The only additional information he could give was that the circus had shifted from Tirupati to Renigunta, and from there to a place called Puttur, and then to Arkonam, a railway junction about forty miles from the city of Madras. He had kept up a desultory correspondence with the proprietor and had received letters from all these places.

THE EVIL ONE OF UMBALMERU

Then the letters had stopped, so that now he had no idea where the circus had gone.

One last thing he told me, and that was that he remembered the tigress had been called Rani.

When eventually we left Tirupati after dark that evening to return to the forest bungalow at Nagapatla, I felt our visit had been most opportune.

Before dawn next morning we drove to Pulibonu, left the car and visited our baits again. Both were alive and well. After that we scoured several *nullahs* and pathways, looking for fresh tiger-pugs and hoping to encounter our quarry. All without result. It was evening when we got back to the bungalow. We had dinner and then went to Rangampet to enlist the aid of a man named Ramiah, who had served me on hunting trips in the Chamala Valley years before. I hoped he would be able to help me now.

Ramiah is a rather extraordinary fellow, at least so far as villagers go. The first time I met him, which might have been eight to ten years previously, he had attracted my attention by his quite unusual interest in matters no other villager would have bothered to know. Ramiah claimed to have discovered a secret herb growing in the valley, the leaves of which, if eaten, would counteract the effects of the bite of any poisonous snake. He said he kept a stock of these leaves, dried and powdered, with him in his hut, and by means of them had saved the lives of many people who had been bitten by cobras and Russell's vipers, and also of cattle that had been bitten. At my request he had brought me a small plant which I had taken back with me to Bangalore and attempted to grow in my garden. Unfortunately, it died. Ramiah had also discovered another herb, a couple of leaves of which, if dropped into a teapot while the tea was being made vastly enhanced its flavour. I had tried this herb and discovered his claim to be true. He had presented me with a smooth egg-shaped stone the size of a tennis ball which he said would always exude a trace of moisture, particularly in the mornings. I had also taken this stone back with me to Bangalore and found that what he said was true. The strange phenomenon had surprised and interested me enough to show the stone to a geologist at Bangalore. But that gentleman, as amazed as I was, had offered no explanation for the strange occurrence.

On one occasion, at the end of a hunting trip, I had offered to pay Ramiah for his services. Instead, he asked me to buy a piece of land at the head of the valley where the forest began, which was for sale cheaply, and allow him to cultivate it, and in return he would serve me any time I wanted when I came to Nagapatla on a shooting trip.

I had done what he asked and bought the land, which was about two and three-quarter acres in extent, for fifty rupees (less than four pounds in English currency). Thereafter, Ramiah had cultivated the land rent free for himself, and had willingly come to my assistance whenever I had called upon him.

So we got Ramiah out of his hut that night and, sitting on his doorstep, I related what I had heard from the refreshment room manager. I had already consulted Ramiah when we had first heard about this killer, but as he had been one of the many who had subscribed to the 'evil spirit' theory, I had not thought it worthwhile to enlist his aid until now.

After relating the story of the escaped tigress, I said: 'I am sure that if any man knows every nook and corner of the Chamala Valley jungle, that man is you. Now think very very carefully. Is there a cave at the foot of the escarpment in the vicinity of the Umbalmeru pool, or within the radius of two or three miles from it?'

His answer came immediately. 'Why certainly, *sahib*. There are—now, let me see—one, two, three, four, and yes, one more, five caves, within about the distance you have said. Two of them are, roughly speaking, to the north, and the remaining three to the east. One of the two to the north is rather high up on the face of the escarpment. I don't think a tiger would readily use it. The ascent is too steep. I know the langur monkeys play around that cave, but they don't live in it either. All the other four would be quite suitable for a tiger to lie up in.'

I was elated and showed my joy. 'Good man, Ramiah,' I exclaimed. 'Will you lead me to each of them?'

'Surely, *Sahib*,' he assented readily. 'I have promised to accompany you anywhere you want in this jungle, and at any time, in return for allowing me to cultivate your land, free of rent, these many years. That promise I will keep, *Sahib*,' he concluded simply.

I questioned him further about these caves and gathered that three of the four he had in mind were rather small. The fourth, which was one of the three caves at the foot of the escarpment to the east was considerably larger than the others and had a name of its own: 'Madapenta', because it was close to a small pool formed by a rill that trickled down the escarpment. *Penta* signifies a pool.

'We will be able to visit all four of these caves in one day, will we not?' I asked him.

'Surely, *Sahib*,' he assented. 'The cave to the north is hardly a mile from Umbalmeru. The three to the east are from two to three miles from the water hole, but within a mile of each other.'

'I will come for you in the car tomorrow morning at cockcrow,' I told him. 'Be ready. With an early start we should be at Pulibonu by daybreak. We will walk the remaining distance to Umbalmeru, and from thence to the caves, beginning with the one to the north.'

'As you say, *Sahib*,' he acquiesced immediately. ' I will be waiting for you.'

Dev and I went back to the forest bungalow as happy as two children. There Dev spent till midnight cleaning and re-cleaning the .12 shotgun. He even cleaned my rifle.

The grey-hackled junglecocks were crowing when the Model T chugged out of the gate of the Nagapatla rest house next morning, and their cousins, the village roosters of Rangampet, had begun to answer them when we arrived at Ramiah's hut. It was almost 5 a.m. He had heard the Ford approaching and stepped out of the doorway as I stopped the car.

We drove the seven miles to Pulibonu, and it was 6.5 a.m. when we halted near the well and set out on our walk along the footpath that formed the right-hand stroke of the letter Y and which ran, very roughly, in a northeasterly direction to end at the water hole at Umbalmeru. We arrived at the pool a few minutes before eight, and the sun was shining brightly in a cloudless sky.

Ramiah told me that from Umbalmeru no well-defined footpath led to any of the four caves we were about to search. We would have to rely on his sense of direction alone.

And Ramiah's sense of direction never failed him. He led the way, armed with his *koitha*, which is a long knife curved at the end, fitted to a bamboo handle about a foot long. It resembled a question mark without the dot at the bottom; but it proved extremely useful when, at times, he employed it to hack a path through the undergrowth.

Very often we met game trails leading in all directions, made chiefly, as I could see from the tracks themselves, by sambar and wild pig, with an occasional trail left by sloth bears, which had dug for roots here and there, and had systematically demolished every ant hill in their eager search for termites. But such things did not deter our guide nor cause him to lose his sense of direction for a moment. Onwards he moved to the north with me just behind him, holding the .405 ready against a surprise attack. Dev brought up the rear with the shotgun.

The land began to rise steadily towards the base of the escarpment which we could see between the trees, frowning down upon us. Soon the larger trees gave place to more bushy undergrowth and boulders lay scattered about, increasing in size and number as we rose ever higher. I had little doubt these had, from time to time, been washed down from the escarpment by rain and the consequent landslides.

Ramiah stopped half an hour later and said in a whisper that we were approaching the first of the caves. We redoubled—if that was possible—the caution we had been exercising since leaving the pool at Umbalmeru. The man-eater might be lurking anywhere, without our knowing anything about it.

Then Ramiah stopped a second time, indicating with a nod of his head, but no spoken word, where the first of the caves lay. And I saw it—the cave, I mean. A pile of boulders had fallen, one upon another, and in doing so had formed a cave. I could see the opening now. Not a large one by any means, perhaps a yard in diameter at the entrance, but big enough to shelter a tiger very easily.

Stretching out my left hand, I touched Ramiah's shoulder. Then I drew him back and took the lead, placing him between myself and Deva Sundram, still at the rear. On tiptoe, and as silently as possible, taking care not to tread on a dried piece of wood or leaf that might crackle, I inched forward till I stood about fifteen feet from the mouth of the cave. Unfortunately the ground before it was hard and stony. Besides, straggling clumps of spear-grass grew everywhere. No tracks would be visible on such terrain.

I made signs to Ramiah and Dev to pick up stones and throw them into the cave. They understood my signals and in a few seconds a desultory bombardment began as they hurled stones, big and small, into the narrow entrance.

Nothing happened. I could hear the thud as each stone fell, and the clatter as it bounced and rolled inside. Certainly, if a tiger was hiding there, it would either charge out upon us or at least demonstrate in no uncertain manner, by growling. But nothing whatever happened. There was complete silence, except for the thud and clatter of the stones. It began to look as if the tiger was not at home.

More stones followed, but without response of any kind. After ten minutes I was sure the cave was uninhabited. I moved right up to the mouth, where the grass and rubble ended and plain earth formed the flooring of the recess. Still keeping a sharp lookout on the dark interior, I stooped down and glanced at the ground for tracks. There were no pug-marks anywhere. The only animal that inhabited the cave, as I could see from his small footprints, was a porcupine; and I knew that no amount of stone-throwing would ever induce him to come out and face the bright sunlight. Being a creature of the night, a porcupine can only be smoked out of his burrow, and that with considerable difficulty. Generally, he will prefer to suffocate under such conditions, if he cannot manage to burrow still deeper.

Just before we turned away, Ramiah pointed upwards to the escarpment. He directed our attention to the second of the two caves he had said lay to the north of the water hole. We could just see the entrance, hidden as it was by the rank grass that half-concealed it from sight. The cave looked to be at least 200 or more feet above us and was perhaps two furlongs away.

THE EVIL ONE OF UMBALMERU

Ramiah had been right. No tiger would attempt that steep climb. Besides, there was another piece of conclusive evidence that no feline lived in that second cave. A langur monkey sat complacently at the entrance staring down at us inquisitively. If a tiger had passed anywhere nearby, certainly if one was living in the cave, the langur would not be there. They are far too cute to take chances.

We made our way down the slope to Umbalmeru and then set out for the three caves that lay at the foot of the eastern escarpment. Once again Ramiah showed himself a good judge of distances. The first cave took us nearly forty-five minutes to reach, by which fact I judged it to be a little over two miles from the water hole. The sloping ground and terrain were much the same, but the cave appeared to be a chasm rather than a regular cave, in that it was open at the top and had been formed by a big slice of the rock face that had fallen in a landslide and lay about ten feet from the base of the cliff. The piece that had fallen looked to be some twenty feet or more in height, and the space of ten feet between it and the escarpment was what Ramiah had called a cave. Being open at the top to admit rain and sunlight, it was thickly overgrown with lantana and long grass.

Although a wonderful place in which to hide temporarily, it did not seem a very likely spot for a tiger to choose to live in for any length of time. For one thing, it was too choked with undergrowth. A tiger does not like to make a home in which he himself might be taken by surprise.

I told my companions to follow the same plan of hurling stones into the recess while I stood guard over them with my rifle. As expected, nothing happened. After a while we drew closer. The ground was too stony and hard to reveal tracks, but the intense bombardment of stones that Dev and Ramiah rained into the gap soon made it clear that the tiger was not there.

THE CALL OF THE MAN-EATER

We skirted the escarpment southward to the next cave, which we reached in about fifteen minutes. It seemed to form the exit of some sort of subterranean passage which led into the escarpment. The opening was comparatively small, at most two feet across. The usual stoning followed and we achieved a negative result for the third time. Once again the ground was too dry and hard for tracks, so we approached the mouth of the passage and set fire to the grass that grew around.

Even if our stoning produced no results, the sight of fire and smell of smoke would bring the tiger out at the double. Still nothing happened. We spent the next ten minutes or so carefully extinguishing every trace of the fire we had made. We knew too well that a single glowing ember would be quite sufficient to start a forest fire that might blaze for days and destroy thousands of acres of timber.

To say we were disappointed would be putting it mildly. We were thoroughly crestfallen. But one cave remained to be visited, the largest of the lot, the one Ramiah had called Madapenta. He told us it was over a mile away.

With little hope of success we set out for this place. Just before we reached it we came to the little jungle pool that gave the cave its name. And here our hopes soared skyward. Clearly imprinted in the mire at the edge of the pool were several sets of pugs, and they had been made by a tigress. Obviously this was her main source of water.

It took another 200 yards, at least, of careful noiseless progress before the cave itself came into view. It had a large entrance, more than five feet in width and perhaps a little over that in height. Lastly, it was clear of grass and undergrowth and provided an excellent view of the approach of an enemy to a lurking tigress within. How excellent this was became clear within the next few seconds. Before Dev or Ramiah could throw the first stone, there came a thunderous growl from the darkness within, and the very next moment out leapt the tigress.

The bright sunlight blinded her for a while. Then her eyes adjusted themselves and she spotted us. She hesitated a brief second, then cowardice, which appeared to be quite strong in this animal's make-up, overcame her. She swerved to her right to make off.

At that instant I acted on the spur of the moment. Loudly and sharply, I called: 'Rani! Rani!'

The tigress halted. She turned to face me. There was ferocity in her countenance; but also a strange expression of bewilderment, recognition and partial submission. But our presence was a riddle to which she never found the answer, for, taking no chances, I fired into her chest, following up, as she toppled forward, with a bullet in her brain.

She was a young animal, hardly full-grown, and obviously thin and underfed. What had turned Rani into a man-eater?

The answer was plain. Years of captivity had rendered her useless at the art of stalking and killing wild game. On the other hand she was conversant only with the appearance and habits of mankind, although she never to the very end lost her instinctive fear of them.

So, in these circumstances she did the only possible thing to keep herself alive. She killed her human victims by surprise attack, and then took the bodies far away, where she would be safe from the danger of pursuit while she fed.

Before closing this story may I add a word of caution that, of course, will only apply to people living in places such as India, Africa and other countries where wild animals can be caught young and kept as pets. I know a lady who brought up a panther cub until it grew too big and too dangerous to be kept any longer. She was passionately attached to the animal, which was equally fond of her. She would not hear of presenting it to a zoo or a circus, as she was convinced that it would be ill-treated at both places. Shooting it, naturally, was for her out of the question. So she took it by car to a certain large jungle and there set it free. Incidentally, she told me later with tears in her eyes, that as the car drove away the panther bounded along behind in an attempt to get back to her.

I wonder if this well-meaning but sadly misguided lady quite realized what she was doing. She had just liberated a very dangerous animal which she had brought up from a cub upon boiled meat, rice, bread, pudding, porridge and what not, omitting to mention such delicacies as sweets, ice-cream and things of that sort. This unfortunate creature was totally unfit to look after itself and catch and kill its legitimate prey. There were just three things that could happen to it, and all of them most unpleasant to contemplate. It might approach the first human being it met in a friendly spirit and be killed for its pains. Secondly, it might starve to death, although this is very unlikely, for when driven by hunger the instinct for self-preservation would become so strong that the panther would eventually kill something. Thirdly, and worst of all, the animal might become a man-eater.

She told me what she had done less than a week after she had liberated her pet. I advised her to scan the newspapers closely for the following month or so. I did the same.

Within a few days we both read a short announcement that told of the strange behaviour of a very emaciated panther that had wandered into a village (which was within a few miles of the place where she had liberated her pet) and gone to sleep inside a grass hut. Then came the sad part. The villagers had closed the door of the hut, poured kerosene oil over the thatch and set fire to it, burning the poor beast to death.

The lady was heartbroken at her pet's horrible end. But I wonder what she would have felt had she read instead that it had become a killer of men, forced to the pernicious habit by her foolishness in setting it free when it was totally unable to fend for itself.

Three

A Night by the Camp Fire

MY WIFE SAYS I AM ECCENTRIC. MY FRIENDS SAY SO TOO. AND I SUPPOSE they are all quite right. But what if I am? I like being eccentric at times.

One of my habits, even to this day, when I get disgusted with the sight of too many people and the awful noise they make, is to jump into my car and drive away to some nearby jungle. There I will leave the car, wander off into the forest, make myself a nice large camp fire as night approaches, and spend the hours of darkness just seated by the blaze. I throw fresh wood on the fire as occasion demands, having already gathered it before darkness fell. Eventually the supply of wood will give out, or I might feel sleepy. In either case there is only one thing to do. That is to go to sleep beside the fire. The embers will keep me warm when the chill and dewfall of early morning might otherwise prove uncomfortable. They will also protect me from elephants and snakes, the only creatures to be feared when no man-eaters are around. With daybreak I will go back to the car and come home and wonder why I did such a foolish and eccentric thing, and what I got out of it.

But I have done it, and will do it, again and again.

Other forms of this madness are to go out to the jungle on moonlit nights, and also on dark nights, and sit behind some tree, or on a rock, or beside a water hole, and just watch and listen.

Those who have had the good luck at any time to sit beside a camp fire, out in the wide open spaces, even where there was no danger from lurking animals or poisonous snakes, might be able to understand my fondness for this pastime. There is a pleasure that comes to one at such times that words cannot describe. It touches some hidden inner chord and sets one's soul afire!

Perhaps it is on such occasions, and in such solitudes, that a man's inner self comes into closest touch with the infinite. I feel very near indeed then to God, far closer than I can feel in any church where the padre, either on the basis of a monthly salary or other means of remuneration, automatically repeats words for the uplift of my erring and sinful self.

However, let me not talk about myself. Perhaps you would like to come with me on one of these night prowls—'camp fire trips' you may call them—into the jungle.

The Studebaker is ready with six gallons of petrol in her tank. She also has a six-cylinder engine and is rated to have horse-power, although how many of those horses are alive after these many strenuous years, I wonder, nor try to guess. Just bring some sandwiches, a water-bottle and if you can get it, a thermos flask of hot tea. I will like you all the better. Your great coat and a cap, too, in case you feel cold, and a pipe, tobacco and matches if you are a smoker. That is all that is necessary. It is 3 p.m., but we have only about fifty miles to cover.

I am taking you to a place called Kundukottai, where there is a nice forest. Two ranges of hills converge there; and two streams, coming from different directions, join together to form one large stream. In the vernacular, the big stream is called Doddahalla (big hollow or big ravine), but I have called it the Secret River. The jungle around this area holds a few animals of every species, except bison. I am told bison were once there also, but they have been shot out long ago, although the forest range officer says they were wiped out by foot-and-mouth disease contracted from the village cattle that graze in the forest. After all, how can the poor man admit the real fact? He is, after all, the range officer.

We are away, and for the first twenty-five miles of our route we spin along a metalled road. At the nineteenth mile from Bangalore it leaves the state of Mysore behind and enters the state of Madras. Exactly at the twenty-fifth milestone we come to the small town of Hosur, which is also the taluk headquarters of that area. From Hosur we branch off the main road and for the next sixteen miles travel along what is known in India as a *kutcha* road—that is, a road made with sand and stones where, for some reason or the other, these two components never seem to be in the proper proportion to make it a good road. One or the other predominates in turn. The stones cut the car's tyres, while the sandy stretches make heavy going. In the rainy season these sandy sections become very entertaining for the motorist with a sense of humour, if there is such a man, for then he will slide and skid from side to side, or perhaps get bogged down to the axle if he is not careful. But this is not the rainy season and we cover those sixteen miles in fair time, to reach the smaller town of Denkanikota, which is the headquarters of two forest range officers controlling different blocks of jungle.

Now we leave the stone-and-sand road and travel on a road that is not a road at all, for this is nothing but a glorified bullock-cart track. About three and a half miles from Denkanikota this track crosses the upper reaches of one of the two streams I have mentioned. There are no complicated and expensive bridges here; the track just splashes through the stream. This is fair enough, unless there has been heavy rain. Then the stream becomes a torrent and the water may rise to a depth of ten feet. When that happens you just go back to Denkanikota and try again after two days, when the water-level may have subsided. Just think how lucky you were to have been on the Denkanikota side. Supposing you had been on the other bank; you would have had to remain there till the flood went down.

Twice more we cross the stream that snakes alongside the track. At the eighth milestone we pass the hamlet of Kundukottai, overshadowed by a rocky hill noted for two things—panthers and the large rock-bee.* And remember that of these the bees are far more dangerous when really roused.

The track now drops sharply into a valley while curving around the spurs of the rocky hill. But we have only a mile more to go, and there, beside the ninth milestone, we must leave the Studebaker after first backing it and turning it around for the return journey—rather an awkward manoeuvre since the track is scarcely wider than the length of the car, with a steep decline on one side.

It is done at last. We place four stones behind the four wheels besides leaving the car in gear, just in case some fidgety

---

* See *The Black Panther of Sivanipalli*, George Allen & Unwin, London.

wayfarer tampers with the controls. Also we must disconnect one of the leads to the battery, since the wayfarer may switch on the lights for you and allow them to burn. Carrying the few things we have brought with us, we must walk sharply downhill to the Doddahalla stream, the two halves of which have united less than a mile higher up, to form the one watercourse which I have named the Secret River.

Indeed, it has secrets of geological interest further down its course. But you will not tempt me to divulge them, for if I did, this beautiful stretch of forest and stream would be invaded and commercialized to their utter destruction.

At last we reach the bed of the little river and find it a veritable fairyland. There is not much water in it at this season; just a tiny trickle that meanders sometimes down the centre of the sandy bed, and at other times curves from bank to bank. Both sides are thickly wooded with towering, gnarled trees—tamarind, *jumlum*, and *muthee* mostly, with here and there a stray flame-of-the-forest, ficus tree, banyan, *neem* and *mhowa*. Between the trees the tall, feathery stems of bamboos bend gracefully over the sandy stretches. Sudden currents of cool breeze now and then rush down the valley and blow along the streambed. When that happens, the branches of the trees and the lofty tufts of the bamboos swing and sway in unison to make a distant soughing sound like a faraway waterfall, or the thunder of the sea on distant reefs in a restless ocean.

It is just 5 p.m., but we have a deal of work to do before it gets dark. First we select a camp site: a spot fairly high up on the sandy bank. And now comes the all-important task of gathering wood for our camp fire. Bear in mind that the more wood we gather the longer the blaze will last, and also the stronger and brighter it will be. There is no difficulty whatever in getting the wood, for it lies everywhere in abundance, thrown up on both banks and even on the wide streambed itself, wedged tightly between boulders and tree trunks that blocked the way when the river was in spate after the rains and carried everything before it—tree-trunks, logs, branches, roots—everything and anything.

It is 6.15 p.m. and we are ready. It is also growing dark. But let us not light the fire just yet, for that will alarm the birds. Rather, let us listen to them awhile: the challenging calls of the grey junglecocks, the wrangling of spurfowl, the strident, plaintive 'meowing' of peafowl, the restless cries of the ever-watchful plover or 'Did-you-do-it', and the distant, provoking crescendo of the 'brain-fever' bird.

Now it is almost dark and the nightjars flit around. One sits on a boulder and is lost to sight in the matchless camouflage that blends with the stone. But we know it is there for we hear it, 'Chuck! Chuck! Chuck! Chuck! Chuck-oooo!' it trills.

Suddenly a distant medley of sound falls on our ears. Not discordant, but strangely thrilling; maybe eerie.

'Ooooo-oooo-ooooh! Woooo-woooo-wooooh!'
'Oo-where? Oo-where? Oo-where? Where? Where?'
'Here! Here! Here! Heere! Heere! Heeeere!'
'Hee-yah! Hee-yah! Heeee-yah!'
'Yah! Yah! Ya-ah! Ya-ah! Heeeeee-yah! Heeeeee-yah!'

It is the chorus of a jackal-pack in their restless hunt for food. The leader calls stridently, raucously—'Oo-where? Oo-where? Oo-where?'—and the pack seem to answer: 'Here! Here! Heere! Heee-yah! Yah! Yah! Yah!'

The long-drawn ululation bursts forth again and is answered by the staccato, raucous, vociferous refrain. The savage call and plaintive reply echo and re-echo from the forbidding darkness of the surrounding forest, rise and fall in crescendo and diminuendo down the aisles of the jungle. The shrieking crescendo of noise passes frantically into a prolonged and

THE CALL OF THE MAN-EATER

indescribable clamour. It permeates the clinging, enveloping, enshrouding blackness. Nothing can restrain it. That wildly beautiful and infinitely savage chorus lingers, dies away and screams again to a crescendo, snivels, abates and swells in turn; an unending medley of outrageous sounds.

Night has fallen. It is time to light the fire, not because of the jackals, for in spite of the forbidding calls they are harmless; not because of a wandering tiger or panther, because there are no man-eaters in this area at present, nor will they hurt you. The reason for the fire is the existence of two different sorts of creatures, one of them very big and the other quite small, which will harm you in no uncertain manner if either happens to come too close: a wandering solitary elephant, and a creeping poisonous snake. We have brought no firearms, and it will not be a pleasant experience in the darkness should an elephant come upon us or a venomous snake find us obstructing his path.

The fire is soon crackling merrily. A few sparks fly heavenward and the glow fitfully lights up the boles of the trees surrounding us, silent sentinels of the watchful wild. The jackals see the glow, or maybe smell the smoke. Their yowling comes to an abrupt end. The fire has frightened everything into silence, except for the wood-crickets which chirp ceaselessly from their shelters among the fallen leaves.

The larger animals will not start moving till after eight o'clock at the earliest, so we have about an hour for a chat. There is no place quite so suitable for a friendly talk as a camp fire. The red embers, the crackle of flames, the occasional shower of sparks as a fresh piece of wood is thrown into the blaze, the acrid smell of smoke that curls upwards in a spiral to the sky above—all these help to give one the feeling of being at home with oneself, with Nature and with God.

A NIGHT BY THE CAMP FIRE

Perhaps you would like me to tell you something about the more intimate and individual natures of some of the denizens of these forests. So far I have told you stories of hunting and shooting them which will give the impression that these animals are without qualification fierce, implacable and unreasonable, given only to the lust of killing and destroying. I thought so, too, in my younger days. But since that far-off time I have kept most of these creatures as pets, admittedly from an early age, but to quite an advanced age in various ways and capacities; every one of them has exhibited traits of remarkable good sense and affection, if only the owner can get to understand their little peculiarities and shortcomings.

Let me try to illustrate my point by telling you about a few of them.

I will begin with Bruno, my wife's pet sloth bear. I got him for her by accident.

I was with a party of friends who had gone to hunt wild boar for meat. There is a place about thirty miles beyond Mysore city where the sugarcane fields are infested by wild-pig, which cause much damage to the crops. The pigs lie up in the sugarcane plantations during the day and we had them driven out by 'beaters' (who are the willing owners of the fields and their hirelings), shooting them as they broke cover between adjoining fields or tried to escape into the surrounding scrub jungle. The arrangement is that half the meat goes to the beaters while we take the rest.

Nearly two years ago, on one such beat, out rushed a sounder of pigs and some of them were shot, while the rest escaped. Everybody thought the fun was over when suddenly there came a loud 'Woof! Woof!' and a solitary sloth bear followed, looking decidedly black and decidedly hot in the midday sun.

THE CALL OF THE MAN-EATER

Now I will not shoot a sloth bear wantonly but, unfortunately for the poor beast, one of my companions did not feel that way about it, and promptly shot the bear on the spot.

As we watched the fallen animal we were surprised to see that the black fur on its back moved and left the prostrate body. Then we saw it was a baby bear that had been riding on its mother's back when the sudden shot had killed her. The little creature ran around its prostrate parent making a pitiful noise.

I ran up to it to attempt a capture. It scooted into the sugarcane field. Following up with the beaters, I was at last able to grab it by the scruff of its neck while it snapped and tried to scratch me with its long, hooked claws.

We put it in one of the gunny bags we had brought for the meat, and when I got back to Bangalore I duly presented it to my wife. She was delighted! She at once put a coloured ribbon around its neck, and after discovering the cub was a 'boy' she christened it Bruno.

Bruno soon took to drinking milk from a bottle. It was but a step further and within a very few days he started eating and drinking everything else. And everything is the right word, for he ate porridge made from any ingredients, vegetables, fruit, nuts, meat (especially pork), curry and rice regardless of condiments and chillies, bread, eggs, chocolates, sweets, pudding, ice-cream, etc., etc., etc. As for drink: milk, tea, coffee, lime-juice, aerated water, buttermilk, beer, alcoholic liquor and, in fact, anything liquid. It all went down with relish.

The bear became very attached to our two Alsatian dogs and to all the children of the tenants living in our bungalow. He was left quite free in his younger days and spent his time in playing, running into the kitchen and going to sleep in our beds.

A NIGHT BY THE CAMP FIRE

One day an accident befell him. I put down poison (barium carbonate) to kill the rats and mice that had got into my library. So did Bruno; and he ate some of the poison. Paralysis set in to the extent that he could not stand on his feet. But he dragged himself on his stumps to my wife, who called me. I guessed what had happened. Off I rushed in the car to the vet's residence. A case of poisoning! Tame bear—barium carbonate—what to do?

Out came his medical books, and a feverish reference to the index began: 'What poison did you say, sir?' 'Barium carbonate'. 'Ah yes-B-Ba-Barium Salts-Ah! Barium carbonate! Symptoms—paralysis—treatment—injections of...Just a minute, sir. I'll bring my syringe and the medicine.'

A dash back in the car. Bruno still floundering about on his stumps, but clearly weakening rapidly; some vomiting, heavy breathing, with heaving flanks and gaping mouth.

Hold him, everybody! In goes the hypodermic—Bruno squeals—10 c.c. of the antidote enters his system without a drop being wasted. Ten minutes later: condition unchanged! Another 10 c.c. injected! Ten minutes later: breathing less stertorous—Bruno can move his arms and legs a little although he cannot stand yet. Thirty minutes later: Bruno gets up and has a great feed! He looks at us disdainfully, as much as to say, 'What's barium carbonate to a big black bear like me?' Bruno is still eating.

Another time he found nearly one gallon of old engine oil which I had drained from the sump of the Studebaker and was keeping as a weapon against the inroads of termites. He promptly drank the lot. But it had no ill effects whatever.

The months rolled on and Bruno had grown many times the size he was when he came. He had equalled the Alsatians in height and had even outgrown them. But was just as sweet, just as mischievous, just as playful. And he was very fond of us all. Above all, he loved my wife, and she loved him too! She had changed his name from Bruno, to Baba, a Hindustani word signifying 'small boy'. And he could do a few tricks, too. At the command, 'Baba, wrestle', or 'Baba, box', he vigorously tackled anyone who came forward for a 'rough and tumble'. Give him a stick and say 'Baba, hold gun', and he pointed the stick at you. Ask him, 'Baba, where's baby?' and he immediately produced and cradled affectionately a stump of wood which he had carefully concealed in his straw bed. But because of the tenant's children, poor Bruno, or Baba, had to be kept chained most of the time.

Then my son and I advised my wife, and friends advised her too, to give Baba to the zoo at Mysore. He was getting too big to keep at home. After some weeks of such advice she at last consented. Hastily, and before she could change her mind, a letter was written to the curator of the zoo. Did he want a tame bear for his collection? He replied, 'Yes.' The Zoo sent a cage from Mysore in a lorry, a distance of eighty-seven miles, and Baba was packed off.

We all missed him greatly; but in a sense we were relieved. My wife was inconsolable. She wept and fretted. For the first few days she would not eat a thing. Then she wrote a number of letters to the curator. How was Baba? Back came the replies: 'Well, but fretting; he refuses food too.'

After that, friends visiting Mysore were begged to make a point of going to the zoo and seeing how Baba was getting along. They reported that he was well but looked very thin and sad. All the keepers at the zoo said he was fretting. For three months I managed to restrain my wife from visiting Mysore. Then she said one day: 'I must see Baba. Either you take me by car; or I will go myself by bus or train.' So I took her by car.

A NIGHT BY THE CAMP FIRE

Friends had conjectured that the bear would not recognize her. I had thought so too. But while she was yet some yards from his cage Baba saw her and recognized her. He howled with happiness. She ran up to him, petted him through the bars, and he stood on his head in delight.

For the next three hours she would not leave that cage. She gave him tea, lemonade, cakes, ice-cream and what not. Then 'closing time' came and we had to leave. My wife cried bitterly; Baba cried bitterly; even the hardened curator and the keepers felt depressed. As for me, I had reconciled myself to what I knew was going to happen next.

'Oh please, sir,' she asked the curator, 'may I have my Baba back?'

Hesitantly, he answered: 'Madam, he belongs to the zoo and is government property now. I cannot give away government property. But if my boss, the superintendent at Bangalore, agrees, certainly you may have him back.'

There followed the return journey to Bangalore and a visit to the superintendent's bungalow. A tearful pleading: 'Baba and I are both fretting for each other. Will you please give him back to me?' He was a kind-hearted man and consented. Not only that, but he wrote to the curator telling him to lend us a cage for transporting the bear to Bangalore.

Back we went to Mysore again, armed with the superintendent's letter. Baba was driven into a small cage and hoisted on top of the car; the cage was tied securely, and a slow and careful return journey to Bangalore was accomplished.

Once home, a squad of coolies were engaged for special work in our compound. An island was made for Baba. It was twenty feet long by fifteen feet wide, and was surrounded by a dry pit, or moat, six feet wide by seven feet deep. A wooden box that once housed fowls was brought and put on the island for Baba to sleep in at night. Straw was placed inside to keep him warm, and his 'baby', the gnarled stump, with his 'gun', the piece of bamboo, both of which had been sentimentally preserved since he had been sent away to the zoo, were put back for him to play with.

In a few days the coolies hoisted the cage on to the island and Baba was released. He was delighted; standing on his hindlegs, he pointed his 'gun' and cradled his 'baby'. My wife spent hours sitting on a chair there while he sat on her lap. He was fifteen months old and pretty heavy, too!

The way my wife reaches the island and leaves it is interesting. I have tied a rope to the overhanging branch of a mango tree with a loop at its end. Putting one foot in the loop, she kicks off with the other, to bridge the six-foot gap that constitutes the width of the surrounding pit. The return journey is made the same way.

But who can say now that a sloth bear has no sense of affection, no memory and no individual characteristics?

I will tell you next about quite a different sort of animal— a hyaena—which is also with us now and is my particular pet. His name is Jackie, and I got him under rather tragic circumstances.

Nearly fourteen months ago I was spending a night in the jungle. But the place and circumstances were different. It was at a spot named Sopathy, a rocky stretch on the Chinar river in the Salem district, and it was a moonlit night. I had not made a camp fire, but was sitting on one of the boulders overhanging a sandy stretch of the river. I was alone and had brought no weapon.

About ten o'clock I noticed an indefinable something moving along the sand in my direction. As it came closer I made out, by the peculiar loping gait, the slanting body and the grey form on which the black stripes were hardly visible in the moonlight, that it was a hyaena. When almost opposite me it halted abruptly and faced about, staring intently away from me at something in the jungle. I could see clearly its large, upstanding, bat-like ears cocked to catch the slightest sound.

Very soon the reason for its behaviour became evident. A wild dog, looking as grey as the hyaena in the moonlight, although it is actually a reddish-brown animal with an almost black, bushy tail, broke cover from the opposite bank of the river that was overgrown with jungle, and advanced on to the sandy bed. Almost immediately it was joined by five others of its kind. The hyaena turned about and tried to slink into the cover of the trees growing near the rock on which I was sitting. But the wild dogs caught the movement and without further ado attacked.

I have had occasion to remark before that wild dogs are fierce and implacable hunters. Except for man, elephants and bison, they will attack anything that moves, including tigers and panthers, and are quite unmindful of the losses they may sustain in the fray, so long as they eventually succeed in pulling down their prey, tearing it to shreds, and eating it while still practically alive. My own experience up to that time had been that wild dogs either regard hyaenas as cousins or beneath contempt and leave them alone. But that night was an exception, for the six dogs attacked the hyaena forthwith.

The hyaena tried to make a run for it, but his shambling feet moved too slowly and in an instant the dogs were upon him. The first attacker came too near. Like lightning, the hyaena switched around, dipped its head at an angle, and closed its vice-like jaws on the dog's neck. I heard the dying wail of the stricken animal when the powerful teeth sank into its throat. The loud crunch of bones followed as the neck snapped like a dry twig. But the other five dogs piled themselves on to the unfortunate hyaena.

THE CALL OF THE MAN-EATER

The *hyaena striata*, to give him his full Latin name, is no fighter. Rather, he is a cowardly, sneaking, skulking creature by nature, that slouches along the jungle, covering enormous distances in his search for carrion—anything that is dead, no matter how it died or in what stage of decomposition the carcass may be. For the hyaena is a scavenger. Very occasionally he may attack, kill and eat a stray goat, sheep or village cur, but that is only when driven by the pangs of extreme hunger. He will try to avoid a fight at any cost.

This unfortunate hyaena, whose plight I was watching, had attempted to slink away, but the dogs had been too quick. Realizing now that it could not escape, it decided to sell its life dearly. While the dogs squealed and 'whistled' in their curious fashion to attract reinforcements of their own kind, with rumbling, throatly growls the hyaena snapped right and left, scoring telling bites on its attackers, who screamed in agony. But the five of them were too many. They covered the hyaena's body, growling, biting and rending the living flesh from the bones. I knew that in another minute the beast would be torn to shreds.

I wanted to help, but I had no weapon with me—not even a stick or stone. For a second I contemplated scrambling down from the rock on which I was sitting and rushing to the rescue while driving the assailants off with shouts. But it was just possible that in their infuriated state they might resent my intrusion and attack. So I stood up from my place of concealment, showed myself, and started whistling and shouting at the top of my voice.

The combatants were so busily engaged in tearing each other to bits that it was some time before they heard the noise I was making. Then, one by one, the dogs ceased attacking the hyaena and turned around to look up at the rock on which I was standing. In the moonlight I could see the hyaena was in a bad way: no longer grey, but bearing large black patches that glistened even at that distance. I knew the patches were caused by the blood that flowed from many wounds. All the five dogs were injured, too. Some of them licked themselves or each other, as they looked at me and then back at their victim.

The hyaena seized the chance, tottered across the dry riverbed and disappeared into the jungle on the other side. A few minutes later the five dogs followed, intent no doubt in finishing the task. But I heard no further sound, and after the disturbance created by the din of the fight, together with the noise I had made, no other animal showed up for the rest of the night.

With daybreak the thought occurred to me to follow in the tracks of the hyaena to see what had happened. This was comparatively easy, for although the ground on the opposite bank was too hard to show footprints, there was a clear trail of blood that had dripped on the grass and had been smeared on the leaves of the bushes. The trail led to a small knoll that was perhaps half a mile away. Close to the summit of this knoll were some large boulders, heaped one upon the other, with spear-grass growing around. Here the hyaena had made a last gallant stand and met death as the relentless pursuers had once again closed in.

One of the red dogs lay dead, stiffening in the long spear-grass that was lank and bent with the weight of the glistening dewdrops that still dripped from the ends of the stems. Only a few bones and the skull of the hyaena remained. Fragments of the grey and black-striped coat lay in shreds around me, most of them dyed a dark rusty-red with blood. But no carcass or flesh were to be seen. The dogs had eaten it all.

Hardly ten yards away was an opening between the tumbled boulders. No doubt it was the den to which the hyaena had been making its way when the attackers had moved in. As I looked upon the scene of carnage, a slight movement at the entrance to the den caught the corner of my eye. I glanced up to gaze into the frightened, sad faces of two baby hyaenas.

So the gallant animal who had fought the previous night against such odds had been a female hyaena, and not a male, as I had thought. Further, she had been a mother and had left two orphaned pups. I could see by their size that they were too young to look after themselves and would starve to death in three or four days. I determined to try to catch them. I retreated downhill the way I had come, in full view of the hyaena's pups. Then I made a detour and approached the hillock from the opposite side. I eventually hid myself behind the pile of boulders and waited for the puppies to come out of the shelter. I knew this would happen very shortly, just as soon as they grew hungry.

My chance came at last. They came out of their den side by side and advanced a few steps to gaze down sadly and wonderingly at the remains of their mother. That was when I pounced. I was fortunate enough to seize one of the pups by the scruff of its neck. But unluckily the other had heard or sensed my approach, and ran back into the cave.

Still holding my struggling captive, I went back behind the pile of boulders and waited for the second pup to come out again. But although I remained for nearly an hour, it did not do so.

Meanwhile, by his constant struggling, the pup I held in my hands became difficult to handle. He bit and scratched and wriggled continuously. Once or twice he almost slipped from my grasp, and I knew if that happened I would never be able to catch him again. So, after another quarter of an hour I reluctantly decided to leave the second pup to its fate and walked back the five miles or so to the village of Pennagram, where I had left my car.

That was how I acquired Jackie, as I called him, for he turned out to be a male, and brought him back to Bangalore. For a few days I fed him on the bottle, with goat's milk, as I have found that cow's milk disagrees with most carnivorous wild animals because it lacks proteins. I supplemented the goat's milk with a few annas' worth of raw, minced mutton that could easily be digested and which at the same time afforded the essential proteins.

Jackie grew apace both in strength and size, soon outgrowing the need for goat's milk and minced mutton. Henceforth his diet consisted of raw beef and bones and it did not matter in the least whether this was fresh or in a high state of decomposition, crawling with maggots and swarming with flies.

Then Jackie met with his first mishap which nearly cost him his life. About thirteen miles east of Bangalore is a little settlement called Whitefield, consisting almost entirely of Anglo-Indian families. In this place a small five-bedroomed cottage, with verandah and kitchen and over half-an-acre of land was for sale for the sum of Rs 5,000, which in English money comes to about £375. My wife fell in love with this place, calling it a 'dinky' little cottage, and wanted me to buy it. I bought it, together with a village cur that had been deserted by her last owner but had remained on the premises. This dog at once attached herself to me. I named her Gypsy as appropriate to her antecedents.

I came to live in this cottage for a few days each week, returning to my home in Bangalore for the remaining days, and I took Jackie with me by car on these visits.

Now this cottage had been lying vacant for some time, and because of that the villagers around had decided to treat it more or less as their own property. Not only did they graze cattle and goats in the compound, thereby destroying the garden, but they had been lopping the trees for firewood and cutting the grass for their cattle, in addition to making the place a rendezvous for the graziers during the daytime. I tried to stop all this, but in vain. The only difference was that, instead of stealing wood by daylight, the villagers came on moonlit nights to do so, while their womenfolk came at break of day to cut the grass, in the manner of the early bird that catches the worm. This led to complaints to the police and one or two 'personal encounter'. So the villagers decided to teach me a lesson.

Now I suffer from many bad habits, and one of them is to keep my dog inside the house at night, rather than let it loose in the compound. I do that because I have previously lost dogs from snakebite or from being carried off by panthers in jungly areas. Thus Gypsy came to be sleeping on a mat at the foot of my bed.

One morning, in the early hours, I awoke to the sound of her growling softly at the bathroom door. It was bright moonlight outside and the time was 3.10 a.m. Now a dog will not growl in that manner without reason. So, taking my torch, I softly opened the door and went into the bathroom. Gypsy brushed past me, halted at the outer door of the bathroom, which was also locked, and still growled ominously.

I was sure there was a snake about somewhere. I then remembered that a section of plank in the door, about two inches wide and three feet or so from the ground, was missing. I stooped down and peered through the gap. What I saw left me with mixed feelings. In the brilliant moonlight stood eleven men—I counted them easily—armed with staves and bamboos. Obviously it was a party of resentful villagers, come to 'beat me up' for my uncompromising attitude.

A NIGHT BY THE CAMP FIRE

Even as I watched, one of the men climbed on the shoulders of another and from there on to the tiled roof which, at that spot, was only about nine feet off the ground. I guessed what he was going to do: remove a tile or two, come through the gap into the house, and then slip the bolt of the outer door to admit his pals. I felt very resentful.

Tiptoeing back to where my .12 bore shotgun was standing in the corner of my bedroom, I slipped two or three No. 8 gauge cartridges into the pockets of my nightcoat and returned to the bathroom. I was toying with the idea of scoring a quick right and left with the No. 8 shot into the legs of the assembly. But, just in time, I realized what would be the outcome; of course, a good many of the fellows would have 'sore legs' from the pellets, and perhaps one or two would have to go to hospital, but that would bring the police into the picture, and any amount or 'red tape'. Why did I fire? Why did I hurt so many men? Was it really in self-defence? I would have to prove that. The men might swear they had come with no evil intent whatever. But they would have a lot of explaining to do as to how and why they had come at that time of night. Altogether it would be a nasty business, requiring my presence at the police station and at court. So I overcame the strong temptation to pepper their legs and decided to fire a shot over their heads.

The report and flash of the gun in that silence caused the nine men who were still standing in a group to make off at top speed. The fellow who had put his companion on to the roof lost his nerve completely and screamed that he had been shot and killed, hastily amending that statement to one that he was dying. He was so afraid that his powers of locomotion failed him and he stood rooted to the spot, yelling at the top of his voice. The eleventh adventurer, who had climbed on to my roof, did not wait to scramble down. He jumped, landed on the ground with a thud, and recovering himself, made off like greased lightning. That broke the spell, and his comrade at last regained his wits and followed hotly in his wake. It all happened in a matter of seconds, and Gypsy and I were then alone.

I opened the bathroom door and went outside to see if any more of the miscreants were lurking about. There was not a trace of them. But there were a few 'souvenirs' left on the field of battle—or perhaps I could more aptly describe them as 'booty'. Three bamboo staves, one solid wooden cudgel which would certainly have broken my thick head had it descended thereon, and, of all things, two pairs of *chappals* or rough leather sandals such as the yokels in southern India usually wear.

The next morning I told the vendors who bring fruit, vegetables and eggs for sale from door to door that, in exactly three mornings from that day, I intended to sell two pairs of good *chappals* very cheaply to the first applicants. On the morning fixed for the sale two 'purchasers' presented themselves for the two pairs of sandals and offered to buy them. I announced that I was selling them at knock-down prices—only one rupee and eight annas each pair—about two shillings! The price was accepted and each man paid his money, took his pair of *chappals*, put them on and went away contented. I had little doubt that they had been the original owners of the sandals which they had discarded on that memorable night. After that there were no more attempts to break into my little cottage, and trespassers of all sorts became conspicuous by their absence.

My purpose in telling you this is to tell you that I became rather fond of Gypsy as a consequence. It all happened a little while before I acquired Jackie, so that when I started to bring him up and down to Whitefield from Bangalore he was quite a little fellow, while Gypsy was a full-grown slut, well on the way to becoming very spoilt.

The first calamity that befell Jackie happened when he tried to steal a bone Gypsy was eating. She bit him, and one of her teeth barely missed his left eye, gouging a deep hole just beneath it. An abscess formed and I thought I would lose Jackie, or at least that he would lose his eye, as he developed a high fever. The vet gave him penicillin injections, four lakh units at a time, till he had five such injections. Then the abscess burst—outwards, fortunately—and his eye was saved as well as his life.

He grew quickly after that and soon outgrew Gypsy. But never once did he attempt to bite her, either in play or anger. He treats her as gently as a lady should be treated, and just loves to romp and gambol with her.

Feeding Jackie now became a problem, for at this time he was eating from eight to ten pounds of raw beef per day, and in Bangalore beef costs eight annas a pound, roughly eight pence! I did not feel justified in spending almost seven shillings a day on buying raw beef for him.

So I kept him permanently at my cottage in Whitefield where, with great tact, I had made friends with the two local butchers, who undertook to supply me with ten pounds by weight of beef, in the form of lungs, guts, tripe, liver, etc., daily, for six annas for the lot. That is, roughly six pence per day for ten pounds of miscellaneous beef!

This arrangement worked well for quite a time, when one day serious trouble befell me and Jackie.

I should tell you that what is termed as 'cow-slaughter' is forbidden in some parts of India, including Mysore state. The slaughtering of cattle is not allowed in these places, although the law does not forbid anyone from eating beef provided he can get it from a place where the prohibition is

THE CALL OF THE MAN-EATER

not in force. As with prohibition of alcoholic liquor, which operates in some states and parts of India and not in others, prohibition of 'cow-slaughter' in one place is an open invitation for brisk business in supplying meat from a neighbouring part of the country or state where that law is not in force. Thus Madras state is allowed by law to supply beef across the border into Mysore state and Bangalore, where cow-slaughter is forbidden. It is said that some individuals in parts of Mysore state, such as the Bangalore district, where the prohibition of alcoholic liquor is not in force, return the favour, although not legally this time, by supplying the prohibited item across the border to Madras state, which is a totally 'dry' area.

This is how Bangalore now gets its beef! But what about Whitefield? The butchers claim they also get their supply of beef from across the Madras border, which is about twenty miles away. But one day the police at Whitefield became suspicious and raided the butchers' houses where the meat was stored and sealed the doors. They said that cattle were being slaughtered on the premises. So, there was no meat for Jackie and he was ravenously hungry. What was I to do?

That night I took a sack and walked to the butchers' homes. The police had sealed the front doors. But are there no such things as back doors, windows and skylights? And tiles can be removed to allow the entry or exit of a human body through the roof, can they not? The gentlemen who had visited me early that morning had given me the idea.

To cut a long story short, I came away with a sackful of beef, for which I had had to pay heavily, slung across my shoulders, and made for my little cottage across the fields, along the outskirts of Whitefield cemetery and then over a hill, till I had reached home dripping with blood that had soaked through the sack. At that time of night, had I been caught I would without doubt have been suspected of murder.

A NIGHT BY THE CAMP FIRE

But I had secured enough meat to feed Jackie for a whole week, although my little cottage stank vilely of rotten flesh after the fourth day. But by then the Police had come to understand that the beef came from Madras, and not from the unwanted cattle of Whitefield itself.

Jackie is with me now and becoming very big, and in appearance repulsive. But he is not at all fierce. On the contrary, his only aim in life is to romp and play. I leave him loose at times and he follows me about, comes out for long walks in the evening and does not harm children, sheep, goats or other dogs. He is passionately fond of little creatures such as puppies, kittens, chickens and the like.

At times his ideas of romping and playing are decidedly boisterous. Although Gypsy is very friendly with him now, she resents too much of his rough play, and she growls at him although he towers above her.

So to serve as a playmate for him I brought home from one of the butcher's houses a female puppy of the breed very definitely known in India as 'pariah dog'. She is about four months old, although Jackie is now over a year, and is approximately one-fifth his size. I have called her Jill. But she gives him all he wants in the way of exercise by chasing him, or being chased herself; romping, playing and even biting him when he becomes a little too rough for her. All this Jackie takes meekly. He is devoted to little Jill, who even snatches the raw meat out of his mouth. Never once has he bitten her; never once has he even growled at her.

Nor has he done either of those things to me. He is rather foolish, with far less intelligence than an average dog. But he is sweet and good-natured, rather like a buffoon among dogs with his grey coat, striped with black, his large head with sharply-pointed ears, the mane of long hair running down his neck and back like a ridge, his short hind legs, and his slouching, shambling gait. So you see, the hyaena is not such a terrible, fierce and loathsome creature as people may think.

We have had about eight panther cubs in all, most of them rescued from their dens after the mothers had been shot. I remember that we lost the first two very shortly after we had acquired them, from gastritis! They also fall very easy victims to colic. Contrary to expectations, a panther cub is extremely delicate and dies easily, being nothing like so hardy as a bear or hyaena. Cows' milk disagrees with them entirely and proves fatal within a few days. Goats' milk seems to agree better, but has to be supplemented, even when they are very young, with a spoonful of minced mutton and mutton blood—not beef. As they grow older, beef can be substituted for mutton, but the quantity given to them at any one time has to be regulated. The need for mutton in the early stages is to compensate for the fact that, as I have remarked in an earlier book, in the wild conditions the mother helps the digestive processes of her cubs by first eating the meat of her kills herself and then vomiting it out for them to eat again. The cubs are gluttonous creatures and will gorge themselves till they can hardly move. That is when the colic sometimes attacks them, and as I have said, when they get colic or gastritis it is fatal.

Panther cubs are extremely playful and mischievous. They can recognize their owner from among other people. Although, as they grow older, their play becomes exceedingly rough, none I have had has been in the least fierce.

I remember one of them, a female which we named Spottie and kept for about nine months. She was a very sweet and intelligent creature. She would stalk my wife or me when we were reading or otherwise engaged when she thought we were not aware of her presence, hiding behind a door, or creeping up behind a chair or a table till she was close enough. Then with mock severity she would charge or pounce upon

A NIGHT BY THE CAMP FIRE

us. On such occasions she never once bit us, but tried her best to be gentle. Yet her claws were sharper than she realized and, as often as not, we would emerge from the game with at least a few scratches.

Some people have the notion that if a panther cub is brought up on boiled meat and soft foods it will not become ferocious. Well, for one thing this idea would not work out, for the cub would probably die! A panther must have proteins, and all the cubs we have kept have been fed on raw meat and given blood to drink as they grow older. Yet not one of them became in any way fierce because of this diet.

The female I have been telling you about, Spottie, died tragically one day, and this is how it happened. My son Donald shot a large sambar stag, and for some reason or other we wanted to see how much Spottie could eat of the carcass. So we allowed her to eat her fill. She gorged till she could hardly crawl. That very night she began to vomit and purge. In a few hours she growled and then screamed with pain and bit savagely in the throes of colic. By morning she was dead.

Sometime later we acquired another cub, this time a male. We called him Spottie II. Benefitting from our earlier errors, we regulated his diet and kept him for over ten months in our house at Bangalore. During all this time he never once harmed a living thing. But we had responsibilities. There were tenants in the house and they had children. The children insisted on coming near the panther. Spottie II loved them and played with them. But we realized we were running a great risk. Finally, very sadly and reluctantly, we gave him to a friend, a Swiss gentleman, who eventually sold him to a German animal-dealer. The last we heard was that Spottie had been sent to some zoo in Europe.

Lately Donald brought home another panther cub. We have had him for about a month and he is not yet three months old. But this one we have called Grumpy, and he is with us now.

Then there is Ella the jackal. She plays with the dogs, cats anything, but loves to hide in dark corners, such as beneath an almirah. Ella gives her 'jackal call' occasionally at nights, but being a vixen she renders what might be termed as 'half notes' rather than the complete and peculiarly attractive full call of the male.

A villager one day brought for sale five jackal puppies, perhaps four to six weeks old, and thinking she might be lonely for want of company of her own kind, I bought them for Ella. That afternoon she was delighted and mothered them in a most touching manner. Around midnight, however, I heard the puppies screaming and found Ella had killed one and was in the process of devouring it. I rescued the other four, and next day, as I had nowhere to keep them, put them with Jackie, the hyaena. They tried drinking milk from him, which disconcerted the poor fellow dreadfully. Since then they have grown quite a bit, and so has Jackie. I kept them together for a considerable time and it was interesting to watch how he took upon himself the serious duty of looking after these four rascals. At feeding time Jackie could hardly finish his meat before the four jackals, who had already swallowed their own share, swarmed around him to steal what remained. Invariably, while he chased one of them away playfully, the other three would gobble up all that was left. Matters became so bad for Jackie that I was compelled to move the four jackals away and put them with Bruno, the sloth bear. He is not so good-natured as the hyaena at meal-times and swipes at the jackals if they come within reach of his paw, although in the afternoons and at night they sleep around and sometimes on top of him in his wooden box.

Meanwhile Ella, the adult female jackal, has grown clever too. She jumps onto the dining table, removes the cosy off the teapot, then the lid, and drinks up all the tea.

We have kept all species of the deer family. They are sweet and gentle, but not so interesting or intelligent as the meat-eaters or Bruno, the bear.

My father had a sambar doe for nearly ten years. He named her Flora. She was his special pet and loved him intensely. But as she grew older she formed a nasty habit of attacking strangers by rearing on her hind legs and striking at their heads with her fore hooves. This was because, being a doe, she grew no horns. Indeed, when she had perfected this technique she would often waylay our Indian cook-woman as she arrived from market. The poor woman would either be knocked down by Flora or run for dear life. In either case she would drop the basket of provisions she was carrying and Flora would eat all the contents except for the meat and the firewood.

I will just mention one more of my strange pets—and I still have her with me. She is Jemima, the python. 'Rock snakes' we call them in India. I caught her by the water-channel in the forest at Yemmaydoddi, and have had her for over seven years. She is quite tame and easy to keep. Don shoots a rabbit for her once a month. I buy a bandicoot—which is a big variety of rat, larger than a guinea-pig—from a man who catches them for me in traps at the market, at the price of four annas per bandicoot, once every fifteen days. That is as often as she eats. One night Don shot a mouse-deer. She swallowed it whole and would not eat again for nearly a month.

Now that you have heard about some of the strange animals and reptiles my wife and I have kept, let us have a sip of tea and nibble our sandwiches; for after this the serious business of listening to what the jungle may have to tell us will begin in earnest.

For a long time there is silence, broken now and then by the crackling of the fire or a loud 'putt-putt' noise, followed by the faint hiss of steam, that comes from the greener bits of wood, or those pieces that have moisture trapped within them. Then, from somewhere on top of the hill, above the road where we have left the car, a horned-owl hoots repeatedly, making a resonant, weird sound which nobody would normally think came from a bird. 'Whooo-oooo! Whooo-oooo!' For a long time there is silence again, broken periodically by the great owl, and now and then by the chirping, flitting nightjars, who do not seem to worry about the firelight.

We hear faint creepings and rustlings in the bushes growing a little beyond our camp fire, and from higher up the bank of the stream. They come in fits and starts—jerkily. But they seem to be always there, never for a moment ceasing altogether. They are nothing to worry about, for they are made by bush mice and bamboo rats which live in thousands in these forests. Harmless and inquisitive little creatures, but for our fire they would be running over our bodies in their search for food, if we sat still enough and refrained from movement. Their presence is one of the reasons why snakes of all varieties, both poisonous and non-poisonous, abound here. The rats and mice, as well as frogs, afford an abundant food supply.

All of a sudden, from somewhere quite far away, we hear it: a cracking, crashing and thudding. Elephants! They are breaking down whole branches of trees merely to eat a few of the succulent new shoots that are just beginning to break at the ends of the stems.

'Quink! Quink! Quink!' A faint, sharp sound comes from the same general direction in which we just heard the branch broken. That means elephant calves; baby elephants!

A NIGHT BY THE CAMP FIRE

But there is no reason to be nervous. If there are babies, it very clearly indicates that their mothers are about. In fact, a herd of elephants; for baby-elephants will not associate with a solitary male tusker. And an elephant herd is quite harmless unless you almost bump into one of the mothers, who will attack you in defence of her calf. But here, seated by the fire, we are as safe as in a house and have nothing whatever to worry about. Should their grazing bring the elephants in our direction, they will smell the smoke of our fire or see the flames, and they will make off without delay.

It is the solitary bull-elephant, wandering all by himself, that is dangerous. Generally, to be alone, he is either 'in *musth*', which is a periodic complaint attacking bull-elephants and lasting for about three months, when they become sexually excited and are turned out of the herd by the other bulls; or he is a confirmed 'rogue' who likes to keep his own company. In either case beware! There exists no fiercer, no more awesome, no more relentless engine of destruction in the whole Indian jungle. But if there had been a 'rogue' elephant about I would have known of it, as the Forest department intimates the presence of such animals to all game licence holders, in addition to issuing notices in the press. Even a rogue elephant, moreover, will hesitate to approach a blazing camp fire.

We listen to the sounds of the elephants grazing. Every little while comes the crack of a big branch, or the sharp snap of a bamboo stem, followed by the peeling, tearing sounds of the leaves being stripped from them by the giant pachyderms. They eat in silence, while a rumbling, like distant thunder, tells that the digestive processes are at work inside those colossal bellies. The calves 'quink' restlessly as they brush against their mothers, worrying them for milk, while at long intervals one of the herd-bulls will roar mildly, a bellowing sound resembling that made

THE CALL OF THE MAN-EATER

by an ox but infinitely louder and more cavernous. It is merely a call of contentment to indicate that all is well; or, maybe, junior has turned his efforts to worrying papa, who is admonishing him gently by·roaring.

An enraged elephant, about to attack, makes quite a different sound. He screams piercingly, and that penetrating 'trumpet' will shake the very earth. It is a veritable call of doom, and there is no misunderstanding the feelings of rage, malevolence, and destruction which are involved in that terrible noise.

A frightened elephant will also scream and trumpet, but there is a wealth of difference in the tone. It is shriller and thinner in quality and volume, and appears to convey the elephant's feelings of fear and trepidation. It lacks that full-lunged menacing shriek that preludes the charge of an enraged bull. After a while there floats to us a dull, hollow thud: the herd has reached the bed of the stream, maybe half a mile below us, and the noise we just heard was caused by one of them turning over a fallen tree-trunk that had been lying there.

The rapt attention with which we have been listening to the elephants is suddenly disturbed by the hoarse, guttural call of a 'barking' deer, which is also named muntjac, kakar or jungle-sheep. 'Kharr! Kharr!' he repeats loudly in alarm from somewhere along the brow of a hill on the opposite side of the stream. A sambar in the valley takes up the note of warning with a startled 'Whee-onk!', followed by an intermittent 'Dhank! Dhank!' as he spreads the news of approaching danger.

Those calls can only mean one of three things: a tiger, the king of the jungle, is on the prowl—or his lesser cousin, a panther. They might also denote the proximity of a pack of wild dogs, the most vicious hunters in the forest, were it not for the fact that the night we have chosen is moonless. Wild dogs hunt by day or by moonlight, but never in the dark.

A NIGHT BY THE CAMP FIRE

So they are not the cause of the alarm in this case; either a tiger or a panther is afoot.

The cause of the hubbub betrays his identity a little later by a grating, sawing sound as he follows in the wake of the sambar down in the valley. 'Ah! Hah!, Ah! Hah! Ah!-Hah!' Disappointed that his presence has been discovered by the two vigilant deer, the panther vents his chagrin in a series of sawing-like, guttural, grating gasps.

All is silent again for a short time. We have almost forgotten about the elephant-herd till the sound of tearing bark reminds us that they are still feeding along the streambed and coming closer to our camp fire in the process. But as foreseen, one of them either smells the smoke or sees the glow of the fire. The elephant strikes its trunk hard against the earth while exhaling air sharply through that organ. The result is a peculiar metallic noise, resembling a sheet of zinc or galvanized iron being suddenly bent in two. That is an elephant's way of voicing its preliminary note of alarm.

Twice more the trunk strikes the ground sharply, and twice more the metallic sound follows. Then the elephant trumpets once—the thin, shrill call of alarm and fear. The youngsters understand it and fall silent. All that can be heard is a faint, indefinable, swishing, brushing sound. It is made by the huge bodies as they try to press noiselessly through the undergrowth on the banks of the stream, the mothers pushing their bigger calves before them, or carrying the smaller ones with their trunks, which they have wound round the bellies of their off-spring before lifting them bodily off the ground. A few seconds later the faint swishing and rustling ceases. The herd has disappeared. Silence reigns once more. We hear no more of the panther or of the deer.

Our fire dies down for the moment, leaving only the glow of burning embers. We strain our eyes into the darkness on the opposite bank of the stream, and for a moment see nothing, as we have been gazing into the fire and our eyes have not yet adapted themselves. Then mysterious little lights appear, weaving singly and in twos and threes among the branches of the trees beyond the reach of our firelight. As the pupils of our eyes expand to explore and penetrate the gloom, we are surprised at the number of little lights that we can see. There seem to be thousands of them, as they flash, scintillate, fade away and then break out again, sometimes in bunches and at other times in myriads when, for a brief moment, they outline and illuminatte the towering trees and their boughs which have until now been indistinguishable in the gloom.

Fireflies! Thousands of them! Now here, now there, now appearing and then disappearing, only to flash forth again, they make a specatacle of ethereal charm which can never be seen in the inhabited parts of the land. No doubt the dampness of the atmosphere in the vicinity of the stream has attracted them. On some occasions, when I have been watching in the jungle, but without a camp fire, I have found the combined brilliance of an innumerable mass of these little creatures great enough to light the surrounding forest and make its details momentarily clear. Though such synchronized flashes occur only at long intervals and last only for a second or so, they are something that must be experienced to be believed, and they bring to one an ineffable sense of beauty and wonder.

We hear nothing more and the hours drag by. In spite of the fire, which we feed with fresh bits of wood from the pile, we can feel the air growing chill, and we can hear the dew beginning to drip from the leaves of the trees growing beyond the circle of warmth generated by the burning wood. I glance at my watch. The hands stand at midnight.

A NIGHT BY THE CAMP FIRE

Would you be interested to hear about some of the superstitions of the aborigines who live in our jungle areas? They are firm believers in the existence of spirits; but with this difference—all spirits to them are evil. Even the spirit of a departed loved one becomes a malevolent entity immediately after death, capable of, and sometimes bent upon, causing grievous bodily harm to the living. For this reason they will shun a human corpse, burial ground or cremation place. To ask an aborigine to sit with you over a half-eaten corpse serving as bait for a returning man-eater is tantamount to asking him to commit suicide. Infinitely worse in fact; for he feels he is certain to meet with a terrible and violent end.

He will explain that you are safe from the evil spirit, because you happen to be a foreigner. Even evil spirits dislike the foreigners, especially if they happen to be white men. But he, being just a miserable, defenceless jungle man, is certain to meet with a violent end, even as he sits close beside you. This anticipated end will invariably take place when the invisible spirit strikes from the rear: then the victim will collapse, become unconscious, vomit blood, and by morning will be dead. If you examine his back by daylight, in spite of his dark skin, he says, you will clearly see the five-finger mark of the spirit hand that struck him down. It will be the ghost of the dead man that will do the deed, as it seeks frantically to revenge its own violent end.

Even in the densely populated parts of the land, the towns and cities, it is quite common to hear that some man was struck down at night while returning home from night-shift at a factory, or perhaps from the late session at the cinema. The victim will say that he felt a heavy hand strike him violently in the back: he will stagger home, tell his relatives what happened and then collapse. He may vomit blood during the night, and the next day he will develop a high fever. But within forty-eight hours, with a few exceptions, he will be dead.

Such occurrences have often come to my notice and I have tried to investigate the causes, but without success. It is significant that it is only the ignorant, poorer working classes that experience such things. Particularly the servant class.

There is also a strong belief that, if a man has eaten or handled pork and goes out at night, if he is barefoot, he stands in great danger of being struck by an evil spirit, which detests pig's flesh. This idea is universal. I heard it first when I was a boy. I remember that I bought a piece of raw pork without delay, told my father that I was going to the pictures, but went to the gates of the cemetery instead, with the piece of pork. There I discarded my shoes, climbed over the gate and walked down the little lane between the tombstones, very fearfully clutching the pork. To this day I have never been so frightened as I was that night. Every single moment I expected a heavy spirit hand to clout me resoundingly from behind. But no spirit had struck me by the time I got back to my shoes. Sure enough, next day I had a fever. It was 'blue funk' fever!

Apart from the spirits of the dead, which are credited with doing these things, the aborigines in the forests, as well as the poorer working classes throughout southern India, are firm believers in what the spiritualists of western countries call 'elementals'. The Tamil name for such beings is *minnispurams*. They are credited with belonging to both sexes—male and female: the male *minnispuram* is comparatively small, is rarely seen or heard, and is benign and harmless, but the female is said to be extremely tall (over ten feet) and is reputed to appear sometimes as a long black figure without head or arms or legs, and sometimes as a tall white figure, similarly headless, armless and legless. Another variety of the female *minnispuram* appears as a midget, gaudily

A NIGHT BY THE CAMP FIRE

dressed in a diaphanous, brightly coloured saree and bedecked with flowers and jewellery. These live in wells, tanks and rivers and are reputed to entice youths to the edge of the water and then to push them in and drown them. All forms of the female *minnispuram* are hostile to human beings, particularly to men.

My friend Byra, the poojaree, told me that he was once poaching for sambar in the Salem district, when one of these female *minnispurams* came upon him. Apparently he was sitting in a 'hide' he had constructed on the banks of the stream, which was dry at the time except for the artificial water hole he had himself made during the day by scooping a deep hollow in the sand. Into this hollow the water had percolated. At dusk he had sprinkled some of this water on the surrounding sand, so that the smell of water would attract the thirsty deer. When that happened, he would kill the first with his muzzle-loading flintlock!

Byra said that it was shortly after midnight when he heard the jingling of bells coming towards him from the left. As there was a curve in the bed of the Chinar river in that direction, he wondered with interest who could possibly be approaching at that time and place. He watched, and shortly what seemed to be a tremendously tall pillar of white mist turned the corner and floated down the centre of the dry riverbed, while the jingling of bells grew louder. Byra said he knew instinctively that it was a female *minnispuram*. He told me that for a few seconds he thought of running away, but if he did that the *minnispuram* might see him and give chase. So he decided to stay hidden.

Meanwhile the tall white pillar approached. It came opposite him, while the noise of jingling bells now changed into a sound more resembling the chink and clank of chains being dragged along the ground. He had just begun to congratulate himself that the *minnispuram* would pass by, when the terribly high white pillar halted on the riverbed directly before him. He heard demoniacal laughter in a high-pitched female voice.

Byra said he fainted. When he recovered consciousness the *minnispuram* had vanished. In its place, clearly discernable in the pale moonlight, stood a hesitant hyaena, which finally ran away. Byra says that if discovered *minnispurams* transform themselves into animals. He did not dare to move till daylight. Thereafter he never again went near that part of the river once darkness had fallen.

The belief in black magic, and the casting of spells, is universal in southern India, particularly along the west coast and in Hyderabad state. The sorcerers are not witches, however. They are men who have learnt the art from their fathers or have surrendered themselves to the practice after long years of initiation.

It is considered a simple thing to have someone 'bewitched' by one of these sorcerers. The cost of the operation will depend on how much harm one wishes to do. The simplest thing is to have the victim made sick, or to lose him his job, or to cause estrangement between husband and wife. A variation is to have him harassed by 'spirit' agencies, which throw stones on his roof at night and sometimes during the day, break crockery, put sand in his food just as he is about to eat it, and at times move the furniture about violently or throw him out of bed.

The worst form of magic is when the victim is made so ill that he dies. In such cases medical aid is fruitless, as no doctor is able to diagnose the malady. I have encountered several cases of 'spell casting' and I will tell you about two of them.

There was Oscar Brown, whom I came to know in 1936. 'Ossie' was a mild, good-natured fellow, jovial, carefree and happy. We became quite good friends. One day Ossie told me a story. He said that about three years previously he happened to be working in an office at Calicut. The staff were paid on the first day of every month, and a number of mendicants had formed the practice of presenting themselves at the office on every payday to get what charity they could from the employees.

Among them was a rather truculent-looking fellow with long hair, who wore a saffron robe. This man never failed to turn up on the first day of each month and demanded, rather than asked for, charity. He behaved as if he had every right to it. This habit had annoyed my friend Ossie, who, one day threatened to hand him over to the police. To that the saffron-robed man had replied: 'You dare to abuse me! I curse you, now. I will put someone into you who will be your constant companion till the day of your death.' With those words he strode away. Ossie went home and forgot all about it.

That night Ossie awoke, and through the mosquito-netting under which he was lying he saw the figure of a very tall black man standing by his bedside. Thinking it was a thief, Ossie sat up and began pulling the netting aside, preparatory to springing out of bed. The figure then stooped over him and the next second appeared to merge itself with him. 'It got right into me,' were Ossie's own words. Then he said: 'Andy, do you know it is inside me now? It lives with me day and night. I cannot get rid of it. It won't go. Sometimes it overwhelms and overcomes me. Then I don't know who I am or what I am doing. Friends say my voice and appearance change. I behave differently, boisterously. To me it is all a blank. When I regain control of myself, I don't remember what happened. I don't remember anything.'

I began to suspect that my newly-found friend was slightly unbalanced mentally. Then I forgot the whole thing.

THE CALL OF THE MAN-EATER

A couple of months later I invited Ossie to accompany me on a short trip to the jungle. By a strange coincidence, we camped on this very river, which I call the 'Secret River', but nearly twenty miles from here, beyond the village of Anchetty, at the spot where it joins the main river, the Cauvery. We had finished our meal and were seated beside a fire, talking about one thing and another. My .405 Winchester rifle, loaded but at 'half-cock', stood five or six feet away against a henna tree.

I forget which of us had spoken last. But I remember I was looking out over the Cauvery river which flowed past us, just a few feet away. And then a strange, gruff voice demanded, 'Who the hell are you? Where am I?'

I nearly jumped out of my skin. I looked at Ossie. Could it have been he who had just spoken? He appeared quite a different person. His eyes shone strangely. His face was twisted and distorted.

'What's the matter with you, Ossie?' I heard myself stutter.

'Don't call me Ossie. That's not my name,' he growled. 'Who are you? Where am I?'

I tried to pacify him. 'Don't you remember?' I asked. 'We came shooting.'

'Shooting? Don't lie! Where's the gun?'

Realization came to me in a flash. Ossie was raving mad, without a doubt. I had heard that lunatics acquire prodigious strength; if he found my rifle he might shoot me there and then. Fortunately he had not seen it, for it was behind him. I tried strategy. 'Behind me, there,' I indicated nonchalantly, pointing vaguely behind my back.

Ossie, or whoever it was that was speaking to me, strode past me, bent upon finding the 'gun', as he had called my rifle. I made a scrambling dive for the weapon. I reached it and swung around. Ossie had turned and was glaring at me.

A NIGHT BY THE CAMP FIRE

Controlling myself as much as I could, I said conciliatingly: 'I have found it. It was lying here.'

'Let me see it,' he had demanded.

'No, I can't,' I lied to him. 'There are tigers and elephants about and I must always have this rifle in my hands.'

He did not answer, but walked across to the fire and started to put it out by kicking river sand on to the embers.

'Stop that, Ossie,' I shouted at him. 'We need the fire. The elephants might come.'

'I am not Ossie,' he replied flatly.

Then he swung around and advanced purposefully towards me. I backed a couple of steps and shouted to him to stop. But he did nothing of the kind.

'I want that gun,' was all he said, and he still advanced.

There seemed no way of stopping him, and I did not care to surrender the weapon. Then a thought struck me. When he was less than five yards away I raised the rifle and fired quickly over his head. He stopped dead in his tracks. Then he shuddered all over violently, as if with ague. Almost mechanically he raised a hand to cover his eyes and sighed. A few seconds later Ossie spoke to me again, but this time the Ossie I knew.

'What happened, Andy?' he asked. 'You look frightened.'

I remained silent, too shocked to speak.

'Oh, I see,' he went on. 'I have had one of my attacks, eh? That other self took control of me. Now do you believe what I told you the other day?'

'Only too well,' I rejoined. 'I thought my last moment had come and that you would shoot me—or force me to shoot you!' Then I added: 'Elephants or no elephants, you won't catch me spending another night alone with you, my friend. Let us start walking to Anchetty. Even if I tread on a snake, it is preferable to the experience I have just been through with you.'

I have related this incident to doctors, who tell me that the symptoms and the shuddering of the patient at the last moment are typical of hysteria. I have told it to others who profess to know something about occultism. They affirm it is a very definite case of 'spirit-possession' and that the shuddering always occurs when the foreign entity leaves the body it has temporarily inhabited. I do not know what to believe.

But the sequel to this story is that Ossie left Bangalore shortly after the incident. Two years later I heard that he died in Calcutta. He had jumped from the balcony of a three-storied building!

The second incident can be related more briefly. A friend in an oil company, stationed at Shimoga, got promotion over a colleague who resented it greatly. The aggrieved man went to a sorcerer in the same town. At the very next new moon strange things began to happen in the promoted man's house. Stones rained on his roof; sand was thrown in his food as he was eating it, apparently from nowhere at all; crockery, tables, chairs and even beds were moved about; his baby son was lifted bodily and thrown down again, fortunately without harm. This went on for over six months, till the harassed man, finding no remedy or help, in sheer desperation resigned from the post to which he had been promoted. Simultaneously, all manifestations ceased.

It is commonly believed in India—this time by many of the educated and higher classes of both Indians and Anglo-Indians—that it is possible for a woman to make a man fall deeply in love with her and become so infatuated that he does not know what he is doing. A certain lady did this to a padre, causing him to desert his wife and three children. The practice is commonly known in India as 'pilling'.

The woman I have mentioned was questioned by a well-intentioned friend of mine, who remonstrated against the

A NIGHT BY THE CAMP FIRE

whole affair. Thereupon the woman, in a spirit of truculence, told my friend in detail how she made the 'ingredients' which caused the mischief and how she had administered it in black coffee. I have the recipe; it is not a wholesome concoction.

But I have not come across the other recipe, which a man should use to influence a lady—that is, excluding the use of the powdered tail of the big lizard known as the 'oodumbu' as an aphrodisiac, about which my old friend Byra, the poojaree, told me a very long time ago, and, of course, the powdered roots of the 'kuloo' water-plant, which I have mentioned in another story in this book.

Speaking of occult matters, I might mention that some years ago my son, Donald, and I set forth from Segur, at the foot of the Nilgiri ghat, to walk the fourteen miles of steep gradient to Ootacamund at the summit. It was past eleven at night when we left, and we had planned to reach Ooty before dawn. But when we were just half-way, at a place named Kalhatti, it began to rain and we took shelter in the travellers' bungalow standing at the end of a pathway just a short distance from the steep road.

This bungalow had long been reputed as haunted. The haunting was said to have originated in the following manner. A severely inebriated *shikari*, a European gentleman, had camped there one night before Christmas. At about 2.30 a.m. he saw what he thought was a sloth bear standing on the verandah of the bungalow. With creditable aim, considering his drunkenness, he had shot the bear, which began to scream. Thereafter he had emptied four more rounds into it from his magazine, and the animal screamed no longer because it was dead. But the only thing wrong with the whole proceeding was that it was not a sloth bear he had shot: it was a man, the bungalow-watcher, or *chowkidar*, himself, put there by the government to look after the rest house.

The local Badagas said it was this unfortunate man's uneasy spirit that now haunted the bungalow on certain nights. I know that when Don and I ran into the verandah to shelter from the rain, we were quite wet and it was bitingly cold. Moreover we were feeling inordinately hungry. Occult subjects were far from our thoughts just then. We wanted to find the man in charge, the one who had replaced the poor fellow who had been shot, to know if he could possibly brew us some hot tea.

So together we shouted: '*Chowkidar*! Watcher!'

But nobody answered us. Then Don went one way, and I the other, around the bungalow to look for him. We met at the back of the building. Apparently the caretaker was not on the premises. Together we returned to the front verandah to shelter from the drizzling rain. A black figure stood at the end awaiting us. We both saw the man distinctly. The next moment, there was nobody there. It was just 2.30 a.m.

But enough of such a topic. It is nearly one o'clock and you look sleepy. Probably you are tired of listening to my tales. In that case we can finish what tea is left in my flask, throw the remaining wood onto the fire and snatch forty winks of sleep. Nothing will come near us, for the embers will continue to glow even when the fire dies down. But you will feel cold, so be prepared for it.

We do just that. We finish the tea, pile all the remaining wood onto the fire till we have a fine roaring blaze, and then curl up in the sand as close as possible to the burning wood. It is uncomfortably hot for the moment, but before long, as the flames become more feeble and only embers remain, we will be feeling the cold.

I awaken several times before dawn. Once I hear the distant calls of frightened spotted deer. Far away in the jungle one of them screams its last, the prey of some successful carnivorous hunter.

Four

The Black Rogue of the Moyar Valley

HE WAS REPORTED TO BE JET BLACK AND I DID NOT ENTIRELY BELIEVE that tale till I saw him for myself. He was black all right, certainly the darkest coloured pachyderm I have ever seen, either in the wild state or in captivity. Also he was exceptionally hairy for a full-grown elephant, particularly around the top of his ponderous head. Elephant calves are all hairy, but as they grow up they tend to lose their hirsute appearance. However, the 'black rogue', as I have called him, although fully grown, had a distinctly shaggy aspect all his roguish days for, above all else, he was very definitely a 'rogue', and a nasty one at that.

But before I begin, let me warn you that this tale has rather a sad and unexpected ending. It closes with an experience I have never had before, and most certainly do not want to go through again.

THE CALL OF THE MAN-EATER

The Moyar river flows from west to east along a deep valley that is all very dense jungle and the home of every species of big and small game of which southern India can boast, with the exception of the 'nilgae' or 'blue-bull', as it is sometimes called, a member of the antelope family that grows to the size of a sambar. Large herds of bison and elephant abound in these forests, and sambar and spotted-deer are plentiful. There are always tigers and panthers in residence, although they are not by any means numerous. This is rather a strange feature when one considers the abundance of game that would serve the two species of felines as food. Perhaps the presence of ticks—both of the large and small varieties—which infest the valley throughout the year, together with the leeches that are to be found in the damper parts, especially during the monsoon rains, keep tigers and panthers from remaining too long in the low river areas. Carnivores detest these pests.

The incident I am about to relate took place in the jungles of Mysore state which fringe that northern bank of the Moyar river, in the Coimbatore district to the northeast, and in the forests of the Nilgiris, or 'Blue Mountains' as they are called, which lie along the south of this rivulet, right up to its junction with another stream known as the Bhavani. Thus you will see that, not only was an enormous tract of jungle involved, or rather several enormous tracts, but also the jurisdiction of three separate Forest departments. The Coimbatore and Nilgiris areas each have their own administration, although both fall within the orbit of Madras state: while Mysore, which was till recently an independent area governed by a maharajah, is now a separate entity with a state government of its own.

Two large game or wildlife sanctuaries exist there. One of them, north of the river, falls within the boundaries of Mysore state and is called the Bandipur Game Sanctuary.

THE BLACK ROGUE OF THE MOYAR VALLEY

Adjoining it, and south of the river, is the Mudumalai Sanctuary in the Nilgiri district of Madras state. The jungles to the northeast, belonging to Coimbatore, are called reserve forests, where hunting is only allowed under licence. There is a proposal to make this portion also a sanctuary, like the other two adjoining it, where hunting is altogether forbidden, so that the three sanctuaries will more adequately protect the game on both banks of the Moyar. The presence of the Bandipur and Mudumalai Sanctuaries gave protection to the black elephant while he was within them, so that he could only be hunted when he happened to cross into the forests of Coimbatore, or went further down the Moyar river into the Nilgiri jungles to the east, towards the Bhavani river and beyond the limits of the Mudumalai Sanctuary.

Due to the abundance of elephants everywhere, the aborigines and other people whose work took them into the jungles of all three jurisdictions were always on the alert. Nevertheless, it was a common occurence to hear of someone being chased by an elephant, while now and again isolated tragedies took place and people were killed. These latter were few and far between, however, and nobody paid much attention to them except to be very careful to avoid coming anywhere within sight, sound or scent of a wild elephant.

How the black elephant first made his appearance or came to be a rogue is obscure. Two versions persist. The first is that a titanic battle was waged, lasting intermittently for two days and two nights, within the precincts of the Mudumalai Sanctuary and was heard by the inhabitants of the little hamlet of Tippakadu, situated on the Mysore-Ootacamund Road. A narrow iron bridge, painted black, spans the Moyar river at this place, and during the afternoon of the second day of the fight the inhabitants of Tippakadu turned out and stood on the bridge to watch two bull elephants battling furiously a couple of hundred yards away on the river bank. They said that both the contestants were enormous animals, but that the bigger of the two was obviously getting the better of the fight, while his opponent, a slightly smaller, very black elephant, was red with the blood that poured from his head and flanks from the many injuries inflicted by his antagonist's tusks.

The other version comes from the village of Tallamalai in the forests to the northeast, belonging to Coimbatore, where an inhabitant proudly claimed the credit of having started this elephant off on his career as a rogue. A solitary bull formed the habit of systematically raiding and destroying the crops in the fields that surround the hamlet. The shooting of elephants, even by the holders of game licences, is strictly forbidden by the government. Nevertheless, exasperated by the damage, this man one night fired at the elephant with his ancient muzzle-loader while it was in the midst of his field. He must have scored a hit, because large gouts of blood were found next morning leading from the cultivated area into the jungle. Of course, nobody followed up the wounded beast.

Many had seen this animal and all said it was a very black, very hairy elephant. Up to that time it had attacked nobody. After being wounded, the elephant left the vicinity of Tallamalai; some said it had gone into the jungle to die, while others thought it had left the locality.

It was over three months later that a herdsman, grazing his cattle, was attacked and killed by a very black elephant. Then the people remembered that an elephant that had been in the habit of destroying their crops, and had later been wounded, was a very black animal. So everyone came to the conclusion that it was this beast that had been wounded, while the owner of the muzzle-loading gun received considerable credit and became very proud of himself.

THE BLACK ROGUE OF THE MOYAR VALLEY

The second story is probably the true one, as it has the incident of the first killing to back it up, although it could equally be possible that the elephant that had received such a beating at Tippakadu had wandered down the bed of the Moyar, emerged in the jungle to the northeast, and come upon the unfortunate herdsman while still in an irritable mood, venting its spleen upon him by trampling him to a pulp.

Sporadic attacks occurred after this in all the three areas I have mentioned. But it is significant to note that the majority were in the Coimbatore forest region. There the elephant smashed a bullock-cart that was being driven from Dimbum to Tallamalai. Miraculously the two passengers in the cart escaped when it was overtuned and fled for their lives, but the driver and one of the two bullocks, as well as the cart itself, received the full fury of the elephant's wrath. The driver was literally torn limb from limb. The elephant had evidently placed a forefoot on his body and with its trunk had wrenched off both arms and a leg. The bullock had been gored through and through by one of the mighty tusks, and its spine was broken by a blow from the trunk. The cart was reduced to fragments.

It was strange that nothing happened to the remaining bullock. When the yolk was broken it had just galloped away, but the villagers said that its escape had not been without reason. It was quite black in colour, whereas the slain animal had been white and brown, and the cartman had been wearing a white *dhoti* or loin-cloth, a white *banyan* (vest) and a white turban. Here seemed evidence enough to emphasize the dislike all wild elephants have for white. Thus, when travelling through elephant country in India you will observe that all mile and furlong stones, normally painted white with black numerals, are black with the numerals generally in yellow. The government has found, to its cost,

THE CALL OF THE MAN-EATER

that wild elephants pull the white stones out of the ground as fast as they are planted.

The two men who had escaped with their lives ran all the way back to Dimbum, whence they had started out, to report the incident. They stressed that the elephant was almost jetblack. They also said that the left tusk was shorter than the right one and curved inwards, while the animal was at least nine feet high, and abnormally hairy. This was the most detailed description of the elephant that anyone had given so far, and was accepted by the Forest department as correct. After all, these two men had been within ten feet when the enraged animal had upset the bullock-cart; they, if anyone, would know what the animal looked like.

The Collector at Coimbatore, which is the headquarters of the district bearing its name, was furnished with this description by the Forest department and asked to declare the animal a 'rogue' and free to be shot by anyone holding a district game licence. But before the declaration was made the elephant struck again, this time about midway between the hamlet of Mudiyanoor and the fairly large village of Talvadi, both situated on an extension of the same track leading from Dimbum to Tallamalai, but about eighteen miles further along it from the spot where the cartman had been killed.

The villager who was attacked was riding a bicycle. He was coming from Talvadi to Mudiyanoor, and was about half-way. And he was wearing a white shirt that hung loosely outside his white shorts. The elephant had evidently seen him approaching and was waiting beside the track; for when he drew abreast, out dashed the elephant upon the cyclist, screaming with rage.

The man both saw and heard the elephant coming, and instinctively did the only possible thing, which saved his life. He threw himself off his machine. Fortunately, at that spot the track ran along an embankment and the villager plunged down this into the bushes and long grass that grew densely on the slope. He disappeared from sight in the undergrowth as the elephant reached his fallen cycle and began to trample it into an unrecognizable, twisted mass of metal, trumpeting lustily and repeatedly in the process. The villager had the good sense to lie quite still. Most probably he was so terrified that he was incapable of movement anyway. The elephant forgot about him in its eagerness to destroy the cycle, which it did most systematically and thoroughly. Finally, tossing it down the *khud* and almost on top of its petrified owner, the pachyderm shambled away.

The villager lay in the bushes for over an hour till he was sure his attacker had departed. Then, smarting from numerous scratches inflicted by the thorns into which he had rolled, he painfully regained the track, where he looked desperately around, expecting to see the ponderous bulk of his attacker at any moment. But the coast was clear. Then the man bolted for all he was worth, running back towards Talvadi, whence he had set forth nearly two and a half hours earlier.

His description of the elephant tallied very closely with that given by the men who had escaped from the cart. He confirmed that the tusks were not uniform in size or setting, and that the elephant was very black. Shortly after this the Collector of Coimbatore issued his proclamation that the elephant was a rogue and free for shooting by anyone with a game licence.

As if he realized that a price had been set upon his head, the black rogue promptly disappeared from the area and was not seen again there till almost three months later. Meanwhile he chased and killed a Karumba within half a mile of the Ootacamund-Mysore state border, but within the Mudumalai Sanctuary, while the man had been poaching honey. This incident, however, was not taken very seriously, as it was considered that the thief had received just retribution for his misdeeds.

The trunk road that leads from Mysore city to Ootacamund, a beautiful hill station on the Nilgiri Mountains, 7,500 feet above sea level, passes through the heart of both the Bandipur and Mudumalai Sanctuaries, which cover the foothills at the northern base of that lofty range. After leaving Tippakadu, the village where the epic battle between the two elephants had taken place, the road begins a climb of about forty miles, passing a place named Gudalur and negotiating many hairpin bends through extensive coffee, tea and chincona estates before reaching Ootacamund. The road is tarred and excellently maintained by the governments of Mysore state and the Nilgiri district of Madras. It carries moderately heavy traffic, ranging from the private cars of the many visitors to the hills, to Ooatacamund.

At Tippakadu another road branches southeast and covers twenty-one miles before reaching Ootacamund by a shorter route. It crosses the black bridge over the Moyar river from which the villagers had watched the elephants fighting, passes three villages named Masinigudi, Mahvanhalla and Segur respectively, and then climbs up a very steep *ghat* road to Ootacamund itself. Although only half as long as the main road, this route is scarcely used because of its extreme roughness and its steepness, especially around the hairpin bends; it is definitely dangerous for all but exceptionally good drivers using vehicles of high horse-power and brakes in tip-top condition.

The main road from Bandipur to Gudalur and the short-cut route from Tippakadu to Segur, at the foot of the steep *ghat,* were periodically visited by the black rogue for three months or so after the Collector of Coimbatore had officially declared him a rogue. But this declaration covered only the forests to the northeast of the Moyar river which, as I have told you, belong to the Coimbatore district. It did not apply to the Mysore and Nilgiri areas, where the elephant had not yet been declared a rogue and was thus still protected. But growing bolder with each escapade, the black elephant hastened his declaration before, sometimes chasing motor cars on both roads.

At Segur he all but added an Englishman, a friend of mine named Collett, to his bag of victims. This gentleman had gone out for an evening stroll with his shotgun and pack of five mongrel dogs, hoping to get a peafowl, junglecock or perhaps a rabbit or brace of partridge for dinner. What he succeeded in bagging I do not know, but towards evening he was sitting on the bank of the Segur river, which is a tributary of the Moyar, his back against a tree and his five dogs round him, when who should come down to drink water but the black rogue himself. He spotted Collett at once and, with his usual shrill scream of anger and hate, charged him forthwith.

My friend had only a shotgun which is useless against an elephant; he had also a permanent injury to his right leg, which made him walk with a slight limp. It certainly prevented him from running or from climbing trees in a hurry. The scene was all set for another murder had not the five dogs, all country-bred, decided to take a hand in the matter by counterattacking the elephant. They ran around him in circles, yapping furiously. This so distracted and enraged the pachyderm that he forgot all about his intended victim and tried to trample the dogs, or seize one of them in his trunk. But the mongrels managed to keep out of reach, and the annoyed elephant dashed vainly in all directions. For no sooner did it concentrate upon catching one of the dogs, than the other four were yapping at its heels. Collett hid behind a tree-trunk and, when the elephant was not looking, managed to reach a footpath in the jungle along which he beat a hasty retreat to the best of his limping ability. Shortly after he had reached his bungalow, the five dogs turned up, all unhurt and panting happily from their exertions.

After about three months the elephant found his way back to the Coimbatore jungles and was not long in claiming another victim there, a villager from a hamlet called Jeergalli which is situated, as the crow flies, about halfway between Mudiyanoor and the deep valley to the southwest through which the Moyar river flows.

Shortly after this incident, an American tourist who was visiting Bangalore came to see me and asked if I would conduct him to some place where he could take movie-pictures of bison. He had visited some of the well-known game sanctuaries of Africa and had a magnificent collection of movie reels of all the game there, including rhino, lion and the great herds of African elephants, which he showed me. He said he now wanted a reel or two of tigers and the Indian bison. I explained that tigers, unlike lions which inhabit open country, live in jungles where pictures cannot easily be taken. But I assured him that it would be comparatively easy to photograph the bison. The outcome of this visit was that he agreed to come with me in his car on a three-day trip, and we started the next morning.

Now I know of no better place than the forests of Coimbatore for photographing bison. Not only are these animals very numerous there, but the jungle is less dense than in some parts of Mysore, and certainly far less thorny. On the way I picked up my old jungle friend and companion, a Sholaga named Rachen, from his hut in the hamlet of Gedesal, and drove on to Dimbum, where we branched off westwards to another hamlet named Honathetti, situated about seven miles along the Dimbum-Tallamalai road. I knew that bison were particularly prolific there.

THE BLACK ROGUE OF THE MOYAR VALLEY

Due to two punctures and other minor delays, it was nearly 4 p.m. when we arrived at our destination. There was hardly time to start looking for bison immediately. Besides, as everyone knows, evening is not the best time for photography. So I told my American friend that we would spend the night under a tree close to the village and start operations the following morning. Meanwhile we got talking to some of the inhabitants of the place, to whom I explained our mission. They were highly disappointed to hear that we had not come on a regular hunting-trip and tried hard to entice us to sit up that night over a water hole to shoot a sambar for them, for meat. Now not only is shooting over water holes forbidden, but is very unsporting, and we tactfully but firmly refused.

A large number of Sholagas from the hamlet gathered around our camp fire after dinner that night, and one of them volunteered to take Rachen along at dawn next day to pick up the tracks of the nearest bison herd. The plan was to follow the herd till it had bedded down for the day and then come back and tell us. Bison do not move far during the hot noonday hours and it would then be a fairly simple matter for us to accompany our Sholaga guides, get up wind of the place where the bison were resting and move closer cautiously hoping to be able to take some pictures before the herd became scared enough to rush away.

Once our plans were made, we began to talk of other matters, and in the course of conversation the black rogue was mentioned. Naturally, his evil reputation had spread far and wide, but he had not so far molested any of the inhabitants of Honathetti, although he had been seen rather infrequently by a few of them. That had happened some months ago, however, and the consensus of opinion was that he had gone away for good. Nobody thought much about him thereafter.

THE CALL OF THE MAN-EATER

It was scarcely daylight when the Sholaga from the village put in his promised appearance and took Rachen with him to look for the tracks of any bison that might have passed during the night. He assured us that he felt confident of finding them, for bison were very plentiful in the low hills and jungle around his village.

My friend had no game licence and I was not particularly keen on hunting feathered game, so we spent the next few hours lounging in the camp while listening to the early morning crowing of the junglecocks and the harsher calls of peafowl. The sun was well up and it was getting decidedly hot when the two Sholagas returned, just before ten o'clock, to tell us that they had succeeded in picking up the spoor of quite a large herd of bison, which they had followed for another two miles till they came upon the animals settled for the day by the banks of a small stream that skirted the base of a hillock. From experience they knew the bison would rest there till evening, before they started moving again.

According to the Sholagas, we had at least four miles to walk to this place. Sholagas, like all aborigines, have a very hazy idea of distances, so that I knew we would be lucky if we reached the place in less than six miles. I remember the sun was abnormally hot that morning, so that it was from sheer laziness that I decided to leave my rifle behind. Carrying it for twelve miles did not seem an inviting prospect. Besides, as I have told you, we had come on a photographing mission, and not to shoot.

We set out accordingly, my friend and I sharing the burden of his camera and auxiliary equipment. It was well over three miles, as I had expected, and not just two miles before we came upon the herd's. It was undeniably fresh. The stems of the grass upon which the animals had fed, and their droppings, indicated that fact clearly.

We started following the wide trail and we had covered another three miles before Rachen and the other Sholaga pointed down the low hillside on which we stood. At least another mile away we saw the shimmer of water, almost hidden by trees, that marked the stream where the herd had decided to rest for the day.

The next thing to do was to test the direction of the wind in order to get up-wind of our quarry. Bison have keen scent, and to approach them down-wind would definitely mean that they would detect our coming and leave cover. Luckily we found that the breeze was blowing uphill; that is to say, from the bison towards us. This meant that we would not have to make a detour but steal downwards upon the herd by following their tracks of the night before.

I have mentioned that the stream was quite a mile away. The hillside sloped gently downwards. It was fairly open, park-like country, with scattered and rather small trees, long lush grass, and a few outcroppings of rock here and there. The Sholaga from Honathetti led, as he knew the way, closely followed by the American and Rachen, while I brought up the rear. The sun blazed brightly down upon us from a steely-blue, cloudless sky. Everything appeared serene and peaceful.

Confident in the abilities of the two Sholagas, as trackers and as men well-skilled in jungle lore, I was walking along thinking of nothing in particular when I happened to notice Rachen glance backwards, the way we had come. He stopped abruptly and uttered the ominous words: '*Dorai, annai varudu*!', which means, 'Sir, an elephant approaches!'

Looking in the same direction, I was dismayed to see that an elephant was indeed heading through the scattered trees and directly towards us. He appeared to be only a furlong away. There was no mistaking the purposefulness of the shambling run. There was no hesitation, no sign of timidity or fear, no attempt to avoid us and slink away. This elephant was bent upon reaching us just as fast as he could.

I knew what would be his next step. As soon as he felt he was close enough he would raise his scream of hate and charge down upon us. A normal elephant would have behaved quite differently. As soon as he had scented or seen human beings, he would have done his best to get away. But this animal was deliberately following us, and there was a sinister, evil purpose about him. Without any doubt, here was the rogue I had heard so much about. Even at that distance, he seemed mahogany-black.

Neither the Sholaga who was leading nor my American friend was yet aware of his presence, for he made no sound as he approached. Fortunate, indeed, that Rachen had looked back and observed him. Otherwise at least one of us would have died very painfully that day!

Desperately I gazed around, looking for a way of escape. As I have said, the trees were small. There was not one that the elephant could not push over easily. But about 200 yards away and to our right, I could distinguish a rock half hidden from view by the boles of intervening trees. I had no means of knowing how big it was or how high. But it was a rock and it was our only refuge.

Refraining from shouting, as I did not want the elephant to hear me and perhaps precipitate a charge, I called softly to my American friend: 'Follow me to that rock to our right. The rogue elephant is behind us. Run for it!'

The effect on him might have been called amusing under less strained circumstances. He stopped dead in his tracks and gazed around confusedly.

'What's that?' he asked. 'Where?'

Running forward, I grabbed his arm and started pushing him towards the rock, while I tried to break into a run myself. Meanwhile Rachen called a low warning to the other Sholaga.

The elephant had been shambling forwards and was only a little over half a furlong away. Undoubtedly he had seen our quickened movements and guessed that his presence had been discovered. For without further ado he trumpeted shrilly. Then he charged!

My friend threw down his camera and the four of us ran, as fast as we could run, for that rock. Regardless of the long grass, the thorns and the intervening trees, we covered the ground at a most creditable speed with the elephant, now trumpeting repeatedly, behind us. Being but a short distance from the rock we managed to maintain our lead and reached our objective about 100 yards ahead of our pursuer.

It was a low, sloping rock, hardly three feet above ground level at one end, and about five feet at the other. But there was no other avenue of escape and we leapt upon the rock almost together. It may have been about thirty feet long. Without stopping, we ran up the slope to the higher extremity. There was a fissure in the rock, from one end to the other. Coarse grass grew in this declivity.

Breathlessly we reached the higher end of the rock and then turned to see what the elephant would do. The infuriated rogue made directly for us, and as we stepped backwards and out of reach of his extended trunk he came to a halt with the bottom portion of his chest against the stone. In this position he continued to trumpet deafeningly, alternately blowing blasts of air at us through his trunk. After a few moments the elephant realized we were out of reach. His next action was to uproot the shrubs growing nearby and, holding them with the tip of his trunk, he tried to flog us with them. Of course, we stepped further backwards, but it did not occur to him to come around the rock to its lower end. Instead he found a piece of loose stone and hurled it at us, narrowly missing my friend.

It took the beast ten minutes to think of reaching us from the opposite end; then things began to happen in real earnest. Evidently the idea came to him suddenly, for he abruptly stopped trumpeting and, with a surprising turn of speed for his bulk, shuffled around the rock to the other end. There he found the rock only three feet high. Placing one ponderous forefoot on the granite, he cautiously tested it for stability and in the next few seconds had climbed onto the rock and was coming straight for us.

It was now that Rachen exhibited a marvellous coolness of nerve and thought. For he called in Tamil: 'Jump down quickly. The elephant will not attempt to follow us that way. It is too steep and he will be afraid of breaking a leg!'

Suiting the action to his words, he jumped, and the three of us followed without delay. My friend then started to run for it, but I caught hold of him and said: 'Stop. He won't attempt to jump five feet to the ground with his ponderous weight; but if we leave this rock he will go around and catch one of us in the open.'

The rogue reached the edge of the rock, where he towered above us—a truly awesome sight! Once more he tried to reach us with his trunk and then waved one forefoot in space as if to try a leap. But he thought better of it and restrained himself while he screamed with hate. We stood beyond his reach and awaited his next move.

After perhaps a minute he swung around and rushed back to the lower end. Hesitating again, he finally stepped down gingerly and turned to come around the rock and catch us. So we drew ourselves up those five feet and got to the top only seconds before he was below us again, and at the spot at which he had first arrived.

Twice more the enraged bull shambled around the rock and climbed up from the lower end. Twice more we leaped down those five feet and stood just out of his reach at the base. It was a game of catch-as-catch-can in real earnest, with the prospect of a terrible death by being trampled upon and torn to shreds if one was late by a split-second, either in jumping down or climbing up again. If there had been only one or two of us in this lively bit of gymnastics, it would not have been so bad. But as there were four, we kept getting in each other's way, particularly when it came to climbing up the five-foot ledge. With an agonizing death as the penalty for being a fraction of a second too slow, it was every man for himself.

Worst of all, perhaps, was the nerve-shattering screaming of the elephant. The very air vibrated with the sound and it required a mighty effort of will not to become rooted to the spot in terror. Fortunately, after the third attempt, the enraged animal either grew tired or came to realize he could not catch us this way. It was a mistake, however, for had he continued we would have become exhausted and sooner or later he would have caught one of us.

But he desisted and now started walking around the rock on which we stood, every now and again rushing up to it and attempting to reach us with his trunk. Each time he did that, we scampered in a bunch to the opposite end, where we would wait till he came around and we scampered back again. While all this was going on I was cursing myself for my sheer laziness in not bringing my rifle. The sun was almost directly overhead and blazed down upon us from a cloudless sky. Waves of heat arose from the rock and shimmered in the still air. Hastily I glanced at my wristwatch. It was almost noon.

Eventually the heat and the sun began to be felt by the elephant himself. He ceased his strenuous tactics and stood in the shade of a tree just a few yards away. There he stayed put. An hour passed in this manner. The granite rock on which we stood became unbearably hot. The heat penetrated the rubber soles of my shoes, so that I could stand on two feet only with difficulty. It was even worse for the two Sholagas, for they were both barefoot; they fairly hopped on the rock as the heat burned the bare soles of their feet.

A crazy idea came to me to try to frighten the monster away. I told my three companions to start shouting for all they were worth, and I joined their chorus of discordant yells. But far from alarming him, our voices caused the elephant to charge us once again, and this time he came straight onto the rock from the three-foot end. In a group we jumped down from the other end and stood out of his reach once more, while he literally danced with rage at the brink above us. All four of us knew that if he but made the leap, one at least of our number would not see the light of another day. But although furious, the elephant was cautious and did not jump. He remained on the rock and screamed and blew air in our faces with his extended trunk.

It was very likely that after a while the heat from the stone began to penetrate even the thick soles of his mighty feet, for he kept lifting his legs up, one at a time, in quick succession. Then he turned and lumbered off the rock from the lower end. In a bunch, the four of us scrambled up the burning stone again. This time we remained silent, watching the brute who was also watching us.

This stalemate continued for another few minutes, then the rogue turned abruptly and shambled over the hillock from which he had come and disappeared from view. I began to congratulate myself that we were well rid of him when both the Sholagas said they thought it was a ruse and that the elephant was only trying to draw us off the rock. So to test this theory, all four of us descended and walked about fifty yards away. Suddenly came a crack and crash of breaking wood, a scream of hate, and there was the rogue charging down upon us from quite another direction. Up the rock we scrambled once more.

The elephant kept us another half hour. Then he walked off again, this time heading for the stream where the bison herd was sheltering. Being downhill, we could see him for some distance till his black form was finally hidden by the intervening trees. Suspecting he was up to his old game, we did not leave the rock, but asked the Sholagas to climb two of the highest of the trees to see if they could catch a glimpse of him if he made a detour and tired to approach from another direction. They did this and after a while signalled that the coast was clear.

When the Sholagas rejoined us, Rachen said that the pachyderm had probably felt the heat and had gone off to the stream for a drink and a bath. After that, he said, it might return and stay by the rock till night fell.

The idea of playing that ghastly game of hide-and-seek with this black monster in pitch darkness terrified me. Handicapped by being unable to see him clearly, I was sure one or other of us would eventually be caught. I suggested we run for it before the rogue came back, a plan which met with unanimous approval.

I asked Rachen to retrieve the American's camera, which he did at once. Then the four of us stepped off the rock and headed for the village. Many were the glances of apprehension that we threw behind us to see if we were being followed as we ran at a jog trot towards Honathetti. But clearly the elephant had really gone for water, for he was nowhere to be seen. Streaming with perspiration and panting from our exertions in the terrible afternoon heat, we reached the village at a quarter to three, glad to have escaped with our lives from a ghastly death.

I was tired and angry. Above all else, I was ashamed. For nearly three hours my companions and I had been engaged in a cat-and-mouse game wherein we had most definitely been the 'mice'. Now that I had my rifle in my hands, weary as I was, I determined to return immediately with the Sholagas and try to find the black elephant once again and continue the game, but this time with the position reversed. I would very soon show this arrogant pachyderm that he was going to be the mouse.

My American friend wanted to come back with us, and if possible take pictures of the elephant's discomfiture. But his presence would have been an unnecessary responsibility, apart from hampering my movements. Very politely, but firmly, I reminded him that he was a photographer and not a hunter. Good sportsman that he was, he understood and did not take offence, although chagrin was written large on his countenance.

Walking fast, and sometimes trotting, Rachen, the second Sholaga and I made for the rock. This time we moved boldly forward through the park-like belt of jungle that surrounded the place and reached it within the hour. There was no elephant to be seen. It was just four o'clock and we had a little over two hours of daylight in which to find the elephant, something that is easier said than done, considering he had the whole jungle before him. But I remembered I had two Sholagas with me. The aborigines, who have lived in the forests for generations, are among the finest trackers anywhere in the world, so there was a reasonable chance of coming up with our quarry.

We moved in the direction in which the pachyderm had disappeared. The jungle was dry, and he had not been feeding but moving directly towards the stream, so that, in spite of his great bulk, his passage through the undergrowth and long grass would not have been evident to an inexperienced eye. But Rachen and his companion had no difficulty in finding it. It was interesting to observe how their trained sight detected every stem of grass that had been bent or broken by the passing animal, and every leaf or twig that had been stamped flat under those giant feet.

Following this trail, it did not take us very long to arrive at the point where the black elephant had reached the stream. Lank reed-like grass grew there and we could clearly see where he had forced his way through it to the water's edge. Rachen strode into the stream, which reached to just above his knees, and at the spot where the elephant had drunk water he turned and began to walk upstream along the trail marked by the crushed reeds and water-plants, while the other Sholaga and I walked parellel to him along the bank.

For some reason the elephant had not crossed the stream, but after wading in the water for about 100 yards had come back to the side on which we stood. Evidently he had drunk his fill, for his plate-like spoor, imprinted at the edge of the bank and still clouded with the muddy water that had seeped in, left the little rivulet after a short distance and led back into the jungle.

We followed this trail closely, knowing that the rogue would now be feeding and that we could expect to hear him before long if he had not already travelled too far inland. It was hot and he might even make for the water a second time for another drink. But that would be a little later, towards sunset, when elephants usualy drink. We had more than an hour before us and could expect to find our quarry feeding inland and at a considerable distance from the river.

As we surmised, the trail turned into the jungle. The elephant had been in no hurry, for he had halted now and again under some of the shadier trees and had evidently been lazing about while sheltered from the sun.

Nearly a mile was covered in this fashion when we first heard the unmistakable crack of a bough being torn down. The branch evidently had a thick layer of bark, for the crack was followed by a twanging sound as the elephant tore the wood from the tree, stripping and pulling the bark from the main limb when it did not break easily. From the volume of the sound and its direction, our quarry was easily a couple of furlongs distant.

If you should ever want to approach anywhere near a wild elephant, the most essential thing is to test the direction in which the breeze is blowing. Having done that, you must work your way into such a position that the wind is blowing from him to you. Should you neglect to do this and approach downwind instead, or even partly downwind, the elephant's keen sense of smell will make him aware of your coming. Then one of the two things will happen. A normal elephant, and often a rogue too, when his instinct warns him that you are no ordinary passing peasant but an enemy, will just fade noiselessly from the scene, and when you reach the spot where he was standing you will find nothing. Alternatively, the elephant may ambush you by waiting silently behind rock, a tree, or a clump of bamboo, till you are very near him, when he will charge at you screaming, flattening every obstacle in his way. This is a favourite habit of rogue elephants, particularly one who has already killed a number of people and has come to realize the utter helplessness of that most obnoxious biped, man!

I tore a handful of grass from the ground, held it aloft in my hand, and then slowly released the broken blades and stems, allowing them to fall to the ground singly. They all drifted from right to left. That meant the wind was blowing from the right and that I was in a midway position, being neither up-wind nor down-wind from my quarry who was directly ahead of us. This was not good enough, so we all turned to the left and made our way forward in single file, as silently as we were able, around the intervening bushes and tree-trunks. We covered over two furlongs in this way when the sound of another crack came to us from a half-right direction. It was fainter this time.

Once again I tested the wind to verify that it had not changed its course. Then we all turned to the front and crept stealthily forward in single file and at angle of ninety degrees to the direction which we had just been following. We might have covered anything up to 200 yards in this fashion when the elephant broke a third branch. This time the sound came from due right. We had detoured enough and were now directly upwind. He could not possibly get our scent unless he himself moved to some other place. Now we had only to be sure we made no noise approaching him, and then he would be at my mercy.

In single file we moved forward, Rachen leading, with me in the centre and the Sholaga from Hanathetti behind me. Judging by the last sound we had heard, the elephant was at least a quarter of a mile or more away. We covered that distance slowly, but heard no further sound. Probably the rogue had already brought down enough branches to provide him with a succulent repast of green leaves and was busy eating them.

A few paces further forward and the ground dropped into a small valley, formed by two low hills. The elephant was clearly in the valley. But such places are unfavourable for stalking an animal with such an acute sense of smell as an elephant, because the hills on either side often cut off any breeze, so that in the still air the smell of human being, particularly when there are three of them together, is carried to the elephant in the motionless atmosphere. That is just what happened, for the elephant got wind of us. Instinctively he knew his enemy was approaching and he slunk stealthily away.

When we came to the place where he had been feeding we found the broken branches and his fresh dung, but of the elephant itself there was no trace. Working together now, the two Sholagas began to follow his track, with me close behind to cover them. It was an easy task. The pachyderm had moved along the little valley which soon ended in the dry bed of a rather big *nullah*. His large footprints, clearly visible in the powdery earth, showed that he had turned down the *nullah*, which obviously led back to the stream from which we had lately come, now well over a mile away. We knew that if he reached the stream he would cross it and probably escape on the other side. Evening had already set in and there was scarcely an hour of daylight left. The only course left to us was to cast caution aside and chase after him to get in a shot before it was too late. So we began to run down the *nullah*.

No doubt the rogue, hearing us and by now thoroughly alarmed, started to increase his pace as well. After half a mile or so I was fairly blown, although the two jungle men with me showed no trace of their exertions. The *nullah* turned in its course and then straightened out. Far ahead of me, and shuffling away for all he was worth, I could see the black rogue—or rather the hind portion of him—heading for the stream. I did not want to fire, as the most I could do was to wound him in the hindquarters, and I do not like wounding any animal, even a rogue elephant, deliberately. So, puffing and blowing and badly out of breath, I followed as best I could.

The elephant disappeared around the next curve. In due course we reached the same bend, turned it, and saw the stream a couple of hundred yards ahead. But just before the stream was the elephant, or rather half of him, for his back was still turned towards us, while his body was twisting and turning, without seeming to make any progress.

Struck with surprise and wondering what could be delaying him, we put on a spurt, or rather my companions did. As for me—well, I could not have put on a spurt even if the elephant had been behind me! However, I drew abreast of them at last, and found that the elephant was stuck fast in a quagmire which reached up to his belly. The explanation was simple enough. The spot where the *nullah* met the stream had become a bog, due to the soft sand in the *nullah* being saturated with the water that seeped into it from the stream. The elephant, scurrying away in fear, had blundered straight into it.

Quicksands, in the true meaning of the term, are I believe, unknown in southern India, although conditions almost approaching them are to be found in some places. For instance, in the upper reaches of the Secret river, above the hamlet of Anchetty in the district of Salem, there is one particular spot where it is positively dangerous to cross at a time when the river is almost dry. I know this to my cost, for I once had tried to cross and had suddenly found myself waist-deep in the ooze. But for the help of two Forest Guards, I think I might have remained there for an indefinite period or even have been drawn under. Very vividly I can still remember how I struggled for all I was worth, but could not succeed by my own efforts in shifting either of my feet an inch out of that clinging slime.

For the elephant, now struggling madly before us, conditions were infinitely worse. His tremendous bulk and weight, coupled with his desperate exertions, made matters worse each moment. Slowly, little by little, he was being drawn down into the ooze before our very eyes. With his trunk he lashed the mud before him to right and left as he tried to find a way to lever himself out. He screamed in sheer terror, while his little eyes were dilated with horror as instinct told him he was doomed. And every moment, inch by inch, he sank lower and lower, while his screams, that had been filled with dread, now took on a piteous note of appeal.

Killer though he had been, his dreadful plight filled all three of us with acute distress. As if it had been yesterday, I remember my own feelings when I had sunk in the wet sand that day on the Secret river. To shoot him in this terrible plight, while struggling for his very life, appeared to be the act of a coward and murderer. A strange and powerful yearning came over me to try to succour him if possible.

But there was just nothing we could do. He was, after all, a wild elephant and to come within reach of that threshing trunk would be certain death. Even as we watched, the spectacle became more and more harrowing. The poor beast was now literally up to his neck in the liquid sand and his back was almost level with its surface. To make the scene even more dramatic, darkness was setting in apace. Escape for the poor animal was clearly impossible. Either he would soon be drawn under and suffocated, which was really the less evil fate, or if his feet found solid ground at the last moment, he could only remain stuck till he starved to death. I could not save him, but I could put an end to his sufferings. And I would have to do that at once, as it would soon be too dark to see.

There is a fatal shot which, if taken correctly, will drop even the largest elephant in his tracks, although it is one that is rarely achieved because of the obvious difficulty of getting the chance to take it: a shot behind the ear, where the bullet will penetrate the brain from an angle unprotected by the enormously thick bones of the forehead. Kneeling down, I aimed carefully behind the left ear, waited for it to stop moving, held my breath, and gently squeezed the trigger.

The explosion had hardly died away when the elephant quivered as if in an ague. The trunk hit the mud with an inert flop, although the tip of it still searched questioningly, like some giant caterpillar groping for a leaf. I ran a few paces to the right, knelt again, and repeated the shot, this time behind the right ear.

A sigh of relief escaped all three of us. At least the poor beast could suffer no more. It was dead.

We came away from that dreadful place and groped our way back to Honathetti in darkness. But the Sholagas, whose village it was, led us there unerringly. Eventually we were back, and I told my American friend of our harrowing experience. But he, not having seen it himself, said he wished he had been there to take photographs, and that he would like to go to the spot the next morning to see if any could be taken.

Filled with a morbid curiosity as to whether those evil sands had finally claimed their victim or not, I accompanied him the next day. We reached the spot, but all we could see was a placid surface of undisturbed wet sand, glinting innocently in the rays of the early morning sun. The elephant had disappeared completely, and the soaking sands held their dark secret.

Five

Jungle Days and Nights

DURING THE MANY YEARS I HAVE LIVED IN THESE ISOLATED PLACES, off the beaten track, various little incidents have taken place, not themselves amounting to adventures, but milestones nevertheless on the long road of memory which often come back to me in my quieter moments. I would like to recount a few of them, some of them rather tragic, others humorous, and even one incident in which I behaved in a downright shameful way.

It took place many years ago, but the memory of that incident still haunts me to this day and I cannot live it down. It is said that making a confession of one's sins will relieve a troubled conscience. So I am going to do that now.

But every evil doer should be allowed to defend himself, and my defence lies in a prologue, an incident that took place earlier, the result of which was very strong in my memory and powerfully influenced me when the second incident occurred.

JUNGLE DAYS AND NIGHTS

This first incident took place about twenty-five years ago. My friend, Deva Sundram, and I had gone out in my Ford to a place named Gummalapur, about twenty-eight miles south of Bangalore, for *khubbar* about panther. Do not let the word *khubbar* alarm you; it is just a simple Hindustani term for news or information.

Gummalapur lies in the Salem district of Madras state and is scarcely three miles beyond the Mysore state border. Two miles west of Gummalapur are many rugged, broken hills, covered with heavy scrub on their lower slopes and granite boulders and little caves at the top. In between these hills winds a narrow stream bearing the somewhat difficult name of Muthiyalamma Holay. It holds water only during the rainy season, is rocky in places, while at others it is full of marvellously soft sand. On both banks the jungle becomes dense and the trees lofty and verdant.

In the days when my father was a lad, and even when I was very young, this forest harboured tiger, elephant, bison and panther, in addition of course to all the normal game animals to be found in this part of the country. But after that the tigers and bison disappeared, shot out by the many hunters who came from nearby Bangalore. The elephants, protected by the government, are still there, but fewer, and are only to be seen during the monsoon months when they trek northwards from the Cauvery river. The panthers remain for a variety of reasons. Firstly, they are common wherever hills occur. Secondly, there is abundant food for them in the many herds of domestic cattle that are driven into the jungle from Gummalapur to graze. Thirdly, people are not as keen to hunt panthers as they are to kill the larger varieties of game.

Deva Sundram and I had gone there to inquire from the local herdsmen whether they had recently lost many of their animals to panthers, and we had also come for a morning stroll in the scrub-jungle in the hope of picking up some feathered game, or a jungle-sheep or pig, to roast for dinner that night.

I forget now what information we got from the herdsmen, but we had crossed the river and walked up a slope in the scrub that soon brought us to the crest of a little hillock. From this eminence we looked across the carpet of jungle below us and scanned the wooded slopes of the higher hills.

Then we saw something, perhaps about a mile away and close to where the border of Mysore state fringes the jungle. Vultures were circling in the sky, many of them. Every now and then one would plane to earth, gliding with outstretched wings to disappear into a small valley in a fold of the hills. It was too far away to hear the rushing, rattling sound made by the wind as it beat against those outstretched pinions. There could be only one explanation. Something was lying dead in the valley. The vultures had located it and were hastening to the feast.

Could it be a panther's kill? Perhaps one of the many cattle that had been taken out to graze in the scrub, and as yet had not been missed by its owner.

With one accord, Dev and I made for the spot. It was not difficult to locate. The hissing, occasionally squawking horde of vultures, struggling and jostling each other on the ground, led us directly to the body. But a very big surprise was in store for us as the huge birds flapped away heavily and took to the air with difficulty. Certainly, a dead body lay there, but it was not the remains of a bull or a cow that had been killed by a panther. It was a human corpse, and as we approached we saw it was the body of a woman.

She had evidently been murdered and then tied to a bamboo pole by her hands and feet, lengths of jungle-vine being used for the purpose instead of the more conventional rope. Then she had been dumped in the jungle, close to the trunk of a large sandalwood tree. The vultures had evidently been feasting for some time, for they had torn chunks of flesh from the body. The eyes had been picked from their sockets, the nose was gone, and holes had been made through the skin of the cheeks and throat, laying bare the bones beneath. But most of the scalp remained, with the long black hair still adhering to it.

The corpse was naked, the birds having torn the thin saree and jacket to shreds. The entrails had been drawn out and devoured, laying bare a deep cavity in her abdomen, and a large part of the flesh of her arms, thighs and legs had also been eaten, so that the white bones could be seen. Had we arrived an hour or so later, we would have found nothing but the bones, picked clean. The vultures would have seen to that.

Dev and I bent over the body, trying to discover how the woman had died. But we gave up that task in a few minutes. The vultures had been at work too long and had effectively destroyed any trace of the manner in which she had been killed; that is, if the murderer or murderers had left any traces at all.

One thing was certain, however. Robbery had not been the motive. A pair of heavy silver anklets still encircled the ankle-bones where the flesh had been eaten away; a ring, which appeared to be of gold, was still on one of the fingers of the right hand; and earrings, undoubtedly of some value, were on the ears. Perhaps she had worn a nose ornament also. But that was gone now—along with the nose! She had a number of glass bangles, multi-coloured and of fancy design, on both arms right up to her elbows.

The smell of decay and putrefaction hung heavily on the still air and Dev, who was essentially an office man, unused to such sights and odours, was on the verge of retching. He clapped a handkerchief over his nose and mouth and backed away.

THE CALL OF THE MAN-EATER

Our cursory examination proved of no value whatever. Obviously, after murdering the unfortunate woman, the culprits had brought the corpse to this remote spot at night rather than risk the trouble and danger involved in digging a grave and burying her. They knew quite well that within a few hours of daylight the vultures would completely obliterate all evidence of the crime. If a bone or two remained, the jackals and any hyena that passed that way the next night would complete the job. All had gone according to plan, except for the most unfortunate and unforeseen fact that that day, of all days, Dev and I had decided to take a walk in the jungle.

Now what were we going to do about it? Obviously, as public-minded people, report the matter to the police. With this in view, we set off on our walk back to Gummalapur. At the top of the first hillock I looked back to fix the location of the valley in my mind in case I should be required to find it again. That done, we hurried on. We reached the village only to find that the one and only policeman had fallen ill and been taken to hospital at the town of Hosur.

Now, as I have told you, this area lay in the district of Salem, belonging to Madras state. Hosur town was the immediate headquarters, but it was also considerably out of our way. Both Dev and I were due back on duty at our respective jobs that afternoon. So we decided to inform the *patel* or headman of Gummalapur village of what we had found and where we had found it, return to Bangalore and send a written report to the Police Station at Hosur by post. As Bangalore itself is in Mysore state, such a report, if made to the police at Bangalore, would be returned with instructions to forward it to the Madras police.

So we told the *patel* and next morning posted a report from Bangalore. Two days later things began to happen in real earnest. A police van turned up at my house with three varieties of policemen in it, all wearing different uniforms. There were police from Hosur, in Madras state, with their tall red turbans. There were police from Bangalore Cantonment, at that time a British-administered sector under Central British government control, in blue and white turbans. And there were Mysore state police in blue turbans with red and yellow tabs.

Then began a perfect avalanche of questioning. Was I Mr Anderson? What was my full name, occupation and income? Where was Mr Deva Sundram? What was his full name, occupation and income? Why had we gone to Gummalapur? How had we found the dead woman? Was she a close friend or merely a casual acquaintance? Why should we have gone to that particular spot? Was the woman alive when we found her? Was she dead? How had she died? Was I sure that one or other of us did not know her before? What was her name? Where had she come from? Was she a young woman? Now came a very important question that I was to answer very carefully; did she bear gunshot wounds? Why did we not report the matter to the policeman at Gummalapur? Why had we failed to do our duty by not proceeding in person at once to Hosur to report the matter there? Where had we been all that day and the previous one? Were we in the habit of visiting Gummalapur frequently?

It took me some time to stop the tide of questions. I pointed out that, in our joint statement, Dev and I had clearly written down all the relevant facts. I went over those facts again.

The inexorable questioning continued. How had we known the woman was really dead? Might she not have been alive; perhaps in a faint? Had we taken steps to render first-aid? Why should the murderers (according to our version and if such ever existed) take the trouble to bind the body to a pole and carry it deep into the jungle? Would it not have been more easy to bury her?

I found myself becoming annoyed. I pointed out that I was not a detective and had made my report as a public-minded citizen. I told them it would have been very easy for us to have said nothing. It was all to no avail. Then came an order veiled in the form of a request. Would I please lead them to Deva Sundram's residence, after which we would both have to proceed to the police station at Hosur.

Now I became really annoyed. I told the three varieties of policemen that I would certainly lead them to Deva Sundram's house, but after that I would not go to Hosur unless they cared to take me under arrest, for which they would require a warrant.

We compromised for the moment by going to Dev's house, where it started all over again. During these questions and answers we suddenly discovered, and with considerable surprise, that the Hosur police had not yet gone to the spot to locate the body. We suggested they do so without delay, giving them explicit directions.

There was some hesitation and much consultation between the three varieties of representatives of the law as to what should, or rather could, be done with both of us. The contingent from Hosur wanted very much to take us back with them, but the element from Bangalore Cantonment did not think it could be done without warrant. The Mysore state policemen remained neutral, ready to assist either way. At last the party drove off after warning both of us to hold ourselves available for further questioning.

Two days later they were back again. They had failed to find any corpse! Not even bones! Not even the bamboo pole to which we had said the body had been tied. Had there really been a body at all?

The result was that I said I would lead them to the place. Dev was busy and could not come. I went in the police van to Gummalapur. From there I set out with the party along the route Dev and I had returned that morning. We climbed the last hillock and I located the valley from it. Finally we reached the large sandalwood tree beneath which we had found the dead woman.

There was no body to be seen; no bones, not a shred of torn saree, and above all, no bamboo pole. Nothing! All the varieties of policemen glared at me with concentrated suspicion. Was this a joke? Was I trying to make monkeys out of them?

I approached the very spot on which the corpse had been lying and searched it closely. There I came across the half of a broken glass bangle and, in a little while, a few strands of long, raven-black hair — undoubtedly hair from a woman's head. I pointed these things out to the policemen in proof of the veracity of our report. I suggested that the murderers were in Gummalapur and had come to know of our discovery when Dev and I had been inquiring for the village policeman on our return that morning. Also they must have heard about our report to the *patel*. Obviously they had returned and removed the remains in order to baffle investigation.

The policemen's reaction to my theory was more unexpected than ever. They wanted to know how I had been able to find my way back and lead them to the exact spot. They also wanted to know what had made me search so as to find the piece of the broken glass bangle and the strands of hair.

I took a deep breath upon hearing these questions and counted up to ten, very slowly. I then told them I would answer through my lawyer. But that made them more suspicious than ever. To cut a long story short, it took nearly three months of correspondence with higher officials, plus two visits to the police station at Hosur, before Dev and I ceased to be regarded as murderers. The solution found by the Madras Police was certainly a neat one. They said the murder must have been committed in Mysore state jurisdiction and the body then brought across the frontier and dumped in the Madras jungles. When it became known that the corpse had been discovered, the culprits had taken it back again.

The Mysore Police strongly rejected this view. Nobody had been murdered their side of the border, they said, adding that the Madras theory was an invention to cover the truth. Wherever the crime was committed and whoever did it, the fact remains that neither victim nor culprits were ever traced.

This was the second time I had suffered from officialdom through making a report of what I had found in the jungle. Once before I had come upon a dead elephant that was only half-grown. It had been shot behind the ear by a ball from a musket. The wound was clearly discernible. I had reported that find to the local Forest department, accompanied by a photograph I had taken of the dead animal, showing the wound. I almost lost my game licence because of that report, because I was suspected of having shot the elephant myself, after which it was said I had made the report to cover up my own misdeed. That case also involved a lot of correspondence. I had to interview a very high official and tell him my story. I still feel he did not believe me. But as the local Forest Guards had placed dry wood upon the carcass of the dead elephant and burnt it because of the stench that spread for about a mile around the spot my guilt could not be proved. So I was graciously given the benefit of the doubt and allowed to retain my game or shooting licence, but under strong suspicion.

Having recounted these two incidents as a 'prologue', I will now go on to tell you about the main occurrence which took place about five years ago, and in which I feel I behaved so very discreditably. Four of us were returning from a visit to a planter friend named Alfie Morrison, the manager of a couple of large coffee estates on the Biligirirangan Mountains. There was the owner of the car we were travelling in; my son's friend, Rustam Dudhwala; another friend named Willie Wollen; my son, Donald, and myself. We had dinner with Alfie Morrison followed by coffee and snacks and a little of his excellent whisky, after which we had been talking for some hours. It was long past midnight when we left his estate, and we had to cover over twenty miles of dense jungle before we reached a place named Punjur. It was a narrow, tortuous road, dropping steeply in places, with bamboo jungle on both sides, the haunt mainly of elephant, bison, and sambar, with an occasional tiger or lesser species of carnivore. Rustam was driving and I was next to him. The other two were behind.

We were about half-way to Punjur. The jungle was particularly dense and heavy. The time was 1.15 a.m. Suddenly, as Rustam turned a sharp bend in the road, we saw a human figure stretched across it, clearly visible in the bright light of the car. He braked hard to prevent running over the man, and we all got out to see what was the matter.

We found that the figure, lying in the middle of the road, was not that of a man at all but of a woman; in fact, of a girl who might have been about eighteen years of age. She was evidently poor, judging from the cheap quality of her red and black saree. Both her saree and her jacket were torn in many places and much of the former was covered with blood. This had not been visible in the lights of the car because, as I have told you, it was a black and red saree and neither colour will show up blood by artificial light at a distance. A closer examination showed the girl had been violently molested and raped. She was quite unconscious, probably from the effects of a blow or other injury. Her bare bosom moved only slightly as she breathed, and her pulse was very weak.

What should be done? The spontaneous reaction of all four of us was to carry her into the car, drive the remaining ten miles to Punjur and report the matter to the police there, and then take her to the hospital at the town of Chamrajnagar, a few miles away. But other thoughts began to filter through. Before us lay a young girl. She had been brutally raped. There were four of us in the car and we were all men! If we took the girl to the police station at Punjur, in that condition and with the circumstantial evidence, including the late hour of the night, the police would probably say the four of us had done the raping. They might even say we had knocked her down with the car and raped her afterwards. Of course, if the girl recovered consciousness, either at the police station at Punjur or at the hospital at Chamrajnagar, she would clear us of suspicion. But would she? What if her attackers had come upon her by surprise? What if she did not know them? Remember, we had no means of being certain where she had been set upon. It might have happened elsewhere and the culprits may have brought her in an unconscious condition in a bullock-cart and dumped her in the middle of the road. In the confused state of mind she would be in when she recovered—if she recovered at all—she might genuinely think we had been responsible and accuse us. Finally, and worst of all, suppose she had been so seriously injured that she never recovered. We would be in a terrible plight with charges of rape and murder against us. We would be in a court case that might drag on for years. We might be jailed. We might even be hanged.

We argued the situation there, in the middle of the road, for nearly an hour, hoping the girl might show signs of returning consciousness, when we would have spoken to her, found out what happened and then taken her into the car. But she never regained consciousness. On the contrary, her breathing became slower and her pulse almost imperceptible.

It was a difficult decision to take, to desert a human being, obviously in dire need and at the point of death, in the middle of an elephant-infested jungle, at dead of night, miles from anywhere and without aid. On the other hand, I remembered the incident of the dead elephant and the murdered woman near Gummalapur. I had been accused on both occasions. Now the evidence against us, although circumstantial, was certainly much greater and almost conclusive. The only defence we could offer was that, had we been guilty, we would have left the girl and not brought her to safety. But even that action could be interpreted as a cunning move to cover our guilt. As the oldest member of the party, I knew I could have persuaded the others to run the risk of what might happen and take the girl in the car to Punjur and then to the hospital at Chamrajnagar. But I did not. Instead, I agreed with them to leave the poor girl where she lay and to continue on our way.

Of course, we never heard what befell that unfortunate young woman. But the action of deserting her and leaving her to her fate is one that fills me with guilt till this very day.

I will now change the mood of these reminiscences by telling you two short stories against myself, stories that show what effect the appearance of a tiger has on the nerves of a tyro.

The first incident took place when I was fifteen years old. My father had taken me to a place named Lingadhalli, in the Kadur district of Mysore state, on a duck and snipe-shooting trip. Dad was never a big game *wallah*, although it was he who taught me how to use a gun at a very early age. He was an excellent snipe shot, at which I am a complete failure even to this day, and was fond of duck-shooting particularly and also other small game.

There are two or three tanks near Lingadhalli which, around Christmas time, hold quite a number of wild-duck and teal, with occasional geese. There are also reserved forests surrounding it which hold tiger and panther. Our armament consisted of Dad's favourite .16 bore double-barrelled shotgun, and an old hammer .12 bore double-barrelled shotgun which he had given me for my birthday that year.

It was reported to me on the afternoon of the second day that a tiger had killed a bull in an areca-nut plantation adjacent to the tank where we had gone to shoot duck that very morning. The owner told me about it, but I kept the matter a secret from Dad. I knew he would not allow me to go after a tiger. My knowledge of big game shooting at that time was practically nil, but when the owner offered to tie a *machan* for me if I made an attempt to shoot the tiger that had killed his bull, I resolved to do or die in the attempt and told him to go ahead.

I told Dad a lie that evening, saying I was going out with a villager to shoot 'flying fox', which is the name given to the large Indian fruit-bat, and said that I would return about eleven o'clock. I fondly imagined I would bring the dead tiger back with me. Leaving Dad in the little Travellers' Bungalow on the plea that I wanted to try my luck at shooting peafowl and hare (rabbits) before going on for the flying fox, I started out a little before 5 p.m. In less than an hour I was alone in the *machan* in the midst of the tall, swaying areca-nut trees, with the dead bull stretched on the ground beneath me.

To this day I can remember that *machan*. It could not have been much more than twelve feet above the ground; a rough, scraggy, unprotected affair. Certainly the kind of *machan* a tiger would easily detect and therefore not visit or come anywhere near. But we have all heard of 'beginner's luck', and it was with me on that memorable evening.

It was dusk when the tiger came, and almost the first thing he did was to look up and see me sitting on that very obvious platform. He snarled and stopped in his stride. I was petrified with terror. Not a muscle would move or obey my command. I wanted to scream aloud in fear. But even that I could not do. The tiger took off with a grunt of alarm and anger as the .12 slipped from my nerveless fingers and rolled off the platform to fall with a thud on the ground beneath. Fortunately the soil was wet and soft, and the gun fell stock-first, so that nothing happened to it. But I was thoroughly disgruntled and hated myself for being an arrant coward, nor did I tell Dad anything about it when I got back to the travellers' bungalow before 8 p.m. that night.

Mortified at what had happened, it was not long afterwards that I went on a hunting trip with another boy, slightly older than myself, named Jerry Barrow. We went to a village a few miles away from the town of Sagar in the Shimoga district of Mysore state. Once again our luck, as novices, was excellent, for within a day of our arrival two tiger kills were reported at two separate spots in the jungle, both scarcely a mile from the village. We tossed a coin and I remember I got the kill to the west of the village. There a fine full-grown cow had been destroyed and partly eaten in the bed of a *nullah* or stream. As fortune would have it, a sapling grew nearby, and, remembering what had happened at Lingadhalli when I had sat on a *machan* twelve feet up, I saw to it that the platform was tied at a crotch in the tree at least eighteen feet above the kill on the bed of the *nullah*. The sapling grew straight up from the bed of the stream and at a right angle to the bank of the *nullah*, which itself at this spot was steep and at least a dozen feet higher than the sandy bed.

I took up my position early and was intently, nervously watchful. All tyros do that. Eventually it began to grow dark, and along with dusk came two tigers—or rather, a tiger and a tigress—walking one behind the other. The only trouble was that they were walking along the high bank of the *nullah,* whereas my present *machan* was about eighteen feet above that same bed. And so it came about that I found myself only six feet above the tiger and his mate. I had sought to improve conditions, but had inadvertently worsened them. At least at Lingadhalli I had been a dozen feet above the first tiger I had ever seen in a wild state. Now I was looking at two of them, and at half that distance! However, I had made some progress by this time, at least so far as my nervous reactions were concerned. I did not let the gun drop out of the *machan*, although sheer blue funk restrained me from attempting a shot.

By a strange coincidence almost the same experience befell a friend of mine, at a place very close by, but many years later. And he, too, behaved like me—and he too was a beginner.

Often, in the course of conversation with other hunters, I hear disparaging remarks about the actions of some novice or greenhorn: of how he would not shoot because he could not shoot, or missed badly because he was trembling like an aspen. Then I confide to my hearers my own reactions on two occasions, in sympathy with those unknown tyros and novices. I can assure you that the mere sight of the king of the jungle in his wild state and in all his majesty, at close range and in darkness, is something awe-inspiring. It is a very different spectacle from the docile, half-starved tigers one sees in zoos and circuses.

Some of our trips have resulted in little incidents with an element of comedy in them; others, which might have ended rather more seriously, turned out rather funny.

JUNGLE DAYS AND NIGHTS

I have been out with all sorts of people. Some have been morose companions, grumbling and complaining at the least inconvenience. Others have been extremely exacting, such as those who insist on eating only home-prepared and cooked food, drinking only boiled water or soda-water, tea and coffee, or sleeping on camp cots under mosquito nets. A third variety, although rare, are of the other extreme; they are so enthusiastic that they want to be on the move right throughout the twenty-four hours. In rain or sunshine, with little or no food at all, and no rest.

That is why, on all serious *shikar* trips, I prefer to be on my own. I have accustomed myself to sleeping anywhere, even in the open under a tree, and to eating anything that may be available, from cooked European or Indian food to an aboriginal diet of berries, roots and even half-cooked meat. As for water, I have had to dig holes in sandy riverbeds, wait till water collects in them, and then lie prone and suck it from the hole I have dug, holding a corner of a handkerchief across my mouth to strain out the finer grains of sand and sometimes the green slime in the water itself.

On one occasion a friend of mine, a major, and two other friends, a doctor and his son, had planned a three-week tiger shoot in a very remote corner of the jungles of Shimoga district in Mysore state. There was a tiny forest bungalow far from any motorable road, and a small village nearby. We had taken along a huge store of provisions, but as three weeks is a long time and we were all permanently hungry and eating heartily, together with the fact that feathered game was not too plentiful and we did not want to alarm the tigers in the vicinity with indiscriminate shooting, our food-stock began to run out soon after ten days. Half rations for everyone was the result.

One night, during the period of scarcity, I heard peculiar sounds coming from the part of the bungalow we had been using as a dining-room. I could just detect a faint rattling and scraping noise. I reached for my electric torch, tiptoed to the door leading to the dining-room, and switched on. There was the doctor's son, stealing food. He had buttered a slice of bread, spread condensed milk over it, and finally sprinkled that with sugar.

I then did an unsporting thing. I 'sneaked'. Feigning alarm, I yelled loudly: 'Doctor, Doctor; there is a thief in the dining-room.'

Out came the doctor, to catch his son red-handed. The lecture that was given the lad was so loud and so long that it kept me from falling asleep for another hour.

Food became scarcer than ever at that camp, but we were loath to abandon it as the tigers had just begun to kill the live baits we had been tying out for them, although we had not had the luck so far to shoot one. It was decided that we should go to the villagers and offer to buy any kind of food from them at any price. The son went first, and returned with one egg. The next day the doctor tried his luck. He came back in a very bad temper. The villagers had told him that the previous day they had sold the young *sahib* seven eggs. The boy had brought back just one. Confronted by his father he confessed he had been very hungry and had eaten the other six eggs, raw, on his way back. The villagers had also told the doctor they had no spare food to sell, for it was scarce and they needed it for themselves.

On the third day, I went. The villagers told me the same thing. They had no chickens to sell and no *ragi* grain either. Everything was required for their own consumption. When the major's turn came to go begging, he decided to do something novel. He invited the whole village to come to the nearby forest bungalow that afternoon to witness a very grand entertainment including dances, such as they had never seen before, performed entirely by himself. It would be a free show, he told them; but a collection would be taken at the end—of food, in any shape or form.

That afternoon a few ancient yokels trickled in and a few young ones. These spectators proceeded to squat on the floor of the verandah. It was an hour before some thirty persons had collected. When he judged that that was about all the audience he would gather, the major went inside and came back with a towel tied around his waist. Then, humming through compressed lips in a very fair imitation of a bagpipe, he executed the highland fling and some reels. Finally, laying two crossed rifles on the floor, he did the sword dance.

I am not sure how much the audience appreciated the show, but for all his efforts not one of them had brought any foodstuff, and the bag Robbie took around for the collection was as empty after his strenuous efforts as it had been before.

Another little incident of another sort happened at Yemmaydoddi, in the Kadur district. Don and I, with a young friend of his, Sonny, had gone there for a few days to show Sonny a tiger, which he was going to shoot. He awoke at 3 a.m. on the first morning of the trip, and I heard him trying to awaken Don and arouse enough interest in him to go for a torch-shining walk in the jungle. It was bitterly cold, and to make matters worse there was a slight drizzle. Don preferred his warm bed, and in no uncertain terms he told Sonny this. I felt sorry for the boy, so in a fit of self-sacrifice I said I would accompany him.

We set forth, Sonny carrying my .405 rifle, which he had borrowed, while I swung the beam of a five-cell torch from side to side in the hopes of picking up the eyes of a tiger. Quite soon we reached a narrow track which runs parallel to a water-channel coming from a big lake, known as the Maddak Tank, about four miles away, and started to walk towards this lake. Fortunately it had stopped drizzling, but it was colder than ever, and pitch-dark.

About halfway to the lake I caught sight of twin spots of light, coming from somewhere in the jungle on the other side of the intervening water-channel. They were fiery red. What animal was this? The eyes were so very red. I used my torch-beam to make the creature move or turn its head to reveal its identity. The twin red lights never as much as flickered. For a moment I swung the torch-beam off them, so as to allow the animal to see us and move, but the red lights glowed on. That solved the problem. They were not the eyes of an animal at all, but the embers of a fire. Some jungle-folk were camped there.

It is a popular, but entirely false notion, that the eyes of wild animals glow in the dark with their own luminosity. They do not. It is only when a bright light is directed on them that the inner surface of their eyes, through the open pupils, reflect the light and the eyes 'shine' with different colours, green, whitish-green, whitish-red, or reddish-white, according to which animal is there, and according to the angle of the light. But the eyes do not shine of their own accord. Therefore, if there is no torch-light no reflecting 'shine' can come from any animal's eyes. Conversely, if there is a 'shine' when there is no torch-light, it cannot come from the eyes of any animal.

As I have said, the solution was simple. We were confronted by the embers of a fire and not by a wild beast. Sonny was standing beside me when I said, carelessly and casually, 'Fire'. The next moment there was a violent explosion, as he fired my rifle. Luckily he missed hopelessly.

There were wild cries of alarm from the rudely-awakened sleepers. 'Aiyo! Aiyo!' they yelled in consternation.

'What the hell are you doing, you fool?' I shouted at Sonny. 'I told you it was a fire.'

'You did nothing of the sort,' he replied. 'You just said "Fire" and I fired.'

Incidentally, this little incident shows with what apparent contempt jungle-folk regard tigers that are not man-eaters. These men were sleeping out in the open, quite unprotected, in an area well-known to harbour tigers.

This fellow Sonny was a dangerous sort of person to go out with. One of those regular Jonahs, if you know what I mean. Once we were driving through a particular belt of scrub jungle near Tarikere, trying to shoot a wild pig for the 'pot', as meat was running low at our camp at Yemmaydoddi. It had rained heavily that afternoon, and as the area was noted for pigs, we were almost certain of coming across one at any moment. It was about 10 p.m. Sonny was seated on the left-hand mudguard of my car with an old .12 gauge shotgun he had borrowed. A friend named Basil Jones was sitting up on the back with another shotgun. Don was next to me, while I was driving. We did not have a spotlight, as that was against the rules, but it was conceded that if a pig ran across the road in the glare of the headlights it could legitimately be shot at.

Suddenly, a boar dashed across the road a few yards in front of the car, brightly lit by the headlights. But Sonny did not see it. He must have been dreaming. We all yelled, 'Shoot', but the pig by that time had gone. We called Sonny all kinds of names and told him to be ready for the next one.

A mile or so later another pig ran across the road. Sonny saw this one all right but was too slow to fire. Basil Jones stood up in the dickie-seat and fired over our heads. Perhaps because of the lurching of the car he aimed short. There followed a sharp crack and the metal aeroplane that decorated the radiator-cap of the Studebaker disintegrated under a shower of pellets.

Just then Sonny began making frantic gesticulations for me to stop. I thought that perhaps Basil had hit the pig and

Sonny had seen it fall. So I braked sharply. Sonny jumped off his seat on the mudguard, ran around the front of the car, and came towards me holding his .12 bore at arm's length.

'Here, take this damned gun,' he said in disgust. 'Something is wrong with it. Before I could press the trigger it went off and smashed your radiator cap to pieces.'

'Let me have a look at it,' I suggested. I took the weapon from him and opened the breach. There were cartridges in both chambers and neither of them had been fired. The explosion of Basil's gun, together with the noise made by the disintegrating radiator-cap, had made Sonny think that it was his weapon that had gone off.

The third incident in which this youngster figured was the funniest of the lot, although it might very easily have ended in a tragedy. This time we were conducting a morning beat for pig in scrub jungle at Bannerghatta, about fifteen miles south of Bangalore. There was an interlude in the beat. Sonny was standing on the bed of a small dry ravine. Another fellow, named Arthur Stanley, was standing at the top of its bank, perhaps ten feet above Sonny and as many feet away. They were talking, and to emphasize some point, Sonny banged the butt of the same .12 bore shotgun, which he had once again borrowed, on the ground. There was a crash as the gun went off, leaping out of Sonny's hand with the force of the recoil, while Arthur Stanley's sun helmet sailed away, its brim shot off at the front by pellets from Sonny's gun.

Arthur promptly fainted with shock. We rallied around and revived him, while we cursed Sonny for a congenital and prodigious idiot. He remained rooted to the bed of the ravine looking at all of us in surprise and wondering what it was all about. Arthur soon recovered from his faint and was still standing at the edge of the ravine, almost at the same spot as when the gun had gone off.

'How could it have happened?' Sonny was asking. 'I had only loaded one cartridge in the right barrel and was gently tapping the butt on the ground when, for no reason at all, the gun just went off.'

And having uttered these words, Sonny began to demonstrate how he had been gently tapping the butt of the gun on the ground when suddenly, unexpectedly, his gun went off a second time. Arthur fell back in another faint as the shot swished past his head.

'I thought you said you had loaded only one cartridge in your gun?' Don asked, in a highly sarcastic tone.

'That's true,' Sonny replied. 'Have a look for yourself.'

With these words he opened the breach of his shotgun. Then his eyes grew wide in amazement. There were two shells in the breach, one in each barrel. And they had both been fired.

We had an amusing experience once in a Model A Ford belonging to Rustam Dudhwala. It happened about thirty miles from Kollegal, in Coimbatore district, in the middle of the afternoon. The nut anchoring the fan worked loose and without warning the fan cut a neat, circular hole in the radiator from which every drop of water soon leaked out. We were in the middle of the jungle and it was evident we would somehow have to get the car back to Kollegal for repairs.

Rustam then had what he called a brain wave. Removing the bonnet completely, he loosened the metal clamps that held the hose-pipe connecting the radiator to the cylinder head. Then he cut one of the spare inner tubes he was carrying right across near the air-inlet nozzle and fitted one of the open ends of the tube on to the metal neck protruding from the cylinder-head, folding the excess rubber around it and fixing the tube to the neck firmly with the metal hose-clamp he had loosened. Down the neck of the hollow tube he poured water from the two-gallon tin he had at the back of the car, tilll the cylinder-heads and half the rubber tube were full. A friend named Willie Wollen was commissioned to sit on the mudguard and hold the free end of the half-filled inner tube in his two hands, while Rustam turned the car around and headed back to Kollegal.

Soon things began to happen. The water grew hot and began to steam. The tube started to swell alarmingly and seemed in momentary danger of bursting. In order to release the pressure and allow some of the steam to escape, Willie loosened his grip at the end of the tube. But he had forgotten that the water-pump was working. Out came not only steam but scalding hot water, all over his hands. With an oath he dropped the whole contraption and away went all the water again. We had a good laugh at his discomfiture, but ceased laughing when he flatly refused to hold the tube any longer. Anyhow, we poured some water down the tube and took turns at holding it while Rustam drove a few miles at a time, stopping occasionally to allow the water to cool. Meanwhile we refilled the two-gallon petrol tin at every stream, tank or well we passed. And so we reached Kollegal at last.

I well remember a certain gentleman I took out with me. He was a bit of a crank. He had read somewhere that condensed milk was rich in food value and provided all necessary vitamins; so he said he would bring no other form of food with him but tins of condensed milk on which he proposed to live for the whole week we remained out. His theories of food value might have been all very well, but he ran into difficulties on the fifth day. Condensed milk itself is constipating. Further, his system was dehydrated by the heat (it was midsummer) and the salt he had lost in perspiration. That evening he suddenly collapsed, saying he was feeling very ill. His temperature shot up and severe stomach cramps set in. But try as he would, he could not relieve himself. The situation became very serious. It was then we thought of using what materials were available. The rubber lead of the foot-pump belonging to the car with the metal connections at each end cut off, and the bulb of the horn filled with lukewarm water and then pressed on to one end of the rubber lead, served as an effective enema. The procedure of refilling the bulb and then emptying it by pressing had to be repeated twice or thrice, but it achieved the required result, thus perhaps saving the man's life. A spoonful of engine oil, grade 40, administered orally, also helped.

I used this treatment once again, years later, at a place named Gerhetti in Salem district, when a rather elderly gentleman named Sells who had come out with me to photograph elephants, suddenly collapsed with sunstroke. We had been out all day in the blazing sun, and when we got back to the forest bungalow at dusk he complained of a very severe headache and giddiness. Soon high fever set in with violent vomiting, and he became unconscious. Treatment with the pump-nozzle of the car, together with hourly cold-water sponge baths, lowered his temperature, and by next morning he was on his feet again.

I had an interesting experience myself when I went out into the jungle several years ago, for a whole week, with my friend Byra the poojaree, an aborigine I had met in the forests of the Salem district in Madras state under rather unusual circumstances.* For the fun of it I had determined to carry no gun nor take any food. I wanted to live on the jungle for these seven days, and on such things as Byra himself could procure from the forest by the primitive means at his disposal.

---

* See *Nine Man-Eaters and one Rogue*, George Allen & Unwin, London.

I had stipulated that Byra himself should not bring his much-prized, but unlicensed, matchlock.

The outstanding thing about this excursion was that I seemed to be always ravenously hungry, every hour and day of the whole period. I am sure Byra found his hands full in having to feed me and himself. As it was, I ate about thrice what he consumed. We swallowed various berries and the yam-like roots of different creepers he dug up; we devoured the combs of wild bees; we ate the small mud-crabs that lived by a pool near the Chinar River; we chewed snails and locusts; we ate the large, long, fat queen-ant from a termite hill that we dug up together. Byra caught two oodumbus (a species of lizard over a yard long, properly called the iguana), which we cooked and devoured; I found it very tasty and very tender.

Yet I was still hungry. With the aid of an ingenious trap, having a noose of plaited horse-hair, Byra caught a jungle-cock. After wringing its neck, he proceeded to make what is known as a 'mud-roast'. I give the procedure, which is really quite simple in case some venturesome boy scout or other person would like to try it out for himself.

There are two ways of preparing a roast without utensils. Of course, whichever way you use it you must first remove the feathers of the bird or the outer skin of the animal which you wish to roast and also its entrails. Thereafter, you can do a 'stick-roast' or a 'mud-roast' as you prefer. A stick-roast is done by driving a long sharpened stick right through the bird or beast. Then two Y-shaped sticks are cut and their ends planted in the ground at such a distance from each other that the ends of the stick which skewers the meat rest on the Y-shaped supports. The stick and its burden can then be rotated. A gentle fire of embers is made beneath, and the skewer-stick slowly rotated by hand to keep the meat from being burnt.

No leaves should be used in the fire, as they will only blacken and smoke the flesh.

This method has several drawbacks. Firstly, it requires constant attention. Secondly, the skewer has to be turned all the time. Thirdly, however careful one may be, the finished roast always turns out dry and partly-burnt, while the inner parts are almost raw. The one advantage is that it can be prepared anywhere in the jungle at short notice.

For a 'mud-roast' the bird or animal is similarly prepared. Then a layer of mud, either from the edge of a stream or pond, or made with the aid of earth and water, is plastered all over the carcass till it is a little over an inch thick. The result is a sort of mud ball encasing the flesh completely. A fire of embers is next prepared and the mud ball placed in it. Then the ball is covered with more embers till it is completely hidden from view except at the top, where the mud should be partly visible. The moderate heat is maintained till cracks are seen in the mud. Another ten minutes is allowed after that, then the mud ball is removed from the fire, taking care it does not disintegrate while doing so. Alternatively, the embers around and beneath the mud ball may be removed, leaving just the ball. Allow this to cool a little and then, with the aid of another stick, break off the covering. The resulting roast will be found very tasty and not too dry, and the meat will be cooked right through.

The disadvantage of this method is, of course, the finding or making of mud of a suitable consistency to cover the flesh entirely. If it has too much large-grained sand, the covering will disintegrate with the heat before the flesh inside has been properly roasted, which will then be burnt. If the mud is too watery it will not adhere to the flesh. But if the mud is of the right composition and holds together, the meat is excellently cooked in its own juices. It is a very successful method provided the game is the size of a fowl or a rabbit, but it cannot be employed for larger game, as the covering of mud will not remain intact in such cases.

Companions who come out into the jungle insisting on drinking only boiled water for fear of germs and dysentery, and in sleeping under mosquito nets because of malaria, prove a nuisance. In my very humble opinion they kill themselves over and over again by imagining the presence of microbes of all varieties. Most important of all, they are not 'mobile'. In a jungle, particularly as far as serious shooting is concerned, it is essential to be able to move anywhere and to move fast, and this means eating whatever is available and drinking and sleeping wherever and whenever one can. A party of hunters impeded with a load of canned provisions and utensils for boiling water, plus mosquito nets and camp cots and regular tentage, becomes cumbersome. Coolies or bearers are required to carry all this paraphernalia. That means more mouths to feed.

I remember that I once took a husband, wife and grown son fishing on the banks of the Cauvery river. I had gone with them in their car. When night fell—a beautiful moonlight night—I made my bed on the river's sandy bank. The cool breezes wafting down the river were refreshing and lulled me to sleep. But my clients woke me up, wanting to know if there was any danger from crocodiles and wild animals. Sleepily, I replied in the negative and dozed off again. But I was disturbed in a few minutes by the noise they were making. These people had brought mosquito nets and poles and were planting the latter in the sand. Cross pieces were tied to the framework, then a snow-white curtain was brought out and tied to the poles at the four corners. Eventually the three of them lay down beneath it to sleep.

But instead of sleeping, every little while the older man would sit up, lift up the mosquito net and shine his torch round and round. I turned on my side with my back to them and once again fell asleep. But not for long. For I was startled by a scream from the lady, followed by much bustling. I rolled over to see the family trio tangled up in their own mosquito curtain, which had collapsed, poles and all, on top of them. The lady was shouting, 'Scorpion! Scorpion!', and the wavering light of the torch was directed upon the river sand a few yards away.

Getting to my feet, I inquired, rather impatiently, as to the cause of the commotion. The lady said that in the light of the torch she was sure she had seen a large scorpion crawling across the sand a few feet away. Taking the torch from her husband, I walked to the spot she indicated. There was no scorpion there that I could find, but she affirmed very definitely that there had been one a few moments before. She may have been right, although I doubt it. However, the scorpion, if there had been one, had disappeared. I searched awhile, but finding nothing I suggested we all might try seriously to snatch a few hours sleep.

But no, they would have none of that. The three of them stoutly asserted that they preferred to spend the rest of the night sitting in their car. Then they did an amazing thing. They draped their mosquito net completely over their car, and, getting under the net, opened the doors and got into the vehicle. This way, they said, they would not be bitten by mosquitoes. Fair enough, I thought; now I will be able to get some sleep. But I was quite wrong. From inside the car, through the windows and the net, they kept shining that infernal torch around and around, and on to me. To make matters worse, after a while they started tooting the electric horn.

'What on earth are you doing?' I inquired testily.

'We hear noises in the jungle,' one of them answered. 'There are wild animals about. You are asleep and so cannot hear, but we can.'

THE CALL OF THE MAN-EATER

With all that commotion, plus the torchlight and the electric horn, I knew no animal would approach within half a mile. But it was not worthwhile to mention the fact. At about 4 a.m. their nerves gave out completely.

'Wake up,' the man called to me, 'and let us get away from this fearful place. It is dangerous for us to remain here.'

Once again I said nothing, but arose docilely and got into the car. Always, when the time comes to leave the jungle and return to civilization, I do so with regret. This time it was different. I was more than fed up and felt relieved when the engine started and we began the return trip to Bangalore.

On another occasion, a very senior officer in a factory where I was once employed asked me if I would take him out to shoot a really large crocodile, as he badly wanted the skin. I agreed, and we left in his car that very night for Hogenaikal, on the Cauvery river, where these reptiles are to be found in reasonable numbers. There were four of us in the party. The officer, his lady friend, my son Donald, and myself.

At about nine the next morning when the sun was becoming really hot we hired a coracle, camouflaged the sides of it with twigs, and started floating gently downstream on the lookout for crocodiles basking on the sandbanks bordering the river. I told the great man that when we saw one, he would have to make a landing ashore, detour into the jungle and stalk the reptile soundlessly till he was close enough to take a neck shot. To approach it directly in the coracle would be to lose it, as crocodiles are very cunning and slide back into the water as soon as danger approaches. Shooting a crocodile in the neck paralyses the spinal column and prevents the reptile from making that last-minute convulsive twist of the body whereby it plunges back into the water, not to be seen again. Either the currents will take the carcase miles downstream or the crocodile will wedge itself between rocks at the bottom of the river and perish there.

But the great man contradicted me sharply. He said that he had read in a book that a heart shot, immediately behind the left foreleg, was the most effective. I tried to point out that there was no doubt that such a heart shot would kill the crocodile, but not before it plunged back into the river and was lost. But he would have none of this.

In due course we spotted a large crocodile sunning itself on a sand bank, and we set our man ashore out of sight and a quarter of a mile upstream. Then I sat in the coracle and watched the scene through my binoculars. For a man of his bulk, he did a marvellous piece of stalking. The bank on which the crocodile was lying rose to some height, and after quite a long time I saw the stalker appear at the top of the bank, lie down and aim carefully. Suddenly the crocodile seemed to rear up on its own tail and then plunge into the water with a great splash. The next second came the sharp report of the rifle.

I ordered the owner of the coracle to paddle quickly to the spot. There my client met me with a wide smile, his face deep red from the heat and his exertions. 'I got him,' he said, 'right behind the left shoulder.'

'I am afraid you haven't,' I answered. 'No doubt you hit him and he will die. But we will never find him.'

'Rot!' he replied brusquely. 'Get some fishermen to throw their nets into the river and we will soon pick him up.'

The coracle was despatched to bring fishermen from the village of Ootaimalai with their nets. These came after an hour and the nets were duly cast. But no dead crocodile was picked up. The river was too deep and the nets did not reach the bottom. Besides, there were the currents to be reckoned with.

'Let us try for another,' I suggested consolingly.

'You don't know me,' said the great man. 'I will never give in till I succeed.'

The nets were cast till evening, but we caught no dead crocodile. At dinner that night I suggested that, as we were due back at work the next day, we should leave at about ten.

'You do not know me,' I was told. 'I will never give in till I succeed. I am not leaving this place till I recover my crocodile.'

Next morning I again suggested we look for another crocodile. My man glared at me disdainfully. The net-casting was begun again, but by lunch-time no carcase had been found. The great man was perspiring copiously and swearing loudly when we sat down for lunch at the table in the forest bungalow. He took off his bush-coat and threw it over a chair, sitting down bare to the waist. Seeing the great personage make himself comfortable, Donald did likewise, removing his shirt before he sat down, also bare to the waist.

Suddenly the great man asked: 'Anderson, how many men work directly under you at the plant?' Wondering at the suddenness of the question, I answered automatically, 'About 110.'

Much to my surprise and dismay, he rejoined acidly: 'It indeed astonishes me how you control them when you cannot control your own son.'

Seeing the bewilderment in my expression, he went on in icy tones: 'You allow your son to sit at lunch-table bare-bodied, with a lady present!'

Before I could answer, Donald cut in. 'What about yourself? Aren't you also bare-bodied? You should set an example instead of doing yourself what you don't want others to do.'

The man's face changed to deep red, then almost purple with anger. 'Damn it man, do you allow this pup to speak to me, your superior officer, in this way?' Then, turning to Don, he added furiously: 'Shut up before I make you.'

That was rather too much for Donald. He was young and very vigorous. 'You old so-and-so,' he answered. 'My dad may be working under you, but I am not. Come outside and I'll feed you to your blasted crocodile.'

I do not know how it was that the great man avoided an attack of apoplexy. Perhaps his friend saved the situation by suggesting we return to Bangalore forthwith, which we did. This man remained my boss for over two years after that, but he never spoke to me again. Don and I still laugh when we think of this incident and wonder how great men can ever be so silly.

Now let me tell you about my friend, Freddie Galiffe, and the wild elephant—half-rogue and certainly a killer—that lived in a corner of his vast estate, and for which Freddie had a soft spot, because the presence of this old monster and his nocturnal ramblings largely discouraged the activities of timber thieves who would now and again raid the more distant parts of his estate for the valuable timber and bamboos that grew there.

Freddie Galiffe owns quite a large estate, somewhere around 600 acres of land about half of which is virgin forest, just within Mysore state and its border with Coorg, which was till very recently a little independent state lying to the west of the larger jurisdiction of Mysore. The ranges of the Western Ghats begin here and the country is wild, rugged and densely wooded. It is inexpressibly beautiful. Large areas are covered entirely with bamboo jungle, and the stems of the bamboos attain really magnificent heights and are extraordinarily stout, sometimes as thick as your thigh.

To the west of Freddie's estate lies a vast area of bamboo jungle called Annay Chowk, meaning 'elephant residence', which is government Reserve Forest and has for long borne an evil reputation for elephants and been the birthplace of many rogues for as long as anyone can remember.

THE CALL OF THE MAN-EATER

'Freddie's Rogue', as I have called this particular elephant, evidently came from Annay Chowk, but for some unknown reason it migrated to Freddie's estate and lived almost permanently in a corner of his land to the west, where heavy jungle and tender bamboos, the favourite food of elephants, prevail. From the description my friend who has seen this elephant many times has given me, the rogue is a very old animal, for the uppermost ends of his ears turn over. Apparently he is over nine feet in height, which is quite big for an Indian elephant.

Not far from the little shack in which Freddie lives is a natural lake, known in India as a 'tank'. Freddie has taken advantage of this tank to build a 'bund', or ridge, on one side, and through a sluice gate he draws water for cultivating several paddy fields where he grows very good quality rice.

Robbers came one moonlit night to rob his paddy. They arrived in a bullock-cart in which they intended to load and carry away the paddy. And they did just that. They stole his paddy, loaded the cart, and drove it away. But by bad luck they met 'Freddie's Rogue' a mile away. He killed one of the thieves, demolished the cart and, strange as it may seem, did not touch the paddy.

On another occasion timber thieves felled a teak tree growing on Freddie's land, lopped off the branches and carried away the straight trunk. There must have been six or eight of them, for the trunk was heavy. Once again 'Freddie's Rogue' appeared around the corner. He squashed one of them flat. Another he playfully tossed away so that the thief's thigh was broken when he hit the ground. The next morning it was his calls for help that brought Freddie and his men to the spot. There they found the heavy teak log, the crushed thief and his injured comrade.

There was a third robbery. This time one of Freddie's sturdy bulls, which he kept for drawing the plough, was the victim. It had been stabled with others behind Freddie's shack; the thieves untethered him at dead of night and led him away. But not very far. Perhaps they had gone half a mile when, like avenging justice, 'Freddie's Rogue' appeared. He chased one of the thieves who, to save his life, came to Freddie's hut for safety, banging frantically upon his door. He gave himself up after confessing his crime.

One day an adventurous couple, who were friends of Freddie's, came to his estate. They said they had decided to live in the wilds for a year and asked Freddie's permission to build a cabin for themselves in some remote part of his estate. It was a strange request, but having nothing to lose by granting it, Freddie good-naturedly consented. But he warned them about the rogue elephant, but nothing daunted, they set about constructing a shack, Tarzan-fashion, among the boughs of a banyan tree and just about twenty feet off the ground. It was really lucky for them that they chose this height.

During the two months or so that it took to construct their hut of split bamboos and leaves, and a ladder for vines by which they could climb up and down to their strange home, they shared Freddie's humble hut. Then at last came the house-warming occasion. The home-in-the-tree was ready. Freddie climbed up into it and pronounced it excellent. That night the adventurous couple spent their first night in their love nest on the banyan tree.

At some time during the dark hours they were awakened by strange noises from below. They peeped down from their front door to see a huge elephant standing on the ground beneath, his extended trunk waving in the air a few feet below them. Fortunately they made no sound whatever, while the pachyderm was not angry but only mildly curious. Without doubt he scented them but failed to discover exactly where they were. He remained below for over an hour, sniffing with outstretched trunk. Had he thought of raising himself on his hind legs, circus fashion, he could have reached them with the end of his trunk and brought their flimsy home crashing to earth. Providentially he did not do so. There is no doubt that by remaining quiet the couple saved their lives, for eventually the elephant lost interest in the structure and wandered off. With daylight they descended, nor did they spend another night in the little tree-hut they had so painstakingly built.

Freddie professes to have a fondness for 'his rogue', as he calls this elephant, and he consistently refuses to send a report to the authorities about him, or to try to shoot the elephant himself on his own land—which is permissible. Freddie claims the pachyderm is an unpaid watchman. It is significant that the thieves now leave Freddie's lands alone at night. It is also significant that Freddie himself will not venture out after sunset. Indeed, the unpaid watchman is doing a fine job! He keeps both intruders and owner behind fastened doors!

Six

The Creatures of the Jungle

MUCH HAS BEEN WRITTEN ABOUT THE BIG GAME AND CARNIVORE OF Africa, and a great deal about tigers, panthers and elephants in India. In this wealth of literature the smaller animals tend to be forgotten.

One of them, the Indian wild dog, which goes under the Latin name of *cyon dukhuensis*, is a most interesting animal, very closely resembling and related to the domestic dog in appearance and habits. In colour it is reddish brown, turning to white on the belly. The hair along the back is dark brown or even black, the tips of the ears often black, with a short bushy tail, having a tuft of black hair at its extremity. Sometimes within and at the end of this black tuft is a smaller tuft of white hair. A male dog weighs over forty pounds and stands almost two feet high. The neck and jaws are massive, the chest deep, but the waist narrow, indicating that the animal is built for speed. It has structural differences from its domestic cousin in its skull and teeth, and it has more mammae. The feet and toes are hairy, and the tracks rather more pointed than those by domesticated dogs.

Wild dogs appear to congregate in packs to a greater extent during the hot weather. Perhaps this has some instinctive connection with the fact that water is scarce in the jungles at that time and the deer upon which they feed are more concentrated in the vicinity of water holes at which they are compelled by circumstances to drink. About October these packs dissolve into pairs; this is the breeding season and the pups are born during the cold weather. They may number about five to a litter, their home being a cave between rocks or a hole in the ground. At weaning the bitch feeds her pups on raw meat that she eats first from a kill, partially digests and then regurgitates for the benefit of her offspring. The young grow rapidly in intelligence and sagacity. From an early age they evince great ferocity at the smell or sight of blood and raw flesh.

Wild dogs have keen senses of sight, hearing and scent, particularly the last-mentioned, which helps them to find their quarry. They attack any living creature in the forest, including adult tigers and panthers, and the calves of bison, but avoid elephants, men, hyaenas and jackals, probably considering the last-mentioned as near cousins. An exception to this general code of behaviour occurred, however, when the six wild-dogs attacked and killed a hyena—Jackie's mother—as I have already related. This proves that there are no hard and fast rules with wild animals. The unexpected often takes place.

I have known of more than one case in the Chittor district of Andhra Pradesh where these dogs have torn a tiger to ribbons after suffering a considerable number of casualties themselves. It is probable that the tiger, accustomed always to be the aggressor and to terrorizing the animals he hunts, is quite at a loss when hunted himself and psychologically defeated even before the dogs drive home their attack in numbers. Panthers and monkeys escape by climbing trees or rocks, but the confused tiger is overwhelmed before he knows what is happening.

Wild dogs hunt by day, favouring the hot hours between 10 a.m. and 4 p.m. They will also occasionally hunt at other times and on bright moonlit nights. I have never known them to hunt on a dark night. While on the chase they make a peculiarly sharp, high-pitched yelp which might be mistaken for a bird-call. Should they be hunting a large animal, like a sambar, the main body of the pack will gallop behind at a leisurely pace while 'flankers' will run ahead to ambush the quarry. Their method of attack is very cruel, as they fasten on to the hunted animal and literally tear him to bits alive. The eyes, nose, throat, ears, abdomen and testicles are favourite points of attack.

Once, when I was sitting on the bank of a dry stream, a full-grown sambar doe broke cover and ran across pursued by wild dogs; her intestines were dragging in the sand and for about twenty feet behind her. Both her eyes had been bitten out, her face was torn in a ghastly manner, and two dogs had their teeth embedded in her flanks and were being dragged along by the still-galloping sambar. There have been quite a number of instances where deer hunted by these dogs have run into a village to try to save themselves from their relentless foes, preferring the company of men to the ruthless destroyers. Unfortunately the villagers, who are only interested in meat, fail to appreciate this and kill the deer for themselves, driving the dogs away.

I was once resting from the noon-day heat beneath a tree at Mamandur when I heard the peculiar yelp of wild dogs.

THE CALL OF THE MAN-EATER

Hastening towards the yelps, I found a full-grown sambar hind standing up to her chest in a pool of water into which she had galloped to try to save herself. Several dogs were swimming out to her, while two had already reached her. One of them had climbed onto her back and was biting her neck. Four rapid shots from the Winchester disposed of four of them, while the remainder ran back into the jungle. The sambar hind still stood in the water, gazing at me with wide, terror-striken eyes. I waded into the pool and went up to her. Then I touched her, expecting she would gallop away. The poor creature was trembling with fear and did not move. I stroked her neck, but she did not even look at me. Her head and large ears were turned towards the spot where the dogs had disappeared. Finally I started pushing her out of the pool in the opposite direction. Even when she reached the bank she did not run till I gave her two sharp slaps on her rump. That seemed to bring her to her senses and she galloped off. She had been badly bitten and several strips of flesh and skin were hanging from the wounds. The canine teeth of wild dogs are curved backwards to a greater degree than those of their domestic cousins. This not only enables them to retain their grip on a running quarry, but helps them to tear out great chunks of flesh when attacking or feeding.

These animals are great killers. They will not eat carrion or decayed meat, nor touch the kills of other animals. Their practice is to slay for themselves, and slay often, so that they may enjoy the warm, red blood and hot fresh meat. They are by far the most destructive creatures of the jungles. For this reason, rewards are paid all over the peninsula for their destruction, with a higher reward for bitches and puppies. The skin and skull must be produced when claiming the reward.

With all their ferocity, wild dogs exhibit a strange friendliness towards a domesticated cousin should they meet one in the jungle. Several times, when out with my dog Nipper, he has come tearing back to me with one or more wild dogs gambolling playfully at his heels—not always puppies, but fully grown animals too. On such occasions I have not had the heart to shoot them, but have stood still to watch what would happen. They have approached to within a yard of me, wagging their tails and fawning at Nipper, making the whining sound that any dog makes when he wants to be friendly. I have remained motionless and they have continued to run round in circles, just out of reach, ignoring me completely but trying to make friends with Nipper. Unfortunately he would never respond but appeared very afraid. Even when I walked away, with Nipper literally between my legs, they would follow closely, wagging away their tails and whining in a friendly manner.

I have never known or heard of a single instance of men being attacked or bitten by wild dogs, but they are strangely fearless of the human race and will stand and look at man without running away when a tiger or panther or elephant would have bolted. I have fired at wild dogs and shot one or two while the rest of the pack lingered in the vicinity. On other occasions, from behind cover, I have shot a dog and, instead of running away, the pack have approached and sniffed at the dead animal. I have been told that under such conditions they will even eat their dead companion.

Once near Dimbum, in North Coimbatore district, when turning a corner of the road in the Studebaker, I came upon a wild bitch crossing the road followed by three half-grown puppies. Not wanting to shoot the mother or the pups, I stopped the car abruptly, sprang out and gave chase. But I had scarcely passed a few yards into the jungle when the three pups left their mother and came yelping around me, zwagging their tails but keeping just out of reach. It was evident from the expressions on their faces that they were just dying to make friends but could not screw up sufficient courage to come any closer. The mother stood aloof, calmly regarding me and her offspring with dispassionate eyes. I am told they can be easily tamed if caught young and make good pets, but I have not, so far, had the opportunity to prove this for myself.

It is a strange fact that the number of wild dogs in any part of the forest is subject to extreme fluctuation. At times a section of jungle will literally teem with them. At other times, not one is to be seen and no tracks are to be found. Some of the aborigines have told me that they are prone to some strange disease, and that at such times they have come upon the dead bodies of a number of wild dogs rotting in the jungle. No animal will go near a dead wild dog to eat it; not even a hyaena or jackal. Vultures are the only creatures that will clean up such carcases if they find them. Personally, I have never come across the dead body of a wild dog that has not been killed by some other living creature, and my own theory is that nature has provided that these animals should be extremely restless and constantly on the move. If they remained permanently in any one locality soon hardly a creature would be left alive there.

I have never heard of wild dogs or hyaenas contracting rabies, but have known of several instances of jackals getting hydrophobia and biting human beings and other animals. Probably due to their excursions into villages in search of offal they have contracted the complaint from a rabid village dog, after which they have spread it among themselves.

There is a village named Jowlagiri at the edge of the jungle in the Salem district, only about forty-three miles from Bangalore. South-west of Jowlagiri and about three miles away is a silent pool in the forest surrounded by rocky hills with heavy bamboo growing in the intersecting valleys. It is a place where panthers often come to drink. The full moon was due one night when I ate an early dinner and motored to Jowlagiri, taking a few sandwiches and Nipper, my dog, which I had procured under unusual circumstances from the village of Devarabetta, only about nine miles from Jowlagiri.* My intention was to sit at this water hole till about midnight on the off-chance of a panther coming along, but more to enjoy the solitude and the moonlight. I reached Jowlagiri by 7 p.m., and the water hole less than an hour later.

But I had been forestalled. Poachers, who had come to shoot an unwary deer that might seek water, were already there. In the bright moonlight I saw two figures wrapped in black blankets scurrying away through the jungle, bent double, one of them carrying a gun. I approached the spot from which they had fled. At the foot of a large tree I found a well constructed 'hide' overlooking the water hole. In their haste to escape the poachers had left an electric torch behind, also a small flask of black powder, a tin box of percussion caps and a cloth bag containing pieces of lead which was the ammunition they used for their flintlock. Considering these articles as the 'spoils of war', I sat down with Nipper in the hide. Just after 10 p.m. Nipper scrambled up alert. Then around the corner came a spotted doe at full gallop, with half-a-dozen wild dogs in pursuit. She ran headlong into the pool to save herself, while the six dogs halted momentarily on the bank.

That was when I opened fire and shot three of them. The remaining dogs began to run away and I was about to fire a fourth round when things began to happen. Something huge crashed down the tree and fell beside me, almost on top of Nipper, who leapt into the air in alarm. It was a human being.

---

* See *Nine Man-Eaters and One Rogue*.

For a moment I was so surprised that I failed to grab him. Like lightning he scrambled to his feet and fled.

Then I realized what had happened. There had been a third poacher fast asleep in the tree above me. He had been oblivious to the departure of his two comrades and my arrival. My three rifle shots had so startled him that he had fallen off his perch. But this was not the end of it. Not by any means. The wretched man had run into the jungle instead of towards a village that was hardly a mile away. From somewhere in the jungle I heard him screaming to his village for help, voicing the most extraordinary falsehoods. He said that someone had come to the water hole and had shot him. He said that he had run away, but was in danger of being followed and shot again. He was imploring his friends to come and rescue him.

Soon I heard answering shouts from the village. In the midst of all this pandemonium I knew there was no chance whatever of a panther or any other living creature coming to the water hole. The spotted doe which the dogs had chased had also run away. I came out of hiding with Nipper and looked at the three dogs I had shot. It was impossible for me to carry three carcasses and my rifle, so I decided to skin the dogs and take only their pelts.

I had already begun this task when Nipper began to bark frantically, and before I quite knew what was happening a large party of men rushed out from the jungle towards me. In the vanguard I counted five musketeers, all pointing their muzzle-loaders straight at me. There were other men behind them, armed with hatchets, knives and staves. Quickly I realized the only thing to do was to appear nonchalant and put up as brave a front as possible. So I continued to skin the wild dog, as if the group's appearance was of absolutely no concern of mine. They crowded round. Then one of them spoke to me roughly:

'Where is the body of our companion whom you have shot?' he demanded.

'Shot?' I feigned great surprise and indignation. 'Your friend jumped down from the tree and ran away. I never shot him.'

'We heard three shots,' he stated emphatically.

'Are you quite sure?' I asked.

'Absolutely certain,' he replied testily, and then repeated, 'three shots.'

'You are quite correct,' I concluded. 'I fired three shots, and here are three dead wild dogs. How could I have shot your friend?'

The logic of this argument sank into them slowly. 'But he called out to us that he had been shot and you were going to kill him.'

'I know,' I answered. 'I heard him too. Your friend is a fool, a coward and a liar. He is hiding somewhere in the jungle. Call out to him now and he will probably answer you.'

All together they began calling and whistling. Soon he answered them. The party of men who had been so belligerent a moment before now looked at each other sheepishly. I knew they were defeated and that I had them in my hands. I determined to press home my advantage by staging a counterattack.

I had left my Winchester in the hide and was unarmed. Slowly I got to my feet and addressed their leader: 'You have dared to accuse a *sahib* of murdering your idiotic friend,' I thundered. 'Remember, I am a licence-holder in this forest and am entitled to shoot here, while he is a poacher, caught red-handed.'

Then, before they could interrupt, I continued: 'I will now make you a sporting offer, because I am a sportsman myself. Either you will soundly beat this man for telling lies, or I will beat him. In addition he will have to carry these three dead dogs to my car at Jowlagiri. If you agree to my terms, I promise you on my word that I shall forget the matter and say nothing to anyone. If you do not agree, I shall not only report him, but your whole village for threatening me with weapons, and shall have your firearms confiscated.'

There was silence while they looked at one another. Then each man told the other to speak. Finally the leader began hesitantly: 'I shall beat the fool myself,' he said, 'and will make him carry the three dogs for you. But will you promise not to report us?'

'I have already promised,' I replied. Then, indicating the hiding place beneath the tree: 'Someone's torch is there, and powder-flask, tin of caps and bag of pellets. Take them, and bring me my rifle.'

A man scampered off to carry out this command. Just then the man who had been the cause of all the uproar walked boldly out of the jungle and jauntily approached us. The poor fellow did not know what was in store for him. As he came within reach, the leader struck him full in the face. He fell to the ground, when another man kicked him viciously. His surprise soon gave way to yells of terror and pleas for mercy. The leader hauled him to his feet by seizing his hair.

'Show me where you have been wounded?' he hissed.

The man timorously answered, 'I heard three shots and I thought I had been hit.'

Eventually they stopped beating him and he was a sorry wreck. Then they loaded the three dead dogs on his back and invited me to sling my rifle around his neck as well. But the weight would have been too great. I knew the three dogs weighed perhaps forty pounds each, and I did not want the man to fall and damage my rifle. So I replied that I always made a practice of carrying my own rifle.

I parted the best of friends that night or rather early morning, as it was past midnight by the time it was all over, with the group of men who had come with the probable intention of murdering me. Then I turned towards Jowlagiri and the car, with Nipper at my heels and the unfortunate poacher, staggering beneath the weight of the three dogs, ahead, just in case he should suddenly drop them and run away.

Another animal about which little has been written is the Indian wild pig, better known as the wild boar. In former times there were stories of how the hardy Nimrods engaged in 'pigsticking'—that is, hunting boar on horseback with spears. A few of these blood-thirsty old hunters varied the sport by maintaining packs of dogs, some of them mongrels, but mostly of bull terrier stock, which they employed to hunt down not only wild boar, but bears as well and, in one instance, even bison. When the hunted animal was engaged by the dogs, the hunter would arrive on the scene and dispose of it, either by shooting or spearing it from horseback.

As a dog lover, I think this so-called sport was decidedly brutal, particularly when employed against wild boar. The most courageous dog has little chance against a fully roused boar, and many members of a pack were torn to ribbons by the tusks of the infuriated pig. And even when the gallant boar was eventually killed, either by shooting or spearing, he was scarcely given a fair chance to show his mettle, engaged as he was in staving off the attacks of a host of dogs.

The wild boar is the most courageous animal in the Indian jungle with the exception, perhaps, of the ratel, a much smaller quadruped, half-mongoose and half-bear. The quality that I admire about him is that when he turns to fight he will fight to the death. There is no running away thereafter, for him. He will either emerge as victor or sacrifice his life. This does not imply that the boar is an aggressive animal, ranging the forest looking for a fight and something to kill. Left to himself he is quite inoffensive. I have many times met wild boar face to face at close quarters and unexpectedly, but never have they assumed the offensive, as a sloth bear would invariably do. They have either stood still or made off to avoid an encounter. But when pursued, pushed amd harried, or when wounded and followed up, they will turn about to fight. That means a charge. Even when a wounded panther attacks, it is not an attack unto death; it is a hit-and-run affair. But the boar will charge repeatedly until it has disposed of its antagonist.

On several occasions I have come across the results of a fight between a tiger and a wild boar. Generally the pig is killed, but it is only after giving an excellent account of himself and seriously gashing his opponent. The copious blood-trail left by the departing tiger has proved this. In a few cases the result has been different: the tiger has been killed or has given up the fight and run away after being severely punished by the boar. Once in Targathy I came upon the remains of a dead boar and a dead tigress, about twenty yards apart. The boar had evidently died first for he was facing the scene of combat; then the tigress had attempted to crawl away, but death had overtaken her. The boar had been bitten through the throat and had died; the tigress's belly had been ripped open and her intestines had fallen through the gap, while the artery in her neck had been slashed by an upward thrust of the boar's sharp curved tusks.

A large wild boar can weigh up to 300 pounds and more, while his curved tusks grow to eight inches in length. He has intelligence and muscle, and the heart of a fanatical warrior. Left to themselves, wild pigs are companionable animals, moving in sounders. They have great love for their young, whom they will defend gallantly. Pigs have fondness for water and are always to be found in its vicinity. Their diet is very varied, ranging from roots, insects, offal and cultivated crops, to lizards, snakes and the kills made by a tiger or panther, as well as cattle that have died in the fields from disease. They are also fond of wild fruit, particularly the acid, jungle-growing mango and figs, and they devour these in large quantities when they fall from the trees. The sow makes a proper nest for herself of sticks or grass or fallen bamboo branches, under which she burrows before giving birth.

The large boars often fight among themselves for the coveted position of leader of the sounder, using their tusks freely and fiercely and inflicting terrific damage upon each other. In the cold weather, and during the rains, they huddle together for warmth, often sleeping on top of one another like a pyramid. I was once motoring from Lingadhalli up the Kemangondi Ghat road. It was pouring with rain. Suddenly the headlights revealed an obstacle before me: what appeared to be a mass of boulders piled one upon the other in the middle of the road, I found was a sounder of wild pigs, huddled together in a pile for warmth from the cold and rain.

Before charging a boar gives two or three loud, sharp grunts. Then his little tail sticks up behind him and along he comes. When cornered, wild boar have been known to charge a solid line of beaters, a feat which even the most ferocious tiger, including a man-eater, seldom attempts. Instances have been known of a wounded boar, when being followed up, making a detour and attacking his pursuers from the rear. I did not believe these rumours till I experienced the very thing myself when I fired at a large boar one morning near Panapatti, on the banks or the Chinar river, but he got away, although I knew I had hit him. Reaching the spot at which I had shot him, I found blood and began to follow his trail. It led across the sandy bed to the bank of the river, and then down a *nullah* between two low hillocks. I was following his tracks in this *nullah,* and could clearly see them leading ahead, when I heard the two familiar grunts from close behind me. I turned around just in time to see the boar charging at me down the bank of the *nullah* a few yards away and from the rear. I was able to shoot him just in time. Had he not given himself away by his grunts, I would not be writing this today. It was clear that he knew he was being followed, so he left the bed of the *nullah,* climbed up the bank and retraced his steps to attack me from behind. All this shows a high degree of intelligence. After I had shot him I verified this by following his blood-trail along the detour he had made.

On another occasion, with my cousin, Stewart Hearsey, and a friend named Willie Thomas, I was beating for pig at Yercaud on the Shevaroy Hills. A huge boar passed me. I fired, but missed. Then Stewart fired, but also missed. Lastly, Willie Thomas fired; he did not miss, but only wounded the boar. At once the pig turned and charged. Willie, who fired his second barrel, failed to stop him. The next instant Willie was on the ground and had been gashed from chin to temple by a slashing thrust from the pig's tusk as he galloped past. Had Stewart and I not been there to put an end to the gallant old boar, he would surely have returned and then Willie's days on this planet would certainly have ended. Willie Thomas, who has shot many panthers and much big game, considers this encounter his closest to death. He still bears the scar to this day.

The sloth bear is a creature that has always interested me greatly. Perhaps this is so because he is quite common and I have often come across him, both in his wild state in the forests and in civilized areas in the keeping of itinerant 'bearmen', who lead trained specimens along and make them wrestle or dance before an audience. The keynote of a bear's nature is absolute unpredictability! You can never know for certain what it may decide to do next. This is the chief cause of the many maulings suffered by people who move about in jungles where bears are numerous. Bears are heavy sleepers, sometimes slumbering in long grass or in holes they have dug. When they sleep they sleep soundly, often snoring in the process. A passing man almost literally stumbles over a bear before it wakes up with a start and finds an enemy so close. Then things invariably happen—to the man.

Bears have very poor sight and poor hearing as well. Their sense of smell seems to be restricted to locating food in the form of grubs, insects, termites, roots and fruit, and they do not seem able to scent the proximity of human beings. When startled, they seek a way of escape. But their reflexes are equally poor and they perhaps feel that their only hope of escape is to down the intruder first. They attack with teeth and claws, always making for the face or chest. I have seen some horribly mutilated faces of people suddenly attacked in this way without provocation. Often one or both eyes have been torn out.

When camping at Mamandur, word was brought to me at night that two men, while carrying honey from the jungle that afternoon, had been attacked by a tiger when crossing a *nullah* and one of them had been killed. I took out a rescue party with lanterns, accompanied by the man who had escaped and who insisted that it was a tiger he had seen, to lead us to the place where the tragedy had occurred. We found the corpse, but one look at the face that had been torn to shreds convinced us that the killer was not a tiger. A careful scrutiny of the sandy ground of the *nullah* showed that a sloth bear with her young had been sleeping by the bank. Not only had the sudden advent of the man startled the mother, but the presence of her cub, whom she instinctively defended from imagined or anticipated assault, had caused her to slay without provocation. When confronted with the evidence, the man who led me to the spot confessed that he had never waited to see the animal. Hearing a growl, followed by his friend's scream of terror and pain, he had started running and had not stopped till he reached the village of Mamandur.

On another occasion I was camping in the Chamala Valley with my son, who was only about fourteen at the time. The valley abounds in sambar and spotted deer; stags of both varieties with good heads are common. For some time Donald had been worrying me to let him shoot a stag. My deer-shooting days had long passed and I had reached a stage when I had ceased killing these beautiful and inoffensive creatures, so I tried hard to infect Donald with my ideas. But being a youngster he was all the more persistent and continued to pester me, so I eventually gave in.

In those days Donald did not possess his own rifle. He borrowed mine and set off before dawn next morning on his blood-thirsty quest. I followed him, but some paces behind, to give him the opportunity of getting the shot he wanted. The Chamala valley has some beautiful stretches of park-like country, which I particularly like. We arrived at one of these spots just as the grey of dawn was breaking over a large hill to the east, known as Monkey Hill. Donald was about 100 yards ahead of me, moving from tree-trunk to tree-trunk in the hope of seeing a stag.

Suddenly I saw him halt abruptly and from the ground, seemingly at his very feet, reared a shaggy black shape which I immediately recognized as a sloth bear. It stood on its hind legs, apparently about to attack him, when mercifully it changed its mind and just as suddenly dashed away with a loud 'Woof! Woof!' Being a mere boy at that time, Donald was as surprised as the bear. To this day he considers it the narrowest shave he has had.

Bears move about at night. Sometimes they may be met in the evening or at dawn — as Donald met the bear that early morning! But once I met one at about two in the afternoon, at the hottest time of the day. The meeting took place in the Chamala Valley. I had gone there with my wife on this occasion, taking my old friend and *shikari*, Ranga, from the Salem district, along with me. We had been for an afternoon stroll to a water hole, known as Gundalpenta, and were returning to our camp near a Forestry department's well at a place named Pulibonu. There were three of us—my wife, Ranga and myself—and Ranga was wearing a black coat, black shorts, and was bare-legged. I was in front, with my wife behind me; Ranga was bringing up the rear.

The path we were following turned a corner. There, some yards away, was a termite hill, and standing up against it and intently looking down one of the holes in the hill was a black figure. For the moment my wife forgot that Ranga was behind her, and thinking my retainer was examining the termite-hill she called out in Tamil: 'What are you looking at Ranga?'

The black figure turned around, and of course it was not Ranga. It was a sloth bear. Surprised at seeing the three of us, he continued to stare at us foolishly, like a short-sighted human.

Then Ranga—the real Ranga this time—called out: '*Karadi*! (Bear!). Hai! Shoo!' Off went Bruin for dear life, muttering an indignant, if startled, 'Woof! Woof!'

Bears are very fond of sucking termites out of their hills. They apply their snouts to holes in the termite hill, or sometimes dig these holes themselves, then blow air into the earth, and finally start sucking for all they are worth. The medley of sound emitted is both curious and amusing. It resembles the buzzing of bees or hornets, and at times the groaning drone of a bagpipe as it deflates. They have a curious habit, too, of sucking their forepaws, which they do assiduously with a persistent humming sound. Some experienced hunters have suggested that it is to soothe their paws when hurt or sore from the effect of constant digging, but I do not think this is so, because our tame bear, Bruno, about which I have written elsewhere in this book, often sucks his paws, though they are by no means sore or hurt from digging. I am convinced there is some sort of secretion from between the toes— whether it be sticky, sweet or salty I do not know— which makes this habit attractive to all sloth bears.

They are very intelligent animals. They have an uncanny intuition that leads them to the different varieties of fruit-trees in the forest when those particular fruits are in season. The boram berry is an example. Especially in the Chamala valley, bears appear in large numbers just after these fruit have become over-ripe and begin to fall to the ground. The same can be said for the wild-mangoes, which are stringy, acid and unpalatable to the human taste, though they are a delicacy to bears; for 'jak-fruit', that do not grow in jungles as a rule but are planted in the cultivated areas bordering the forest; for sugar-cane, that is set in large squares on agricultural ground; and particularly for the jamun or *jumlum,* grape-like purple berries that fall in thousands from the parent tree in July and August each year, to carpet the ground with a purplish-black, slightly astringent fruit.

Jumlum trees grow densely along the banks of the Chinar river in Salem district, and bears turn out in large numbers during those months to gormandize the fallen fruit. In my earlier years I shot a few, but soon found this a tame and unsporting pastime. I would visit the trees in the afternoon with my assistants, Ranga and Byra, and one or two more men if available, and gather the fallen *jumlums* into an immense heap at the foot of one of the parent trees. The more fruit we could gather and the bigger the heap, the better for my plan.

THE CREATURES OF THE JUNGLE

I would come prepared with a very powerful catapult made of rubber cut from an old inner tube from a bus or lorry, and a pocketful of smooth pebbles, gathered from the riverbed. Climbing into the tree before sunset and on moonlight night, with my rifle in case of eventualities, I would await the coming of the sloth bears. Around eight o'clock they would turn up, one by one; large, black, grumbling, rumbling and lumbering creatures. What a spread they found awaiting them! I am sure they must have thought they were in Paradise! Soon the mound of *jumlums* would have four, five or more bears tucking into it.

And now came the time for some fun. I slipped my hand into my pocket, felt for a suitable pebble, fitted it into the leather sling of the catapult and took careful aim at the biggest of the bears beneath me—perhaps only twelve to fifteen feet away. I stretched the rubber to its utmost and then let fly. The pebble hit the big, black bear hard on the back of his neck, then all hell was let loose!

'Damn this fellow at my side,' he apparently thought, as he bit viciously his innocent neighbour.

'You want to fight, do you?' the neighbour questioned as he bit his next neighbour in turn. And so it went on, till there was a mass of fighting bears below me, screaming their heads off, while I sat as quiet as a mouse in my tree. Somehow they sorted themselves out with yells of protest, squeals of pain, and many grunts of indignation. There was much snuffling and shuffling and huffing, but after some time they forgot the silly incident and settled down once again to gorge upon the fruit spread before them.

Then the catapult spoke for the second time, and the yelling, screaming, biting and tearing black mass of bears went for one another once more, this time for longer. But finally they settled down to eat and tried to overlook each other's nastiness. Then the catapult let fly a third time! That really was a fight! Eventually some of the bears broke away and began to wander off. The place seemed to them unhealthy.

But suddenly one of the bears looked up and saw me. So this was the nigger in the woodpile! Pandemonium reigned as he screamed with fear and indignation. His hysteria spread to the other bears and they all screamed and yelled in unison. Only once did one of the bears think of doing something about me. He rushed to the foot of the tree and began to climb up the trunk. I thought I would have to shoot him with my rifle, which I had brought with me as a precaution. But I made a final attempt to drive him away. Using the catapult once more, I hit him squarely in the face. Protesting loudly to the whole jungle, he fell to the ground with a thud. Then he scrambled hastily to his feet and, still complaining vociferously, bounded away.

This habit of biting one another when one of them has been hurt is common behaviour with bears. Should two be together and one be wounded by a gun or rifle shot, he or she will invariably attack the other savagely. Sloth bears can climb trees easily when they want to. They go up after beehives, which they knock down to the ground and then devour. They have also been known to drink toddy from the pots fixed on date palms to collect the fluid. This intoxicates them to some extent, as do the thick petals of the *mhowa* flower when it falls to earth. Although they can ascend trees without much trouble they find difficulty in descending. Sometimes they try to slide down backwards. At other times they just let go and thud to earth. Apparently they never seem to hurt themselves in that way.

Although they are irritable and get easily excited, sloth bears are most affectionate towards their young and each other. When alone and wounded, one will scream aloud in complaint and tell the jungle all about it. His companions will add to the screaming out of sympathy. They have known to try to succour one another and I have heard of the case of a male bear trying to remove the dead body of his mate that had been shot. Female bears carry their young—there are generally two cubs born at a time—on their backs till they are quite big, and will defend them at the cost of their own lives. All bears, including the males, have a patch or tuft of very long hair on their backs, just behind the shoulder blades. Presumably this is to provide a better 'grip' for the cubs when mother is travelling fast.

It is a mistake to think that the sloth bear is purely vegetarian, confining his diet to roots and yams, together with insects. This is very definitely not so. More than once, when sitting over tiger and panther kills, Bruin has turned up and started to devour the carcass, even when it was getting fairly high. Bruno, our tame bear, is very fond of all kinds of flesh, especially pork, venison and the flesh of wild ducks.

The claws, particularly on the forepaws of a sloth bear, are white, very long (almost four inches) and very powerful. The tracks made by his hind feet closely resemble a human footmark without the toes. The body of the animal, after it has been skinned, looks very much like a human body, and very well muscled.

Bears must feel the heat to some extent, clothed as they are in long and thick black hair. They are fond of water and often dig holes in the sand of dry riverbeds in an attempt to reach the little that will percolate through. They are noisy creatures and make a variety of sounds. When moving in pairs, but at a distance from each other, they maintain contact by a constant medley of very curious sharp, gurgling cries. Should one of them locate a nest of insects under a log of wood or a stone, he or she will immediately call the other bear by a series of squeals and happy squeaks.

THE CALL OF THE MAN-EATER

A very curious creature of the Indian jungle is the five-toed pangolin, which goes under the somewhat formidable Latin name of Manis pentadactyla. Averaging about three and a half feet in length, of which about half is his tail, he is encased in an armour of thick, overlapping, sharp-edged scales, and rolls himself into a ball when touched. The pangolin is very rarely seen and most people, even experienced hunters, do not know of his existence. This is because he is entirely nocturnal, to the extent that he rarely emerges from his hole in the ground before 1a.m., and not on every night, moreover, but only occasionally. His actual den is at the end of a tunnel and about ten feet below the surface. It is useless to try to dig one out, for the deeper you dig the deeper the pangolin goes. You will never be able to catch up with him, for nature has provided him with claws particularly suited to burrowing.

The best way to see or catch a specimen is to look for his tracks in the mud of a water hole, where they form a peculiar parallel row of sharp indentations or holes as he approaches the edge to drink. Having found the water hole you will have to sit up night after night, and all night, during the period of moonlight, until you catch a glimpse of him rolling from side to side over the mud till he reaches the edge of the water. This peculiarly rolling gait is due to the fact that the pangolin walks upon the knuckles of his feet, the claws of his forefeet being turned inwards, while the soles of his hind legs are turned outwards and upwards. The rows of parallel indentations that betray his passing are formed by the backs of the inwardly-folded claws.

When he is clear of the shrubbery and is in the middle of the mud, it is comparatively easy to rush upon him; he will then curl himself into a ball at once. Although inoffensive otherwise, a pangolin can cut your hand badly with the edges of his razorsharp scales by a quick jerk of his body or tail.

THE CREATURES OF THE JUNGLE

Should you allow the pangolin to regain the cover of the jungle, he might escape you, for he has a habit of 'lying doggo' in a clump of thick grass or a bush till you have passed, when he will crawl out in the opposite direction and move away at a pace equal to a fast walk.

When caught, a pangolin generally makes a hissing noise, as does the oodumbu or iguana. In moving, the scale rustle faintly against one another like the quills of a porcupine. When hurrying away he will keep the tail off the ground so that it will not become an impediment. As might be expected of an entirely nocturnal animal, and one that lives deep underground, he cannot see very well in bright sunlight. I have noticed the same thing with a hyaena. Pangolins are said to be powerful swimmers, although I have never seen one in water. But I have observed that, when burrowing beneath boulders, they have been strong enough to move the stone away despite its weight.

An animal for which I have a special affection is the hyaena, perhaps for no better reason than that most sportsmen appear to regard him with contempt, unworthy even of a photograph or bullet. This prejudice is so great that many hunters of my own acquaintance seem to have closed their minds—and their eyes—to his very existence, and declare that hyaenas are rare in the forests of South India. I really do not know how they can be so wrong, as I know of scarcely a jungle where hyaena tracks are not to be found in the sandy bed of a river, or traversing ravines and *nullahs*.

Only one special species of hyaena is to be found in India — the striped hyaena, Hyaena striata. A fully-grown specimen is almost as tall as a Great Dane, with a head considerably larger and broader. It is ash-grey in colour with black stripes, and has a black patch over the throat. It has large, long, pointed ears, a broad forehead, an immensely powerful jaw, broad chest and tremendously thick and strong forelegs, ending in large hairy paws. The back tapers considerably to a miserably weak haunch and hindquarters, and inadequate, puny-looking hind legs. Its spoor is therefore very distinct from that of a panther, although the pugs are about as big, because the hyaena's forepaws are about twice the size of its hind paws and are round, whereas the latter are elongated. The impressions of a hyaena's toe-nails, which are not retractable, are clearly visible in the tracks, whereas the pug-marks of a panther are quite different. The panther's front and hind paws are of about the same diameter, while the ball of the foot is much larger than a hyaena's, and the claws are retractable and therefore do not show.

I am convinced that the hyaena is an extremely unintelligent animal. He has very poor sight (particularly in the daytime), poor hearing, and (here I differ from other writers) a sense of smell which is only mediocre. I have carried out many tests with Jackie by throwing a piece of strong-smelling meat only a few yards away, when he has been unable to locate it. There is no doubt he could faintly smell the meat, for he ran aimlessly about in circles in his unsuccessful efforts to find it.

A habit I have noticed in Jackie when taking him for a walk is that every few minutes he will shuffle around in a circle, and almost always in an anticlockwise direction. But perhaps the most peculiar of his many unusual idiosyncrasies is that, every now and again, when he passes a bare stump of a tree, or a pillar or post, or a bush, he will literally dance around it, anticlockwise, with his forelegs stiff and hind legs doubled beneath him, hindquarters just off the ground. Then he will stop and for a few seconds his whole anus will protrude, as if about to pass a motion. But he emits gas instead and then straightens up and continues his way. The purpose may be to enable the wild hyaena to find his way back again by sniffing at such spots, although the theory is weakened considerably by the fact that his sense of smell is so poor.

But if his sense of smell is really so poor, how does a hyaena in the wild state locate dead and putrefying animals in the jungle? Perhaps the smell has to be brought to him on the wind before he can locate a kill. I am fully aware I am here entering upon highly debatable ground, because hyaenas all over the world are credited with great ability to scent death and decay at a great distance, but the experiments I have made with Jackie have led to a quite different conclusion.

There is no doubt that a hyaena is very much attached to his own den, which may be a hole in the ground or between rocks or boulders, or a small cave, and that he inhabits the same place for years. I know of a pair living near Gundalam, on the Secret River, that have lived in the same small cave for over five years and have brought up several families there. Unlike all other animals, the same pair remain together for a long time. To some extent I have proved a hyaena's liking for a particular home by the fact that I had Jackie at my little cottage at Whitefield for several months, where I had given him a spare bathroom to live in. Though I left the outer door open night and day to enable him to go outside to answer the calls of nature (he never once attempted to run away), he did considerable damage to that small bathroom by breaking down the brick wall at all four corners to burrow holes, and by biting at both the inner and outer doors. So I removed him eventually to my house at Bangalore, after having an island dug for him in the compound, surrounded on all four sides by a trench four feet wide by four feet deep. On the island I had a large brick house built for him, with a roof of zinc sheets. Steps led down from the island to the trench, to enable him to go down and race around if he wanted to. But as soon as I put

Jackie in his new home he went completely off his food for almost a fortnight, although he drank water.

Now it cannot be argued that it was me he missed, for I went with him to Bangalore. I maintained the same feeding-times, at midday and sunset, and gave him the same food, beef that was several days old and crawling with maggots. I even thought he might be missing the companionship of his playmate, Jill, my mongrel at Whitefield, so I brought Jill to Bangalore. Jackie was immensely pleased to see her, wagged his tail affectionately, and started to romp with her in his usual hearty and rough manner. But for all that, he would not eat his food. As might be expected, he lost weight and began to look miserable and thin, so that I was on the verge of giving in and taking him back to Whitefield. However, it occurred to me to cut his meat up into small pieces and to try feeding him a piece at a time. It was fifteen days before he consented to nibble even a little bit, just as it was becoming evident he would soon die of starvation. Then, little by little he began to eat again, although it was another fortnight before he returned to his normal hearty appetite. There is no doubt in my mind that this month of self-imposed starvation came about only because I shifted him from his little bathroom in my cottage at Whitefield, to which he had become attached since a puppy. He missed his den.

During my efforts to overcome his total refusal of food, I let him loose within the bungalow. With my back turned for a minute, the first thing he did was to chew up Donald's alarm clock, greatly to my son's indignation. Jackie tried to make friends with my wife's pet, Ella the jackal, and wanted to play with her; but, although about one-sixth his size, she began to bite him savagely, though he did not bite back. I have already mentioned that both Gypsy and Jill, my dogs at Whitefield, although they used to play with him freely, at times would lose their tempers when he was too rough and would bite him. Never at any time did he attempt to retaliate upon animals that were far smaller than himself and infinitely weaker.

I have mentioned that the trench surrounding Jackie's island was only four feet wide and four feet deep. I had noticed while he was with me in Whitefield that because of his short and weak hind legs he was not able to jump more than two feet either up or across. But I think there is a good reason for this strange disproportion of the hyaena's build. I often watched Jackie while he was eating. He would hold a bone firmly between his powerful forelegs, doubled his hind legs beneath him, and then use the slope or slant of his disproportionate body as a lever to enable him to tear great chunks of flesh from the bone. He could not have acquired the necessary purchase or leverage with the straight back of a dog.

Should you approach the den, particularly when there are pups inside, the hyaena will generally become frightened and utter a deep-throated growl of a peculiarly vibratory, humming nature, continued for a long time. If much terrified, for example by the appearance of a tiger at a kill where he has been robbing, he will voice a loud, snarling yap, something like the short growl made by an angry tiger or lion, but not so loud. If you are watching while he does this, you will notice that he literally trembles with fear. Often he will pass urine involuntarily. Should the intruder be less dangerous than a tiger, say a panther or bear, the hyaena may howl (perhaps 'yowl' is a better word to describe the sound) in a dismal, mournful manner. Should you be sitting-up over a kill or a water hole and should the hyaena discover your presence, he will either run off at once, when you may hear him pitter-pattering away over the dried leaves, or he may become tremendously agitated, when he will produce a medley of noises that can only be described as 'chattering'. Most often, he begins with a hiss of disdain, a sort of derisive, spitting sound: 'Cheey! Shee-ay!' quite frequently uttering, before or after, a series of surprised and vehement exclamations: 'Ha! Ha! Ha! Ha!' Then, as he warms to his indignant protest, come other peculiar noises: 'Garrar! Gurr-rr-aa! Guddar! Guddar! Guddar! Goo-doo! Goo-doo!'

Weird sounds indeed! But there is nothing whatever to be afraid of. The poor hyaena is just a bunch of nerves and is hoping you will end the same way. He is merely trying to drive you away with his clownish noises. He tries so hard to frighten you that he succeeds only in frightening himself. He will certainly not attack you, in spite of the pandemonium he creates.

This brings us to an often-debated question. Can a hyaena drive a tiger or a panther off its legitimate kill? Or, should he be caught in the act of robbing a kill, will the hyaena run away when the tiger appears, or will he attempt to frighten the real killer away? In my experience, there is only one answer: the hyaena will not wait a moment, he will just vanish.

But a pair of hyaena will make a cacophony of sound. It is a war of nerves. Sometimes a panther cannot tolerate the strange medley of noise and slinks away voluntarily. But should the panther be determined to hold his ground, a shouting match ensues until the nerves of one or other gives way. If the panther becomes threatening, the hyaena or hyaenas hesitate no longer; they bolt. For after all they are nothing but large, clumsy, unintelligent dogs, and in a straight encounter a panther would be able to dispose of them with ease. They are far too slow in their movements and too stupid to be able to withstand a determined attack, especially as a panther is an animal that can move like lightning. Even if two or three hyaenas were there they would lack the intelligence to co-ordinate their actions and fight together.

With a tiger, even half a dozen hyaenas would not stand the ghost of a chance. Although far larger, heavier and stronger than the wild dogs, they lack the latters' keen intelligence, swiftness of movement and almost suicidal courage. Yet it is strange that wild dogs do not as a rule molest them. It is a common sight to observe jackals and hyaenas feeding on the same kill. At such times they ignore each other's presence completely, while keeping a sharp lookout for the sudden return of the rightful owner of the kill, who would undoubtedly take immediate reprisals.

Despite their ungainly build, hyaenas can in emergency put up a fair turn of running speed. To an observer. they appear to assume a galloping gait, much like a horse, and run askew. Perhaps this is because the hyaena holds his head at an angle when travelling fast, so giving his whole body a crooked appearance.

Hyaenas are the scavengers of the jungle, doing useful work by devouring kills and dead animals that would otherwise decompose slowly and pollute the atmosphere. Particularly in dense forest, where vultures cannot operate, because the heavy vegetation prevents them from 'spotting' the kill, hyaenas, jackals, wild pigs, and sometimes a bear, all help to clear away a decomposing carcass rapidly.

Hyaenas eat only dead animals. Occasionally they may kill a fawn, a calf, dog or goat—always an animal far weaker than themselves. A hyaena's way of killing some small, defenceless animal is to sidle up to it, suddenly dip his head at an angle and grab the smaller creature by the throat. There is no denying the tremendous strength of those jaws or the grip that can crack a bone or bite through it with the greatest of ease. But the hyaena lacks the courage to attack any living creature unless it be far smaller than himself and quite defenceless.

THE CALL OF THE MAN-EATER

A hyaena has a long mane of greyish-black hair from the back of the neck to the root of the bushy tail. When alarmed or excited or angry, this mane stands erect, increasing the height of the animal by about six inches and giving it a peculiarly flattish appearance. Despite a fierce and hideous face, the eyes have a peculiarly soulful expression. Although such a vile feeder, the hyaena's whole coat is extremely clean and free of any odour. In this respect they differ from vultures, which really stink. I have also found Jackie singularly free from ticks, fleas or other vermin, or at least he carries far fewer than the felines and deer. A full-grown male weighs over six stones and the bitch about a stone less. She gives birth to four or five puppies at a time and as usual with the young of carnivorous animals, no sooner are the eyes opened than they supplement their diet of mother's milk with partially digested raw meat, eaten by their mothers and then vomited out for their benefit. Although nocturnal in their wild state, I have come upon hyaenas basking in the morning sunlight at the entrances to their dens or caves. Occasionally, and especially in the foothills or the Nilgiris around Segur and Anaikutty, I have found them in broad daylight, lying up in thick grass or under a thorny bush beneath which they have made a burrow.

The first story in the book concerned an active partnership between a jackal and tiger. It may well be asked whether this is a common occurrence, for the question has been hotly debated for years by very experienced Indian hunters. My own opinion is—and it is only opinion and therfore not necessarily correct—that a jackal, being a highly intelligent creature, first attaches himself to a tiger or a panther as a parasite, knowing fully well that he is thereby sure of finding food, because the tiger or panther must kill to eat, and eat to live. By their very nature and by their habit of leaving the kill during daylight, the big cats also leave sufficient pickings for the parasite. During all this time the jackal takes very good care to keep its distance, and the tiger or panther may not even be aware of its existence in the earlier stages. As time goes on, the jackal—always the more intelligent of the two animals—finds that the habit of following its host about from kill to kill continues to pay very high dividends. It may therefore happen quite naturally that the jackal adopts the practice of voicing a call should it come to discover a prospective victim, thus relaying the information to its host. The tiger or panther, although not actually relying upon the jackal to find its food, has by this time become accustomed to its presence and, being primarily a hunter after large prey to keep itself alive and provide a hearty meal, does not worry unduly about a creature which would not provide of itself nearly enough for a square meal. When the jackal begins to call, the carnivore knows something is afoot and is made aware of the presence of a victim.

It is commonly thought that tigers and panthers have a keen sense of smell, but this is definitely not so. Neither animal eats at the spot where the kill is made. Invariably it drags its victim to a shelter of some sort, such as a bush or *nullah*. When coming to eat a second time, the killer does follow the drag-mark by sniffing along the ground. It seems to remember exactly where it has left its kill, as it may return from any direction quite irrespective of which way the wind is blowing, and does not necessarily retrace its own footsteps. Further, I have often sat on the ground for both animals, in 'hides' of one description or another, and by remaining absolutely still, I have, regardless of the direction of the wind, had them approach to practically within touching distance without becoming aware of my presence. Even a half-developed sense of smell under such conditions would have warned them of my proximity, but they have remained completely ignorant while I kept quite still and made no sound. This in itself clearly shows that neither animal has any sense of smell whatever, although they possess the keenest sight, detecting the slightest movement, and the acutest hearing, picking up the faintest sound. The marvellous night-sight of both tigers and panthers enables them to conduct a soundless stalk through the densest jungle on the darkest of nights, an attribute that in itself makes them formidable enough without additional gifts.

The uninitiated townsman might be tempted to think that the bold colours of a tiger and the even more vivid coat of a panther would make them both extremely conspicuous in a jungle. But they are not. The tiger, which hunts invariably at night or in the evening, becomes invisible when he 'freezes' or crouches motionless, his skin blending with the background of bushes, grass, trees and earth. The panther is even less conspicuous, even in broad daylight; he can lie so flat to the ground, under a bush no longer than himself, or on a background of dried leaves and grass, that again, unless he moves, he is quite invisible. This blending of colours is one of the main hazards in following up a wounded animal of either species; the hunter is liable almost to tread on it before he becomes aware of the creature's presence.

I have often been asked if it is really possible for a man to call like a tiger with sufficient realism to bring a tiger near. Have human lungs the capacity to utter such a tremendous sound? The answer to the last question is a very definite 'no'. Human lungs can never equal those of a tiger. But that means only that a man cannot call loud enough to attract the attention of a tiger some distance away. If the tiger is near, a well-imitated call can certainly bring him nearer. The factor that really attracts the tiger is curiosity. So long as one is experienced enough and skilled enough to imitate a tiger's call closely, even if the timbre differs somewhat, he will be drawn by a curiosity to find the 'tiger who is making that funny noise'.

The same can be said of a panther or many other wild animals. After all, in America various gadgets are sold that imitate the cries of moose, deer, wild-buck and various birds. I have a cousin who, with the aid of a blade of grass, can call exactly like a junglefowl or a spurfowl, and regularly lures these birds before shooting them. The only difference in imitating a tiger's call is that no instrument is used; but the principle is the same.

Tracking is a fascinating art, and, compared with some of the aborigines with whom it has been my privilege and pleasure to go out, I would regard myself as an absolute tyro at the game. An observant person who has seen many tiger and panther tracks may be led to ask: 'Why is it that a tiger sometimes leaves a double track, one that shows the pugmarks of all four feet, while at other times he leaves a single track as if he had only two legs like a man? And why does a panther, particularly the average-sized animals living close to villages, invariably make a double track only?

I think the answer is that the tiger, out for a casual stroll and not on the hunt, just ambles along serenely and leaves a double track. As soon as he becomes aware of the presence of a quarry and begins stalking, he exercises caution: he slows his pace and probably 'feels' the ground with each forefoot before placing it, thus making certain that he does not tread on a twig or leaf that might crackle and betray his presence. As an added precaution, he brings up his hind foot and places it in exactly the spot that his forefoot vacates as he takes the next step forward. Of course, he follows this practice instinctively and not by deliberation.

As to the panther, who 'creeps' the last stages of his stalk, with his belly close to the ground, he perhaps has no

THE CALL OF THE MAN-EATER

opportunity of placing his hind feet in the spots vacated by his forefeet. A fact that appears to bear out this conjecture—and let me emphasize once again that it is, after all, nothing more than conjecture—is that, whereas one can trail a tiger to the very spot from which he launches his final attack, it is seldom possible to do this when following a panther's spoor. The last few feet of the trail become indistinct, indicating the panther had begun to creep.

Another question I am asked is whether a tiger can really imitate a sambar's call, and if he does, whether it is in order to ambush a sambar. The answer to the first part of this question is very definitely yes. I have heard it happen. But to answer the second part of the question is difficult, for I have heard a tiger call like a sambar when approaching its kill, a young bull, in a stretch of jungle near Tagarthy where there were no sambar at all. On another occasion, in the Chamala Valley, a tiger called like a sambar when approaching his own kill, a dead buffalo, and when only a few feet away from it; in that stretch of forest there were many sambar.* But this tiger was not hunting; he was returning to his own kill. Both these examples appear to indicate that the 'pook' made by the tigers, although closely resembling the call of a sambar, more like that of a doe than a stag, were not made with the object of decoying a real sambar. The call may therefore express anticipation, contentment, hunger or enjoyment. Perhaps it is a call inviting a tigress to the feast, or it may be a kind of mating call, although I do not think so myself, as in neither of the cases mentioned was a tigress near.

The tiger—and I am now referring to the ordinary male and not to a man-eater—is generally an inoffensive beast and

---

* See: *Nine Man-Eaters and One Rogue*.

will do his best to avoid man. Even should a human being intrude upon his privacy, the tiger will slink off. So will a tigress for that matter, although she is more apt to growl or show some degree of resentment. There is an exception to this general rule, however, and that is at the time of mating and especially in the act of mating. Tigers are very fierce then and are apt to attack on sight, and will persist in their attack till they kill the man who has intruded upon their privacy. It may be a desire to 'show off' to the tigress, although I think it is due rather to the high degree of sexual excitement into which they lash themselves. Anyway, one can hardly blame the tiger for resenting being spied upon at that particular moment.

I had rather a narrow escape when accompanying a friend, a German photographer who wanted to wander into a tiger sanctuary at night and take flashlight photographs. I tried to dissuade him on the ground that tigers are far from being photogenic, but he was adamant. It was early in October when we went, somewhat ahead of the regular mating season, which extends from the end of November till the end of January, and we were both on foot and unarmed, except for the flash-light camera, since in a sanctuary shooting is strictly prohibited and one cannot wander with a firearm of any description.

But as luck would have it, we suddenly came upon a pair of tigers. Fortunately they were not actually mating, but they resented our intrusion nevertheless. They growled, and side by side left the little clearing where we had surprised them and advanced on to the track along which we had just come.

The impulse was very strong to show these tigers what we could do by way of a sprint. But had we given in to that temptation, I am sure the pair of lovers would have been equally tempted to pursue us. So we 'retreated according to plan', which means a pretty fast walk while flashing the torch constantly behind us. Nevertheless the resentful pair followed us for well over a mile. At one particularly nasty spot, where the track traversed a deep and overgrown ravine, they galloped up to about twenty-five yards behind us. We coughed loudly and began to talk at a pitch that would have done credit to any public orator. This caused the enterprising tigers to fall back once more, and so we made our way out of a situation that was certainly for a moment a matter of touch and go.

The tigress usually goes into isolation before the cubs are born, because her mate has an inclination to kill and eat his offspring. She generally chooses a cave, although occasionally she may litter in a ravine or other overgrown spot. On an average, three to four cubs are born. These are fed on milk, and later on vomited meat, till they can digest stronger food. As they grow older they accompany the mother on her foraging expeditions. Then, after a while, papa rejoins them and the parents start teaching them the art of killing by breaking the neck of their victims. In this process much wasteful slaughter sometimes takes place; as many as four or five cattle from one herd are slain merely to give the juniors a lesson or afford them some practice. The young tigers frequently make a mess of the job, succeeding only in mauling their victims rather than killing them outright.

When the cubs are half-grown, one sometimes meets a family party of tigers, consisting of the male, female and several large cubs. I myself stumbled across a family of four one night at a place called Kodihalli near Tagarthy, when I was out for a night walk. They had just drunk at a stream and ascended the bank. First mama appeared. She saw me, growled, leapt across the track and began a peculiar vigorous mewing. This brought out the two cubs, who were about the

THE CREATURES OF THE JUNGLE

size of spaniels. Seeing the torchlight, they were not in the least alarmed, but advanced a few feet playfully. At this unseemly behaviour, mama protested loudly by growling. Papa, who was in the rear, thought this behaviour intolerable. He sprang on to the path in front of them to block their progress and roared menacingly. That roar had the desired effect of not only frightening the cubs back to mama, but myself almost to the point of shooting him. I was glad I did not do so when I realized his intentions were merely to admonish his playful offspring rather than to attack me.

Tigers have certain habits peculiar to themselves, in which they differ from panthers. Some of them—not all—make a practice of standing on their hind feet against the trunks of certain soft-barked trees, reaching as high as they can, and cleaning the claws of their forefeet by raking them through the soft bark. Their method of passing their dung is also different. In this respect a panther is a true cat; he will scratch up the earth beside a jungle pathway and afterwards carefully cover his excrement up. But not a tiger; he will scrape a patch of ground bare, about a foot square, sometimes right in the centre of the path. While doing this he appears to 'dance' in a crouched position with his hind feet together, trembling visibly. When passing their dung they hold their tails up ludicrously high. The dung is a sticky, black, tarry substance, and is left uncovered.

Another difference on which I have had occasion to remark is their way of feeding. Tigers start on their kills at the rectum, often biting off the tail of the animal to facilitate proceedings. Then they make an entrance and, inserting a paw into the carcass, scoop out the intestines and stomach, which they generally remove a few feet before eating. Panthers on the contrary are dirty feeders, and get the stomach and dung of their kill mixed up with the meat. But a large 'thendu', or forest panther, eats in the manner of a tiger and not like his smaller brethren.

Tigers are intolerant of the heat, which is not the case with panthers. They delight in lying up in cool and shady places, and may be seen submerged in a rill with only their heads above the surface. They are also fond of swimming and frequently cross rivers. The panther, which is a truer cat in every sense of the word, detests water even to the extent of curtailing his hunting expeditions on a rainy night. The only circumstance that will force him to swim a river might be a pack of wild dogs hot on his trail, or a forest fire. Under compelling conditions he can swim quite well.

Another difference in habit between the two animals is revealed during the series of meals each makes on any large animal he has killed. In between each gorge a tiger apparently must drink a good deal of water. Knowing this, it is fairly easy to locate the presence of the killer at the nearest water hole or stream to the kill and organize a 'beat' accordingly, provided the hunter is the type of man who prefers beating to sitting up in a *machan* and awaiting the tiger's return. But this is not so with a panther. He does not require nearly so much water, so he is difficult to locate.

Tigers often get into fights with bison, wild boar, bears and even members of their own kind. They are fond of eating porcupines, but they do not always emerge unscathed from such an encounter. A few miles from Tagarthy I found a dead tigress with a number of porcupine quills in her face. Tigers will also kill panthers, and for this reason jungles where tigers are plentiful hold few panthers, who give way to their larger and more powerful cousins. Panthers are also not nearly so belligerent or courageous, and instances are known where even a village cur that has been attacked has turned on the panther in sheer desperation and the attacker has decamped.

THE CREATURES OF THE JUNGLE

Tigers are inordinately fond of pork, while panthers appear to consider monkey-meat a delicacy. Both felines will go to extraordinary lengths to procure these respective titbits and show great reluctance to abandon a favourite kill. Indeed, the tiger becomes really belligerent if one attempts to drive him off a succulent wild-pig, and a panther will demonstrate violently over the carcass of a langur monkey. After killing their prey, at least as far as my experience goes, I have not found a tiger suck the blood from the animal while retaining his grip on its throat. Perhaps this is because they kill quicker, the neck of the victim being quickly broken, while a longer and more painful death by suffocation is the lot of the panther's prey. A panther often sucks the blood of its victim.

Tigers are far more fastidious in their food than panthers, and it is therefore a great mistake to tie up a very old, emaciated or diseased bull or buffalo as bait for a tiger. Once, while at Anaikutty, the only bait I could procure was a bull suffering from the last stages of foot-and-mouth disease and at death's door. Pug-marks, the next morning, revealed that the tiger had come, walked around the bait, sat down in front of it, and from various scratches in the ground I could deduce that he even set about playing with it. But he never killed or even hurt the sick bull, which succumbed to the disease the next day.

Tigers will sometimes drag or carry their kills, even a very heavy animal, up and over considerable obstacles. I have used the word 'carry', for that is exactly what I mean. One rainy afternoon a tiger killed a large brown bull in the middle of a cultivated field hardly two furlongs fron Tagarthy village. He carried this animal, slung across his back with one hoof trailing along the wet ground, for nearly half a mile down hill into a jungle ravine. Another tiger dragged a large ploughing-bull to a fence, and leapt over it with the dead animal. Panthers sometimes drag their kills, such as a deer or goat, into a tree, probably to protect them against other predatory animals.

Tigers sometimes have a funny way of resting on a hot day. They will lie on their backs on the cool sand of a *nullah* under the shade of a tree, and fall asleep with all four legs up in the air. They are also fond of taking sand-baths and of rolling on dry leaves. Perhaps they do this to scratch their backs and rid themselves of ticks. These pests are always to be found in large numbers on a tiger after it has been recently killed.

Tigers are great hunters and cover many miles a night in search of food. Moreover, they have a habit of following a specified 'beat' of territory which may extend up to a hundred miles, always repeating the same route in the same direction. This habit, as I have remarked in my earlier stories, is of considerable help in plotting the probable time of return of a man-eater to a particular locality, and the estimate is always correct to within a week or two.

It has been proved that the tiger is a comparatively recent immigrant into India, which before his arival was largely inhabited by the Asiatic lion. Then the tiger came down from the north—from Siberia and Manchuria—and the lion slowly began to lose ground before that more active animal. The tiger has slightly diminished in size and become rather richer in colouring, assuming a russet brown with black markings in place of a greyish colouration, but still with the black markings of the original immigrants. But he has not yet been able to conquer his intolerance of the heat, which forces him to drink water frequently and to lie up in cool places, often submerging himself in a pool.

As far as evidence can show, the panther, like the sloth bear is a true inhabitant of the country and has been in India from the earliest traceable times. Panthers are widely distributed throughout the world. Not only are they found in South America as thickset jaguars, but in Africa, the Middle East, Asia Minor, Persia, throughout India and Ceylon, Burma, Malaya, Indonesia, Indo-China, China and also Manchuria. With such a wide distribution it is to be expected that the animal will vary considerably in size, shape and habits, according to the territory. But fundamentally they all belong to the same species. Since I am concerned only with India, and in particular with South India, I can only confine my remarks to the local variety.

The panthers of India vary considerably in size and colour. Large specimens of the 'thendu' or jungle panther attain up to seven feet six inches in length and weigh upwards of 160 pounds. They have a rich, tawny coat with large rosettes and long fur, particularly below the belly, and large squarish heads. Such panthers can kill fairly big animals; for example, a well-developed domestic bull, a sambar hind, or even a pony of moderate size. Their manner of killing is the same as the tigers', in that they usually break their victims' necks rather than strangle them to death. And they begin to eat from the hindquarters, in the same way as a tiger does. Invariably these large specimens inhabit fairly forested areas.

At the other extreme we have the village or 'monkey panther', an adult animal, rarely over five feet long and weighing around sixty pounds. They are generally of a palish yellow colour, with small rosettes, short hair and small, roundish heads. Their diet is very comprehensive, and includes a variety of small creatures such as dogs, cats, goats, fowl (both domestic and wild), rabbits, birds, lizards, and even frogs and crabs. They are found in the vicinity of villages, among rocks, and in sparse scrub though the small panther may sometimes occur in deep jungle, just as a thendu may sometimes live in scrub or on a hillock near a village.

Because of this sharp contrast, it was long contended that there were two distinct animals. That theory has now disappeared: there is only one animal, its appearance and diet varying according to its surroundings.

Black panthers occur on rare occasions. They are scarcely jet black, but rather an extreme dark brown when viewed at close range. Even at a distance, when they appear quite black, the rosette markings are still visible when light falls on them at an angle. Black panthers are not a distinct species. They are examples of melanism, and occur generally in the jungles where the rainfall is heavy and the vegetation dense. Occasionally they occur in other forests, too. A normal mother may have a litter of two or three cubs, one of which may be black. It is curious that its melanism should recur only among panthers and not tigers, but cases have been recorded of tigers that are almost white, and of sloth bears that are almost brown or even grey.

A noticeable characteristic of panthers is the way their tails vary in length. The small panthers seem to have longer tails, and the larger panthers to have shorter ones. Panthers can tolerate great heat and do not require much water. In fact, they actively dislike water. I have often observed, when looking at pug-marks, that a panther will make a considerable detour to avoid crossing even a few inches of water or mud, unless of course he has to wade a stream. Tigers have no compunction about wading or swimming and often welcome an opportunity.

In my opinion, a panther is by far the more intelligent animal. There is a definite purpose about his actions. For instance, around about 5 p.m., before the sun begins to set and the air to cool, a panther will lie prone on a rock on a hill-top, scanning the country below for prey, such as goats, sheep, dogs, etc., as they return to their villages. Seeing a likely victim, he will stealthily drop downhill by the shortest route, stalk his prey, and kill it within a matter of minutes. Of course, tigers are great hunters too; but their hunting seems to me a matter of instinct combined with wonderful skill, rather than of forethought.

A pantheress with cubs will defend them desperately. Tigresses, surprisingly as it may seem, will sometimes desert their offspring, although I had a very uncomfortable experience once to the contrary.* Panthers are particularly fond of catching and eating monkeys, piglings and porcupines, although they will give an adult wild boar a very wide berth. As regards porcupines, however, at Gummalapur in the Salem district I came upon a burrow which, by the tracks in the soft sand at its entrance, was occupied by both a porcupine and a panther. This burrow was on the banks of a stream known as the Muthiyalamma Holay. I made it my job to sit in a tree immediately overlooking this spot the same evening, because I wanted to satisfy myself as to the truth. The poojarees had frequently told me that porcupines and panthers lived together, but I never quite believed these tales as I knew these creatures to be instinctive enemies. It was a comparatively lonely spot, and just before 6 p.m. out came the pantheress, an adult of average size. Later dusk fell, but it was quite dark before I heard a rattling sound, made by the quills of the porcupine, and shone the beam of my torch in time to see a large specimen emerging from the same hole, between rocks on the riverbank. Do not ask me for an explanation of this strange fellowship, for I cannot give one.

Panthers are much more versatile than tigers. They can live in fairly open country with little scrub, so long as there is shelter among rocks and boulders. They move about much

---

* See: *Man-Eaters and Jungle Killers*, George Allen & Unwin

more in daylight than do their larger cousins. They are also great climbers. I remember that at Muttur many year ago I shot one that had climbed to the top of a giant *muthee* tree, in which it had cornered a terrified young monkey. Panthers are also less afraid of a light, particularly if it happens to come from a lantern or other oil-lamp.

Following up a wounded panther is often more dangerous than following up a tiger, for two reasons. His colour blends with the jungle and makes him invisible until almost trodden upon, and he rarely gives a preliminary warning growl, as does a tiger. Fortunately, to offset this the panther frequently lacks the courage to charge home. He attacks vigorously, but swerves off at the last minute. Even when he pounces on a man, it is just to scratch and bite violently for a few seconds. Then he bolts. He does not stop to kill the man, as does a tiger.

There is one great difference between a man-eating tiger and a panther that has formed the same habit. Once a tiger acquires a taste for human flesh he will become a permanent addict; he will go on killing people till he is killed. A man-eating panther will never take to eating human flesh alone, nor will he depend on it; he will continue to kill and eat his normal food as well. Sometimes he will cease man-killing altogether for long periods and behave like a normal panther. But sooner or later he will recommence his depredations against the human race. This makes him all the more dangerous and difficult to find and shoot. Even when he has shot a panther in the belief that it is the man-eater he has been after, the hunter can never be certain he has not killed just an ordinary panther, and that the culprit is still not at large. The only test is time—and the fact that no more human beings are killed in that particular area.

Panthers, living as they do, much more in contact with the human race, are far more audacious than tigers. I remember many years ago having dinner with my uncle, aunt and cousins at their home at Yercaud, on the Shevaroy Hills, while the seven cats they owned were eating from as many plates on the verandah of the bungalow. We heard an unearthly yowl from one of the cats and rushed out to see a panther leap off the verandah with one of them in its mouth. Thereupon we made a great hubbub and released the dogs. Somehow the cat escaped, but minus one hind leg. Martha, for that was the cat's name recovered from her wound and lived on three legs for many years. There are many instances of pet dogs being carried off literally from between one's feet when out walking in a jungle. And more than once I have sat in the midst of a poultry farm for a sneaking 'monkey' panther that had developed the habit of having chicken for supper several times a week.

Panthers are generally shot from *machans* when over their kills and rarely in a beat. They are too clever and too cunning to be driven, and can hide too well. This is another example of their superior intelligence. One exception to this general rule, however, is their habit of returning to a kill even after being fired at and missed. Tigers rarely do this. I have heard of another case where a panther returned to its kill where a lighted lantern had been placed a few yards away, though I was not present to witness it.

I think it is rather unfortunate on the whole that this animal is classed as 'vermin' by the government and the Forest departments in the various states of India where, in some places, no licence is required to hunt him. Although the species is still very numerous throughout the country, I feel it deserves a better fate. The spectacle of a well-marked panther stalking through jungle dappled with sunlight and shade is even more beautiful than that of a tiger. It is the most handsome wild animal in India. The call of a panther—a guttural, sawing, rasping grunt—is heard when the male calls to his partner, and sometimes when he approaches his kill. It is a distinctive sound and remarkably loud and far-carrying for an animal of such moderate size. In the jungle, panthers exact a heavy toll of the small species of deer—spotted deer, jungle-sheep and mouse-deer—which form their staple food, together with wild sows and piglets. The larger boars they leave severely alone. In village areas the diet is changed to include domestic goats and dogs; in some villages the dog population has been completely wiped out by an enterprising panther or two. At the Jowlagiri forest bungalow I walked out on to the verandah one night and almost stumbled over a panther that was lying there eyeing Nipper, my dog, who was asleep under the dining table. Apart from the animals listed above, panthers will kill smaller creatures and birds of all descriptions. In turn they are frequently killed and eaten by tigers, so that in a locality where the latter exist permanently, panthers are exceptionally shy and cunning and are sometimes not to be found at all. They will be tempted to rob from a tiger's kill, but while doing so are very much on the alert against the sudden return of the rightful owner. Finally, they will eat carrion and feast on carcasses in a very advanced stage of decay. I have found that tigers do not do this in southern India, nor as a rule will they return more than once to do so, for they are tremendous feeders and by that time, if undisturbed, have eaten all there is. But panthers return to their kills two and even three nights in succession.

These reminiscences would not be complete without something about that magnificent giant among wild animals, the elephant, which has been with mankind, in some form or other, from prehistoric times. There are only two distinct species of elephant in existence today, the African and the Asiatic although there are variations to each of these two main divisions. The African elephant is the larger animal, often attaining a height of twelve feet at the shoulder. In appearance he differs considerably from his Asiatic cousin. He has enormous ears for one thing, and very long and heavy tusks. His back is concave, with a distinct saddle, and he has only three toes on each hind foot. His forehead recedes sharply, and this, with his long ears, gives his head a rather pointed appearance. Even the females have tusks. But the Asiatic elephant differs in a number of ways. The largest of them reaches to no more than ten feet in height. The ears are much smaller, and the tusks are shorter and not nearly so heavy, nor so thick. In some cases the back is convex, with a slight hump, and in others relatively level. There are four toes on each hind foot. The trunk is not so ringed nor so rugged as in the African species, with a slight depression at the top between the right and left halves of the skull; there are noticeable hollows at each temple. The females never grow tusks.

As with the African variety, the Asiatic elephant also has its pigmy variety in some countries, such as Ceylon and Malaya, where both males and females are without tusks. Tuskless males, called muknas, are sometimes found among the herds of the larger variety in India, although not very common in South India. The fact that such tuskless bulls are not necessarily alone, but live with tusked males in a normal herd, is evidence enough to counter the theory that they are a variety on their own, although there is no explanation why their tusks have never grown. Such tuskless males seem to develop into more bulky animals than do most males with normal tusks.

The idea that a 'rogue' elephant is mad is quite wrong. It is also often thought that a rogue elephant is always an elephant in a state of *musth*. Actually these terms refer to three quite different conditions affecting a male elephant. The condition of *musth* is only temporary, lasting from a few weeks to three months, and corresponds to rut among stags. It is directly connected with a state of sexual excitement, and passes away after the condition has subsided. This period of *musth* mainly attacks male elephants, during which time they are restless, quarrelsome, excitable and quick-tempered. They fight with the other bulls in the herd, who sometimes combine to expel them till the fit subsides. But this is not always so, as *musth* elephants occasionally exist in a herd on amicable terms with the others and particularly the very young calves.

An elephant in *musth* is invariably a very dangerous creature to meet. He is liable to attack without provocation and on sight. Being a natural and periodic condition in all elephants, tame males also become *musth*, and when that happens they are not put to work but are kept securely chained by their hind legs till the attack passes off, when they return to normality. The condition is a glandular one. The temples become swollen and puffed. The overflow discharges through orifices in both cheeks, situated between the temple and ear, and runs down the elephant's face as dark oily matter. There is also a seminal discharge. An animal in *musth* emits a peculiar odour because of these secretions. Many accidents have occurred and people have been killed by tame elephants when in a state of *musth*. Generally the *mahout*, or elephant-driver is the first victim.

A rogue elephant has little the matter with him. He has become a rogue because he has lost his fear of human beings and has formed the habit of pursuing and killing them without provocation. The reasons are many. To begin with, when in a state of *musth* he may have attacked people, chased them and perhaps killed a couple. This has caused him to lose his inherent fear of the human race and to realise how very helpless they really are. So he continues his habit even after the *musth* condition has long passed off. Or he may have had a fight with another elephant or elephants and been expelled from the herd. In a paroxysm of impotent fury, he may have come across some unfortunate human being, who fled at his approach, causing him to give chase and finally kill him. Thereafter he has found this an amusing pastime. Thirdly, he may have been so wounded or harried by humans that one day he turned the tables by attacking and killing one of his molesters. Realizing from that moment that humans can be killed easily, he lost no chance in putting an end to one at every opportunity.

The 'rogue' condition in an elephant is akin to that of a tiger or panther becoming a man-eater, except that I do not know of any rogue elephant that has eaten any part of his human victim. My friend Freddie Galiffe, however, tells me that a small rogue elephant shot recently just outside the limits of the Annay Chowk Reserved Forest, and not far from his estate, had a human thigh-bone in its stomach. I have not been able to verify this for myself, but such a find, if authentic would be unique in the annals of rogue-elephant history.

A mad elephant is one that has become mentally deranged. The animal may have contracted hydrophobia through the bite of a mad dog (in which case we cannot really say that it became mentally deranged in the accepted sense of the term), or it may have fallen victim to heatstroke or overwork (in which case it is still not really mentally deranged). Personally I have never come across an instance of this sort, although I have read of such cases occurring in the stables of Indian potentates who kept elephants, and in the government *kraals* housing elephants that work in the forests.

Elephants have poor sight, but a very good sense of hearing and a truly marvellous sense of smell. For this reason, any attempt to approach a wild elephant for purposes of observation, photography or shooting, can only be made from a direction that is upwind. Otherwise a long stalk will end with the discovery that the quarry has long since decamped. It is said that wild elephant can smell each other three miles away, and a human being one mile away, if he is downwind.

Twice the circumference of the forefoot of an elephant gives its exact height at the shoulder, a fact that is always used in estimating the height of rogue elephant that have been proscribed for shooting and in identifying those shot with measurements that have been recorded previously from the tracks of the rogue. When an elephant collapses after being shot, the most certain indication that he is really dead is the protrusion of the penis to its fullest extent outside the sheath.

These animals live for well over a hundred years, and there is a case on record where an animal has reached 150 years of age. Indications of old age in an animal are generally its lanky and underfed condition (the teeth have been so worn that they cannot masticate the food, and the droppings therefore consist of undigested leaves), hollow cheeks and sunken eyes and temples, ears that are considerably turned-over at the top edges and ragged at the bottom, and a condition of hairlessness with a sallow, very-crinkled hide. Authorities on the subject state that for the first fifteen years or so the top edges of the ears are perfectly erect. Then they begin to turn over at the rate of an inch for every thirty years of life, but I have no personal knowledge of the correctness of this assertion.

Those who have constant dealings with elephants consider them very intelligent animals, although a few hunters are inclined to disagree. Judging from their habits in the wild state, and the number of purposes to which their services can be put when tamed, they are decidedly clever and sagacious. But they have one undeniabe feature: their lack of courage, amounting to arrant cowardice, for creatures so huge. A mature wild boar, when aroused, has many times the courage. An elephant may attack a man by surprise, relying on his mighty bulk and blood-chilling, frenzied trumpeting to strike terror into the victim. But let a man stand his ground, clap, shout and wave his hands, and the elephant will invariably swerve off and bolt at the last moment. Not so the wild boar. He charges home, right to the smoking muzzle of a rifle, with several bullets in his body—unless, of course, one has already succeeded in piercing his brave heart or some other vital spot.

Many elephants suffer from a form of leucoderma: the skin becomes speckled by white patches, especially on the trunk and ears. To posses such an animal is considered very lucky, although they have an unsightly appearance. Perhaps the superstition is only a reflection of the fact that the so-called 'white' elephant are considered very important for religious purposes among Buddhists in Siam as well as in Burma.

The female elephant breeds about once in every two and a half years, while the period of gestation averages twenty months. She is fond of her calf, which makes her dangerous if encountered suddenly when her offspring is in the vicinity. I had cause to know this only too well when I took out a party of Americans working with me in Bangalore to photograph a herd of these animals. Unfortunately, the beaters who were to drive the herd along the bed of the Secret River, not far from Anchetty, in a direction that would make them pass the concealed cameramen, fell foul of a female with a calf. She promptly charged them and they broke back towards the place where the rest of us were comfortably seated, bringing the infuriated female behind them. I can assure you we all ran very, very fast that day, leaving a considerable portion of our clothing and ourselves on the thorny shrub through which we dashed. Luckily the calf could not keep up with the pace set by us and by its mother. It began to squeal at being left in the lurch and this caused the female to abandon the chase and return to her youngster. Otherwise there would have been a nasty accident, for none of us was armed, since the shooting of any elephant except a declared rogue is very strictly forbidden.

When on the march, females and their calves head the herd, tuskers bringing up the rear. It is the mothers that regulate the halting places according to the availability of grazing and water in relation to the ages of the calves. When a calf is born the whole herd delays its march for a week till the baby is strong enough to keep pace with them. Bull elephants make but little attempt to defend their young when danger threatens. On the other hand, they frequently head the line of flight. While fording a river, the mother holds her offspring before her on the surface by supporting it under the belly with her trunk. They can swim with ease for long distances. When encountering obstacles or going uphill, she frequently pushes her baby in front of her. Calves drink milk from their mothers for many months, until they are comparatively big. They do this by sucking with their mouths and not through their trunks; the mother's breasts are located immediately behind her forelegs.

Herds are constantly on the move as the grazing becomes exhausted. They drink water twice daily, just before sunset and at dawn, but enjoy water-baths as well as sand-baths at other times during the day, especially in the hot weather, if opportunities occur. They are very affectionate towards each other and solicitous of the welfare of their young at all times, and a herd behaves like one big happy family. The members are often relatives, due to constant inbreeding. I have never watched them mating, because I have never had the chance; but poojarees have assured me that the male endeavours to cross the female only after persuading her into a depression, or on to lower ground, to facilitate his performing the act, which he does in an almost erect posture behind the female.

When digesting their food they make a variety of sounds, including a low, rumbling, thunder-like noise; a bellow resembling that made by a domestic bull, but infinitely louder, when they are contented; pig-like squeals when they are particularly happy; a short, sharp trumpeting when alarmed or attacking; and sharp rapping sound as a warning to an intruder and to alert each other. This last is made by striking the trunk against the ground while blowing air through it sharply.

Elephants even suck their fingers—represented by the tips of their trunks—when in doubt. It is amusing to watch a bewildered elephant stand with the tip of its trunk in its own mouth while wondering what to do next, for all the world like some timid little boy sucking his thumb.

Unlike deer, who shed their horns periodically to grow another pair, elephants retain their tusks for life. Should one of them break in a fight, the animal goes through the rest of its life with a damaged member. It is a mistake to think the tusks are employed for pushing over trees; the elephant does that by placing his forehead against the bole and pushing hard while using the weight of his body. Elephants are most careful, when going downhill, not to trip or slip for fear of breaking a leg. They are very conscious of their own weight and the injuries they may incur by falling on a decline, or by placing a foot into a hole, or by stepping into a bog or mire and becoming stuck. For this reason, if a man is chased by an elephant, he has far better chance of escaping by running downhill, rather than uphill or on the level. Elephants cannot jump, either horizontally or vertically, for at no time will they trust themselves with all four feet off the ground. For that matter, they do not run in the accepted sense of the word,

THE CALL OF THE MAN-EATER

but use a fast shuffling stride which might reach a speed of a little over fifteen miles an hour. They can maintain this pace steadily for some miles.

A fairly good runner can outpace a pursuing elephant for a reasonable distance, but it is problematical how long he could maintain his lead, particularly when fleeing through dense or thorny jungle, among tree-trunks, clumps of bushes and especially thorns. Precious time is lost in going around such obstructions, and considerable damage is done to one's person and clothing in trying to negotiate the barrier, while the pursuing pachyderm just crashes through.

No discussion about elephants would be complete without a mention of that intriguing question: where do elephants die? A wealth of superstition and conjecture has arisen over this question in all countries in which these ponderous animals exist in their wild state. In Africa, for a long time, they believed in the existence of secret elephant cemeteries, and more than one expedition has set out to find the treasure in ivory that must be there. But none succeeded. In Ceylon, Burma, Malaya and Siam the same question is asked and the same belief is held. But no proof has been forthcoming in any of these countries.

The aborigines of southern India are divided in their beliefs in this matter. The karumbas and poojarees support the 'secret-cemetery' theory, while the Sholagas contend that elephants never die at all, which is obviously incorrect, for every living thing must die. But the former theory is equally untenable, because there is no corner of the jungles of southern India that has not been trodden by the foot of man. There are no unexplored places there.

Where then do elephants die when they grow old? In all my years of jungle-wandering, I have never come upon the carcass of an elephant that has died a natural death. I have found a small female that had been killed by a pair of tigers.

And of course the Moyar valley rogue got caught in sinking-sand. But none of these endings can be described as natural death. So the question remains unanswered and the fable continues. At most, we can conjecture or suggest a possible solution, of which there may be more than one.

Twice have I found elephant bones in the mud and ooze of the Cauvery river when the water sank abnormally during an excessively hot and dry season. One of these was a section of the spinal column. This I found at Hogenaikal. The other was a thighbone picked up at Sangam. Both these places harbour elephants and are on the banks of the Cauvery river. Do aged elephants, when they find dissolution approaching, deliberately commit suicide by drowning themselves? The idea is improbable, as they are instinctively powerful swimmers. Further the urge to live is strong in all creatures. It is possible, however, that they grow so feeble with old age as to be unable to cope with the current, and are therefore drowned by accident. This is, I think, the most likely solution of the problem, as in every country where elephants occur there are large rivers winding through the forests; they are fond of water and keep swimming across them, and at last the day comes when they are too feeble to keep themselves afloat, so they perish in the turbulent currents.

The second theory is that elephants do die in remote parts of jungle where vultures, hyaenas, wild pigs, bears, porcupines, ants, termites and fungi all combine to destroy carcass and bones completely before the advent of the next human passerby, which is very occasional because of the remoteness of the spot. This is a quite possible solution although I do not think it is the correct one. At some time or the other somebody would surely have appeared in time to find the carcass, if not the skeleton. Even the latter, except those of elephants known to have been killed, seem never to be found.

The third theory is that elephants live to such a great age—over 150 years in fact—that by the law of averages they never die natural deaths, but meet, sooner or later, with a violent end. In such circumstances as I have said, their remains are frequently found. In fact the stench given off by a decomposing elephant carcass advertises its presence for miles. The objection to this last theory is that, even so, there are extraordinarily few carcasses, skeletons and bones found even of elephants that have died unnaturally, to account for the number of these animals that must pass away each year in every country in which elephants have their habitat. This is particularly so in Africa, where there are many thousands in the wild state today, while the number of carcasses and skeletons found of creatures that have died from unnatural causes is quite disproportionate to the total number of deaths that must occur each year.

Seven

The Sulekunta Panther

THE PANTHER OF SULEKUNTA WAS A 'THENDU', A HINDUSTANI TERM indicating a 'forest-living panther of large size'. It was an exceptionally big thendu at that.

I first heard of this beast through Muniappa, one of my *shikaris*. The word *shikari* means 'hunter', generally one who has made it his profession, and Muniappa was such a one in every sense of the word. In addition he was an out-and-out poacher. I use the verb 'was', because Muniappa assures me his poaching days are over. Well, that is what he says; but I for one do not believe him. Muniappa is an awful liar.

Many years ago this man was responsible for creating a man-eating tigress, which commenced her depredations at Jowlagiri in Salem district and then visited Sulekunta and other places. Well, all that is another story.* I just mention

---

* See: *Nine Man-Eaters and One Rogue*.

THE CALL OF THE MAN-EATER

it to acquaint you with the fact that Muniappa had been a poacher and done his quota of mischief in days gone by. But he is nevertheless a fairly reliable *shikari* and certainly knows the jungles within a radius of ten miles of his own village of Jowlagiri like the palm of his hand.

Sulekunta is a little hamlet in the forest of the North Salem division, and lies about seven miles southeast of Jowlagiri. It boasts a varied type of jungle; heavy forest with much bamboo growth in a deep valley intersected by a stream known as the Battaiamaduvu Halla. This stream itself flows eventually in a southeasterly direction and is a tributary of a larger rivulet known as Doddahalla, which I have called the Secret river and about which I have already written.

Sulekunta hamlet is on rather raised ground, surrounded by a few fields devoted to the growing of *ragi* and *cholam* grain. Around the fields in every direction is scrub jungle. Low hills surround the area and these are very rocky, consisting in many cases of piled boulders interspersed by glades of long, barbed spear-grass. Between the patches of grass and often in dense clumps, lantana and wait-a-bit thorn grow profusely together.

The area was once abundantly stocked with peafowl which fed on the rich red plums of the cactus plant. But the Forest department introduced the cochineal insect, which feeds only on the cactus plant and destroys it. The experiment has proved outstandingly successful and the cactus is rapidly dying out, but with its diminution the plumlike fruit is becoming a rarity. Hence the peafowl have moved to other regions, although there are a good many birds still to be found in the area. These encroach upon the fields in the mornings and evenings, from whence their plaintive cries echo across the valleys and hills. The sandalwood tree grows prolifically there, although for some reason or the other the plants in the region seem to suffer excessively from the attacks of the 'spike' insect and are mostly unhealthy.

THE SULEKUNTA PANTHER

However, to return to my story, Muniappa sent me a postcard one day, written in the Tamil vernacular, saying that a tigress had killed three head of cattle within the space of as many weeks quite close to the hamlet of Sulekunta. He invited me to come and shoot it. I cannot read Tamil, so I had the postcard translated by an Indian friend. I particularly asked him if he was certain that Muniappa had said the killer was a tigress, or might he have meant a tiger, or possibly a panther. My informant was quite definite and confirmed that Muniappa had clearly written that the killing were the work of a tigress. So I did not answer the summons, for I was not interested in hunting a tigress which was, after all, only doing her legitimate killing for food. I got my friend to reply for me in Tamil, thanking Muniappa for the information but saying I was not particularly interested.

I heard nothing more for about a month, when I received a further postcard from Muniappa, once again in Tamil. This conveyed the fact that the tigress had since killed four more head of cattle, making an average of one victim per week since her arrival in the area, and stressing that I should not fail to come and shoot it. Once again I sent a reply, stating very emphatically that I had no desire to shoot a tigress that was after all, only taking her natural food and harming nobody in the process. A fortnight later Muniappa turned up in person. He arrived just as I had finished lunch, and said he had travelled by bus, having left Jowlagiri at dawn. Considering that Jowlagiri is only about forty-three miles from Bangalore, you will have some idea of the slow rate of travel of what are known as the 'third-line bus services' in southern India. Muniappa said he had come to urge me to go after the tigress. I replied that I was scarcely interested and suggested that he shoot the animal himself. He said that he could not do so, for he had no game licence.

THE CALL OF THE MAN-EATER

I answered, rather bluntly, 'You should know me better by now Munniappa. Do you think I believe you for a moment?'

Muniappa hesitated for a while, and then answered: 'It is no use trying to deceive the *dorai*. He knows very well. The fact is, my muzzle-loading gun is scarcely effective against a tigress.'

'I seem to remember that you shot a tiger with it once,' I replied, 'and that little bit of shooting started quite a big bit of trouble. Isn't that so?'*

He was silent for a minute and then said, 'I don't want to take another chance. This time I want to make certain the tigress is killed.'

His words awoke my curiosity. 'Why are you so interested in this tigress?' I asked.

Finally, in typical eastern fashion, and seeing that my cross-questioning had cornered him, Muniappa came out with the truth. It appeared he had borrowed a hundred rupees from one of the more influential men in his village, as he had required that money for the purchase of a good bull to draw the plough on his field. He had had two bulls previously, but one of them had died and it was essential that he made good the loss immediately, as two bulls, and not one, were required for ploughing.

The creditor had begun to press for the return of his money, but Muniappa had none. To cut a long story short, this creditor had agreed to release him from the debt if he (Muniappa) could supply a good tiger-skin, freshly shot, which the creditor in turn intended to present to another man, an official this time, in return for a special favour.

Of course Muniappa gave me details of the creditor and of the man to whom he wished to present the tiger-skin; also

---

* See: *Nine Man-Eaters and One Rogue*.

THE SULEKUNTA PANTHER

of the nature of the special favour. But this has no bearing on the story itself. I pleaded that I was busy and could not get leave for another month, which was a fact. But Muniappa persisted in pestering me till I compromised by agreeing to answer any summons from him that arrived after the next five weeks had elapsed, as I was fully engaged during that time. He was fairly satisfied and stated that, when this period had passed and a kill had occurred, he would arrange to have it covered by branches as protection against the vultures and would cycle the twenty-three miles from Jowlagiri to the district headquarters of Hosur, whence he would send me a telegram. Upon receipt of the mesage I would go at once by car. Pending my arrival he would return and put up the *machan*, so that all I would have to do would be to shoot the tigress when she appeared. He pleaded his cause so well that not only did he succeed in getting me to give him the bus-fare for his journey to Bangalore, but also for the return journey, as well as two rupees for the telegram that he would send and something more for himself.

Five weeks had just passed when I received the telegraphic summons. As agreed, I answered it promptly, so that about ninety minutes later I stopped the Studebaker in front of Muniappa's little house in Jowlagiri. I found him squatting at the door, awaiting my arrival. He had just got back on his bicycle from Hosur. He explained that the tigress had killed a large brown bull within a mile from Sulekunta the previous evening. A runner had brought the information as it was getting dark. Muniappa and the runner had returned to Sulekunta by lantern-light, and he had spent the night there. At dawn he had visited the dead bull and found that the tigress had eaten almost half of it. Muniappa and his Sulekunta friends had covered the carcass with leaves. Then he had given them instructions where to erect a *machan*, after doing which he had half-run these seven miles to Jowlagiri, jumped on a bicycle, and had covered the twenty-three miles to Hosur in two hours to send me his telegram. The message had come fairly quickly and I had responded quickly too, so that it was now just after 3 p.m. and I was faced with eight miles to walk, and then had only to sit on the *machan*, which no doubt would be ready and awaiting me, and kill the tigress when she turned up. It was all that simple.

We started for Sulekunta without further ado. On the way I questioned Muniappa about the terrain where the kill had taken place. He said the bull had strayed into a belt of dense bamboos, where it had met its end. Then I asked him if he had observed any particulars about the kill itself, and whether he had found pug-marks to corroborate that the killer was a tigress.

'No,' he answered; 'I could find no pug-marks, as the area is carpeted thickly with fallen, dry and decaying bamboo leaves. Besides, there was no time for me to hunt further afield for tracks, as I had to hurry back to send the telegram. But the killer is a *pilli* (tiger) all right, for the bull's neck was broken, which is a sure sign. It must be a tigress, for the people of Sulekunta say so.'

With that illogical argument I had to be content, so we did not waste time in further conversation. With all our efforts, it took two hours to reach Sulekunta, and some more time to arrive at the dead bull. My watch showed exactly 5.30 p.m.

We removed the leaves from the carcass. As Muniappa had reported, the bull's neck had been broken and the rear half had been devoured after the entrails had been removed a few feet. All indications pointed to the handiwork of a tiger —or tigress! The myriads of fallen and died bamboo leaves precluded any hope of seeing pug-marks.

Then I turned my attention to the *machan* itself. As might have been expected, having been left by a second party to a third party to construct, the result from my point of view was far from satisfactory. To begin with, it was one of those bamboo-tree-*machan* affairs, by which I mean that it was constructed at the top of a clump of bamboos. Of course, that was nobody's fault, as the bull had been done to death in a belt of bamboos and there was no other tree nearby on which to tie the platform. But such *machans* have many disadvantages. Unless they are constructed very carefully and cleverly, they are apt to be very conspicuous. This one was no exception.

Every single bamboo stalk had been lopped off at the height of about fifteen feet, the cut pieces having then been shaved of their leaves and placed crossways to form the floor of the *machan*. As a result, that particular bamboo clump had an obviously beheaded appearance and clearly revealed the platform on top of it. Secondly, the crosspieces were too few and some of them were several inches apart. The whole structure looked most insecure, and I knew it would sway and creak horribly. Thirdly, no attempt had been made to camouflage it from below or from the sides. It was just a bare platform, erected at the top of an abruptly shortened clump of bamboos.

Time was running out, however, and it was too late to do anything about it. After removing the leaves from the dead bull, I scrambled onto the platform with my rifle and usual night equipment.

My worst fears were immediately confirmed. Straight away, my weight tipped one end lower than the other, so that the whole structure went askew at an angle of almost thirty degrees from the horizontal, and I felt it sway ominously. Muniappa cut a few green bamboo fronds and stuck them between the crossmembers beneath me in an attempt to conceal the structure from below. But it was a poor effort, and now that the time was almost six o'clock, nothing more could be done by way of camouflage at the four ends of the platform. Then Muniappa went away and I spent one of my worst nights ever. The bamboo pieces cut into me from below. Each time I moved, the whole structure creaked and swayed. The *machan* appeared to go still further askew with my weight and every movement I made. Hence I was forced to remain immobile for fear that the crazy structure might collapse or tip further down at one end and so steeply as to make it impossible to remain there.

Although sitting over a kill is regarded by many as an irksome and tiring ordeal, to me it has always been a source of considerable pleasure. Perhaps this is because I am, above all else, a lover of nature. Far from dragging monotonously, I have found that time passes, if anything, too quickly. I am so absorbed in the wonders of the night, be it moonlight when the soft, silvery moonbeams outline the jungle in a ghostly brilliance quite different from its appearance by day; or a dark night, with the fireflies flitting fitfully around, while the stars in the heavens twinkle serenely with a radiance sufficient to outline the surrounding bushes and landscape. There is so much to listen to, even if one cannot see the myriad forms of life that crowd the forest night. So much is there to learn, if one has only the desire and ability.

But this night was an exception in every way. It was as black as pitch, the darkness being accentuated by the heavy clouds that fled low across the sky. But the jungle was as silent as the grave. No animal or bird voiced the faintest sound, nor did a frog croak or cricket chirp among the dark swaying aisles of bamboos.

I knew the reason for these unusual conditions. A storm was brewing. It was eight o'clock when the first harbinger of the downpour made itself felt in the bamboo grove. The wind started to blow. I could hear it coming across the tops of the bamboos, beginning as the far-off roar of a distant ocean. Eventually it reached me with the impact of a giant hand. The tops of the feathery bamboos bowed low beneath the onslaught, while the cut stems below me began to bend to the breeze. This caused the crossmembers of the platform on which I was sitting to creak and, what was worst of all, to separate increasingly. The tilt became more acute as the mutilated bamboo stems shook and tossed with each gust.

And then came the rain! Often in the jungle, especially in hilly regions, you can hear the rain falling before it reaches the ground. I heard the distant murmur as the condensing clouds began to spill their contents towards the thirsty forest below. This soon became a continuous roar as the rain struck the jungle, and the roar advanced with growing intensity as the wall of water rushed towards the spot where I sat. A final gust shook the broken bamboos below. They strained with the impact, and then a sheet of water enveloped me. Vivid flashes of forked lightning streaked earthwards, followed by the earsplitting crashes of the thunder. In a moment I was drenched.

But I had little time in which to lament my discomfort, for a still greater calamity befell me. With the next onslaught of wind the ropes holding my crazy platform either slipped or gave way, and I felt the structure heel over to an angle of forty-five degrees as I, and all my equipment, slid down the impossible slope.

I let go the rifle as I felt myself falling. I recollect hearing it clatter against the bamboo stems and then fall with a dull thud to the ground. The cut ends of the tossing bamboos sought to impale me as, sprawling awkwardly, I sought desperately for something to hold on to. One of these cut ends ripped through my shirt at the back, while another almost gouged out my eyes. I clutched fearfully at the latter, striving to push it away as it tore my forehead. And in the midst of the confusion, from below me came a series of coughing roars and the sound of a heavy body rushing through the undergrowth.

I yelled at the top of my voice while I frantically clung with both hands to the bamboo before my face. My legs and body were wedged between the stems, while my full weight was borne by both arms. In this position I held on for dear life, continuing to shout for all I was worth to drive away the tigress which I now knew was beneath me.

It was much too evident what had happened. She had returned to the kill just as the rain came and had decided to shelter at the foot of the bamboo-clump in which my most insecure *machan* had been built. As likely as not the wind, rain, thunder and lightning had all combined to distract her attention from spotting that very obvious platform on which I was seated and which she would no doubt have seen at once had conditions been normal. But that was when the ropes holding my *machan* gave way. My rifle and other equipment had fallen all around her, while I had started floundering among the stems above.

She must have been badly frightened, and annoyed too. No wonder she had roared so terribly in strong protest. But the question was: had she run away, or was she still lurking below?

I was in complete darkness, having dropped my torch with the rifle. Also I could not hold on much longer. My hands, face and back were torn, the wet bamboo began to slip from my hands, and my legs and body slid a foot or so downwards. Then I become wedged between the stems. I was well and truly fixed, and I was helpless in every way.

As I have told you, the platform had been erected at a height of about fifteen feet from the ground. It must have tilted about two feet lower. Then I had slipped downwards at least a foot more before I became wedged. I was therefore about three feet lower than the original fifteen. My height is 5 feet

7½ inches. As a result my legs were hanging not more than about six feet above the ground. Of course I did not do all this mental arithmetic just then. But I did enough to realize I was in great danger should the tigress decide to attack. For any tiger could now reach me without effort, while I was held tightly among the bamboos, unarmed and in pitch darkness.

Can you blame me for shouting? I did not do so merely to frighten away the tigress. I suppose when one is really terrified, the spontaneous reaction is to shout—rather, I should say, to scream. So I continued to do just that for quite a while, most unrestrainedly and unashamedly. Then I managed to regain control of myself and began to think things out. I remembered having heard the sound of a heavy body rushing through the undergrowth. Undoubtedly, that had been the tigress. But had she rushed right away, or had she just leapt to the shelter of some other clump after bedlam had broken loose around and above her?

As I calmed down I realized with great thankfulness that the tigress was after all just a normal cattle-lifter and not a man-eater. My screams must surely have frightened her more than ever. Having reasoned thus far, I felt fairly certain she had run away and that I would be safe enough if I descended to the ground. But the point was that I could not descend, I was caught firmly between the swaying stems.

The next few minutes were extremely harrowing ones. Finding myself held so firmly, the obvious thing to do was to draw myself higher up the stem to which I was clinging in order to free my feet and lower extremities. I started to do this while groping with the toes of my canvas shoes for the slightest foothold to support my weight, even for a few seconds, to relieve the terrible strain on my arms.

I do not know how many of you have seen or examined a bamboo stem, or frond as it is generally called, very closely.

There are projections along it from which the leaves branch out. Some of them are spiked, but they are all relatively strong although only as thick as a man's middle finger. These sharp spikes pierced the thin rubber soles of the canvas shoes I was wearing and cut their way into my flesh. But they were strong enough to support my weight. With considerable effort I regained the foot or so I had lost. As I did so I felt my legs come free. Soon I was clinging to only one stem, which supported my entire weight.

While all this was happening the storm continued with unabated fury. Lightning flashed, the thunder rumbled and crashed, and the rain descended in solid sheets. The wind grew stronger, if that were possible, and tore its way through the bamboo grove, whipping off branches here and there that swished past my face as they were carried away by the breeze. Suddenly a tremendous blast, stronger than any of its predecessors, seized the tops of the bamboo. It struck the mutilated clump, causing the stems to bend further than ever, and the stem to which I clung broke sharply below me. I felt myself falling as my body crashed its way through the other stems, and a second later, still holding the broken bamboo in my hands, I hit mother earth with a resounding thump.

Instinctively I scrambled up and with my feet groped in the intense darkness for my fallen rifle. But it was quite some time before I found it, and I went twice around that clump of bamboos before I did so. I could feel the end of the muzzle clogged with mud and the first thing I did was to clean it.

I had not brought a greatcoat with me because the weather had been warm; only a pullover. This had fallen to the ground with the rest of my things and very foolishly I did not think of searching for it, a lapse for which I was to suffer intensely before that night was over.

THE SULEKUNTA PANTHER

The next thing I did was to press the button of the torch that was fastened to the barrel of my rifle. Nothing happened. I felt along the torch itself till I came to where its lens would have been, but there was neither glass nor bulb. Both had been smashed in the fall. I was in pitch-darkness. And the rain continued with unabated force.

I have mentioned that the bull had been killed about a mile from the hamlet of Sulekunta. A mile is no great distance, but to reach that hamlet in those conditions would be tricky, for apart from the rain and darkness, I had a bamboo jungle to contend with. Those who have been in such jungles at night will understand what that means, for the bamboos grow in clusters, each cluster only a few feet from its neighbour. As a rule no trees grow between, nor large bushes either, the intervening ground being covered with grass, minor undergrowth, or just a deep carpet of fallen, decaying bamboo leaves. Even in bright daylight one clump of bamboos looks like any other, and I knew that, in pitch-darkness, intensified by the bamboos themselves, the overcast sky, the pouring rain, the absence of any star to guide me, and the impossibility of keeping a match alight even if I could strike one on the sodden box, once I left the clump on which I had been sitting, I might wander all night in circles without getting any closer to Sulekunta. I might even wander further away from the hamlet.

By this time I had ceased to worry about the tigress. If she had been anywhere near and had wanted to attack me, she would have done so already. Otherwise, no animal would venture out in a storm like that. Even wild elephants, a few of which generally inhabited these mixed jungles, where the bamboo grew to provide them with tender fronds, would not brave these elements, but would seek such shelter as they could find, huddled together beneath the clumps. Of course, it would be just too bad if I was unlucky enough to walk right into one while groping in the darkness. That was a chance that had to be taken.

I waited for the next flash of lightning, and it was not long in coming. After that momentary illumination, I faced the direction in which I judged the hamlet to be. I walked a few paces with outstretched hands that soon met the spiky obstruction caused by the next clump. I felt my way around it, and when I judged I had walked about half way around, I tried to continue in the proper direction. A few minutes of this sort of thing made me realize its utter hopelessness. To begin with, when I walked around each clump of bamboo I had no means of judging whether I had circumvented half of it, or less, or more; so that each time I set out for the next clump I might be walking in almost any direction. I then decided that there was no alternative but to wait for the storm to pass. I sat on my haunches at the foot of the next clump. The ground was about six inches deep in water and mud, so I placed my rifle across my knees and awaited events.

It was ten o'clock before the heavy rain eased, but a sharp drizzle prevailed till almost midnight. The thunder had long since ceased and the flashes of lightning became fewer and then stopped altogether, leaving me in inky blackness.

So long as it had rained heavily I had not felt the cold unduly. Paradoxically, the water had seemed comparatively warm. When the drizzle set in I felt chilly, and when after midnight the drizzle ceased, that was when I really started to feel the cold. What with the drop in temperature towards the early hours of the morning, together with evaporation from my soaked clothing, I began to freeze. In no uncertain manner I cursed myself for failing to look for my pullover. Eventually I removed every stitch of clothing, walked to and fro, leaped up and down, flung my arms and legs about, and did everything

I could to keep the blood circulating in my chilled body. I tried to light a match, but the box and its contents were sodden. The sky remained overcast, without a star to guide me on another attempt to reach Sulekunta. And so I passed what was without a doubt the most uncomfortable night ever. Blue with cold and with chattering teeth, I witnessed the dawn break through the clouds of vapour that rose from the saturated jungle.

With daylight I was able to gain an idea of the general direction in which the hamlet lay and set out for it. Imagine my surprise when, scarcely a minute later, I passed the beheaded clump on which I had been sitting the night before. Although I had been tempted many times during the hours of early morning, when I felt that I would freeze to death, to blunder forth a second time, at that moment I heartily congratulated myself for having remained where I was. Eventually, wearing my still soaking trousers, I reached the little village, where I found Muniappa anxiously awaiting me.

Before telling him what had happened, I asked him to make a big fire of straw, wood, dried cow-dung—in fact, anything that would burn—without a moment's delay. Soon a healthy blaze was started and I sat close beside it, my saturated shirt spread on the ground beside me next to my pants, while I wore Muniappa's turban around my waist. It was a feeling of pure bliss that crept over me as the heat penetrated every part of my body. Then, as Muniappa placed a small pot of water in the midst of the fire, preparatory to making tea, I told him the tale of woe.

An hour later I started the seven-mile walk back to Jowlagiri and my car. I now had a personal account to settle with the tigress of Sulekunta. Although she was undoubtedly innocent of the intention, she was, I felt, responsible for the terrible night I had just endured. At Jowlagiri I left Muniappa with money for another telegram in case the tigress should kill again, when he was to inform me without delay. Then I returned to Bangalore, a sadder but a much wiser man.

The same evening I suffered a sharp attack of ague, followed by high fever. The exposure had brought on a bout of malaria. To malaria bronchitis was added three days later, and this in turn developed into pneumonia. It was then that the telegram came from Muniappa: the tigress had killed again at Sulekunta. Of course, I could not respond. I told my wife to write to Muniappa, telling him of my condition, and that I would contact him when I was fit to answer a further summons. But it was a whole month before I felt I could risk another night in a *machan*. And that, of course, against both my wife's and the doctor's orders. Meanwhile I wrote and told Muniappa that I was well again.

Nearly another month passed before I received the next telegram. Briefly it informed me that a cow had been killed near Sulekunta. Thirsting for revenge, I set out for Jowlagiri once more, but this time with a raincoat and two pullovers, together with a spare torch, batteries, bulbs and matches, wrapped in an old oilskin tobacco pouch to protect them from the wet. I had learnt my lesson: from that time I have always carried these additional articles with me.

When Muniappa met me at Jowlagiri, he told me that the killer was a very big panther—a thendu—and not a tigress as he had imagined. He said he was certain of this because he had clearly seen the pug-marks in the sand beside the kill. To say I was very disappointed would express my feelings lightly. Then Muniappa said something that made me think deeply. He said that he now thought that there never had been a tigress, and that this thendu had alone been responsible for the many kills that had occurred at Sulekunta. He reminded me that we had seen no pug-marks near the bull over which

THE SULEKUNTA PANTHER

I had sat. Both he and I had concluded the animal had been a tiger because the bull's neck had been broken and it was the villagers of Sulekunta who had said it was a tigress. He also reminded me that thendus kill and eat in the same manner as tigers.

The thought that I had been through all that dreadful ordeal for the sake of a mere panther was distinctly galling. However, having come so far, I set out with Muniappa for Sulekunta. The kill, this time a fully-grown and white cow, lay at the fringe of the same belt of bamboo. In my letter I had told Muniappa to build no more *machans* on bamboo trees. Thus I was left with selecting the spot where I intended to sit and constructing my hide in the short space of the one remaining hour of daylight. It was exactly five o'clock.

In those early days I had not made the portable *machan* which I carried about with me in later years to meet just such an emergency as this. So I had to work really fast if I wanted to be in place by six o'clock. The kill had been made at the fringe of the bamboo belt and was much closer to the hamlet. The bamboo grew less thickly there and was interspersed with a few trees and a considerable number of lantana and other bushes which had spread in from the adjacent scrub jungle.

Glancing around quickly, my eyes fell on a large lantana bush some twenty yards away. It was a few feet apart from its neighbours and seemed the ideal place. Muniappa had brought his curved knife for cutting wood, so we set to work in real earnest. From the edge of the lantana bush furthest from where the cow was lying we hacked a small passage leading to its centre, which we then cut away also, retaining for camouflage use all the branches and twigs we removed. I crawled through the passage and sat in the centre of the bush. Then, level with my head, Muniappa cut a rectangular opening directly facing the dead cow. We made the space in the middle of the bush large enough for me to sit in comfortably, together with my raincoat, pullovers and a flask of tea. Taking up my position, I aligned my rifle through the rectangular opening and at the kill to test the angle and direction of fire.

We had worked fast and it was still ten minutes to six when Muniappa, after a scrutiny from all angles to check if anything had been overlooked, pronounced himself satisfied. Then he went away. It was quite warm under the bush which, together with the earth beneath, still retained some of the heat of the day. This caused me to perspire a little, but as it grew dark this slight inconvenience passed away and I was as comfortable as I could expect.

There were the usual jungle sounds of sundown, dominated by the screeching of myriads of those small green parakeets with purple heads that abound in the vicinity of bamboo frests, where they feed voraciously on the dried bamboo seeds. Batches of the 'seven-sister' birds, which is the colloquial name for the Indian 'babbler', fluttered from bush to ground and back again, chattering vigorously, and a couple of mynas winged around the clearing, snatching at the insects that began to show up in the grass as it cooled. In this task the mynas had an active competitor in a solitary hoopoe that hopped about on the ground, raising his crest of comb-like feathers of a rich light-brown hue, and dipping it again from time to time in his pursuit of insects. As a background of sound to this nearer chorus came the distant cries of peafowl, the challenging crow of the junglecocks, and the squabbling of spurfowl; all three, together with the parakeets, are particularly fond of localities where the bamboo grows thickly, providing them with both food and dense cover in which to hide from their natural enemies—man, and the members of the cat-tribe.

At length darkness fell. Although there was no moon, the sky was completely cloudless and was soon filled with myriad stars. The starlight shed a diffused light over the ground in front of me, so that the dead cow, as I looked at it through the opening we had made in the lantana, still remained visible as a faint blur on the ground although it had lost its shape. The patches of white on its coat helped to reveal those parts of the carcass, whereas the brown patches were nearly invisible. The minutes passed quickly enough and it was 7.45 when I thought I heard a slight sound to my right. It seemed like a faint sigh, or maybe a stifled yawn. Then, seconds later, came a faint scratching.

What could have made it? Not a panther, nor a tiger for that matter. Very likely a mongoose was nosing around. That would account for the scratching noise I had heard, but not for the faint sigh or stifled yawn. The minutes sped by and then the scratching was resumed. This time it came from behind me. Something was clawing gently at the lantana bush in which I was seated. It seemed to have discovered the freshly-cut branches and twigs that had been loosely placed there by Muniappa and was investigating; perhaps even trying to remove them. Whatever animal was busy there, it was either extraordinarily brave or exceptionally curious. I became curious too, and I turned my head slowly to glance over my left shoulder.

The scratching noise ceased abruptly. Had the animal been able to detect that slight movement, even through the intervening twigs? For a considerable time nothing happened. Then the scratching restarted, more insistently and more quickly this time. From the darkness in which I sat the leaves and twigs of the bush behind me were outlined faintly against the background of the star-dusted sky. I saw them vibrate and move. The creature now seemed to be making a determined effort to remove the loose twigs. Then I heard the faint hissing sound that is the unmistakable snarl of a panther in doubt.

Slowly I drew the rifle back from the rectangular aperture before me, and half-turned my body around. That was when the panther ceased to be in doubt or even to be curious. There came a series of quick, deep growls, followed by a rush and a thud, as the panther backed out and leapt for the shelter of some other bush or a clump of grass.

My memory flew back to that rainy night just two months earlier, when I had slid off the tilting *machan* and had almost been impaled on the lopped ends of the bamboo stems. I had heard this very same growling then, followed by the rush and thud as an animal had leapt away. I wondered if Muniappa was right. Could it have been just a panther that had been sheltering under the bamboos when I had fallen on top of it, and not a tigress—or a tiger—as I had thought?

Well, whatever animal had made its rush on that occasion, I had no doubt whatever that in this instance I was dealing with a panther—and a thendu at that. And now it had discovered my presence and had gone, and there was little chance that it would return. Luck was entirely against me. I looked at my wrist-watch; the time was 8.20. The night was still young, so I decided to wait till midnight and then return to Sulekunta.

As chance ordained, however, I had not heard the last of the thendu for that night. Obviously hungry, certainly curious, and angry at being spied upon, it came back in a half-circle and, without revealing itself, started uttering the well-known sawing call of a panther from the jungle in front of me and immediately beyond the dead cow. Panthers often make these sounds when returning to an animal they have killed, but this one had not done so up till now.

I remained quite still and the effect on that thendu was amazing. He walked around the area in a wide circle, taking care to keep out of sight, till he got behind me. Then, as if conscious that he was at an advantage, redoubled—if that was possible—his sawing, alternating with snarls. At one stage he ceased abruptly and silence reigned for a while. Either he had gone away or he was preparing to attack. But panthers, even the large thendus, do not do that sort of thing unless they have become man-eaters, and I knew this animal was no man-eater. For there had not been a single report of any person having been molested by tiger or panther in this area since the reign of the Jowlagiri man-eater.[*]

The doubt was settled a little later when he worked himself around to a direction in front of me but half-left, and from there he began to call again. This gave me the hope that if I remained absolutely still he might become bold enough to advance upon the kill, or at least show himself for a minute or two. But it turned out a futile hope. Finally, he abandoned the task of trying to terrify me with his calls and departed, his grunts of disapproval and disappointment gradually fading away in the distance.

I remained till midnight without any sign of his return, and then, deciding he had gone for good, I stepped out of my hiding place and walked the short distance to Sulekunta, where I woke up Muniappa and told him what had happened. Muniappa said that he thought I had done wrong by coming away and that I should have remained in hiding, as he was certain the panther would return in the early hours of the morning. He even suggested that I go back and re-enter the lantana bush. But I was of a different opinion, being just as confident that the thendu would not return, because, all his efforts to dislodge me having failed, he would hardly be so foolish as to come back and show himself, when I might still be concealed.

---

[*] See: *Nine Man-Eaters and One Rogue*, George Allen & Unwin, London

Muniappa challenged me to a bet on this issue. I accepted it and suggested a stake of five rupees—about six shillings. He said that was too high a figure, but he was prepared to bet me a rupee that the thendu would return. I accepted the challenge.

It was agreed that I should walk back to Jowlagiri alone and spend the rest of the night in the small forest rest house there, while Muniappa would remain at Sulekunta, inspect the kill early next morning to see if the panther had come back, and then follow to Jowlagiri and report.

I spent a late morning at the Jowlagiri rest house and awoke to see Muniappa peering in at me through the iron bars of the little window which I had left open. The time was 8.30 a.m. Getting out of bed, I went out on to the verandah, where Muniappa told me he had won his bet and come to collect his money. The thendu had returned and eaten well, but he said he thought there was enough left over for a third meal. That would mean that the panther would be at the kill that very evening. Muniappa also said that he had taken the precaution of covering what remained of the carcass with leaves, in order to hide it from the vultures.

Beckoning him into the bedroom of the rest house, I solemnly handed over the stake money of one rupee and then told him I would prepare some tea for him if he would take my camp-kettle to fill at the little stone-lined well about a hundred yards behind the bungalow. He did that with alacrity, and soon the roar of my Primus stove told us both that refreshment was on the way. Without bothering to shave, I buttered some cold *chappaties* and opened a large tin of sardines to keep them company. Being a caste man, Muniappa would have nothing to do with my buttered *chappaties* and sardines, but he accepted the big mug of tea I offered him. Then we tried to chalk out a line of campaign for the forthcoming night.

Now I did not favour the idea of sitting in the bush again, for I was almost certain the panther would inspect it carefully before approaching his kill, if he did return at all. If he found me inside, which he was sure to do, he would repeat his performance of the night before. True he had come back in the early hours of the morning, as Muniappa had predicted. But I felt he would not have done so had I returned to the bush the previous night, as my henchman had suggested, or had I remained there. So a plan began to form in my mind, but I did not tell Muniappa, whose opinion it was that I should reoccupy my old hide. Instead, I told him to go to his house in the village of Jowlagiri, half a mile from the forest rest house, eat an early lunch and be prepared to return with me to Sulekunta at exactly one o'clock.

Eating a cold lunch myself, I left the bungalow at twelve thirty and walked to the village to collect Muniappa, but my retainer had not even started on his meal when I arrived. However, by dint of much cajoling, I managed to get him on the move by one-thirty in the afternoon. It was blazing hot, but we maintained a brisk pace, reaching what remained of the dead cow at exactly three-thirty. We were both streaming with perspiration. I then began to seek for the means to put my secret plan into operation. You will probably have guessed what I was looking for: a convenient tree, overlooking the bush inside which I had sheltered the night before, quite regardless of whether the kill was visible from the tree or not.

As soon as he realized what was in my mind, Muniappa told me plainly that he did not think it a very good plan. Fancy sitting up over an empty bush! To him the whole idea was stupid. We found a tree—a half-grown *jumlum*—about thirty yards away. It commanded a fairly clear view of the lantana bush, but from it nothing could be seen of the dead cow, because the latter was at a right angle to a line drawn between the *jumlum* tree and the lantana bush. The three points represented the three corners of a right-angled triangle. That was why I had not selected the *jumlum* in the first instance in preference to the bush.

Choosing a convenient branch, I instructed Muniappa to erect a *machan*, which he did quite efficiently within a little over an hour, concealing the platform on the four sides as well as from below with leaves from the same tree. While he was busy I let him into the second phase of my secret plan, by hanging a spare khaki shirt inside the lantana bush where I had sat the night before.

It was ten minutes to five when I climbed into the *jumlum* tree and told Muniappa to wait for me at Sulekunta. He departed with a rather glum expression. Plainly he thought that I was very silly; but as he walked away he did what I had previously instructed him to do: he talked aloud to himself so that, should the panther be lurking in the vicinity, he would gain the impression that the man who had been near his kill was now going away. I sat perfectly still and silent. The next hour or so would prove whether I was right.

The sun had not set and it was quite bright when a large thendu walked gingerly out of the jungle to the right, halted some twenty paces from the bush, and stood regarding it intently. He was at right angles to me, absolutely motionless and broadside on, presenting a perfect shot—either behind the left shoulder or at the neck, as I might prefer.

Very slowly I raised my rifle, fitted the stock comfortably into my shoulder, and started to align the sights on the panther, which remained quite still, staring into the bush. What a perfect picture he presented, his gloriously spotted hide a thing of beauty! Each rosette was clearly visible. His cocked ears and slightly tilted head were ready to catch the faintest sound or movement from the bush. Only the tip of his ringed tail twitched spasmodically from side to side, registering the nervous tension which was not at all evident in his bold posture

THE SULEKUNTA PANTHER

I had almost squeezed the trigger when I thought of the two nights of excitement and entertainment with which this animal had provided me. Was I now justified in butchering him in cold blood when he was quite unaware of my presence, and when he had committed no crime? Twice he had had me at his mercy, but had done nothing. Now he was at mine. What was I going to do about it?

I hesitated another moment—and was lost!

Lowering my rifle, I called pleasantly to him, 'Good evening.'

He looked up at me, very startled. Then he returned my greeting. 'Wroof! Wroof!' he said, and was gone!

I listened to the familiar and always delightful calls of the birds as they went to roost, and returned to Sulekunta at about 9 p.m., with the news that the panther had not shown up. I admitted to Muniappa that I had erred greatly in not listening to him by sitting over the kill. He nodded in a superior kind of way and said rather haughtily: 'I told you so, but you would not listen to me. You thought you knew better. The next time you will do well to remember that I, Muniappa, the best *shikari* in Jowlagiri, know all about the animals of the jungle and their ways.'

It would never do to let my retainer think his *dorai* had become suddenly soft and sentimental. Better to be thought wrong, than to be considered a maudlin idiot. But I never regretted my last-moment decision to spare the life of that beautiful animal.

Incidentally, I do not know if that official did Muniappa's creditor the favour that was required of him. Probably not; because he never got the tiger's skin—nor a panther's, for that matter. But I do know this much: Muniappa never paid his debt of one hundred rupees. He told me so, many years later, blaming me for being the direct and only cause of his dishonesty, because I failed to shoot the panther and procure the pelt.

Eight

From Mauler to Man-Eater

THIS STORY IS THE SEQUEL TO TWO EPISODES I HAVE RECORDED IN THE earlier books of adventures. The first of these began when a tiger began to behave very strangely by mauling the graziers of the hamlet of Rajnagara, at the foot of the Dimbum escarpment in North Coimbatore district in what is now known as Madras state. The unique feature was that this tiger never bit any of its human victims nor was there any authentic proof that it had killed or eaten anybody. It merely rushed at its victim and, when close enough raised itself on its hind legs and severely mauled him with the claws of its forefeet in the region of the head, chest, back and arms. I attempted to bag this elusive animal, but failed completely.

Then the scene changed to a very much wider area of operations, varying from sixty to one hundred miles north and northeast of Rajnagara. A tiger killed and carried off a boy at another little hamlet in the jungle, called Pegepalyam.

FROM MAULER TO MAN-EATER

That boy was the first of several victims, some of whose remains were recovered. The bodies bore unmistakable evidence of having been severely mauled by the claws of the tiger which had attacked them, while teeth marks, other than where the flesh had been eaten, were conspicuously absent. In one case, two men who had climbed up a tree saw their companion actually being mauled by this tiger, which attacked him on two separate occasions, clawing him across the face the first time, and killing him with a blow of its paw the second time, before it carried him off.

The human remains that had been found indicated that there was apparently nothing wrong with the animal's teeth or jaws, as had at first been conjectured. For he had eaten a good meal from each, which would hardly have been possible with impaired teeth or a broken or otherwise maimed jaw.

His constant mode of assault, however, which was by clawing and striking with his forepaws and not by biting, appeared to indicate beyond doubt that this animal was none other than the earlier 'Mauler of Rajnagara' that had strayed northwards into an area of jungle far larger than his original habitat. My son Donald made two attempts to bag this beast, the first at Pegepalyam itself, and the second near the road between Lokkanhalli and Bailur, in the very area where I had encountered the Ramapuram Tiger some years before.* But he had met with bad luck, for on both occasions this tiger had not returned to the remains of the human victims he had killed and over which Donald had, with the utmost difficulty, persuaded the bereaved relatives to allow him to sit.

Naturally, both Donald and I scanned the newspapers keenly for further reports of man-killing, besides receiving such reports as the Forest department sent us from time to

---

* See: *Man-Eaters and Jungle Killers.*

THE CALL OF THE MAN-EATER

time. From these sources scanty news trickled through at long intervals. Human beings began to fall victim to a tiger in scattered areas and in the most remote north-eastern corners of the Kollegal taluk in North Coimbatore district, just south of the Cauvery river, which separates it from Mysore state on the northwest and the Salem district, which is a part of Madras state, on the north and east.

Two definite and authentic items of news eventually arrived. The first was a report that, while grazing her cattle, an old woman had been carried off by a tiger which never so much as touched any of the browsing herd. Her remains were never found. This happened at a cattle *patti* named Gulya. The second report was that a man grazing cattle had been attacked and mauled, but not killed, at another *patti* named Alambadi just across the Cauvery river from Salem district; in this case it was reported that the herdsman, who was standing in the midst of his cattle while the animals were feeding in the jungle looked up in time to see a tiger spring from an adjacent bush and regardless of the beasts all around, come straight at him. He yelled at the tiger, and as it came within reach he pluckily swung at it with the wooden staff he was holding. It appears that the tiger then reared up on its hind legs and severely clawed his chest and arms, knocking him down. But among the man's cattle were five buffaloes, and these animals happened to be grazing nearby. As buffaloes often do, the five of them joined together and charged the tiger, which turned tail and fled. Although severely injured the man was able to stagger back to the *patti* where there were several other herdsmen to succour him.

A *patti* is a patch of jungle which has been let by the government to a number of herdsmen for kraaling cattle at night that have been licensed to graze in the reserved forest. These animals are permitted to feed during the day in the jungle within a radius, generally, of three miles around the *patti* in any direction. The grazing period lasts for about six months out of twelve: after the monsoons and during the hot dry weather, when there is no fodder to be found near the villages. The licence costs four annas per animal for the six months, which works out to about one shilling for three head of cattle for six months. This breaks down to two-thirds of a penny per animal per month for the right to feed all day within an area approximately twenty-eight square miles.

However, to get back to our story: because the scenes of these two incidents, and Alambadi in particular, were close to the Cauvery river, with Salem district on the other side, with reasonably good roads and communications, the news spread quicker and in greater detail, so that we heard about it in Bangalore within a month of the incidents in question. This is not a long time for such conditions and such remote areas. It was therefore reasonably certain that this tiger was not entirely devoted to man-eating. He was following the general practice of man-eating panthers, attacking human beings only when an exceptionally easy opportunity turned up or perhaps when the mood seized him. At other times he was obviously living on wild game, as there were no more than the usual number of cattle being killed in the area by tigers and panthers.

Time passed and we were beginning to forget about this tiger when reports came in quick succession that two persons had been killed and eaten at a small hamlet with the rather curious name of Bejahahai. It was reputed that the body of the first victim was never recovered, but the second was found after it had been half-devoured. This man had been badly mauled and clawed about the face and chest.

Donald agreed with me that at last we had something concrete and authentic to work upon. The elusive tiger of

Pegepalyam, which we suspected to be no other than the mauler of Rajnagara, appeared to be again at work. According to the map, the hamlet of Bejahahai was situated almost 3,000 feet above sea level in a valley to the east of the highest mountain peak in Kollegal taluk, named Ponnachchi Betta or Ponachi Malai, itself nearly 5,000 feet up. Donald had long determined to shoot this tiger and solve the riddle of its strange habit of mauling its victims before killing them. So he decided to set out on a month's 'safari', as he called it, to accomplish his objective. What follows is Donald's story, as he told it to me:

After receiving reports of the two human kills that had taken place at Bejahahai, I decided at all costs to get the tiger that had been responsible, especially as I was sure it was the same beast I had tried unsuccessfully to shoot almost a year before at Pegepalyam.

There were two curious things about this tiger. The first was that he was reported to claw the people he attacked rather than bite them. The second was that he never returned to a human kill; I had already sat up for him over human bodies without success.

So I got things ready in a hurry and collected as much cash I could, nearly 300 rupees, to pay for my baits and general expenses while I was out on safari. Although this was a good deal of money, it was well worth spending if I could shoot this tricky animal that had proved such a menace for so long. So at five o'clock one morning I set out in my car, which although old, had proved itself over and over again as very good for jungle work.

I stopped for a couple of hours at Pennagram to pick up Dad's old *shikari*, a fellow named Ranga, whom I regarded more as an old friend than a servant. I then made a diversion down a jungle road to a place called Muttur, seven miles away

FROM MAULER TO MAN-EATER

in a valley on the banks of the Chinar river, where I persuaded Byra, another old *shikari* friend, to accompany me too. Byra is a poojaree, an aborigine who was born and bred in the jungle. Dad and I have known him for many years. Although he is pretty old, I still think he is even better than Ranga when it comes to jungle knowledge and work. He is certainly a better tracker.

We motored back to Pennagram and then turned due west, to cover another ten miles to a hamlet named Hogenaikal, on the banks of the Cauvery river. There are some water-falls here which have become famous for religious reasons, at least so far as the Hindu faith is concerned. Years ago another very good *shikari* lived here, who had at one time got into trouble with the government through shooting an elephant on one of his poaching trips. He also knew me from an early age, but he was now dead. A mile from Hogenaikal is a village named Ootaimalai, where Dad has a one-roomed brick hut which he used in the old days as a camping place when game was plentiful in the area and he came regularly on hunting trips. Conditions have changed since then, however, and there is not much to shoot in the locality.

I left my car in front of his hut and in charge of the local Forest Guard. Then I distributed all the kit I had brought between Ranga, Byra and myself and we set out to cover the rest of the journey to Bejahahai, about 9½ miles, on foot.

First we walked three miles down the road that led north-westwards from Ootaimalai, along the banks of the Cauvery river, towards a place named Biligundlu. At the third mile there is a ferry across the river, and we had to use this to reach the Alambadi cattle *patti* on the further bank. Incidentally, this ferry is not a regular wooden boat, but a circular, basket-work affair, perhaps eight feet in diameter, covered with tough buffalo-hide and hardly drawing six inches of water.

THE CALL OF THE MAN-EATER

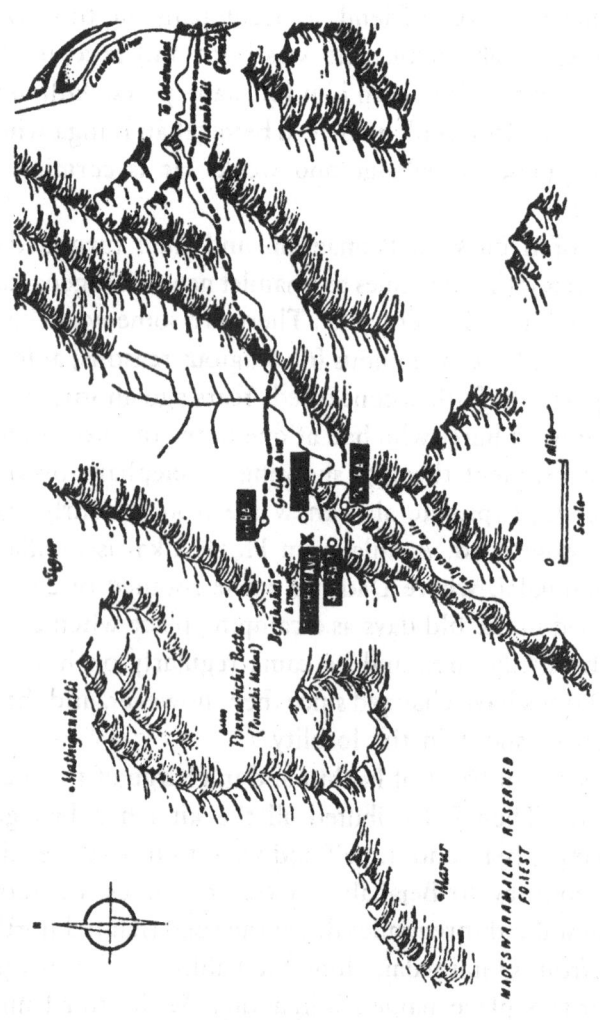

FROM MAULER TO MAN-EATER

These leather-cum-basketwork jobs are known locally as coracles. They are controlled by one man with a short wooden paddle; he is highly skilled in negotiating the strong river currents and in avoiding the sharp edges of rocks that often lie just below the surface. When we set foot on the opposite bank near Alambadi we were in Kollegal taluk, which is a part of North Coimbatore district and has quite a separate Forest department administration. Alambadi was one of the places at which this tiger had seriously mauled a man some months earlier. I tried to get more information about the animal from the herdsmen living in the *patti*, but I could gather very little.

Two facts were prominent, however. The first, that everyone was terribly scared and walked about in fear of their lives. The second, gained from those who had seen the man who had been mauled, was that he had been severely clawed about his shoulders, chest and back, but had not been bitten anywhere. The poor fellow had since succumbed to his wounds as a result of blood poisoning.

The place for which I was bound was the hamlet named Bejahahai, on the eastern slopes of a mountain chain about ten miles in length, running almost north and south, which has its highest peak at a point named Ponachi Malai, about four miles from the northern end. A stream called Gulyatha Halla rises somewhere south of this chain and flows in a northeasterly direction, joining the Cauvery river a little north of Alambadi. There is a footpath from Alambadi to Bejahahai, which more or less follows the tributary I have just mentioned for about five miles, and then turns westwards for the remaining mile and a half to Bejahahai. The three of us set out along this footpath. It was close on three in the afternoon. The sun was really fierce, and walking along the narrow and stony track was arduous. We crossed the tributary about half-a-dozen times; it became increasingly rocky and boulder-strewn as the land rose perceptibly towards the mountain chain ahead.

Our trek was not altogether uneventful. We had practically completed the first five miles and were at the last river-crossing before the pathway left the stream to turn westwards to Bejahahai, when we came upon a herd of elephants resting from the heat beneath the shade of the *muthee* and tamarind trees that grew along both banks of the tributary. They were not feeding at the time and so we did not hear them, and as the breeze was blowing down from the hills, past them and towards us, they did not scent us. I was wearing rubber-soled boots, while Ranga and Byra were barefooted. Hence they did not hear us coming, with the result that we almost walked into their midst. Pandemonium broke loose as the elephants scented and spotted us simultaneously. As if to show how cowardly these huge beasts really are, even when in large numbers—there might have been about thirty in all—the herd rushed away headlong, the shrieks of the frightened females being exceeded by the terrified trumpeting of the tuskers. The piglike squeaking of the calves, bundling as fast as they could at their mother's heels added to the confusion. What was most amusing was that the big tuskers, whom one might expect to put up a rearguard action to protect the cows and babies, actually jostled them aside and vied with one another in showing a clean pair of heels. In a few moments, where there had been many elephants and much noise, there was nothing but a deep silence.

We reached our destination without further event at about five in the evening. Although it was a comparatively long time till sunset, the whole area was already in shade, for the sun had sunk behind the frowning ridge of the mountain chain. The actual peak of Ponachi Malai towered to the northwest, a little over a mile away.

FROM MAULER TO MAN-EATER

Bejahahai was like all jungle hamlets, and consisted of about a dozen huts clustered together. Most of them had walls of thorn and roofs of dried jungle grass, the thorns and the grass being kept together with spliced bamboos tied with lenghts of dried jungle vines. One or two of them, which were clearly 'better-class' buildings, had three foot walls of dried mud, plastered with cow dung, but with the same roofing of jungle grass. The cattle-pens which adjoined the rear of each hut had low walls of woven bamboo, topped by a stockade of thorns. The latter were necessary to keep out marauding panthers and tigers.

Our advent caused quite a stir. Two or three dozen men, wearing nothing but wisps of rag around their loins, barebreasted women with tattered and torn sarees, and pot-bellied children, affected by enlarged spleens owing to the ever-present malarial mosquitoes, timidly stepped out of their huts or stood in the doorways to watch us suspiciously and rather fearfully. One or two of the men salaamed nervously.

We came to a stop in the centre of this group of hovels. Obviously, if I expected them to answer questions, the first thing to do was to set the inhabitants at ease. With that in view I judged that Byra would be the best person to speak. For one thing he was an aborigine himself, and these scared folk would understand him. I knew from experience that Ranga was rather haughty towards people whom he considered his social inferiors, and would call them by such disparaging names as 'jungle monkeys' and 'stupid apes'. If I spoke to them myself they would perhaps become even more nervous. Certainly they would not believe me.

I told Byra to introduce us. Never have I been so flattered as by his words. Byra said that I was a great hunter who had shot hundreds of tigers, elephants, panthers and similar insignificant creatures, and that hearing of the plight of the inhabitants of Bejahahai I had come many miles to deliver them. He said that an essential contribution from them would be all the information and help I could get. His speech was a bit long-winded, but I must say it accomplished its purpose. Smiles crept over some of the faces surrounding me. But anyway, the tension clearly eased.

I can speak Tamil and Hindustani, and understand some Kanarese. Most of my hearers were Tamil, although I could make out a few Sholagas who, like Byra, are aborigines and have inhabited the Coimbatore forests from time immemorial. So at this stage I took an active part in the proceedings by addressing the gathering in Tamil. As simply as I could, I told the people that my purpose was to rid them of the terrible menace that had come into their lives. I also told them I was confident of success. There was but one condition: that I should receive their unstinted and active co-operation. I said that I expected every able-bodied man in the village to assist me to the utmost. My simple speech appeared to have the desired effect. Villagers in India do not applaud by clapping their hands as do the people of the West. But they do something as good, if not infinitely better. They smile, even laugh in approval. The inhabitants of Bejahahai smiled widely that evening.

Having won their goodwill, I began questioning them about the tiger. I asked if any of them had seen him, if there was anything distinctive about his methods or appearance, if he had any particular or peculiar habits or any favourite locality in which he was likely to be found. Several of the simple folk replied that they had seen the man-eater, but from their generally contradictory answers it was soon evident that either there were many different-looking tigers about the place, or that the people were saying they had seen this beast just to please me.

FROM MAULER TO MAN-EATER

As one might expect, the majority proclaimed that he was an animal of colossal dimensions, with a head about two feet in diameter and a body at least twelve feet long. One or two of the women who said they had glimpsed the marauder prowling near the outskirts of the hamlet were emphatic that this was a tigress and not a tiger. But in one respect they were all in close agreement: that it would be quite useless for me to attempt to shoot the man-eater. He, or she, was protected, they were confident, by a forest goddess that sat astride the neck and accompanied the animal on its hunting forays. Indeed, they were quite sure that the goddess led the man-eater directly to each unsuspecting victim.

While this harangue went on, I noticed that one man, who squatted on the ground slightly apart and never so much as opened his mouth, wore a rather cynical smile while the rest tried to outdo one another in their wild statements. He was a middle-aged fellow, clearly a Sholaga, and wore only the briefest of loin-cloths. Thinking he might not understand the Tamil I spoke, I asked Byra to question him.

But the man interrupted by saying: 'I can understand you, *dorai*, and I shall speak as soon as these liars around us have stopped talking.'

Those words had a silencing effect and the throng ceased jabbering at once. The Sholaga then began to speak and his words were as unusual as they were dramatic.

'For one thing, *dorai*,' he said, 'the man-eater is male and not female. I know this for certain, for just three days ago, when I had climbed up a tree to catch an oodumbu that was sheltering in it, he came out of the jungle and calmly squatted down at the foot of the tree, waiting for me to descend. I shouted at him and hurled twigs, but he only growled and glared up at me menacingly. I thought he would never go away, but towards midday, when the sun reached its zenith and the waves of heat danced above the ground, he became thirsty and suddenly walked off into the jungle. I thought it was a trick and that he would be hiding in the undergrowth, waiting for me to descend. So I remained in the tree for another two hours. Just as I was wondering what I should do, there was a great hubbub and a pack of about a dozen wild dogs chased a sambar stag into the clearing beneath my tree and tore him to bits in a few moments. Then they started feeding on the carcass. This I knew was my only chance. No tiger, not even a man-eater, will dare to show itself in the face of a pack of wild dogs. If I came down from the tree and made my escape the dogs would not harm me, while the chances were that the tiger had fled long ago.

'So I did that, *dorai*. The dogs stopped feeding, stood up, and looked at me inquiringly. But not one of them ran away. It was as if instinct told them I was unarmed and helpless and that they could kill me if they wanted. And while they were still looking at me I stole off and managed to return to the hamlet without harm, although I do admit I was terribly afraid, once I got away from the presence of the wild dogs which had actually been the means of saving my life, as I was sure the man-eater would have returned to the vicinity after slaking his thirst in one of the few remaining pools that are fast drying up in the streambed.

'Well, *dorai*, I saw the animal clearly. It is not such a big tiger as these people try to make out, but only of average size. But it has quite a long tail. I noticed that particularly, as it kept twitching it from side to side while glaring up at me. And that glance, *dorai*! I have never seen such diabolical hatred in the eyes of any living creature as I saw in the eyes of that tiger.'

'How is it that you did not return and tell the other villagers what you had seen?' I asked suspiciously.

The Sholaga remained silent for a while. Then he said: 'There is a reward for the death of this animal. I intended borrowing my uncle's muzzle-loading gun and trying to shoot it. My uncle is due back in this village the day after tomorrow. I wanted the reward, for I am a poor man. Nor would I have told you about the incident, but my stomach was turned at hearing the silly tales these villagers have been telling you.'

A murmur of anger and protest rippled through the throng, but the Sholaga continued. 'This tiger has no magic nor goddess to protect it, *dorai*. But it does have brains, much more brains than most of the people standing here. However, if the *dorai* is really in earnest and means to shoot it, I will help him. For I have brains, too; more brains than the tiger or these folk around us.'

And that was how I made the acquaintance of Lotta the Sholaga—outspoken and unusually arrogant and self-opinionated for a simple aborigine. But as I was to find out very soon, he knew his jungle and its inhabitants intimately, and he was a tremendously brave man, too. I told him I would welcome all the assistance he could give me, whereupon, in token of agreement, he came and stood at the side of the two henchmen I had brought along with me.

As there was little more information to be gained from the inhabitants of the hamlet, I led my three followers into the jungle for about a furlong, where we squatted on the ground to work out a plan of action. By the time all this talk was at an end another forty minutes had elapsed: it was exactly 5.40 p.m. It was too late to tie out live baits, an operation which includes the complex but very essential task of selecting the most likely places in which to tether them, and the erecting of *machans* in advance, if possible, at those same places, so as not to cause a disturbance later on, should a kill have been made.

Lotta told us that the tiger's pug-marks were frequently to be seen in the morning, leading across the dry sands of the Gulyatha Halla stream, and that these tracks were invariably found just south of a hillock about 500 feet high that rose sharply from the left-hand or northwestern bank of the stream, a little over a mile away, coming from the same direction as we had that very evening. In fact, the pathway we had followed to Bejahahai, after leaving the stream, had passed this same hillock on its northern side. He told us there was a small cave near the top of the hillock in which he believed the man-eater lay up during the day. Although the whole hillock was clearly visible from the bed of the stream five hundred feet below to the southeast, Lotta said the cave itself was hidden from view by a large intervening boulder. According to him, the lower two-thirds of the hillock were covered with jungle, but the higher slopes were comparatively bare, consisting of tumbled boulders, piled on top of each other. Therefore, anyone approaching the cave would be at a disadvantage. Not only would he be visible to the tiger from above, but however silently a man might climb he was bound to make some sort of noise in negotiating the rough terrain and in jumping from boulder to boulder, or in trying to pass between them.

We asked Lotta what made him think the tiger used the cave on the hillock as a shelter. He answered that, apart from the frequency of the tracks that crossed the riverbed and seemed to come from the hill and lead back to it, he had several times heard the langur monkey's cries of alarm on the hill, generally too. Also, about four nights ago, a tiger had called from somewhere on the hillside.

Byra pointed out that none of these happenings in themselves conclusively proved that the man-eater lived on the hill, but that all the facts put together, plus the presence of the concealed cave Lotta had mentioned, suggested it might be so. The only way of settling the question was to climb the hill and investigate the cave, if possible. So we determined that early next morning we would procure two live baits and tie one of them on the streambed to the southeast of the hillock, where the tracks appeared so often, and the other on the footpath along which we had just come, and which, as I have already told you, passed the hill on the northern side. In addition, just after midday, when the sun was at its hottest, I determined to climb the hill and try to find the cave. In doing so it was possible that I might stumble across additional evidence that the tiger lived there. There was also a slim chance that I might catch a glimpse of it—perhaps even be able to get in a shot.

Daylight was fading fast by the time all this was discussed and settled, and so we withdrew to Bejahahai to camp for the night. The problem of accommodation arose. I had brought no tent with me because of the extra weight to be carried on our long march. Besides, it was the last week of March, when not only is the weather very dry but growing uncomfortably hot. Dad and I generally camp under the trees at all times except monsoons. Lotta offered us the use of his hut. It would have been rude to refuse, but as I stood at the tiny, low entrance and looked into the small, dark and rather smelly interior without ventilation of any kind, I politely but firmly said that sleep would not come to me in such a warm and enclosed place, and that I would prefer to sleep outside. Now anyone who has tried to sleep in close proximity to any hamlet in southern India will at once agree with me that it is well-nigh impossible. Not only is the ground covered with refuse and filth of every description, but it is freely used as a latrine by the inhabitants after darkness has fallen. So to avoid the refuse we walked to an open spot about 150 yards away and decided to sleep there for the night. Lotta said he would stay with us, and I lay on the ground while my three followers gathered wood and soon had a fire burning merrily.

The first item on the programme was to brew some tea, and while the water was boiling I ate a little of the cold salt beef and *chappatties* I had brought from home. Then, as I sipped the hot tea, I listened to the tales my three friends had to tell me. And indeed I was happy. The starry sky above, as it began to pale with the glow from the rising moon, the flashes of fireflies against the sombre background of jungle trees, the towering and serrated outline of the Ponnachchi Betta mountain chain to the west, the homely flickering light of our camp-fire with its slumber-inviting warmth, and the wisps of smoke that curled and eddied and finally disappeared in the darkness—all contributed towards that happiness.

Ranga and Byra had been taught to read the time from a watch, so at eight o'clock I took off my wristwatch and handed it to Ranga, instructing him to remain awake and alert, and to feed the fire till ten-thirty. Then he was to awaken Byra whose guard-duty would extend till one. Then came my own turn, till three-thirty. Finally, I would hand over the responsibility to Lotta (who did not know how to read the time) till the dawn came at six.

I fell asleep immediately and awoke only when Byra gently shook me by the shoulder at one o'clock. I saw that the other two men were fast asleep and Byra soon joined them. The fire had died down to a few embers and there was not much wood left to keep it alive. Finally, despite the season, it became decidedly chilly. My watch passed uneventfully. An elephant trumpeted in the distance, and a sambar stag called three or four times closer by. But the calls were not of sufficient duration to indicate the passing of a carnivore. Perhaps something smaller had frightened him, for the stag soon got over his fear and fell quiet. I began to feel sleepy again and was glad when my watch showed three-thirty. I awoke Lotta, whispered to him to husband the few remaining sticks so as to keep the embers alight till dawn, and fell asleep once more.

It was past six-thirty when I awoke to find my three assistants busy with a large fire they had built, on top of which I was glad to see the kettle boiling for tea. Then we set to work in real earnest. By dint of much bargaining, I managed to hire two brown bulls for ten rupees apiece. The man who hired them made it plain that he could not sell the animals outright, since he was not their owner. The true owner lived in a faraway village and had entrusted him with some thirty-five head of cattle for grazing over a period of six months. His salary for this was three rupees a month (4s. 6d.) plus as much milk as he might want to drink. No wonder he was tempted to hire them to me for a few nights for twenty rupees, which represented almost seven months pay. But he made it clear that if either of the animals was killed I would have to pay a hundred rupees in compensation. In addition, nobody should be told he had lent the animals for bait. He would tell the owner that the bull had been killed by a tiger while grazing. No doubt the owner would fine him by stopping two or three months' pay, but as he had received a hundred rupees from me, he would make a profit of at least ninety rupees. Such is the simple logic of an otherwise honest jungle-man.

We retraced our steps along the path by which we had reached Bejahahai the previous evening, and after covering a little over a mile found ourselves just to the north of the hillock Lotta had described. Just as he had said, more than half of the lower portion was jungle-clad, but beyond that the hill was bare of vegetation except for a few thorny bushes between the piles of boulders.

A tamarind tree beside the track provided an ideal site for the first *machan*, to be tied some fifteen feet above the ground, which is about the ideal height. We tethered one of the bulls by a foreleg to a stake driven into the ground in the middle of the path; then my companions set to work on making a *machan*. As all three of them were well skilled in jungle-craft, I did not have to tell them what to do. Indeed, the completed structure, which took about seventy-five minutes to erect, was a work of art and so well camouflaged that it was barely visible even from a distance of thirty feet.

From the tamarind tree we followed Lotta along a short cut through the jungle and reached the stream (Gulyatha Halla) within half a mile. Turning up-stream for another quarter mile, we found ourselves due southeast of the hillock and at the place which Lotta had described the evening before. His story needed no corroboration, for within a few minutes Ranga found a fresh set of tiger pug-marks leading across the sands of the tributary. Clearly the tiger that had made them the night before had descended from the hillock. A few yards away a half-grown plumfig tree provided another suitable place for the second *machan* to be tied. An hour and a half later this had been done, and we tethered the second bull to a stake driven into the bank of the stream just below the tree.

It was now past noon and the next step in our campaign was for me to climb the hillock and try to locate the cave. As far as the two live baits were concerned, there was nothing more to be done except to hope that the tiger would kill and eat one or other of them during the coming night—or the night after that.

Quite a sharp argument arose among my three retainers as to which one of them should accompany me, each of the three insisting that it was his particular duty. Ranga was very emphatic, claiming he had carried me when I was two months old and so had known me longest. Byra was equally insistent, saying that when it came to 'smelling' a tiger at close quarters, he was the most competent, and that therefore he would be of the most use to me. Lotta, although only recruited the day before, claimed that clearly he was the most eligible as he alone knew the position of the cave.

Obviously the man to take with me was Lotta, for his claim was the most justifiable. But here a tricky situation arose. The complexities of the eastern mind are somewhat difficult to fathom at times, and I well knew that, if I chose the new man to come with me, I would deeply wound the feelings, pride and affections of my two old henchmen. And to select either one of them in preference to the other, would cause even deeper hurt to the one left behind. So I made up my mind quickly. There was nothing for it but to go alone.

I announced my decision as nonchalantly as possible and asked Lotta to indicate, from where we stood, the approximate position of the hidden cave. A renewed outburst was the result, all three proclaiming that such an undertaking was extremely dangerous. In fact, realizing my embarrassing position in having to choose between them, all three volunteered to step down to allow me to choose between the other two. But this did not make matters any easier. I still had to pick on one of the three to the detriment of the remaining two. Besides, having said I intended to climb the hill alone, to change my mind now would show that I was afraid. So I said very firmly that I had made my decision: I would go alone.

Rather sheepishly Lotta pointed out a boulder standing a few yards from the summit of the hillock, and told me that the entrance to the cave lay right behind it. He suggested that, rather than approach the cave from directly below, I would do well to climb the hill at an angle till I reached the top, and then creep along the summit till I could overlook the cave, which I ought to have no difficulty in finding if I kept the boulder as a marker.

With these instructions in mind I said no more, but crossed the stream to the opposite bank and began the ascent. The jungle that clothed the lower two-thirds of the hill effectively shielded my approach if the tiger happened to be lying near the entrance to the cave. By the same token, it hid the tiger in case he happened to be lying in the undergrowth, waiting for me to come near enough to spring upon me.

I went forward very warily, intently scanning every thicket and bush ahead. Of necessity my progress in this fashion was rather slow, so that it was some time before I saw that the undergrowth was becoming perceptibly thinner as I approached the higher part of the hill where the boulders predominated. But at last I reached it, only to find that I was now considerably worse off than when negotiating the jungle-clad area. I was clearly visible to any watcher from above. The tiger could creep down upon me, and merely by lying in wait behind one of the boulders he could pounce upon me as I drew abreast; or he could wait for me to pass and then attack from the rear. But having committed myself to the task, there was nothing for it but to go on.

Some of the boulders were quite large, being ten feet high or more. Others were small, about three feet high. In many cases it was difficult to pass between or around the smaller ones as they were jumbled together. Often I had to climb on to one and jump from it to the next. That made me very conspicuous from above. Besides, I was bound to make some noise in my movements, in spite of my rubber-soled boots and the infinite caution I exercised. At this stage I regretted my foolhardiness and began to wish that I had brought one of my companions with me.

However, my luck held out and at last I stood on top of the hillock, almost at its right end. I had now to creep along the summit towards the other end till I came in sight of the boulder that hid the entrance to the cave. This I did, standing on tiptoe from time to time to see if I could see the boulder. But a fresh difficulty arose. From my position I could only see the top of each boulder and not its base, which was hidden from my view by the curvature of the hillside. And there were so many boulders that I had no means of identifying the one that Lotta had indicated. In this dilemma I still advanced, when quite unexpectedly the problem was solved for me.

Suddenly a large grey shape shot out from behind a rock just in front of me and bounded away. Startled out of my wits and thinking it was the tiger, I had raised my .470 to my shoulder. Then I saw that it was a solitary langur monkey. He leapt from rock to rock towards the other end of the hill and in a few moments had disappeared from view. The langur's presence seemed very reassuring. Had a tiger been in the vicinity, I knew quite well that the monkey would not have been there. More rapidly, and with less caution, I advanced towards the place where the langur had vanished.

Then a strange thing happened. The langur gave a cry of alarm; 'Har! Har! Haar!' The next instant he reappeared and came bounding back. In a series of prodigious leaps from rock to rock, he dashed past and was lost to sight behind me.

Now why had the langur called in alarm? Why had he dashed back so wildly, almost on top of me?

More cautiously I approached the spot where the monkey had reappeared. As I drew nearer to the end of the hill and could look over the edge, I caught sight of the upper half of a boulder. It came more into view as I advanced, till soon I could see it wholly, and then I knew it was the boulder that Lotta had indicated from the streambed. I was standing at that moment above the cave itself. The realization came to me in a flash. The langur had cried out and bounded back because he had probably seen the tiger lying at the entrance of the cave, or had come to realize the proximity of his age-old foe. The question that now arose was whether the tiger was outside or inside the cave, and the only way to find an answer was to go still closer.

So I crept forward, inch by inch, till I came to the edge of the hill and the land fell away sharply before my feet. Dropping to my hands and knees and craning forwards, I was at last able to see the entrance to the cave—a narrow opening in the rock, which I judged to be about five feet high and perhaps a yard wide. No tiger was to be seen. I pondered what I should do next. I was tempted to call out or to throw down a pebble, in order to make the tiger charge out and so show himself. But I curbed myself in time. The tiger might not be at home. Moreover, stone-throwing would needlessly frighten him. He might come out from a second cave connected with the first, of which Lotta knew nothing, and then just run away to some other part of the forest, where the job of coming to grips with him would have to be started all over again. All said and done the wisest course seemed to be not to give myself away or to frighten him, but to withdraw quietly and let events—in the form of his taking one or other of the two baits—take their own course.

So, as silently as I had come, and glancing back every now and again against a surprise attack from the rear, I retraced my footsteps to the point where I had first reached the summit of the hillock, and continued down the further side till, eventually, I stood among my followers on the bed of the stream. We remained in camp that evening so as not to disturb the jungle unnecessarily and made a point of going to sleep early, although we continued to keep watch, one at a time, just as we had done the previous night. This time we took the precaution of gathering in advance a large pile of brushwood, among which were some quite big logs, so that the question of having to husband our stock should not be repeated.

Dawn found us on the way to examine our first bait—the bull we had tied on the pathway leading to the hamlet. He was well and unharmed. Nor were any pug-marks to be seen along the track. We followed the same short cut to the stream and our second bait. But that animal was also alive, but with this difference: casting around, we found that the tiger had seen him. He had come as close as fifteen yards, squatted on the streambed and closely scrutinized the animal, no doubt wondering whether he should kill it or not. And then, for some unaccountable reason, he had just walked away. His pug-marks on the soft river sand told us the story as clearly as if we had been watching him.

With nothing to do, we returned to the hamlet to find that Lotta's uncle had turned up on schedule, bringing his matchlock with him. The presence of the gun (not of the uncle) urged Lotta into action. He put before me an idea which had his definite recommendation. Rather than spend a third night in camp, doing nothing, he strongly advocated I should beg, borrow or steal two more cattle for bait and tie them at the two remaining sides of the hill which were roughly to its east and west, and that I should sit over one of them, while he did the same with his uncle's matchlock over the fourth bait. He reasoned that, as the tiger had closely approached but not taken one of the first two baits, having clearly become suspicious, it was very likely he might do the same with baits numbers three and four if he came upon them after descending from the cave on the hillock. So Lotta suggested that I should sit over the live bait to the west, while he sat over the bait to the east. Then either of us might find a chance of shooting the tiger while he was examining the bait. Of course, if the tiger happened to kill either of these two new baits it would be all the better for us in ensuring an easy shot.

By nature I am a restless person and the idea of remaining inactive day and night while waiting in the hope that the tiger would take one of the first two baits did not appeal to me at all. Several times I had toyed with the idea of trying to flush him out of his cave, but Byra and Ranga had cautioned me against the plan in case we succeeded only in frightening the tiger away. Under these circumstances I welcomed any plan that savoured of action and immediately fell in with Lotta's idea. Entrusting him with the task of procuring two more bulls, and that quickly, I began to prepare a hasty lunch out of some of the tinned provisions I had brought with me.

Lotta succeeded more quickly than I expected and by noon turned up with a half-grown black bull and a buffalo heifer. The four of us soon set forth with Ranga and Byra carrying my greatcoat, water-bottle, sandwiches and an empty beer bottle filled with tea. There was also my torch equipment, which could be fastened to my rifle with two clamps. Lotta brought up the rear, driving the bull and the heifer.

I admit I acted rather selfishly in choosing the eastern side of the hillock in preference to the western, as suggested by Lotta, as I had reasoned the tiger was more likely to approach in this direction, since it overlooked the stream. I also selected the buffalo heifer in preference to the black bull as tigers are sometimes rather shy of a fully black animal. Secondly, having refused one of the baits last night—a bull—I hoped the tiger would not refuse a young buffalo.

Next came the task of finding a suitable place in which to sit, and this presented some difficulty as the jungle growth on the lower two-thirds of the hill consisted mainly of bushes, grass and trees that were neither high enough nor strong enough to bear my weight in a *machan*. I was soon forced to face the fact that there was no suitable spot whatever on this part of the hill, unless I was prepared to sit on the ground in a bush, which would be very hazardous.

The idea then came to me to climb a little higher, among the rocks that were piled in profusion on the upper slopes. We did so, and in a little while came across a formation that seemed to suit my purpose admirably. Two boulders, each over twelve feet high, touched a third wedged in between them and a little higher than the first two being about fifteen feet high. The three rocks were at an angle to one another of slightly less than ninety degrees. The space in front was open and overlooked the hillside and the Gulyatha Halla rivulet below. If I sat at the base of the centre and highest of the three rocks, after getting my retainers to cut thorns and wedge them firmly into the spaces between the bases of the three rocks, I would be quite safe against attack from the rear. To get at me the tiger would have to jump on to one or other of the three rocks, which he could easily do, but even then I would not be directly visible to him owing to the curvature of the boulders. He would have to leap down into the amphitheatre in the centre first, and then turn to find and attack me, which would leave me time enough for a shot.

The only other way in which he could get at me would be to come around from the exposed area in front, where I intended to tether my buffalo heifer, at a spot about fifteen yards away. I reasoned that, even if the tiger discovered my presence and had brains enough to sneak around the outer edge of the rocks, he would find the heifer confronting him, which would be a definite deterrent. He might make up his mind to kill it; he might walk around to inspect it; but its presence would definitely confuse him and confuse his original plan of attack. Lastly, the buffalo would be visible to the tiger from the top of the hill and would serve to attract him. Of course, if he tried to creep through one or other of the spaces between the rocks, he would need to clear away the thorns and the noise would afford me ample warning.

I was therefore very pleased at my good fortune in finding such an excellent and comparatively safe hiding-place. I explained my plan to my three companions, who unanimously agreed that it was a really good one. While I sat at the entrance keeping guard over them with my rifle, they scurried a short way down the hill and came back carrying quantities of cut thorns, which they proceeded to wedge tightly into gaps at the base of the boulders. Finally they tethered the heifer by its forefoot to a stake they hammered into the earth at a spot exactly twenty paces from where I was going to sit.

It now remained to find a suitable place on the other side of the hill for Lotta to hide in with his uncle's ancient matchlock. I wanted to help in this and so, rather than walk directly across the hill from where we stood, or climb over its crest as a short cut, when in either case the tiger might see or hear us and take alarm, we descended to the base of the hill in single file and made a detour, walking along the streambed for a short distance and then through the intervening jungle, led by Lotta, before climbing the hillock again on the opposite face.

The conditions here were exactly the same as on the eastern side. There was no tree big enough for a *machan* on the lower slopes and so we climbed higher, into the zone of the rocks and boulders. It was too much to expect to find such an ideal 'hide' as the one I had secured, and after clambering over and stumbling in between the heaped rocks, Lotta finally selected an almost flat slab of rock that was slightly higher on the end that faced the summit of the hillock. He said that this was all to the good, and that he would lie prone on top of the rock and tie the black bull in front of the higher end, from where it would be in uninterrupted view of the tiger, whose cave was around the corner or shoulder of the hill, out of sight of the flat rock and considerably higher up.

It was now about 4 p.m. and too late for us to go back to camp. The upper surface of the flat rock, being to the west of the hillock and directly exposed to the rays of the afternoon sun had become far too hot for Lotta to take up his position immediately. So we all helped in tethering the black bull, and then left Lotta with his matchlock sheltering in the shade on the lee side of his rock. He said he would climb up at about five-thirty, as soon as the rock had cooled.

Once more Ranga, Byra and I slithered down the hill, detoured through the jungle and down the bed of the stream, and came to the place where I would have to start climbing to regain the three rocks where I was going to sit. Here I parted company with my two servants, after giving them strict instructions that they should return to the hamlet and remain there till morning, when I would come back to them.

It was a few minutes after five when I got back to my hiding-place. The heifer, quite undisturbed, was resting on the ground, half asleep. The sun had already sunk below the crest of the hillock to the west, so that it was comparatively cool at the foot of the rocks and entirely in the shade, particularly as I was sitting to the east of them and had the rocks between me and the ridge of the hill over which, as I have just said, the sun had already set. There being no jungle in the immediate vicinity, hardly any sounds reached me other than the distant twittering of the hundreds of *bulbuls* that fed on the clusters of blue-black lantana berries at the foot of the hill. Lower yet was the belt of greenery which denoted the tamarind, *muthee* and *jumlum* trees bordering the stream. From that direction I heard the occasional cries of jungle fowl and spurfowl as the cock-birds sent out their evening challenges to their rivals before settling down for the night.

It grew quite dark soon after six o'clock, although I could still see the trees that grew along both banks of the stream far below me, the scrub jungle in the middle distance, and the heifer only twenty yards away. I remember comparing the scene to a picture on a cinema-screen, where the spectator in the audience sits in darkness while the screen is illuminated. But very soon that picture faded, too; and then all around me was a dense, heavy blackness, relieved only by the few stars that twinkled directly overhead. The rocks around me seemed to shut me in from the usual and pleasant sounds of the jungle.

Then, just as my watch showed ten minutes past eight, the silence was rudely shattered by a sudden, distant, wailing scream, followed in a second or two by the deep boom of a muzzle-loading gun. Then there was complete silence till, in another half minute, a distant sambar doe, somewhere in the valley below, as startled by the sounds as I had been, began to utter her resonant cry of alarm, that echoed and re-echoed down and across the dells and the jungle-clad aisles of the forest, to fade into nothingness in the mountain fastnesses.

I sprang to my feet. Without doubt something terrible had happened to poor Lotta. The weird cry I had heard, although it had sounded inhuman, could only have come from his lips. The report of a muzzle-loader, quite distinct to experienced ears from that of a rifle or breech-loading gun, could only have emanated from the ancient musket he was carrying. The fact that the scream had come first indicated that Lotta had either been attacked or severely frightened and then had fired in self-defence. But Lotta was not the sort of man to be easily frightened.

It was doubtful whether Ranga and Byra, back at the hamlet over a mile away, would have heard the musket-shot, particularly as it came from the other side of the hill. They would certainly not have heard the scream. And I had emphatically instructed them not to leave the village. So there was but one thing to do—and at once. I would have to go to Lotta myself, and see what aid I could give him.

With the help of the torch that was clamped to my rifle I stumbled downhill through the scrub jungle to the bed of the stream, up which I ran for a short distance. I did not know the short cut leading across the belt of jungle to the spot at the foot of the hillock from where we had started climbing to reach the flat rock, for it was the Sholaga himself who had led us along that path. So I followed the only alternative, which was to cut across from the stream to the foot of the hillock towards the west, and start climbing in a half-left direction that would, sooner or later, bring me within hearing-distance of the injured man, who would answer me if he was still alive.

I felt myself trembling with excitement and nervousness as I forced myself to climb upwards through the scrub belt, flashing the beam of the torch from side to side in fear that the man-eater might ambush me at any moment. Finally the scrub petered out and those awful rocks began. I could see the top of the hillock outlined against the starry sky and, keeping this to my half-right, I pressed forward as best I could in that difficult terrain. In a few moments, judging that I was within earshot of Lotta, I began to call his name as loudly as I could, conscious as I did so that I might succeed in accomplishing one of two things—either in driving the man-eater away or in attracting him to me.

For quite a long while there was no answer to my calls. Then I heard a feeble groan. I stopped walking to catch the direction from which the sound had come, and shouted again: 'Lotta, where are you? Answer me, and I will come to you.'

I heard a subdued moan, followed in a few seconds by a faint cry, '*Dorai*, I am here. I can see your light. You are going too high up the hill. Walk forward, but come a little lower.'

The voice had seemed to come from very far away, but I stumbled on Lotta within a hundred yards. He had fallen to the base of the rock on which he had been lying, but had managed to cling to his matchlock, although he could not reload it. The Sholaga had been badly clawed down his back, buttocks and thighs. Very fortunately he had not been bitten.

In a whisper he told me that the tiger had evidently seen him from somewhere on top of the hill and had worked around to the rear, while he had been lying on the sloping rock facing uphill, where we had tied the black bull. Without warning it had sprung on to the rock from behind and then had jumped on to his back and begun to claw him. Unable to turn around or point his weapon, he had just pressed his finger on the trigger. The roar of the explosion, and no doubt the flame and smoke from the black powder, had evidently frightened the beast, for it had sprung away, knocking him off the rock in doing so. Lotta had been lying at the foot of the boulder, expecting the man-eater to return at any moment, when he had seen the light from my torch and heard me calling his name. Had he fallen to the left of the rock instead of to its right, it would have come between him and me, and he would never have been able to see my light.

A closer examination by torchlight revealed that, although severely and deeply clawed, and bleeding profusely, no very serious or dangerous wound had been inflicted. The man was obviously suffering from severe shock and was in great pain, but there was no trace of a bite.

I pointed out to him that we would have to get back to the hamlet somehow, as no help would reach us till morning. At first Lotta said he could not stand, but as the effects of shock wore off I drew him to his feet; after abandoning his matchlock, which he was loth at first to do, he clung to my neck with both hands. I supported him with my left arm while I held my rifle, with the torch still alight, in my right hand. In this manner we began a nightmare journey down the hill.

With difficulty, and only after a long time, we reached the streambed, where Lotta collapsed with exhaustion. From there I carried him on my shoulders, fireman's lift fashion, and by the time we got back to the hamlet I was dead beat, while the cells of my torch, that had been burning for so long, had grown very dim.

We awoke the inhabitants and all became a bustle of excitement as hot water was prepared. I then washed the Sholaga's wounds as best I could and poured on to them raw crystals of potassium permanganate, followed by iodine. It was crude treatment, I knew, and he groaned with pain. Finally, I injected the contents of two phials of penicillin procaine, which totalled eight lakh units, into his buttocks. Dad and I always make a point of carrying a hypodermic syringe, penicillin, iodine, a sharp knife, bandages, cotton-wool and other items of first aid on our *shikar* trips, to meet such emergencies.

It was past 3 a.m. when I told the headman of the hamlet that he would have to press eight able-bodied men into service early next morning to carry Lotta on a *charpoy* to the Cauvery river and, after crossing by ferry, on the Ootaimalai, from where I would take him in my car to the hospital at Pennagram.

THE CALL OF THE MAN-EATER

I was falling asleep from sheer exhaustion when Byra came to me with a dramatic idea. '*Dorai*,' he said, 'let us make a last attempt to kill this tiger. After being frightened by the explosion from the muzzle-loader it has probably gone back to its cave and is hiding there. You go to sleep now. I will call you when the junglecocks begin to crow. We will go back to the stream and climb the hill as day breaks. You creep along the top till you reach the point at which the langur sprang back, overlooking the entrance to the cave. After allowing you sufficient time to get into position, I will come along the hill from one side and momentarily show myself before the cave. The tiger, provided it is inside, will probably growl first before he attacks, which he will then do by charging out. I will step back and hide flat against the rock so as not to get in the way. You shoot him through the back from above, with both barrels of your rifle. I have spoken.'

'Nonsense,' I began remonstrating, when Byra broke in: 'Go to sleep now quickly, *dorai*; you have hardly two hours in which to take some rest.'

And I was so tired that I fell asleep before I could argue.

Promptly at five Byra awoke me, and true to his promise I could hear the junglecocks crowing, although it was quite dark outside. Still undecided as to whether I was being wise or foolish, I followed him. The torch gave out long before we reached the bed of the stream. Believe it or not, although I had been most careful to check all the equipment I had brought with me from Bangalore, this most important item—extra torch batteries—had been overlooked. But I had the utmost confidence in my old jungle friend, Byra, and so I kept behind him as we groped through the heavy belt of trees and eventually found ourselves on the dry sands of the stream. Here we sat for another half-an-hour, till dawn began to break. Then I removed the torch and the clamps from the barrel of my rifle, as these would now be a needless impediment, rechecked the rounds in the two barrels of my .470, and began to follow Byra up the hill.

When we had almost reached the top, he took me by the arm and whispered: 'You go on from here, *dorai*. Make no sound whatever. Creep along till you reach the summit. Then turn to your left and continue until you are directly above the cave. Lie down there and be ready with your finger on the trigger. I will give you plenty of time before I show myself. When you shoot, fire both barrels to make sure.'

Then, without another word he disappeared behind a boulder. With many misgivings I did as the little old man had told me. To reach the top of the hill and work my way along the ridge to the left was easy enough. But to recollect the very spot to which I had followed the langur monkey was a very different matter. Thrice I misjudged the place and, looking down from above, saw no cave. Then I remembered the rather tapering boulder that served to hide the cave-entrance from sight when standing on the streambed. At last I spotted it, and keeping it in view as a marker, soon recognized the exact place from which I had overlooked the mouth of the cave after the langur monkey had rushed back. Once more the cave was directly below me.

Now another thought began to worry me. Had Byra given me enough time to allow for the three mistakes I had made in finding the place? I had heard no sound, so nothing could have happened. Silently I lay down on the bare rock above, so that the muzzle of my rifle overhung the narrow entrance to the cave. And there I waited and waited. But still Byra did not appear.

Then abruptly, before ever I was aware of his proximity, the little man came into view from below and to the left of me. Calmly but gingerly, so as to make no sound before the right moment had come, he walked towards the narrow cave-mouth, stood before it, kicked a loose stone with his foot, and cleared his throat. Like lightning, after that, he nipped back the way he had come and disappeared from my view behind a ledge to the left.

Events followed quickly. The ground on which I lay seemed to rumble as if with an approaching earthquake as the tiger growled within the cave below me. Then he roared loudly, and the next second had dashed into view from out of the very bowels of the earth.

As the man-eater hesitated for a moment, not knowing where the man who had so impertinently disturbed his privacy had gone, my first shot took him behind the neck. He somersaulted and fell on his back, the white of his belly turned towards me—all four legs threshing the air wildly. My second shot went through his chest.

He had hardly stopped twitching when Byra reappeared around the corner, and with hands on hips smiled up at me broadly, the smile of one whose plan of campaign has worked out to perfection. In great excitement, I slid down the rock from above, arriving in a most undignified manner, all of a heap, at Byra's feet and uncomfortably close to the tiger which we were both not quite certain was really dead. There we waited for about five minutes. Then Byra threw a stone that glanced off the animal without bringing any response. That told us what we wanted to know; the tiger was dead.

And now the moment for unlocking the secret which had puzzled Dad and me and a host of others for practically five years. Why had this tiger formed the habit of scratching and clawing, rather than biting, its human victims when it first attacked them?

The mystery was solved at last when we examined the dead animal. The whole of its nose had been blown away by an old gunshot wound, probably caused by a .12 shot-gun or perhaps a muzzle-loader, which had also shattered the bone at the bridge, extending from the nostrils to between the eyes. What must have been a ghastly and extremely painful injury had healed marvellously, but the tiger had doubtless never forgotten to associate that terrible wound with the human race, and so had taken great care to keep the organ out of the way and safe from possible harm every time he attacked a man. This could be the only explanation, as such cattle as had been killed by this tiger had been done to death in the normal manner, with teeth as well as his claws. Besides, he had eaten normally. The wound, as I could see, had healed perfectly. Therefore it was very unlikely that he still suffered pain in the act of biting. Assuredly, but for this injury, he would have remained like any normal tiger, quite harmless to the human race.

In great exultation we hurried back to the hamlet and told the good news. Lotta was loud in his congratulations. Every man, woman and child of Bejahahai turned out and climbed the hill to see the dead man-eater for themselves.

It was a joyful procession that walked back to Ootaimalai a little later, with Lotta on a *charpoy* carried by eight men, and the skin of the tiger, rolled in a bundle, on Byra's head. Although the jolting must have caused the Sholaga considerable pain he never complained or murmured once, but was garrulous in his praise of me as the slayer of the tiger, and of the little old poojaree, Byra, whose jungle cunning had brought about its end and whose fearlessness had flushed the man-eater from its den.

I felt guilty for having delayed the medical attention that would otherwise have been rendered Lotta earlier by my action in going back for the tiger. But I am glad to say he made a quick and easy recovery. Nothing Byra did could have raised him higher in my estimation. My admiration for him was at its peak. Old Ranga was a bit crestfallen that his competitor had managed to steal a march over him on this occasion. But the two of them, joined now by Lotta, are always awaiting us as faithful friends, companions and assistants, ready to serve Dad and myself at any time.

Call of the Man-Eater collects stories and anecdotes of Anderson's [adv]entures in the southern jungles of undivided India. Frequently sought [by] tormented villagers, Anderson would comb riverbanks and jungle [path]s to hunt down panthers and tigers well known for their slaughter of [hu]mans. He negotiated the dangerous terrain carefully with a .405 [Win]chester rifle, a Studebaker car, and some help from friends and native [info]rmants. Sometimes he domesticated these wild creatures, as in the [cas]e of the hyena, jackal, bear, barking deer and a few snakes, which the [hun]ter-writer tamed and kept as pets around him.

Non-fiction

ISBN 978-81-716-7469-5

₹195

www.rupapublications.com